Rita Bradshaw was born in Northamptonshire, where she still lives today. At the age of sixteen she met her husband – whom she considers her soulmate – and they have two daughters, a son and six grandchildren. Much to her delight, Rita's first attempt at a novel was accepted for publication, and she went on to write many more successful novels under a pseudonym. Rita has now written over twenty-five novels using her own name and is a *Sunday Times* bestselling novelist.

As a committed Christian and passionate animal-lover Rita has a full and busy life, but her writing continues to be a consuming pleasure that she never tires of. In any spare moments she loves walking her dog, reading, eating out and visiting the cinema and theatre, as well as being involved in her local church and animal welfare.

Rita Bradshaw

Skylarks at Sunset

HEADLINE

First published in 2007 by
HEADLINE PUBLISHING GROUP

First published in paperback in 2007 by
HEADLINE PUBLISHING GROUP

First published in this paperback edition in 2023 by
HEADLINE PUBLISHING GROUP

1

Cataloguing in Publication Data is available from the British Library

ISBN 978 1 0354 0312 7

Offset in 11.2/15pt Bembo Std by Jouve (UK), Milton Keynes

Printed and bound in Great Britain by Clays Ltd, Elcograf S.p.A.

Headline's policy is to use papers that are natural, renewable and recyclable
products and made from wood grown in well-managed forests and other
controlled sources. The logging and manufacturing processes are expected
to conform to the environmental regulations of the country of origin.

HEADLINE PUBLISHING GROUP
An Hachette UK Company
Carmelite House
50 Victoria Embankment
London
EC4Y 0DZ

www.headline.co.uk
www.hachette.co.uk

For our first granddaughter, Georgia Faye Anderson, born 31 March 2006 – the most exquisite, beautiful and precious little girl in the world, and baby cousin for Sam and Connor. Thank you, darling Faye and Roy, for letting the doting grandparents be so involved on that special day, and praise and thanks to the Lord for making everything so perfect (even down to the dinner, Faye!). Dad and I love the three of you so very much.

Contents

PART ONE

1932 – Jiggery-Pokery

Chapter 1

'Are you man or mouse? That's what I want to know. By all the saints, you know how things are. How do you think we're keeping our heads above water when businesses are going down right, left and centre, eh? Answer me that. Not by standing in line while some outfit like Stratton's or Clark's cuts us by ten per cent.'

'I know that.'

'I'm not sure you do.' Abe Fallow glared at his son before sitting up straighter in the big leather chair. Putting his two square hands flat on the shiny surface of his desk, he said, 'Look, Cecil, we've done this before an' we'll do it again before we're finished, it's nowt. We're not doing anything wrong, just smoothing the way, oiling a few wheels, so to speak.'

'Jim Clark doesn't see it that way.'

'I don't give a monkey's cuss what Jim Clark sees. I'm not going to lose this contract. We need it.'

The tall thin man on the other side of the desk blinked,

and ran his hand through his thick dark hair. His voice low, he said, 'Old man Clark is one thing, Jim's another. He's dangerous. Since he came into the business he's got his finger in lots of pies.'

'Aye, I know that right enough which makes it all the more important we don't give in to his bullying. He's nothing short of a gangster and a thief, in my opinion.'

Cecil stared at his father. When they offered bribes and jiggled the figures on tenders, his father called it oiling the wheels; when Jim Clark did the same he was a thief and a gangster. 'He might be particularly sore about this one because it was already theirs, bar the ink on the contract. And . . . and he knows we sent a second tender a week ago.'

'He can't. Randall told me he'd scrap our first one and put the second in its place on the quiet, no questions asked.'

'Apparently Jim's got a niece in the office at Randall's. And he knows all right.'

'He's bluffing.'

'There's something else.' Cecil swallowed, wetted his lips, then said, 'It seems Daniel sent the second tender into the general office without marking it for Maurice's eyes only. The girl saw it but thought nothing of it until Clark's got the call to say they were out of the running. She told her mother, Jim's sister, who phoned Jim . . .'

There was a long pause during which Abe's face turned a mottled shade of red. 'You damn fool! You let the lad take care of things?'

'I told him to send it for Maurice's attention and marked confidential. He must have forgotten.'

Abe swore profusely but he kept his voice down, conscious he was in his study at home rather than the office. Emily would have a blue fit if her afternoon bridge club, who were at present meeting in their drawing room, heard him, hoity-toity dried-up sticks that they were.

Cecil took a deep breath and dared to say, 'This wouldn't have happened if you'd let me tell Daniel how things are, clue him in. I don't see why you insist on keeping him in the dark now he's left university and has come into the business.'

'Don't you take that tone with me, lad, and I don't have to explain meself to you.'

'I'm not saying you do, only that—'

'You do as you're told an' keep your mouth shut, all right? And this is your fault, not Daniel's, let's be straight on that. Now, as I see it, you'll have to shovel your own muck regards Jim because in spite of what he thinks he knows I'm not backing down on that job. Like I said, we need it. You do damn well out of me, lad,' Abe stabbed a finger at his son, 'an' don't you forget it.'

Cecil's face was white, his mouth tight, but before he could reply there was a knock at the study door and a moment later it opened revealing a tall, thin woman in a black dress and cap. A sharp pair of eyes took in Abe's glowering face and Cecil's pinched one, then the woman said, 'They've gone and she said for you to join her in the drawing room for tea and cake. Shall I say you'll both be in in a minute or two?'

'Aye, yes.' Abe flapped his hand and the woman departed, closing the door soundlessly behind her.

'If you hang on to this contract, Jim won't forget it, he's got a long memory.'

'Oh, I'm hanging on to it all right, lad.'

'Word is they need the work even more than we do.'

5

'Tough. I've not got me philanthropist cap on the day.' Abe rose to his feet, indicating the discussion was at an end.

Cecil stood up too, his face sullen. 'You might blame me but Daniel hasn't got a grain of interest in what he's doing and he's got worse of late. You'll have to have a word with him because he takes no notice of me. Couldn't wait to get out of the door today and wouldn't stay an extra minute. Where is he anyway?'

Abe shrugged. 'Out,' he said shortly. The truth of the matter was he didn't know where Daniel was but he, too, had noticed a change in his younger son the last few weeks. Perhaps it was time to have a word with him. His eyes narrowed. Aye, in view of this with Randall's, it was more than time. He could be wrong but his gut feel told him Daniel had his eye on a lass and at twenty-one that was only to be expected. He'd have preferred the lad to confide in him of his own accord but now he had a good reason to probe.

His mind made up, he led the way into the drawing room where his wife was waiting; Cecil, as always, followed in his father's footsteps.

Chapter 2

When was he going to come? She had been here ages now, or at least it felt like ages. Of course it was her fault, she'd left far too early for their rendezvous but it was such a beautiful day and the desire to be free of the stench and grime of the town had been irresistible. But whenever he came, she would say she had only just arrived, she didn't want to appear too forward.

The slender fair-haired girl sitting in the thick grass starred with buttercups and forget-me-nots and white clover could have been any age between fifteen and twenty. Her slim arms were clasped round her knees upon which her chin was resting, thick-soled shoes peeping out from beneath the bleached cotton dress she was wearing and her hair fastened in a decorous knot at the back of her head.

The view in front of her was one of rolling fields and low hills, the odd farmstead and small cottage dotted here and there. It was no coincidence she was looking this way. The opposite direction brought home the truth that the outskirts of the fast growing ward of Bishopwearmouth wasn't as far away as she would have liked.

Although to be fair, it was the comely part of Bishopwearmouth, she reasoned. Names like Lindon House and Ashbrooke Grange indicated residences of some note, all surrounded by tree-lined grounds manicured to perfection by an army of diligent gardeners. It would be necessary to walk some way, past Willow Bank Lodge and then Ashbrooke Grounds with its genteel pavilion and lawn tennis courts before the grids of mean terraced streets began to emerge. These streets rapidly became denser if an easterly direction was taken until, once past the orphan asylum and what remained of the old town moor, the East End of Sunderland stretched. This ward consisted of a grim tangle of decaying houses and factories built right to the edge of the harbour and its quays, noisy saw mills and industrial works competing for space with notorious public houses and gin shops.

Don't think of all that now. The girl shifted, lifting her gaze to the high blue sky and watching the skylarks as they swooped and dived in the clean pure air, their sweet song touching something deep inside her soul. Make the most of each moment of this afternoon. Don't waste a second.

She brushed a wisp of pale silky hair from her face. An onlooker would have said it was a striking face, beautiful even, the high cheekbones covered by smooth creamy skin, emphasising the unusual combination of dark brown eyes and fair, almost silvery hair. Her nose was straight and small, her mouth a full rosebud.

When in the next moment she realised she was again thinking of the squalid surroundings she'd left just an hour before, she made a sound of sharp impatience in her throat.

What was the matter with her? She had looked forward to this afternoon all week and now it was here she felt too het up to enjoy it.

She rose to her feet, shading her eyes with her hand as she turned and looked back over the town from the summit of the hill she was on.

It was that row with Constance that had done it. Never one to hide her feelings, her sister had been fiercely resentful when she'd refused to allow her to accompany her today. But how could she have done? How could she have said she was meeting a lad? Constance couldn't keep a secret at the best of times and for the moment she didn't want her friendship with Daniel Fallow to become common knowledge. She could not have said why; she couldn't explain it even to herself except by acknowledging that it was too new, too precious.

Hope Woodrow stood a minute or two more before shaking her head at herself and sitting down again. Daft, she was. She admitted it. Daniel was a grown man of twenty-one and his family were something in the town. Didn't they live in a great big house off Ryhope Road and keep a housekeeper? This thing between them couldn't go anywhere. Perhaps even now Daniel was thinking of ending it. Maybe he wouldn't turn up today. He'd probably see that as letting her down lightly before anything happened. But something *had* happened.

Hope closed her eyes on the thought, squeezing them tight as her heart pounded. She had fallen in love. It had happened the first time she'd met him and she didn't care if people said love at first sight was a fallacy, she knew how she felt and it was love all right. If only they were from the same background, the same part of town though. Everything would have been simple then. As it was, they were worlds apart. And to cap it all he'd told her his family were Catholics although he'd also said he didn't go in for all that incense-swinging and whatnot.

Her lips turned up at the thought. He'd made her laugh that day although she'd known she shouldn't have, he'd been somewhat irreverent about the Church and its practices. But Daniel could always make her laugh, that was one of the things she loved about him. Her Aunt Jinny would get on with him like a house on fire, they had the same way of looking at a situation and finding something funny in it when no one else would.

Hope's smile died as she thought of her aunt. She felt bad she hadn't told her about Daniel. She'd never kept anything from her Aunt Jinny before and the deception didn't sit well on her conscience.

Her surroundings faded away and Hope lost herself in her thoughts. She could still vividly picture the day thirteen years before when she and Constance, who hadn't been a year old at the time, had made the journey to their aunt's house in the East End. The memory was tied up with her mother collapsing on the hall floor, the telegram informing her of her husband's death at sea clutched in one hand. That same day the baby her mother had been expecting had come much too early. There had been a lot of coming and going followed by a profound silence, or at least that was the way Hope recalled it. And then her aunt had arrived at the neighbour's house where she and Constance had been taken.

Hope plucked a blade of grass, chewing on it as her thoughts meandered on. Her aunt had sat the bewildered four-year-old child she had been then on one ample knee, hugging her tight as she had gently explained that her mam and the babby had gone to be with her da in heaven. She and Constance were going to come and live with her, Aunt Jinny had finished, and they'd have lots of cousins to play with. That would be nice, wouldn't it?

And so the transition from Hartlepool where her mother and father, a respected sea captain, had settled had been accomplished. One day she'd been living a quiet sheltered existence with her mother and baby sister; the next she'd found herself in the menagerie that was her aunt's two-up, two-down terraced house in the worst part of Sunderland.

But it was a nice menagerie, she told herself, disloyalty piercing her. And it didn't matter that it wasn't clean or that there wasn't room to swing a cat. She'd thought when her eldest four cousins had left to get married things would improve and they had in a way, but with the remaining three being full-grown men it didn't always feel like it. What would Daniel think to her home?

The uncomfortable feeling of disloyalty pricked again. As though in answer to it, she reached for her straw bonnet which she had discarded on arriving at their trysting place. She pulled it firmly on her head. Her aunt and uncle were good respectable folk and that was all that mattered. Anyway, Daniel wasn't uppity in spite of living in a grand house and having been to university and everything, he hadn't seemed at all bothered when she had explained her circumstances to him. And he hadn't tried it on with her, he'd been a perfect gentleman to date. Six times they had met and he hadn't even kissed her yet. That showed he respected her, didn't it?

Aye. It did. She answered her own question with a bob of her head. And she knew he liked her in *that* way, it was in his eyes every time he looked at her even though he hadn't spoken it out.

Nevertheless her thoughts disturbed her. She again rose to her feet, smoothing out the creases in her dress nervously. He had to be late by now even though she had got here early. She would wait a minute more, then she'd go. She wasn't going to let him mess her about however much she liked him, no good came of letting a lad walk all over you. She might not have courted someone before but she knew that much.

'Hello, Hope.'

The quiet voice brought her spinning round and there he was. Tall, grey-eyed and as smart as a whistle in grey flannels and a light cloth jacket.

'Hello.'

'I didn't know if you'd be here yet considering I'm ten minutes early.'

He was ten minutes early? And she had been thinking . . . She felt foolish. Wetting her lips, she said, 'I caught an early tram. It's such a bonny day I couldn't wait to get away from the town.' And then she blushed scarlet. Would he think she was insinuating she couldn't wait to see him?

'I know what you mean.' Shrugging off his jacket he walked over to where she was standing. He laid the jacket on the grass and gestured for her to sit on it. 'You feel you can breathe out here. Who was it who said God made the country and man made the town. William Cowper, I think. Anyway, it's a sentiment I can agree with.'

Hope said nothing to this. She had no idea who William Cowper was. She sat down carefully, folding her legs neatly under her so her shoes were hidden. They were ugly shoes, stout and serviceable, but the only ones she possessed along with her winter boots. She hoped the grass wouldn't stain his lovely jacket or her shoes mark it.

Daniel sat on the grass beside her and she was aware of the overall length of him and the nice clean smell emanating from his clothes and skin. She didn't look at him but directed her gaze at his shoes. They were beautiful, brown leather and clearly of the best quality with an intricate pattern all around the laces. They were further proof of the different worlds they inhabited. None of the lads in the streets where she lived could have dreamt of wearing such shoes, it was all the dock workers, miners, shipyard workers and the like could do to keep their hobnailed boots soled and heeled these days. With the Depression beginning to bite more and more, the dole queues were getting longer. Only the pawn shops did a roaring trade.

'I've missed you.'

Surprise brought her head swinging round, her eyes meeting his. It hadn't been so much what he had said as the way he had said it. She stared at him, her cheeks burning. 'It's only been a few days,' she managed at last.

'A few lifetimes.' He took her hand, his eyes roaming round her face. 'But I have to know, Hope. Do you feel the same as me? I don't want to rush you, I know you haven't had a lad before but I need to know—' He stopped abruptly. 'I need to know,' he finished softly.

She didn't know how to answer him. The look she had seen before in his eyes was now all over his face, lighting it from within somehow, but she still wasn't sure of exactly what he was saying.

Was he asking her to be his lass, all above board and proper? Or something else? She knew from the talk at the laundry where she worked that you had to be careful. Lads could say one thing and mean another.

And then he disabused her of that idea when he said, 'I want you to meet my parents, Hope, and I want to get to know your Aunt Jinny. She sounds a canny body.'

He exaggerated the last two words, his accent ridiculously broad, and Hope gave a weak smile, her earlier fears coming to the surface. 'Daniel, my Aunt Jinny's isn't anything like your home. I mean—'

'I know what you mean.' His finger on her lips stopped her from saying more. 'And it doesn't matter. How could it? It's *you* that matters, you and me. You do see that, don't you?'

'Oh aye, aye, I do, but—'

'No buts.' His voice was firm. 'But you still haven't said if you feel the same as me. You do, don't you? Do you, Hope? Say you do.'

She nodded. 'Of course I do.' She didn't question what he felt; if it was half of what she felt for him, it would be enough.

'Oh, Hope.' His voice was even softer, trembly, and when he whispered, 'May I kiss you?' she leant towards him which was an answer in itself.

It was only his mouth that touched her, he made no attempt to take her in his arms, but his lips were warm and firm and she breathed in the smell of him, her eyes shut and her heart racing. He didn't prolong the moment and in her innocence she wasn't aware of the control he was exercising when he drew back after a moment or two, his voice shaking slightly as he said, 'I know we only met a few weeks ago, Hope, but I can't imagine you not being in my life now. Do you know what I mean?'

She nodded, her lids lowered. The kiss, gentle and restrained as it had been, had rocked her to her foundations. She had never been kissed on the mouth before. No one at home indulged in any physical shows of affection, it just wasn't their way, and on the rare occasions when her aunt kissed her, it was a quick peck on the cheek.

'I shall always remember my first sight of you at this very spot. I thought an angel had fallen from heaven.'

He was smiling as she raised her eyes shyly to his.

'An angel in a straw bonnet of course,' he added, 'reading a book. You were very stiff with me that day.'

'I didn't know you,' she said reprovingly although her eyes were laughing at him.

'And now you do.'

Aye, now she did and she couldn't believe her good fortune.

They'd met every Saturday afternoon for the last six weeks, the knowledge she was going to see him again carrying Hope through each week in a rosy haze. Even her work at the northern laundry seemed less taxing, although when it was her turn to check in the dirty washing, it still had the power to turn her stomach. But the walk home from St Mark's Road on the west side of town to her aunt's house in Moorgate Street seemed shorter and the frowsty smell of the laundry which clung to her clothes did not bother her as much as usual.

And then Saturday lunchtime came and she was free of the laundry for a whole thirty-six hours. She would fill up the old tin bath in the scullery, strip off the clothes she'd worn all week and scrub herself from head to foot. Then she would have a bite to eat and escape the East End.

The luxury of a tram ride to the outskirts of Bishopwearmouth was part of the Saturday treat, along with the bliss of only having her library book for company. After the incessant noise and chatter at work and home all week,

Hope ached for solitude. In the winter she'd tramped for hours, often frozen to the marrow but relishing the cold clean air, but in the summer it had been heaven to find a quiet spot and sit and read, the scent of warm grass and flowers in her nostrils and the skylarks serenading her overhead.

'No book today?' Daniel was smiling; they both knew her routine had changed since she'd met him although she had continued to bring a book for outward appearances.

'I forgot it.' She wrinkled her nose. 'Constance was being awkward. She wanted to come with me.'

'I didn't think Constance liked walks in the country.'

'She doesn't but her best friend's got chickenpox and she decided she was bored.'

'Oh dear, poor Constance.' In spite of his words his tone stated he wasn't interested in discussing her sister. His gaze tight on her face, he said softly, 'Will you come out with me tonight, Hope? I thought we could go to the Regal. There's a new Laurel and Hardy film showing and the stage show is very good. I could come and call for you, it would be a good opportunity to meet your aunt and uncle.'

She stared at him, the magic of her first kiss evaporating like the morning mist before the sun. There was nothing in the world she'd like more, but how could she accompany Daniel to somewhere as grand as the Regal in Holmeside? Everyone knew the Regal was the biggest and most luxurious cinema in Sunderland, but even if he'd suggested one of the less stylish picture palaces she still had nothing to wear that wouldn't let him down.

Money was tight at home with her uncle and Bart being out of work, and although Dennis and Norman were still earning, their wages at the shipyard had been cut to near half.

She stumped up fourteen of the sixteen shillings she earned each week to her aunt. She had never had an item of new clothing in her life that she could remember, all her things came from the second-hand stalls at the Old Market and even then she couldn't afford any of the really nice stuff.

'What's the matter? Wouldn't your aunt and uncle approve?'

Hope swallowed. 'It's not that.'

'What then?' There was a pause and then he said quietly, 'Aren't you comfortable about the idea of walking out with me, Hope?'

What could she say? Over the last six Saturdays they had talked and talked about all sorts of things and she had learnt so much about him and his family. He spoke so casually about his mother's dinner parties and bridge club and the tennis matches he and his friends enjoyed and – oh, a whole host of things she had no experience of whatsoever. How could she tell him she only had two sets of working clothes to her name, along with her Sunday outfit which had seen better days? Some of the girls at the laundry were able to put several shillings a week aside for a clothes club and she'd seen them out in new togs, dressed up to the nines some of them. But she knew what an uphill struggle it was for her aunt to make ends meet and they were always weeks and weeks behind with the rent. And Daniel didn't even work, or at least not properly, she amended. He had told her he was working in the office at his father's engineering works for the moment since leaving university, just a few hours each day, but that he was toying with the idea of training to be an architect or something along those lines.

'Hope?' His eyes were gentle and steady as they looked into hers. 'Be honest. You won't hurt my feelings if you want to carry on the way we are for a while.'

It would be easy to grasp the line he'd thrown and the words were hovering on her lips but she found she couldn't voice them. He wasn't uppity, Daniel, he had no side and that had amazed her at first. In spite of his background he was ordinary. No, not ordinary. He was anything but ordinary but . . . Hope gave up trying to put a name to it and took her courage in both hands. 'I'd like to come out with you but I haven't got anything to wear,' she said quickly before she lost her nerve. 'Not for somewhere like the Regal.'

'Oh, Hope.' He was completely taken aback, surprise evident in his raised eyebrows and slightly open mouth. And then, in a voice that brought burning colour into her cheeks, he said, 'You would look stunning in sackcloth and ashes. Don't you know that? Whatever you wear looks lovely on you, you're one of those women who have a natural grace and elegance any amount of money can't buy. You're beautiful. Utterly beautiful.'

She had to restrain herself from wriggling with embarrassment. No one had ever referred to her as a woman before, and certainly she'd never been told she was beautiful. But Daniel thought she was, and he wanted her to go out with him this evening. The glow from within was reflected in Hope's voice when she said, 'If you're sure then.'

'I'm sure. In fact I've never been so sure of anything in my life.'

She fiddled with a sleeve of his jacket, a heat in her body which had nothing to do with the hot summer's day. Daniel Fallow wanted her to be his lass. Even knowing where she came from and that she worked in a laundry and hadn't had a proper education, at least not like he had, he still wanted her to be his lass. She felt as light as thistledown.

'That's settled then.' The lilt in his voice brought her eyes to his and suddenly they were both laughing. They sat quietly for some time after this before he said, 'I'll call for you at six o'clock. That will give us time to talk to your aunt and uncle, and tomorrow afternoon you must come and meet my parents.'

She was startled now, her voice high as she shook her head and said, 'Not tomorrow, Daniel.'

'Aye, tomorrow.' Grinning, he pulled her to her feet. He did not let go of her hands once she was standing but tucked one through his arm and slung his jacket over his other shoulder. 'You're my girl and I want the world to know about it but there'll be hell to pay if I don't tell them at home first. So tomorrow it is. Right? I shall tell them tonight I'm taking you out and that you're coming for afternoon tea tomorrow. Oh, Hope.' He pulled her closer and for a moment she thought he was going to kiss her again, but instead he said softly, 'You don't know how happy you've made me. Come on, I'm going to walk you home and all the way this time. All right? No argument.'

She made to protest; for the last six weeks she had only allowed him to accompany her part of the way home, just to the edge of Mowbray Park. Then she thought better of it. If he was going to call at the house this evening then he might as well get some idea of what he was letting himself in for. She just hoped Mrs Finnigan wasn't sitting on her doorstep as she was prone to do on warm summer evenings. With her man's cap, layers of raggedy petticoats and a predilection for stout which she'd send one of her numerous offspring to fetch in the old grey hen, Mrs Finnigan's name was a byword even in the East End. When she got going she could

19

make old Nick himself blush, or that's what her Aunt Jinny said.

As they left Tunstall Hills and made their way northwards past the farm and old quarries, she felt very self-conscious about her arm being in his, but as he seemed unconcerned she gradually began to relax.

'Do you want to take the tram?' As they neared the tram stop he looked down at her. 'You must be tired after working so hard all week.'

Hope smiled at him. 'I'm not tired and I like walking.' How could she prefer sitting in a creaking old tram with lots of other folk when she could walk in the warm sunshine with her arm in his? Anyone seeing them would know they were a couple and the knowledge was heady.

'So do I.' He smiled back at her and not for the first time since she had met him she asked herself what it was that made him so attractive. He wasn't exactly handsome, his face was too thin and his nose too big for that, but his eyes were lovely. A deep grey fringed by black lashes beneath a head of wavy black hair, but it was their expression that caught her every time. There was a kindness in them, a gentle warmth that made her heart race. She had read in one of her books that the eyes were the window to the soul, and she believed that in Daniel. He was a good man, honourable, but he wasn't stuffy. Not like Clarence Irvin, the vicar's son. She knew Clarence had had his eye on her the last six months but she'd rather die than step out with him.

The thought of Clarence brought home another major problem. 'What will your parents say when they find out I'm not a Catholic?' she asked abruptly. 'Will they mind?'

His hesitation was all the answer she needed, and further

proof was provided when he didn't answer her directly but said, 'They'll probably be the same as your aunt and uncle, I suppose.'

There was no reply to this. From a bairn she had been taught to view all Catholics with deep suspicion; the chapel-goers, the Salvationists, the Quakers, even the Jews were one thing, more misguided than bad, whereas the Catholics . . . On high days and holidays, in particular St Patrick's Day, she had seen lads who were pals the rest of the year fight like cat and dog on the side of Protestant versus Catholic, often until blood ran. Her own male cousins, Bart, Dennis, Norman and William, the latter having recently wed and moved in with his in-laws, had regarded it as a badge of honour to bloody as many Catholic noses as they could. And Enid, Rachel and Mary, their sisters who were all married now, had been as bad, egging the lads on and acting as though they were heroes when they came home tattered and torn.

Whether Daniel had picked up on her train of thought she didn't know, but now he said, 'It might help in the case of your aunt and uncle if I say how I feel. What do you think?'

Hope considered this for a few moments. The last time they'd discussed their respective religions a couple of weeks ago, Daniel had confessed that since being at university he didn't know what to believe. 'Except it's not in a God who decrees every non-Catholic is consigned to the everlasting flames. Not that I think your side's got it right either,' he'd added. 'In fact the narrowness of denominational belief seems at odds to me with the vastness of creation and the natural world. Why should the power that can cause an oak tree to grow from a tiny acorn and keep the rhythm of the tides in perfect accord insist on having a label pinned to it? It's not feasible. It's man's doing. In all the debates we had at university I didn't hear one good reason for such segregation among people who claim to believe in God, Son and Holy Ghost.'

Remembering now how shocked she had felt when he had first spoken, Hope said, 'It's perhaps best if we let my aunt and uncle and the lads get used to the idea we're walking out before you say anything. It'd be enough if I let them know you're not sure about staying a Catholic. They could understand that. They're always going on about how the priests try to dominate folk.'

'Aye, all right.' He stopped, turning her to face him. 'I don't mind what you believe, Hope. Maybe I should but I don't. It doesn't matter. In the long run it's how we feel about each other that counts, isn't it? How many couples do you know who have been married for years and go to church every Sunday but are as miserable as sin together?'

She stared at him, her brows coming together. She couldn't truthfully say she agreed wholeheartedly, everyone knew you should marry someone from the same faith, and yet he had a point. Who did she know who was really happy together, or at least happy in the way she wanted to be when she got married? Even people who had been married just a short while like William and his wife argued and talked rough to each other, but then that was because things were bad with the Depression and all.

No, no it wasn't.

As had happened more and more since she had met Daniel, her mind baulked at the easy answer, challenging her to think clearly.

The spectre of the means test and the dole and the dreaded

words 'laid off' made life worse for the folk she knew, but the filth and grinding poverty evident in every street in the East End had been there for decades, long before unemployment and soup kitchens. It sapped the will from birth, she'd seen it, and she didn't want to live like that. She *wouldn't* live like that. They'd call her an upstart if she dared voice what she felt, but from a little bairn she'd known she wanted to get away. The decay and dirt stifled her. It made her feel as though she was drowning, and she was often conscious of taking long breaths the further she got away from the East End, as though emerging from deep water. And yet her friends, even her cousins, didn't feel like that. Enid, Rachel and Mary had all settled close to their mam, and William's in-laws were just a few doors down.

'Don't look so worried.' Daniel smiled, stroking her face with the tip of his finger before tucking her arm through his again as they began to walk on. 'It'll all work out, I promise. No one is going to spoil things unless we let them and I don't intend to let that happen. How about you?'

Hope shook her head, drumming up a smile in reply although the rational part of her brain told her that family mattered, whatever Daniel might say. She knew his people wouldn't approve of her. Oh, her Aunt Jinny and Uncle George might object to Daniel being a Catholic, in fact she was sure they would, but it wasn't like his parents would be. They wouldn't want him to see her again once they knew, and she'd die if that happened. She wished they could continue with their Saturday afternoon meetings for a while longer. Everything would change now.

It was as they passed the old bandstand on the town moor, its tiered rails hidden by the layers of washing drying in the bright sunlight from the houses close by, that Constance popped up in front of them. She emerged like a jack-in-the-box from a group of squealing children intent on a game of bray the cuddy, the rusty tin they were endeavouring to beat with their sticks landing at Daniel's feet.

Constance's brown eyes were alight with curiosity, her gaze not moving from Daniel as she said, 'You're back early the day, our Hope.'

This was the beginning of it and it would get worse. Her family might or might not rally round, but the news she was courting a lad from the posh end of town – and a Catholic to boot – would spread like wildfire round the backyards. And Hope knew what some of the old wives were like once they got their teeth into someone. The very same neighbours who had clucked in sympathy at the plight of the 'poor wee orphaned bairns' when she and Constance had come to live with their Aunt Jinny, and who had shown them nothing but kindness since, would be the first to put the knife in.

Hope didn't know how she'd come by the knowledge but it was probably instinct that told her that folk hereabouts would take it as a personal affront that she, of all people, had 'aimed high', as they'd put it. Someone they'd always been comfortable feeling sorry for, someone even less fortunate than themselves walking out with a lad from one of the big houses in Ryhope? Well, it was clear what he was after, wasn't it! And they would use the fact that Daniel's family were Catholics as justification for their disapproval, whatever their religion. The unwritten rule that you didn't take up with someone from the opposite side would unite both camps, which was funny in a way if you thought about it.

'Hello, Constance.' Hope tried to keep her voice ordinary.

Turning to Daniel, she said, 'This is my sister, Constance. Constance, this is a friend of mine. Daniel Fallow.'

'How do you do?' Daniel's voice was cheery and he smiled at the pert-faced girl in front of him as he held out his hand.

There was a moment of hesitation on Constance's part and then she took his hand for just a moment, her gaze swinging from Daniel to Hope and then back to Daniel. She giggled, then turned and whirled off after the pack of children who had resumed their game.

'Sorry about that.' Hope had gone red. 'She usually has better manners.'

'She's just a bairn.'

'Hardly, she'll be fourteen in a couple of months and starting work as a housemaid at the Grand.'

'Please don't let it concern you.'

Daniel sounded faintly perplexed. He thought she was making a fuss over nothing, Hope told herself, and maybe she was, but it wasn't nothing to her. She had so wanted his first contact with her family to go well, and Constance had behaved worse than any of the raggedy urchins hereabouts. You'd think she was three instead of thirteen.

In Prospect Row she kept her gaze straight ahead, her cheeks burning. The blazing sunshine seemed to highlight their dismal surroundings and the rotting mess in the gutters rather than making it better, the smell of fish from the harbour competing with human excrement. The backyards always stank to high heaven in the summer but today, owing to the heat-wave, the smell from the privies was particularly foul.

'The next one's Moorgate Street, isn't it?' Daniel said.

'How do you know?' She was surprised into looking at him.

'I've been round here before.' He glanced about him as he spoke. 'It's a bit grim but there's worse.'

She didn't know of any but the relief he had known what to expect was enervating, robbing her of the ability to speak for a moment. He had known where she lived, he'd seen it and yet it didn't matter. He had still asked her to be his lass.

At the top of Moorgate Street Hope stopped, withdrawing her hand from his arm. 'It's better if you don't come all the way with me now so I can tell them first,' she said, her voice lighter than it had been during the walk home. 'Ready for tonight, you know?'

'If that's what you want.'

'It is.'

'Go on then, I'll watch you down.'

He smiled at her and Hope smiled back before walking away. She felt self-conscious as she made her way down the street, knowing he was watching her. Outside the house she glanced back and Daniel waved immediately. She lifted her hand to him but did not prolong the moment; a couple of women were chatting on their doorsteps across the road and she knew their eyes were on her.

Inside the house Hope stood for a moment in the narrow dingy hall, her heart racing. Her uncle and the lads would be at the football but her aunt would be in the kitchen, she was rarely anywhere else. After taking off her hat and coat Hope smoothed her hair and then opened the kitchen door.

'Hello, hinny.' Her aunt was stirring something on the big black range and she waved her hand as she said, 'I've just made a brew. Pour us a cup, would you, lass? I'm parched.'

Hope did as she was told and it was only when she was sitting at the scrubbed kitchen table that she said, 'Can I talk to you a minute, Aunt Jinny? Before the others come home?'

'Aye, lass.' Jinny's voice was relaxed but her gaze had narrowed on Hope's face. She left the stew and came and plonked her large frame on a chair opposite. 'Trouble, lass?' she said softly.

'No, not really. At least . . .' Hope's voice trailed away. Taking a deep breath, she said, 'I've met a lad, Aunt Jinny. A nice lad. He wants us to start courting but his family's well-off, his da has his own business and everything. And . . . and he's a Catholic, or rather his family is. He doesn't hold with the Catholic thinking. He wants to come and meet you and Uncle George tonight . . .' She paused for breath, adding lamely, as she took in her aunt's wide eyes and gaping mouth, 'What do you think?'

Her aunt didn't answer immediately. She blinked a couple of times, shut her mouth and swallowed hard before she said, 'I've never bin a drinkin' woman but right at this moment I could do with a drop of the hard stuff an' no mistake. By, lass, you've fair took me breath away. Look, you start at the beginnin' an' I'll get us a bite of sly cake while we're talkin', all right?'

Hope nodded, and then as her aunt stood up she reached across the table and touched her arm. 'Thanks, Aunt Jinny,' she said softly. She might have known she could rely on her Aunt Jinny. Her uncle and the lads were a different kettle of fish, but come what may, she wasn't going to give up Daniel. Not while she had breath in her body.

Chapter 3

Daniel remained leaning against the wall of the house where he'd settled himself, his hands in his pockets, after Hope had disappeared. His gaze went up and down the dismal street for a few seconds before it fastened on a group of shabbily dressed bairns playing a skipping game with a bit of old rope they had found, their bare feet as brown and hard as tanned leather. One small boy had his bottom hanging out of his tattered trousers and another child, a little girl, had running sores from nose to mouth.

Daniel stared at them. How on earth could they appear so happy when every one of them looked undernourished and crawling with lice? Poor little devils. They didn't stand a chance in life, not being born round here.

'Got a penny to spare, mister?'

One of the bigger lads who looked to be all of seven or eight had noticed him watching them and now approached, one filthy hand extended, his wide grin showing blackened stubs of teeth. Daniel was about to refuse, then suddenly thought, why not? The lad wasn't begging, not really, he was just making the most of an opportunity which had presented itself.

'Aye, all right.' He delved into his pocket and found the rest of the group had magically gathered round him in the blink of an eye, eyes wide and eager smiles on their dirty faces. After placing a penny in each grubby paw, Daniel turned and walked away, their excited chatter behind him making him smile. A penny and you'd have thought they'd been given the earth, but then a penny had to go a long way round these parts. His smile died and he quickened his pace, not slowing until he was well past the town moor and Hendon junction. When he reached Hendon cricket ground he stopped and mopped his brow with his handkerchief before he continued to walk on, his mind on Hope. He hated leaving her there. From the moment he had taken it upon himself to go and see where she lived a couple of weeks ago, the desire to whisk her away out of it had been overpowering. Did she have any idea how strongly he felt about her? How he wanted her to the point of distraction?

No, of course she didn't. And he didn't want to rush her either. She was like a child in some ways, innocent, unawakened, certainly with regard to the physical side of love. And he wouldn't want it any other way. But those couple of relationships he'd indulged in at university with modern young women who had been absolutely determined to experience anything and everything had proved to be a mixed blessing. Exhilarating and instructive certainly, but where was the off switch when you needed it?

He smiled ruefully. If he went to confession Father McHaffie would be quick to point out that all sin had its price, and in this, if nothing else, Daniel had to admit the Church had a point.

The sun was still hot on his head but without the power of noonday. Now the stench of the East End was out of his nostrils, Daniel found he was enjoying the walk. He'd just have time for a bath and a change of clothes once he was home; he'd have to break the news about Hope tomorrow morning. That would do.

He refused to acknowledge he was procrastinating. As a little niggle of conscience made itself felt, he justified himself by arguing that as long as there was a bit of time before his parents were due to meet Hope, what did it matter? In fact it would give his mother in particular less time to stew.

When he reached Ryhope Road his surroundings became markedly pleasanter. Before his surreptitious visit to the East End, he had never given much thought to the area in which he'd been brought up since the age of four or five, but now he found himself appreciating the scents and colours in the grounds of the houses he was passing. Some of the establishments were very substantial detached properties, homes of the town's more affluent figures. Others, like his own, were somewhat less grand but provided well-to-do families with fine accommodation, discreetly high laurel hedges and long drives, all of which gave the overall impression of well-mannered wealth.

He turned into the pebbled drive of his home, passing between two open wrought-iron gates secured by drawbolts. As his gaze went to the two cars parked in front of the solid looking house, he groaned softly. Cecil was here. This meant his father had undoubtedly been informed he'd messed up on the tender for Randall's, although he still didn't see why it was such a disaster that he hadn't marked the envelope as Cecil had ordered. But that was Cecil all over, making a drama out of the least thing he did wrong. He wouldn't be at all surprised if his brother had called round merely to drop him in it, what with his father not being in the office this morning. He would have admitted his mistake over breakfast tomorrow, that had been his plan, but he might have known Cecil would try and get in first. Oh aye, his brother would be making a meal out of this if he knew anything.

As Daniel walked up the drive, his face settled into an expression which made him appear far older than his years. At the front door he stood for a minute and mentally steeled himself for what might be awaiting him. Then he opened the door with his key and stepped into the large square hall. He cocked his head towards the drawing room. They were in there, he could hear them. Or he could hear his father at least.

'You're back early, lad.'

Daniel hadn't noticed the housekeeper walking down the central staircase but now he smiled at the thin figure in black. 'I'm not staying long, Annie. I'm seeing someone shortly.'

'Oh aye?' A pair of beady black eyes surveyed him and the severely plain face with its hooked nose broke into a smile. 'Do I know her?'

'Who said it was a her?'

'You did. Not in so many words but you've been different the last few weeks and I thought it might be a lassie. I'm not daft, you know.'

No, Annie wasn't daft. Daniel stepped forward as she reached the bottom of the stairs and took one of her hands in his. He said softly, 'No one knows yet and I think I'm in hot water about something else, so keep mum till I tell them tomorrow, but you're right, I've met someone. The thing is, she isn't from round these parts, Ryhope I mean. She's from the East End.'

'The East End?' Annie Croft's voice had risen but now she moderated it as she whispered, 'Ee, your mam'll go mad. You know that, don't you? She'll go mad, him an' all. They're having another dinner party this coming week.'

Daniel closed his eyes briefly. 'Who is it this time?'

'The Sheltons are bringing their daughter, the youngest one.'

'Olive? She looks like a horse and horses are all she's bothered about. Even if I was interested in her, which I'm not, I wouldn't stand a chance unless I had a mane and plaited tail and a nose even bigger than this one.' He touched his face as he spoke, his voice wry.

'Oh you.' Annie nudged him with her elbow and they grinned at each other. Then she bent forward, her voice conspiratorial. 'Cecil got here some twenty minutes ago. I don't know what it's about but your da wasn't too happy. With him, I mean. So if that has a bearing on your hot water . . .'

Nothing in this house escaped Annie. In fact Daniel thought she knew more about him and his brother and two sisters than their mother did. In one of the spontaneous gestures of affection which had characterised him from a child, he leant forward and kissed the housekeeper on her cheek. 'Thanks, Annie,' he said softly. 'I'd better go and face the music.'

'Aye, all right, lad.' Annie patted him on the arm, her face tender. 'Your sister and her husband will be here shortly, by the way. They're coming for dinner but your mam wanted cocktails first.'

They looked at each other, a long look. Daniel knew Annie would never say a word against either of his parents but now, as he'd done often since going away to university and having his eyes opened, he wondered how she stood his mother's airs and graces. Annie had known his mother and father from childhood. The three of them had lived in the maze of terraced streets close to the workhouse in Chester Road, and he knew they'd all been snotty-nosed urchins without a pair of boots between them because his father had told him so. But for his da having the Midas touch, likely he and his siblings would be living in those streets too, but from small beginnings his father had risen to own a very successful engineering works that was still doing well even in the current climate. And Daniel was proud of his da, more than proud, especially because his da wasn't ashamed of his beginnings like his mam was. Annie had to wear a black dress and little cap, and he and his brother and sisters had to call their mam Mother, and dress for dinner even when they were on their own – all this smacked of pretension. But his mam couldn't see it. She would never see it.

'Go on then. Get it over with.'

Annie gave him a little push with the flat of her hand and then laughed, her hand going over her mouth as he growled playfully, 'Hey, who do you think you're shoving, woman?' before walking across the deep red carpet and opening the door into the drawing room.

Four pairs of eyes looked his way. His father was standing with his back to the fireplace which contained an elaborate flower display. Cecil was seated with their mother on a long chesterfield directly opposite, and his younger sister, Rosaleen, was curled up in a chair next to the seventeenth-century writing desk his mother was so fond of. It was Rosaleen who said, 'Are your ears burning, Daniel? They should be. We were deciding why you disappear so mysteriously every Saturday afternoon.'

'Shut up.' Abe didn't look at his youngest child as he spoke but kept his eyes on Daniel. 'Where've you been?'

'Here and there.' It was facetious but Rosaleen's amusement and the fact they'd been discussing him had caught him on the raw.

'Aye, no doubt. Let me put it another way. What was so important that you couldn't put it off when Cecil told you about the pig's breakfast you made with Randall's tender? Not that he,' Abe jerked his head at his elder son, 'should have left the sending of it to you anyway. Not with you not knowing your arse from your elbow half the time in the office.'

His mother made a sound in her throat at this use of the English language, but after a glance in her direction, his father's eyes returned to him. Daniel knew it wasn't the moment to tell them about Hope but something in him was already savouring their shock when he made it clear he did not intend to stand by and meekly let his parents choose his future spouse as his elder brother and sister had done.

The thought brought Daniel up short, shocking him. He hadn't been aware until this moment how deeply he resented the procession of young women, most of them daughters of his parents' friends, who had been paraded before him over the last three years under the guise of dinner parties. Without pausing to consider his words, he said, 'I was meeting someone. I've met her every Saturday afternoon for the last six weeks actually.'

34

Their reactions were what he'd expected and yet, no, that wasn't quite true, not in his father's case. Cecil was gaping at him and Rosaleen clapped her hands, squealing something about him being a dark horse and the quiet ones were always the worst, while his mother glared at him. But he couldn't quite make out what his father was thinking, except, as he put it to himself, he didn't seem very surprised.

Instead of firing a barrage of questions at the top of his voice, his father said quietly, 'Six weeks and you've only just brought yourself to mention it, lad? Why is that?'

'I didn't see the need, I suppose.'

'Didn't see the need?' His mother reared up as though someone had prodded her with a pin. 'Are you mad? Who is this girl?'

'*Emily*, I'll handle this.'

His father's voice cut off his mother's volley as effectively as turning off a tap, but only for a moment. Swinging her head to meet her husband's gaze, Emily Fallow delivered a look which would have floored lesser men. 'Did you hear what he said? Did you?'

'Of course I heard, I'm not deaf.'

'Who is she?' Cecil found his voice. 'Someone you met at university?'

'No she's not, as it happens.' Daniel's voice was clipped. The university gripe again; Cecil couldn't let it alone. It wasn't his fault his father had flatly refused to agree to Cecil furthering his education, couldn't he see that? When his mother, in an effort to keep the peace between him and Cecil, had first told him the reason for his brother's resentment, he had felt some sympathy for Cecil. He would be the first to admit that Cecil was brighter than him and a whiz with figures and it must have been galling when his father had drummed Cecil straight into the business at the age of four-teen instead of listening to his brother's pleas, and those of his teachers, that he be allowed to continue with his studies. But his sympathy and understanding had worn thin as time had gone on, not least because of the spitefulness Cecil had displayed since the moment he had heard a place at Edinburgh University was secure.

Daniel took his eyes from Cecil and spoke directly to his father when he said, 'Her name is Hope Woodrow and we met by chance while out walking.'

'By chance?' Again his mother interrupted. 'You mean you weren't properly introduced? You picked this girl up?'

For crying out loud! Who did his mam think she was kidding? Anyone would think they were all descended from the nobility, listening to her.

'Don't be so terribly old-fashioned, Mother.' Help came from an unexpected quarter as Rosaleen spoke. Although only sixteen and therefore a year younger than Hope, his sister seemed a decade older to Daniel. Rosaleen had been spared the Fallow large nose and thinness of face which was just about passable on the male members of the family but on Bernice, his elder sister, made for acute plainness. Instead, as his mother loved to point out to all and sundry, Rosaleen took after her, being blue-eyed and chestnut-haired with a button nose and pretty face. She had been their mother's favourite from birth, and had been hopelessly spoilt.

'People don't worry about being introduced these days,' Rosaleen continued airily. 'There are heaps of new people at the tennis club this season and absolutely no one stands on formality. It's just not done.'

'Is that so?' Abe's brows drew together. 'Well, all I can say is that if this is what this fancy finishing school your mother persuaded me to send you to teaches you, I'm wasting me money.'

Ignoring her father, Rosaleen eyed Daniel interestedly. 'Is she one of the Newcastle Woodrows? There's an Eleanor Woodrow at the school.'

He couldn't care less who was at her precious school. Daniel looked at his father as he said, 'Hope and her sister were orphaned as very young children. An aunt in the East End took them in. And you might as well hear the rest. They're not Catholics.'

This silenced even Rosaleen. For a moment or two the silence was absolute. Then Abe broke it, his voice sharp and clipped and his face grim. 'Right, I think you an' me have got some talking to do, lad. In private, in the study, now. An' you,' he swung his glance to Cecil, 'I'm not finished with you yet, not by a long chalk, but it'll wait till Monday morning. Get yourself home to that wife of yours.'

'I don't see how you can blame me for Daniel's mistake.'

'Aye, you've said, but who runs the business? You or me? Now unless you want to feel me toe up your backside, get moving.'

There was a moment when Daniel thought Cecil was going to stand up to their father for once in his life. But then he got sulkily to his feet and after a muttered, 'Goodbye, Mother,' walked out into the hall.

Daniel glanced at his mother as Abe followed Cecil out of the room. Her face could have been set in granite, the expression at odds with the pretty, almost babyish features. There was no point in saying anything, he knew that, but in spite of himself he said, 'Hope's a nice girl, a really nice girl. If you give her half a chance, you'll see that.'

'I have no wish to see it, Daniel. Or her.'

He straightened, his face taking on the expression it had worn on entering the house. 'I see. So that's the way it's going to be, is it?'

'What did you expect?' Emily snapped back, her colour high.

'That you might act like a proper mother for once.'

'Don't speak to her like that. You know she only wants the best for you.' Rosaleen got up and went to kneel at her mother's side. She took her hand as Daniel stared at them both. They were as alike as two peas in a pod. In his mother he could see Rosaleen in thirty years' time.

Biting back the harsh retort hovering on his lips, he turned on his heel and left the room, banging the door behind him. It was a petty gesture, futile, but it stoked up the anger burning inside him and he needed its strength when dealing with his father.

Abe was just shutting the door on Cecil. The sharp grey eyes narrowed on Daniel's face. 'Come on, lad,' he said quietly. 'Let's discuss this without an audience, just you an' me.'

The tone wasn't what Daniel had expected after his father's last words in the drawing room. He felt his resolve weakening and he couldn't afford to be weak. Forcing a belligerence which didn't come naturally to him, he said, 'Why bother? You and Mother have already made up your minds about Hope and you haven't even met her yet. Nor will you, according to Mother,' he added bitterly.

'I care about you, lad. That's why I'm bothering. You're young still, gullible. If some lass has got her eye on a meal ticket—'

'It's not like that.' Daniel's hands were clenched at his side, his face burning. 'You couldn't be more wrong. She doesn't *think* like that. We got friendly before I even told her about the business and everything.'

Abe could have pointed out that the way he dressed, the quality of his clothes and general air of well-being would have spoken for itself. Instead he said, 'You say she doesn't think like that so come an' tell me how she does think. I can't know if you don't tell me, now can I? Talk to me, lad.'

Daniel stood undecided for a moment and then accompanied his father down the hall to the study. Once they were both seated they stared at each other for a moment or two before Abe shook his head. 'Take that look off your face, Dan. I'm not your enemy, far from it. Surely you know that. I thought there was enough between us for you to be able to talk to me about anything.'

'Aye, there is, but . . .'

'But what?'

Daniel shrugged. This wasn't going at all the way he had thought. He had expected his father to shout and bellow and he could have coped with that by shouting back, but this quiet, almost hurt attitude . . . 'I knew you'd be against it.'

'If I remember rightly you said the same about university but I backed you there, didn't I?'

'This . . . this is different.'

'Aye, lad.' Abe's voice was flat. 'This is different. I take it this lass is not just some passing fancy?'

'No, she's not.'

Abe nodded. 'And were you planning on introducing us sometime?'

'Tomorrow.' A thread of eagerness came into Daniel's voice.

'I told her this afternoon that I'd bring her to meet you all tomorrow afternoon. I'm meeting her folk tonight before we go out. You'll like her, Da, I know you will. She's bonny but it's not just that. She's special, wonderful.'

Abe watched the light come back into his son's eyes as he talked on. It was a minute or two before Daniel ran out of steam, and it was only then that Abe said, 'If you're meeting the lass's family tonight, you'd better move yourself, lad. It wouldn't do to be late, now would it? And tell her we're looking forward to seeing her tomorrow, all right?' His lips smiled.

The light dimmed as Daniel said, 'What about Mother?'

'Leave your mam to me, lad. An' frankly, you couldn't have expected much more from her, springing it on us like you did.'

'I know, I know. I didn't want to tell you like that.'

'Aye, well, it's done now.' As sounds registered from the hall, Abe added, 'Your sister an' Rupert have arrived, if I'm not mistaken. Your mam'll be faffing about her blasted cocktails if I don't make an appearance. You cut along.'

'Da?' As Daniel stood up and Abe joined him, Daniel put a hand on his father's arm. 'Thanks.'

'Nowt to thank me for.' But Abe patted the hand on his arm before they walked into the hall.

Annie was standing a few feet away. She looked at Abe and said, 'She sent me to tell you she wants you in there. She's in a bit of a stew. But I didn't like to interrupt you and Daniel.'

Abe ran an irritable hand through his grizzly grey hair, the action expressing his thoughts on the evening ahead more effectively than words.

'And I'm to bring in the canapés once you're in there.'

'Canapés?' It was a snort. 'By all the saints, she's had you making canapés now? Bits of nothing, they are.'

'It's what you do if you serve cocktails.'

'Aye, mebbe, but I'm a beer and chitterlings man as you well know. Times were we'd have thought we'd landed in heaven if we'd had tuppence worth of chitterlings and a full belly. Me mam'd turn in her grave if she saw them canapés.'

Annie didn't reply to this directly, but her voice was soft when she said, 'You go in to her and I'll bring the canapés through. Oh, and I've run you a bath, Daniel. Thought it'd save you a bit of time.'

'Thanks, Annie.' Daniel nodded at her before taking the stairs two at a time.

It was only when he had disappeared into his room that Annie looked Abe straight in the face. 'So? What do you think?'

Both the words and the manner in which they were spoken suggested the two were used to speaking frankly. Abe answered in like vein when he said, 'What do I think? That he's a damn fool. That's what I think, lass. I'm long enough in the tooth to know the sort who's got her hooks into him. They're ten a penny in that area. Likely she sees Daniel as a way of getting out of the muck, an' while I can't blame anyone for wanting something better, there's ways and means. Let her find some other charlie who's still wet behind the ears, but not my lad. Not while I've breath in me body. What good could come out of it, I ask you? And the lass not even a Catholic.'

'She's not of the faith?'

'No, she damn well isn't. It appears you didn't know it all for once then.'

Abe's tone brought Annie stiffening, her voice sharp when she said, 'He only told me about her tonight, if you're wondering, Abe Fallow, although to be truthful I've thought something was up for weeks the way he's been.'

'Aye, me an' all, but I didn't think he was barmy enough to take up with some lass who's no better than she should be. I thought it was a girl at the bottom of things but I expected it to be one of the lasses from the tennis club, someone like that.'

'Did you take that tack with him?'

'Don't be daft. He's like some knight or other defending his lady. Lady! Huh!' They stared at each other. Then Abe said, 'I might be like a bull in a china shop half the time but I can play it canny when I want to, don't you fret.'

Annie dug her teeth into her bottom lip. 'Canny or not, he's twenty-one years old, don't forget. He's lived away on and off for nigh on three years and I dare bet we don't know the half of what he got up to.'

'Meaning?'

'Meaning he's not the lad he was.'

'No?'

'No. And don't look at me like that, I'm only telling you what's under your nose. At his age you'd been married for twelve months and Cecil was on the way.'

'Aye, and I was working all hours an' robbing Peter to pay Paul often as not, but he's not me, is he? He wasn't dragged up in the gutter and I'm glad of it. The last thing I want him to do now is to mess his life up.'

'You might not be able to stop him. He's more like you than you give him credit for.'

'You're saying I should stand back and watch this little huzzy get her hooks further into him?'

'No, of course I'm not saying that.'

'I should damn well think not.' Abe glared at the woman he considered as much a part of his family as his own children, and whose advice he secretly valued more than that of his wife. 'It's got to be nipped in the bud, any fool can see that, but there's more ways of killing a cat than drowning it. If I meet him head on in this he'll dig his heels in, I see that. I didn't need you to tell me.'

Annie ignored this. 'What are you going to do then?'

'Have her round tomorrow like he wants but I'll make sure she knows I'm on to her little game. I'll see to it she's way out of her depth and if she's a grain of sense she'll bow out gracefully. I haven't got to where I am today without learning a bit about what makes folk tick.'

'I could give Father McHaffie the nod at Mass tomorrow morning and see he "accidentally" pays a visit after lunch?'

'Now you're talking, lass.' Abe's face split into a grin. 'He could put the fear of God into the devil himself, Father McHaffie. Aye, you do that, Annie, but not a word to Emily. She can't act to save her life and she'll give the game away to Daniel if she knows owt. I'd better go and do the honours,' he added hastily, 'an' you bring them canapés in. That'll put the smile back on her face. An' thanks, lass,' he added softly. 'You're a good un.'

Annie nodded, but it was some seconds after Abe had closed the drawing room door behind him before she moved. And then it was slowly, her shoulders bowed as though beneath a great weight.

In the kitchen she did not immediately pick up the elongated plate holding the selection of canapés. Instead she walked over to the long mirror fixed on the far wall next to the big oak dresser holding the family's weekday crockery. Emily had insisted on installing the mirror so Annie could check her appearance before she served at the table when they had guests. It was rare Annie took advantage of it. She never looked at herself once she was dressed in the mornings, not if she could help it.

Annie stared at herself now for a full ten seconds, one finger tracing the curved outline of her beak of a nose and pointed chin. 'Be grateful he sees you as a friend and confidante and you're part of his life,' she whispered. 'You prayed in the beginning that if you could just be near him it'd be enough, and you've had that. It's you who runs his house and practically brought up the bairns and he knows it, even if he's never said. For all her fluffy hair and big blue eyes, she couldn't keep this house running as smoothly as you do. Not that she has to. She just smiles at him and he's putty in her hands.'

Her hand dropped to her side, her fingers clenching as she turned from the pain in the dark eyes looking back at her.

She walked across to the table and picked up the plate of canapés, staring down at the fancy bits of pastry with their different fillings. Her voice held deep bitterness when she murmured, 'Canapés . . .'

Chapter 4

It was exactly six o'clock when the knock came at the front door. Hope cast a quick glance at her aunt who nodded back. 'Go on then, hinny, let him in. Don't keep him on the doorstep in case he turns tail an' scarpers. An' you three,' Jinny's glance took in her sons sitting sullenly at the kitchen table, the remains of their evening meal still in front of them, 'you remember what I said. Keep a civil tongue in your heads or I'll skelp you, big as you are. Your da an' me can deal with this, it don't need you chippin' in. Isn't that right, George?'

The small man puffing away on his pipe did not reply to this, but his mild blue eyes met his wife's and their expression must have satisfied Jinny, because she turned to Constance sitting beside her and said, 'You help me start to clear the table, lass. With them three rantin' an' ravin' we're all behind.'

When Hope opened the door and Daniel smiled at her, a thrill of pride surged through her, washing away the leaden feeling her cousins' reaction to her news had produced. He looked lovely, not just smart but . . . She couldn't find a word to describe the feeling that was sending little shivers down her spine.

He bent his head, his voice a whisper when he said, 'How did your aunt take it?'

She was glad she could whisper back in all honesty, 'She's fine, my uncle too. What about your parents?'

'My father said to tell you he's looking forward to meeting you.'

'Come in, they're waiting.' She pulled him over the threshold, wishing her aunt had cooked something less pungent than herring for dinner but they'd been cheap, eight a penny the night before when one of the old fishwives down at the docks had wanted a quick sale for the remains in her basket so she could get off home.

Daniel didn't say a word as he followed her down the gloomy passage; the jocular ease of manner he normally assumed seemed to have fallen from him. She could understand that. She was going to be scared witless tomorrow when she met his folk. She just hoped Bart, Dennis and Norman wouldn't go for him; with her Aunt Jinny there, they probably wouldn't dare. She threw open the door, standing to one side and beckoning for Daniel to walk into the kitchen. 'This is Daniel, everyone. Daniel, this is my Aunt Jinny and Uncle George and my cousins, Bart, Dennis and Norman. You've already met Constance, haven't you?'

'Pleased to meet you.' Daniel wasn't sure whether to offer to shake hands, but as none of the men had got to their feet or even moved, he merely nodded at each one in turn. When his gaze rested on Hope's aunt, he saw she was smiling. She was also one of the fattest women he had ever seen in his life; her shape made her appear as wide as she was tall and her huge breasts strained the seams of her faded brown blouse. Her husband looked tiny by comparison, small and sinewy, but the sons took after their mother; they were big and hefty, and they didn't look overjoyed to see him.

'Come in an' take the weight off, lad.' Jinny moved away from the range where she had been standing and pulled out a chair from beneath the table. 'There's still some tea in the pot if you'd like a sup afore you go.'

'Thank you.' He didn't want any tea but he didn't like to refuse.

'An' so you an' Hope met out Tunstall way on one of them walks of hers? Times were as a bairn I used to pick black-berries there near the old quarry but I daresay it's all different now. Our mam used to make pies with 'em and send me sellin' 'em round the doors hopin' for a bit of housekeepin' but ten to one me da'd nab the money for his beer. Graspin' swine, me da was. Never liked you, did he, George?'

Jinny didn't wait for a reply but continued, 'George stood up to him, see? He weren't scared of me da like most folk were and me da knew it. Little bloke me da was but nasty with it.'

Daniel couldn't imagine anyone much smaller than Hope's uncle but Jinny was talking as though her husband was six feet tall. Perhaps he was in her eyes. Daniel decided he liked Jinny. He also thought there might be a covert message in the fat little woman's words regarding the stance he should take.

'Here, lad.' Jinny pushed the cup she'd been filling with stewed black tea towards him. 'Get that down you.'

Daniel glanced round the table for milk and sugar. There was none. Surmising, rightly, that the family did without such luxuries, he took a sip of the tannic brew, forcing himself not to flinch as his tastebuds curled up in protest.

'Hope tells me you're takin' her to the Regal?' said Jinny as Constance sidled in from the scullery where she had been washing the dishes and stood staring.

'Talking of which, we ought to be going,' Hope cut in quickly, feeling she couldn't stand it a minute longer. Her cousins were sitting like lumps of wood and Constance was standing with her eyes popping out – what would he think of them all? And her uncle hadn't said a word, not that anyone could when her aunt got going. But Aunt Jinny was only trying to make Daniel feel welcome in her own way.

'Aye, all right, pet.' Jinny smiled benevolently. 'You two enjoy yourselves. You're only young once.'

'Thank you for the tea, Mrs Craggs.' Daniel stood. 'It was nice meeting you all.'

It was at this point George took his pipe out of his mouth. 'You an' all, lad.' And then he added, with a quietness that gave added emphasis to his words, 'You make sure you look after her, all right? Me an' the wife might not be her natural mam an' da but we love her like our own an' she's a good lass. One of the best.'

Feeling he had caught a glimpse of the straight-talking individual who had stood up to Jinny's father, Daniel returned the steady blue gaze. 'I know that, Mr Craggs, and I'll look after her. It will be a privilege.'

Scarlet with embarrassment, Hope all but dragged him out of the kitchen and into the hall, snatching her hat and coat from the rickety hooks in the wall near the front door but not stopping to put them on until they were some distance from the house. 'I'm sorry.' She didn't look at Daniel as she

48

spoke, taking her time doing up her coat buttons. For her uncle to speak like that! As though Daniel had asked for her hand in marriage or something.

'What for?'

'My uncle.'

'He loves you, Hope.' Daniel stopped, forcing her to stop too and meet his soft gaze. 'And he's absolutely right to say what he did.' His eyes moved over her flushed face under the straw bonnet and the rush of love and desire that flooded him made his voice gruff when he said, 'I can understand he wants to protect you. So do I.'

She stared at him, not speaking, aware he was saying much more than the mere words conveyed. His meaning was in the deep husky quality to his voice and the way he was looking at her. For a shining moment the scene in the kitchen was forgotten and with it the mean dirty street in which they were standing. Suddenly this evening was filled with magic and anything was possible. Even . . . even Daniel falling in love with her.

'Come on.' He took her hand, tucking it through his arm as he had done that afternoon. 'Like your aunty said, we're out to enjoy ourselves and we're only young once, remember.'

Hope giggled. 'She liked you, I could tell.'

'I liked her. And your uncle.'

'Did you? Did you really?' Her mouth was unsmiling now.

Again he stopped but this time, careless of the women gossiping on their doorsteps and the bairns playing in the shafts of sunlight slanting across the dusty pavements, he took her face in the palms of his hands. 'How could I not like them when they love you?' he said very softly. 'They're good people, I can see that, but even if they weren't I'd like them because they love you. I came alive the moment I met you. Before that I realise I was only half alive, do you know what I mean?'

She nodded, unaware she was holding her breath.

'I love you, Hope. I've been waiting to say it for weeks, since that first Saturday.'

'Why . . . why didn't you then?'

'I didn't want you to think I was spinning you a line. You might have thought it was too quick.'

No, she wouldn't, because she had felt the same.

And as though he had read her mind, he said, 'Tell me how you feel. Say it.'

'I love you.' Her face was aglow, the rigid barriers of class and religion swept away. 'I always have, even before I met you.'

That sounded silly but Daniel nodded. 'Since the beginning of time,' he murmured. 'Always and for ever.'

They stared at each other, wonder in their shared gaze. It was Hope who said, 'Do you want to go to the Regal?'

'Not if you don't.'

'Could we just walk instead? We could look round the Winter Garden and watch the bowling in Mowbray Park. It's such a lovely evening.' And find a quiet park bench away from the main paths. She didn't want to share him with lots of other people, not tonight. She wanted his whole attention.

'That's fine by me. We can do the Regal another evening.' And then he added, his voice husky, 'We've the rest of our lives to do things together, after all.'

The next afternoon when Daniel came to collect Hope for tea with his parents, the enchantment of the previous evening had been swallowed up by harsh reality for both of them. Before church Hope had endured her three cousins going on and on about the folly of continuing to see Daniel, and then she had seen Bart talking to Clarence Irvin before the service. Immediately afterwards Clarence and his father had made their way over to her and the others, the Reverend's face sorrowful and Clarence's aggrieved. A painful few minutes had ensued from which Hope had emerged upset and guilt-ridden, even though she told herself she'd done nothing to be ashamed of.

On Daniel's side, it had become evident to him that as far as his mother was concerned he had done something unfor-givable in asking Hope to be his lass – or 'that chit from the East End' as his mother had put it. Her terminology had caused a row between them which had shook the rafters, with the result that he had said far more than he'd intended. He'd further compounded his fall from grace by refusing to accompany the womenfolk to Sunday Mass, a move he regretted with hindsight. Not because he felt any guilt about refusing to attend a church he'd long since felt at odds with and in which his father only put in an appearance on high days and holidays, but because his decision had given his mother further ammunition against Hope. He was kicking himself for not having had the courage of his convictions months before.

Hope was waiting in the hall for Daniel's arrival; as soon as he knocked on the door she joined him outside. She was wearing her Sunday best under her summer coat, a pale lemon frock with a dark brown belt and collar, but as the dress had been second-hand when she had bought it twelve months before, she was only too aware it was past its best.

This worry paled into insignificance when Hope caught sight of the large gleaming automobile parked in front of the house. All the bairns in the street were gathered round it, running mucky fingers over the shining paintwork.

'My father offered us the use of his car,' said Daniel, taking her hand as he spoke.

Hope almost groaned out loud. This flamboyant show of wealth would make things harder in the coming days with the more spiteful neighbours. And then she looked into Daniel's face and saw the pleasure his father's gesture had given him. Forcing a wide smile, she said, 'That was nice of him, I've never ridden in a car before,' her chin lifting as though she was already doing battle with Mrs Finnigan and the rest.

'I think it was because my mother's played up a bit about things,' said Daniel, feeling he had to give her some warning as to the situation at home but hating having to say it. 'She's mad at me because I didn't say anything about us sooner,' he added lamely.

Hope nodded but said nothing. His mother was angry about far more than that and they both knew it.

Once Daniel had helped her into the car and closed the passenger door, Hope became aware of a sea of twitching curtains. This, combined with the overall grandeur and strangeness of her surroundings, held her as taut as piano wire. She wanted to put her hands to her hot cheeks as Daniel joined her but instead she sat perfectly still and straight after smiling at him nervously. They had been travelling for over a minute or so before she felt sufficiently in control of herself to make conversation. 'I didn't know you could drive a car. It looks very difficult with all those knobs and things.'

'Da taught me a couple of years ago,' Daniel said airily. 'There's not much to it once you get the hang of things although it'll be a while before I take on Malcolm Campbell. Two hundred and forty-five miles per hour he reached last year. Can you imagine that?'

Hope couldn't. She had no idea of the speed they were travelling now but compared to the lumbering trams it seemed terribly fast. She had never felt so scared in her life but the feeling of exhilaration was stronger. She hoped her Aunt Jinny had seen her drive off, she'd be tickled pink. Her mouth turned up momentarily at the thought. Almost immediately, though, the enormity of what the afternoon entailed crowded in on her again. And his mam was against her. Daniel's mother hadn't even met her yet but she was against her, maybe the others too for all she knew.

In no time at all they were on Ryhope Road and now Hope felt physically sick with nerves. For the life of her she couldn't respond to Daniel's conversation with anything other than monosyllables. These big grand houses and everything so quiet and still, no bairns playing games in the street or neighbours chatting over the backyard wall. It was another world, another universe.

When they drew to a halt some way down the road and Daniel left the engine running, Hope stared at him in surprise. 'I want to say something before we arrive,' he said softly, reaching across and taking one of her hands which was stone cold in spite of the warmth of the day. 'It's just this. I love you and you love me. Nothing else matters. *Nothing*. I've told them all that so they know how the land lies, all right? And I'll be at your side every minute.'

If he had thought to make her feel better, it wasn't working.

Panic had clamped her mouth shut and frozen her limbs.

'You know that bit in the Bible where it goes on about a man leaving his father and mother and taking a wife and the two become one? I even quoted that at them this morning.' Daniel grinned.

Finding her voice at last, Hope said shakily, 'I bet that went down like a lead balloon.'

'It's there in black and white, though, and they can't argue with it, or the fact I have to make my own life independent of them.'

'I suppose not.' She looked at him, her eyes enormous in the whiteness of her face and suddenly he pulled her to him, knocking off her straw bonnet as he kissed her so soundly she was gasping for air when he finally drew away. The chill in her body was swallowed up by the warmth of his love and for a moment she felt she could take on a hundred Fallows and win.

Chapter 5

'The car's here.' Abe had had Annie stationed in the hall for some time while he kept an eye out for Daniel's return. 'Now don't forget what I told you. Don't give her time to get her bearings. However hard-boiled this girl is, I want her to see from the outset she's bitten off more than she can chew in taking me on. You look the part in that black dress an' cap thing, I'll say that for Emily. So stand on ceremony, all right?'

'Don't go on,' said Annie stonily. 'I know what to do.'

'Aye, all right, lass,' said Abe soothingly, aware he had put his foot in it but not sure how. 'It's just that with Emily getting the lad all riled up, it's made things harder. I told her how he was an' to play it canny for the time being but she couldn't contain herself, I suppose. Been awake half the night she has, worrying about him.'

Worrying she'd lost her chance to marry Daniel into the higher levels of Sunderland society, more like. Annie wondered how such an astute and intelligent man could be so dim when it came to his wife. Taking a deep breath, she said, 'Go into the drawing room then else they'll be in before I have a chance to open the door.'

'Aye, aye.' Abe straightened his already straight tie. 'I've enough on me plate at the moment without this,' he added, as much to himself as Annie.

Daniel was just helping Hope out of the car when Annie opened the door. She watched the two young people approach and although her face was deadpan she was experiencing some disquiet. The lass didn't look hard-boiled. In fact, but for Daniel's arm round her waist, she didn't look as though she'd make it to the house. Furthermore, she seemed little more than a bairn.

'Annie, I'm glad you'll be the first one to meet Hope.' Daniel's voice was over-hearty and he must have realised this because it was less ebullient when he continued, 'This is Annie, Hope, the rock of the household. Annie, meet Hope, my young lady.'

Abe had told her to be cool and restrained but it wasn't as easy as she had expected. Daniel had mentioned the girl was seventeen but it was a young seventeen and it didn't seem right to cold-shoulder her when she was obviously scared to death. How a lass like this one would cope with Father McHaffie she didn't know.

The next moment the decision as to how to greet Hope was taken out of her hands as Annie found herself elbowed out of the way by Rosaleen who had come up behind her. 'You're back then,' she said, addressing herself purely to her brother as though he was standing alone. 'All the clan have arrived since you've been gone, Cecil and Gwendoline, Bernice and Rupert, all dutifully gathered for the big event. Mother's holding court of course, it's very civilised.'

'Shut up, Rosaleen.'

'Why?' Rosaleen's voice held malicious amusement. 'She

must know what she's let herself in for surely?' She allowed her eyes to rest on Hope for the first time. 'You do, don't you?' she added, a small smile playing about her mouth.

Annie watched the two girls taking stock of each other and she couldn't help thinking that for all her expensive education, Rosaleen had the manners of a guttersnipe. But then Daniel's lass would have to face far worse than Rosaleen if she was serious about holding on to the lad, so perhaps Rosaleen was doing the girl a favour in the long run. And then she found herself taken aback when Hope held out her hand, her voice steady as she said, 'I think we were interrupted, Annie. It's very nice to meet you.'

Flustered out of her aloofness, Annie smiled. 'Aye, likewise, I'm sure.'

'And you must be Daniel's younger sister.' Unsmilingly, Hope offered her hand again. 'How do you do?'

There was a moment of hesitation before Rosaleen responded. After shaking Hope's hand she turned on her heel, throwing over her shoulder, 'They're waiting in the drawing room for you. Or perhaps we should say the parlour. You know the old saying, come into my parlour, said the spider to the fly . . .'

'I'm sorry about her, Hope.'

Daniel was clearly mortified but Annie thought she detected a note of amusement in Hope's voice when she said, 'Don't worry. At least it lets Constance off the hook.' Turning to Annie, she explained, 'Constance is my sister and she can be a handful too.'

'Is that so?' Annie nodded. 'Well, come in, lass. Let's have your coat and hat.'

Once divested of her hat and coat, Hope smoothed her

dress, the action betraying her nerves. Annie looked at the slim young figure and again she felt extremely uncomfortable. She knew Emily was wearing a new frock of wool and crêpe de Chine which she had bought from an exclusive dress shop she favoured in Newcastle. Fifty-five shillings it had cost, just three shillings less than two weeks' unemployment pay for a man with a wife and two school-age children. And she knew exactly why Emily was wearing it today and how she would eye the young lass up and down.

Daniel took Hope's arm. 'We'll see ourselves in,' he said, opening the drawing-room door before Annie could protest and leaving her regretting the part she'd played in arranging for Father McHaffie to call.

Hope's first impression of the room in which she found herself standing was that it could have come out of a book, a book featuring the interiors of grand houses. She just had time to take in the fact that the carpet wasn't a square in the middle of the floor but went into all four corners and that the room was simply enormous, before her gaze focused on the stout middle-aged man coming towards them.

She knew immediately this was Abe Fallow, even before he said, 'Here you are then an' this must be Hope. Well, well.' He was standing in front of her now, hand outstretched. 'I'm Daniel's father.'

His hand was hard, his grip firm, and although he was smiling, the grey eyes remained cold and speculative. He turned, still holding her fingers as he said, 'This is Mrs Fallow, Daniel's mother.' An extremely smart woman in a pale blue dress came forward reluctantly.

'How do you do?' The carefully made-up face was still pretty, quite remarkably so, in spite of the faint lines radiating from the corners of the eyes and mouth, but the forced smile was chilly.

Hope had no time to reply before Daniel's father, letting go of her hand, waved at the remaining five individuals watching her so closely. 'That there is Cecil, our eldest, and his wife, Gwendoline, and next to Gwendoline is my youngest daughter, Rosaleen. And then we have Bernice and Rupert. Rupert's a town councillor and a very useful man to have in the family, isn't that so, Rupert?'

The plump, rosy-cheeked man, who was the antithesis of his gaunt, pale wife, bobbed his head, his smile wide as he said, 'As you say, Abe. As you say.'

'So there you have it, that's the lot of us. Come and sit down. Annie'll be bringing the tea trolley now you're here.'

Hope sat down in the chair Daniel's father had indicated. It was set at an angle to two large leather sofas occupied by Cecil, Gwendoline and Rosaleen on one, and Bernice and Rupert on the other. Daniel's mother resumed her seat next to Rupert and all six faces surveyed Hope without smiling. Abe was standing in front of the fireplace, swaying gently as though warming himself although there was no fire in the grate. Hope felt she understood how a plaintiff before the bench must feel and she wondered if that had been their intention.

When, after a moment's hesitation, Daniel did not take one of the other chairs but came and perched on the arm of hers, Hope could have kissed him. She knew immediately his mother didn't like it. Emily's mouth pulled tight and she glared at her son. Daniel seemed unaware of his mother's disapproval. He put his hand on Hope's shoulder and glanced at his brother. 'What have you done with Edward?'

'My mother has taken him out for the afternoon.' It was

Gwendoline who replied, adding, as she looked at Hope, 'Edward is our little boy. He's three years old.'

Gwendoline's voice was what her Aunt Jinny would describe as la-di-da, and although Cecil's wife was dressed quite plainly, it was clearly an expensive plainness. Hope smiled at the older woman but said nothing.

'I suppose Edward will come back with umpteen presents.' Rosaleen nudged her sister-in-law. 'Your parents spoil him.'

'Not at all.'

Gwendoline's protest and the ensuing dispute was interrupted by the arrival of Annie with the tea trolley. Hope glanced at the plates of dainty cucumber sandwiches, cream cakes, little fancy pastries and other delicacies. She swallowed. The china cups and plates were so fragile it didn't seem possible you could actually use them, and there were tiny silver forks and thick cloth napkins and all sorts. She wished the ground would open and swallow her, she was sure to be clumsy and make a mess of things. Why, the cost of the food on this trolley would keep her Aunt Jinny in scrag ends and vegetables from the market for a week, and Daniel was used to this sort of going-on all the time. However could she have imagined they had a chance together?

Her gaze left the trolley, rising to meet Abe's some feet away. The grey eyes were sharp, penetrating; it was as though he was reading her mind. Suddenly Hope was absolutely sure Daniel's father was against their seeing each other every bit as much as his mother was. He might have pretended to go along with the idea, offering Daniel the car and inviting her to tea, but those eyes told her he didn't want her to have anything to do with his son.

Hope felt the colour sweeping over her face and she had

the urge to jump up and run out of the room. To get as far away from this beautiful house and its occupants as she could.

And then the warmth of Daniel's hand on her shoulder pierced her hurt and embarrassment.

Daniel didn't care about elaborate tea trolleys and china cups and eating fancy cakes and pastries with silver forks. He had never once made her feel she wasn't good enough for him by word or action. He loved her. Just as she was, he loved her. So she could either let his father and the others bully her out of his life, or she could stand her ground and show them she was every bit as good as them.

'A cup of tea, lass?' She looked up and Annie was standing in front of her, blocking out the others. And the dark eyes were kind.

Hope nodded. 'Thank you.'

'And something from the trolley? Sandwich, a pastry maybe?'

'Just a sandwich please. I had a big lunch.' It was a lie. She had been unable to eat a mouthful of food since she had woken up.

Annie was just handing Abe his plate when a knock came at the front door. Hope happened to be looking their way and she saw the glance that passed between them, her finely tuned senses telling her the visitor was not unexpected. When, a few moments later, Annie opened the drawing-room door, saying, 'It's the Father,' before standing aside for the black-robed figure to enter, she knew she had been right. The priest's visit was not by chance and the housekeeper had known about it. She had thought that Annie wasn't like the rest of them but she had been wrong.

'Father McHaffie, what a pleasure.' Emily had risen hastily

to her feet, all smiles. As a raggedy, snotty-nosed child she had been taught to hold all priests in awe by her illiterate and deeply superstitious parents. They were holy, their word sacrosanct, one step down from the Almighty Himself. The fact that she had risen to a position in society where she could now entertain priests socially and with all manner of niceties never failed to create a whole host of emotions in her breast. Abe's refusal to attend Mass regularly was a constant thorn in her flesh admittedly, but Father McHaffie and Father Ferry spoke so civilly to him when they did see him that it wasn't the issue it could have been.

'Come and have a seat, Father,' said Abe, drawing one of the big leather chairs into the circle. 'You're just in time for afternoon tea.' In spite of his benevolence, Abe had little time for this particular priest, considering him bigoted and egotistical, unlike his fellow priest, Father Ferry. Father Ferry was a thinker, someone who wasn't frightened by one of the flock having different ideas to his own. For that reason it had had to be Father McHaffie who came to the house this afternoon. The situation needed fire and brimstone from someone who was narrow-minded enough to carry it off.

'Thank you, Abe.' Father McHaffie settled his tall bony body into the chair with a thin smile, his cold eyes resting on each member of the family as he nodded a greeting.

Hope had felt Daniel's hand tighten momentarily on her shoulder at the priest's entrance and now, as Father McHaffie looked at her, she heard Emily say in a rush, 'This is Daniel's young lady, Father. Hope Woodrow. He's brought her to meet us this afternoon.'

'Is that so?' Father McHaffie inclined his head slowly. 'Good afternoon, Miss Woodrow.'

'Good afternoon.' She didn't add Father because she didn't know if she was supposed to, not being a Catholic.

'Here we are, Father.' Annie had entered the room again with an extra cup and saucer already holding tea, which she handed to the priest, adding, 'Can I get you a sandwich or cake?'

'No thank you, Annie. I had sufficient lunch and I shall have my evening meal after six o'clock Mass.' The cold, almost opaque blue eyes swung to Hope again and, without any preamble, the priest said, 'I presume you are not from this district, Miss Woodrow? I don't recall seeing you in church.'

'Hope lives with her aunt and uncle and their family in the East End,' Daniel cut in before Hope had a chance to reply. 'She and her sister were orphaned when they were very young.'

'Is that so? I'm sorry to hear that, Miss Woodrow. Life's trials can begin at an early age to be sure but that would explain why I haven't seen you before.' Father McHaffie took a sip of his tea but apart from Annie leaving the room, no one spoke or moved. 'Remember me to Father Taylor when you get the opportunity, would you? It is St Patrick's you and your family worship at?'

He knew she wasn't a Catholic. He was playing with her, like a cat with a mouse. 'No, Father McHaffie,' Hope said very clearly, hoping her voice didn't reveal the trembling in her stomach which had begun when the priest had entered the room. 'I attend Holy Trinity Church.'

'Holy Trinity?' The priest's sparse eyebrows came together and he raised his gaze to Daniel. 'What is this, Daniel?'

'Hope and her family are not Catholics, Father.' Daniel's chin was now jutting out at a fighting angle.

'I see.' The pale eyes swung to Abe. 'And you are happy with this?'

63

'Daniel is twenty-one years old, Father. I cannot influence him one way or the other.'

'In the matter of his immortal soul I think you should try.'

Daniel now got to his feet, drawing Hope up with him and putting a protective arm round her shoulders. 'You might as well know I don't hold with the Church's teachings on a whole host of things and haven't for some time, the loss or otherwise of my soul just for falling in love with someone from a different denomination being one of them.'

Father McHaffie's eyes narrowed. 'Whether you "hold" with the Church's teachings is irrelevant but it is my duty before God to warn you that if you and this young woman are contemplating a future together, you will be damned unless she converts. And so, incidentally, will any children from your union. Do you want that responsibility, Daniel? Think long and hard before you reply.'

'I don't have to think about it, Father. I understand what you are saying and I would have been surprised if you'd seen it any other way. But I don't believe the way you do, the way you all do,' he added, his glance taking in his family, 'and I'm done pretending. Frankly, I wouldn't want Hope to convert even if she agreed to it. In fact, I—'

'Daniel, please.' Emily had risen to her feet, along with Cecil.

The note of anguish in his mother's voice silenced Daniel, but only for a moment. He said, 'I'm sorry, Mother, but that is how I feel, and let me make it clear once and for all, this matter has nothing to do with Hope. I thought it all out months ago.'

'I find that hard to believe.' Father McHaffie had entered the fray again, his voice icy.

Daniel's eyes swung to the priest and his face was as set and angry as the older man's. What he might have been tempted to say no one ever knew because Hope took a step forward at this point, speaking not to Father McHaffie, or Emily, but to Abe who was silently watching. 'I'm sorry it had to be like this,' she said quietly, her face white, 'but you're doing your son a great disservice if you imagine he hasn't thought long and hard about what he believes. And I might not worship like you do or come from the best part of town, but my family is every bit as good as yours, Mr Fallow. Good afternoon.'

Her eyes left his startled face and with Daniel's arm round her once more they walked across the room. Daniel opened the door and she had passed through into the hall before she heard him say, 'I shall never forgive you for this, never. You didn't give her a chance.'

Oh no, they would never accept her now. Biting her lip to hold back the tears, Hope watched Daniel close the door and she saw his face was dark with rage. He fetched her hat and coat from the ornate coatstand under the stairs where Annie must have placed them, and helped her into her coat without speaking. Hope found she was holding her breath and praying no one would emerge from the drawing room before they were out of the house, and then Daniel had opened the front door and they were stepping into hot sunshine.

'I shouldn't have said that to your da, about my family being as good as yours.'

'Oh yes you should.' Daniel stopped, turning her into him before cupping her face in the palms of his hands. Tenderly now, he said, 'It's the truth, Hope, and I'm so sorry for what happened in there. I should have got you out as soon as Father McHaffie walked in. The man's a fanatic.'

'I think they knew he was coming.'

'No, no, he often calls by. Father Ferry does too.'

She didn't press the point. Her face straight, she looked at Daniel and said, 'I don't want you to fall out with your family because of me.'

For answer he bent and kissed her, a long, hard kiss, and when he finally raised his head, he traced the outline of her mouth with one finger, murmuring, 'Nothing and no one is going to separate us, Hope, so the choice lies with them. I love you and we are going to be together. They'd better get used to it.'

Chapter 6

Bernice sat very straight and still beside her husband on the drive home to their large and pleasantly situated house on the outskirts of Bishopwearmouth. She was always still around him. If it had been within her power she would have made herself invisible.

She kept her gaze trained on the view through the side window of the car so as to avoid the chance of seeing his hands on the steering wheel. His fat, greasy-looking hands which went with the fat, greasy-looking whole. She couldn't ignore the smell of the sickly sweet scent he wore, however, and it coated her nostrils like glue.

When the car stopped outside the substantial natural stone house, Bernice was out of her seat like a shot. She had long since ceased waiting for her husband to open the door for her and help her alight. That meant he had to touch her and her mind as well as her body shrank from the possibility.

In the early days, before they were married, she had put Rupert's desire for physical contact down to the fact that he cared for her. She had soon been disabused of this. Her wedding night had been a time of terror. Not that Rupert had been violent, his tastes were of a more subtle, perverse nature, but Bernice had been as innocent as a lamb and horrified by what he had done and what he had insisted she do to him. Even in her ignorance she had known that such things were not normal.

It had been some months later, months of agonised shame when she had dreaded the night hours and the times Rupert would demand she fulfil her wifely duties, before she had found out the truth about the man she had married. She had called for her mother for a day's shopping in Newcastle but on leaving the house her mother had stumbled and twisted her ankle. When her mother was comfortable and the ankle bandaged, Bernice had called for a taxi and returned home. There she discovered that the housekeeper had been given the day off and found Rupert entertaining two heavily made-up women of dubious character, brazen and loud. All three were cavorting in front of the fire in the drawing room, as naked as the day they were born. She could still picture the depravity she'd witnessed if she let the guard she kept on her mind slip for a moment.

During the ensuing scene she had learnt her marriage had been a sham from the start. Rupert had married her for a cloak of respectability when her father had offered her to him on a plate. Rupert could enjoy his dalliances at the various bawdy houses he visited, knowing the world saw him as an eminent councillor and happily married man; her father had gained an important and influential contact within the council, which he used to his advantage and she . . . she had nothing. She didn't doubt that her father knew nothing of the sordid side of Rupert's life, but nevertheless her marriage had been a business transaction as far as he was concerned, nothing less.

And so had Cecil's. Gwendoline's father was a big cheese in the town and Abe Fallow had been determined to bring him on side. They were all puppets as far as her father was concerned, pawns in the game he played.

Bernice's mouth pulled tight with the nature of her thoughts and on entering the house she made for the stairs after a cool 'Goodnight' to her husband. In her room she locked the door. Not that she thought Rupert would bother her. From the day she had caught him out, he'd made it plain that as long as she presided over his dinner parties and fulfilled her social obligations, that would be all he asked of her. As Catholics, divorce was out of the question, not that she could have brought herself to reveal to another soul the travesty that was their marriage. She would rather die than suffer such humiliation.

She walked across to the bed and sat down, her hands resting in her lap as she gazed unseeing across the room. Her father would never allow Daniel to marry that girl; somehow he would see to it they were separated, as he had done with her and Thomas. Her father was a master of subterfuge.

Bernice unfastened the first few buttons of her high-necked dress, and opened the clasp of the cheap silver locket which had been under her clothes. She sprang the little catch and then gazed at the two tiny faces therein; herself, smiling and not looking so plain for once, and Thomas, his square, blunt face split by a huge grin. He had won the locket for her at the Michaelmas fair and she had paid for one of the street artists who had been present to paint their miniature portraits then and there. It was the only thing he had given her in their six-month association. As one of her father's engineering labourers, his wage was poor. His own father had died a couple of years before, so he was the sole breadwinner for his mother and six younger siblings. But she had loved him, and he her.

She snapped the locket shut and swayed backwards and forwards for a few moments, her eyes tightly shut. But for his mother sending her that letter she would never have known why the family had left Sunderland so suddenly. 'My lad hasn't been thieving,' his mother had written in an almost illegible hand. 'I just want you to know that. Your da's at the bottom of this trumped-up charge. But my Tom can't risk being sent down the line and so all he could do was to skedaddle like your da told him to. There's me and the bairns to provide for, see. Don't think too badly of him 'cos he thought a bit of you, lass.'

The letter had come six months after Thomas had disappeared from her life but it had carried no address. It had been too late by then anyway. Heartsore and not caring what happened to her, she had married Rupert the previous week.

Bernice's eyes snapped open. She had been stupid, so stupid. And cowardly. She was still cowardly. If she'd got an ounce of Daniel's girl's courage she would have confronted her father with the letter and left Rupert that same day. But she hadn't. And now she was destined to live her life alone, without Thomas, without children. With Thomas by her side she would have dared to defy convention and marry a man the world thought beneath her, but without him she was the meek downtrodden mouse she'd always been.

But it didn't have to be that way for Daniel.

Bernice began to pace the floor. She would keep her eyes and ears open over the next weeks, talk to her mother, find out what her father was planning. Because he *would* be planning something, she was sure of it. And whatever it was, she'd foil his scheme by letting her brother know what he was about. If nothing else, she'd have the satisfaction of seeing her father lose for once. Her hands clenched as she thought about the man she hated.

When she thought of her father, and she often did, of his driving ambition and ruthless determination to ride roughshod over anyone foolish enough to stand in his way, she wondered why he was so well thought of by the majority of people. But then she had been the same once, before Thomas's mother's letter had opened her eyes. And then there had been no going back. And with the knowledge had come discernment. She knew full well why her father had allowed Daniel to go to university: a son who could boast such an education would be an asset socially. A scholar in the family lifted them a step higher, it was all about prestige. This was the driving force in her father's life, her mother's too. Oh yes, she knew them only too well.

She began to undress slowly, her movements automatic and carrying a certain heaviness. All the life had gone out of her that day three years ago when, desperate that Thomas hadn't come to their meeting place for several nights running, she had swallowed her pride and gone to his home in one of the backstreets of the town. Another family had been in residence and she had received short shrift from the man of the house who had clearly been drunk. It had been his wife who had followed her a few yards and told her that the previous family had left the district suddenly. Too suddenly, the woman had added darkly. Been up to no good, she'd be bound.

And then the next week her father had invited Rupert to dinner . . .

Bernice climbed into bed and buried her face in the pillows. As she did most nights, she cried herself to sleep.

Chapter 7

The dappled light and shade that spoke of autumn twilight combined with the scent of wood smoke and the low murmur of insects would normally have proved soothing to Hope. Ever since she and Constance had joined in the hop-picking at Springwell Farm on the outskirts of Bishopwearmouth, she had loved it, even looked forward to it year by year in spite of the hard work involved. The farm was owned by an uncle of one of their old schoolfriends, which was how they had first heard about it, and initially they had gone along because they would get paid by the bushel for their work. The fact that the farmer's wife provided bottles of cold tea and great slabs of baked bread pudding full of fruit and brown sugar, sticky and extremely satisfying, was an added bonus. It more than made up for their rough and stained hands at the end of the day and the long walk home, their sixpences for the day's work clutched in tired hands.

This year, though, everything was different. For one thing Constance wasn't with her. Her sister had had her fourteenth birthday some weeks before and had been taken on as a house-maid at the Grand Hotel in Bridge Street, and there had been no question of Constance asking for the Saturday off or working extra hours the next week. But the reason for the agitation Hope was feeling as she left the fields with the other women and children who had come for the hop-picking was not connected with her sister, but with Daniel. They had been seeing each other for over three months now and it was eight weeks since the awful visit to his home, but somehow, in the last week or two, she felt he'd changed. She couldn't put her finger on it but something was different.

So immersed was she in her thoughts that she walked straight past the object of her musing, and it was only when Daniel caught hold of her arm, saying, 'And how's the bonniest lass in the whole of Sunderland?' that she realised he had been waiting for her.

'Daniel, what are you doing here?' They had arranged to meet later that evening. 'Is anything wrong?'

'How could anything be wrong when you're mine? I just wanted to be with you, that's all. Seven o'clock was too long to wait so I thought I'd see you home and make sure no handsome farmhand had won your heart.'

'Silly.' She nudged him with her elbow and then, conscious of the interested glances coming their way, she said, 'Come on, let's walk.'

'You're not walking home after a day like you've had. The car's parked in the lane.' His voice was faintly apologetic. He knew how Hope felt about their using his father's car. Since the disastrous Sunday afternoon when she had met his family, she had made it very clear she wanted no favours from his father. 'I thought you'd be tired,' he added lamely.

'I am.' To be truthful she hadn't known how she'd manage the walk even to the tram stop. She had enjoyed the day in the heady hop-impregnated air as much as ever but she hadn't had much sleep the last few nights and it had caught up with her. 'Thank you,' she said softly.

In the car Daniel didn't start the engine immediately. It was only when the last group of workers, consisting of a mother and her seven children, the youngest an infant in a dilapidated perambulator, had passed them and the lane had settled into a hazy dusty silence, that he said, 'I want to ask you something, Hope.'

'What?' She turned in the seat and stared into his serious face. The day in the fruit-laden air under a hot sun and strong breeze had tinted her skin rosy pink and burnt her nose, despite the protection of her straw bonnet. 'What's the matter?'

'I told you, nothing's the matter.' And then he shook his head impatiently at himself. 'No, that's not true, but it has nothing to do with what I'm going to ask you. Not the quintessence of it at least.'

She didn't know what quintessence meant. It was another thing she'd look up in the library when she had the chance, as she had done with William Cowper and his poems a few weeks ago.

'Hope, you know I love you?'

She nodded, the fear of losing him suddenly paramount although she couldn't have explained why except Daniel looked so very sombre.

'Then will you marry me? Will you be my wife?'

Her brown eyes opened wide, for a moment she couldn't take it in. She had been waiting for this, dreaming of it from the first day they had met but never really believing it could happen.

'Will you, Hope?' he asked softly.

'Yes, oh yes.' She flung herself into his arms, careless of the controls of the car. This man, this wonderful man wanted her as his wife. Not as his lass, someone who could be got rid of with the words, 'I don't want to see you any more,' but as his wife. They kissed until she was breathless, each of them murmuring incoherent words of love that went on and on.

It was some time later and the evening shadows were now stretching across the lane, the sky turning to charcoal when Daniel said, 'We have to talk, Hope.'

Her head had been resting on his shoulder for a little while, their hands entwined. Hope had been content for the moment to go on for ever, just the two of them in their own world where no one could touch them. Now she raised her head and moved fully into her seat, but left one hand in his. 'What is it?' she said quietly.

'My sister came to see me last week, Bernice. She phoned and asked to keep the meeting secret, all very cloak and dagger. She wanted to give me — us — some advice, or rather to warn us.' He paused, obviously finding it difficult to go on. 'I hadn't realised she was for us but she is. She liked you, apparently, she wishes she had half your pluck.'

'Did she say that?'

Daniel nodded.

Hope stared at him. She couldn't really say Bernice had registered much with her that Sunday afternoon eight weeks ago, except as a silent figure at the side of her portly husband.

'She told me my parents are planning to send me on a trip abroad under the guise of broadening my horizons.'

'To get you away from me,' Hope said flatly.

'I'd refuse to go of course, there's absolutely no question about that, but . . . Well, I suppose it brought home they're not going to change their minds about things. Bernice is quite sure they're determined to separate us. She told me she'd met someone years ago who they deemed unsuitable and the next moment she was married off to Rupert.'

The words chilled Hope, she felt sick at just the thought of losing him. But Daniel wasn't like his sister, he wouldn't let that happen. And then she remembered the look on Abe Fallow's face and fear gripped her. He was a strong man, a ruthless man, and Daniel was so nice. Nice people, gentle people like Daniel, were no match for men like Abe Fallow.

'Don't look like that.' Daniel lifted her chin with one finger so she met his eyes. 'But I had to tell you because of what I've got in mind.' Now he began to talk in a different tone and Hope sensed excitement in his voice. 'I was going to wait to ask you to marry me until I'd got a job, a proper job, not working for my father. I'm like a fish out of water there. I made some inquiries about training to be an architect but with the way the country is, it's hopeless. But I could work somewhere else and keep trying until things pick up. I've got a good degree, it's got to be worth something, hasn't it? We could rent somewhere, somewhere small, just for a while. But we'd be married, no one could break us up. The thing is, the way I see it we'd have to be married in a registry office.'

Hope's hand jerked in his. A registry office? She didn't know anyone who had got married in a registry office. You weren't really married, not in the sight of God anyway, if you didn't get married in church. That's what all the neighbours would say.

'I know it's not what you'd choose but it's the only way and it can be soon. You wouldn't convert, and I don't want you to, and your minister wouldn't be happy marrying us, would he?' He waited for Hope to shake her head before going on, 'So a registry office is the answer. And no one would get wind of it like they would if it was a church. I've made inquiries, it would only take about ten days. I've got a bit saved, not much but it would start us off. What . . . what do you think?'

Hope's head was whirling. Whatever anyone said, a registry office was legal. She would be Daniel's wife. His *wife*. And if they didn't do this, his father might win and succeed in breaking them up. Somehow he would find a way. She didn't think about Daniel's mother here, instinct told her Emily wasn't a threat in the same way as Abe. Daniel's mother didn't want them to get married any more than Abe did, but Emily came right out and said what she felt. Abe Fallow was cunning. Furthermore, Daniel loved his father in a way he didn't his mother. He had never voiced this but Hope knew it to be true, and she was uneasy about the strength of the bond between them and the power it gave Abe.

She took a deep breath and spoke from the heart. 'I would marry you anywhere, Daniel Fallow,' she said softly, her eyes shining. 'And as soon as you want.'

He bent over and kissed her again before drawing a small box out of his jacket pocket. 'I want you to have this even though you can't wear it yet with having to keep things secret.'

Hope lifted the tiny hinged lid and stared at the engagement ring the box held. It was a half hoop of pearls and rubies and it was exquisite. 'It's beautiful,' she said breathlessly, refusing to acknowledge the tiny voice in the back of her mind that said they would probably need the money the ring had cost in the next little while.

He reached for her hand, took the ring out of the box and slid it onto her third finger where it sat in twinkling splendour on her stained skin. 'I love you, Hope,' he said huskily. 'I always will, I promise you that.'

'And I promise you I'll always love you.' Suddenly the fact that he had bought her a ring in the midst of all the uncertainty and turmoil was infinitely precious. He was her Daniel, her love, and whatever the future held they would see it through together once they were married. 'But, Daniel,' she put her hand on his arm, 'I have to tell my Aunt Jinny we're getting married, my uncle too. I couldn't get married without them being there, and Constance will have to know. They won't say anything to anyone, not even the lads if I ask them not to.'

'Are you sure about that?'

'Quite sure,' said Hope firmly. 'You don't mind, do you?'

'Darling, I just don't want anything to go wrong.' Daniel took her hands, drawing them against his chest. 'But if that's what you want, so be it. They can be our witnesses, how's that? And perhaps your aunt might know of a couple of rooms somewhere we can rent till we're on our feet. You won't mind that? Starting off small? I promise you it won't be for ever and—'

She stopped him by reaching up and placing her lips on his. It was the first time she had instigated such intimacy, normally it was Daniel who took the lead, and the gesture conveyed more than any words could have done. As his arms went round her and he held her tight, Hope knew she would marry him tomorrow if she could. The furore that would undoubtedly arise on the Fallow side, the reaction from her cousins and not least the stigma of a registry office wedding paled into insignificance beside the knowledge that Daniel loved her and wanted her to be his wife.

Chapter 8

Abe parked his car near the almshouses at the back of Holy Trinity Church and began walking. It had been years since he had been in the East End but nothing had changed. It was still the same labyrinth of filthy alleys and narrow courts of back-to-back terraces with smells so ripe they could knock you backwards. Mind, he'd had some good times here as a lad when he and Emily and a few other young couples had ventured this way on a bank holiday. He'd say one thing for the East End, they could put on a good procession.

He stopped in Prospect Row, his eyes turning to the town moor but he was seeing it as it had been over thirty years ago on the night he had proposed to Emily. There had been a ragtime band playing and the moor had been full of dancing lads and lasses, the boiled crab and kipper sellers and hot potato man doing a roaring trade. They hadn't had two farthings to rub together but they'd been happy then. His eyes narrowed. What was he saying? They were still happy.

He hunched his shoulders into his thick neck and then

straightened, as though throwing something off. Aye, they were happy enough, he reaffirmed, but you couldn't stay young lads and lasses for ever. With marriage came responsibilities. When their Cecil had been born he'd barely had the money for the midwife and they'd been thankful for the neighbours bringing in the evening meal for a day or two. Bug-infested wallpaper and one room to call their own, that was what Cecil had been born into. And he'd sworn then, when they'd nearly lost the babby to bronchopneumonia or whatever the quack had called it, that he'd have them out of that damp hole by the end of the year. And he had. And if he'd taken a few short cuts to get them where they were now, so what? He'd do the same again, by, he would. God helps those who help themselves. Like he'd said to Cecil when Clark's went down the pan last week, it could just as well have been them. They had needed the Randall's contract every bit as much as Jim Clark and his father, and if Jim couldn't see it that way he, for one, wouldn't lose any sleep over it.

Walking swiftly now, Abe turned into Moorgate Street. The weather had changed over the weekend, the heat of Saturday breaking in violent storms throughout Sunday and now, on Monday morning, the air was cold with a bite to it. Nevertheless, there were still a few bairns playing hopscotch with a Cherry Blossom tin, not one of them with a coat and one little lassie wearing boots so large they flew off her feet when she hopped to the next chalked bay, a chunk of bread and dripping clutched in her grubby hand.

Abe didn't pause until he reached Hope's door. Then he glanced up and down the street before he grasped the dull brass knocker and brought it down hard on the flaking wood.

He couldn't see anyone looking out from behind net curtains but that didn't mean they weren't. The street he had grown up in wasn't so very different to this one and you only had to sneeze for it to be common knowledge. For that reason he had left the car some streets away, knowing it would be sure to bring comment. If he could get away with this without Hope and therefore Daniel being any the wiser, all to the good.

It was a moment or two before the door opened and then a woman of enormous bulk seemed to fill the entrance. Abe cleared his throat. 'Mrs Craggs?'

'Aye. Who's askin'?'

'The name's Abe Fallow. I'm Daniel's father. I wondered if we could have a quiet word, Mrs Craggs?'

For a moment Abe thought Hope's aunt was about to shut the door in his face. Then, her face stiff now, she said, 'You'd better come in then.'

The hall stank of cabbage and something else, something undefinable but which brought back memories of his squalid childhood. Abe followed the waddling figure down the passage and into the kitchen. The room was crammed full with a large kitchen table and six hard-backed chairs in the centre of the stone-flagged floor, a six-foot-long wooden scarred settle against one wall and a rickety dresser against the opposite one, but it was homely, the fire in the black-leaded range and the enormous clippy mat in front of it warming.

'You've just missed me husband.' Jinny turned to face him once they were in the kitchen. 'Him an' the lads have gone to see if they can get set on.'

Abe nodded. That suited him just fine. Hope's uncle might be a proud sort, sometimes all that men in his position had left was their pride, but women were more reasonable, especially when it was left to them to make a penny stretch to two. 'No matter,' he said quietly. 'You'll do as well.' Better, in fact. 'I suppose you know why I've come.'

A pair of shrewd eyes looked him over. 'I can guess. You're about to tell me you don't want our Hope to have anythin' to do with your lad. Right?'

Abe didn't answer this directly. Instead he said, 'Can I sit down?'

Jinny nodded, watching him as he pulled out a chair but making no effort to offer him a cup of tea as she would have done with any other visitor.

'You know Daniel's a Catholic?' Abe had been reared among straight-talking women like Jinny and he knew there was no point in procrastinating.

'I know he's been brought up as one. Accordin' to the lad he's not too sure what he believes these days but it's not in all the Hail Marys an' paraphernalia your lot go in for.'

'Aye, that's true enough but by the same token he wouldn't commit to Hope's church. Doesn't that bother you?'

Jinny's arms folded over her massive stomach. 'The way I see it he's not committin' to anythin' except our Hope an' that's no bad thing.'

'You don't really believe that.'

Jinny looked hard at Abe. 'If you've got somethin' to say then say it.'

Abe looked down at the table for a moment. Hope's aunt was clearly baking this morning, two loaf tins full of dough were warming by the range and if he wasn't wrong she had cut off some dough from the main batch of bread after its first rising and there was stottie cake cooking in the oven.

It had been years since he'd had stottie cake; Emily considered the distinctive textured bread beneath them these days but the smell was making his mouth water. Raising his head and looking directly at Jinny, he said, 'Hope's a grand lass and she'll make some lad a fine wife but you know as well as I do mixed marriages never work. All right,' he flapped his hand as though Jinny had been about to speak, 'I know what Dan's saying now but it's not unknown for a young man to have doubts about his faith. They don't last. Dan's a Catholic, take it from me, and he's already made it plain there's no chance of Hope converting. Marriage is hard enough as it is without starting off with everything stacked against you.'

'An' it don't help she's from the East End. Say it, it's what this is about at bottom. You don't think Hope's good enough for your lad.'

Abe closed his eyes and shook his head. 'No, no.'

'Yes, yes.' Jinny was standing slightly bent towards him now, aggression emanating from her. 'I wasn't born yesterday. But let me tell you, Mr High an' Mighty Fallow, if your Daniel's lucky enough to get our Hope it'll be him who's done all right for himself. She's worth a dozen of them sorts you get at the tennis club an' the other fancy places your lad goes.'

Abe held up his hands as though in protest. 'I have nothing against your niece, Mrs Craggs. Far from it.'

'Aye, an' pigs fly.'

Abe tried to hide the rising anger in him, losing his temper would get him nowhere with this one. Instead he forced himself to smile. 'I assure you, I'm just as concerned for Hope in all of this as my son. It's just that for the life of me I can only see heartache ahead for one or the other of them, especially her. The longer they see each other, the harder it'll make it when the thing comes to an end. And it will. Looking at it realistically, it will. And whereas for a lad there'll be an element of folk thinking he's sowing his wild oats, for a lass the gossip could be something different.'

Jinny seemed to swell in front of his eyes. Her jaws clenching, she took a step towards him. 'My lass is a good girl an' any that say different'll get my fist atween their eyes. There's bin no sowin' o' oats, wild or otherwise.'

'I didn't mean—'

'I know what you meant an' you can take your bad mouth out of here. It comes to somethin' when I'm visited in me own home to be insulted. Let me tell you, m'lad, it's a good job Mr Craggs isn't present 'cos you'd be out the door with his boot up your backside.'

Damn it all, this hadn't gone as he had expected. What was the matter with the woman? Frustration uppermost, Abe cast caution to the wind. 'Look, Mrs Craggs, I came here today believing you to be a sensible woman who's got Hope's best interests at heart,' he said, rising to his feet. 'She's a canny lass, I can see that, bright as a button and it seems to me given half a chance she'd go far. If she took a shorthand and typing course, something like that, she could do well for herself but I know how you're fixed. I was thinking I might be able to help . . .'

Jinny was still now, her face set. Her voice was flat as she said, 'What are you sayin'?'

Abe prided himself on being a good judge of character. It was this attribute, along with his sharp business acumen, which had enabled him to rise from poverty to plenty in the early years. He looked at the blowsy woman in front of him and wondered how much it would cost to buy her co-operation. He didn't doubt he could achieve this, everyone had their price and when you were living hand to mouth necessity made you as cunning as a cartload of monkeys. He cleared his throat, prolonging the moment. 'I'm thinking you would like to see the lass do well, that's all, and I've had my days of making a penny stretch to a shilling. I know what it's like. If Hope went on some course or other, there wouldn't be her wage coming in so I'd expect to reimburse you as well as pay for her tuition.'

'In return for what?'

At last they were getting somewhere. The old biddy was smelling the pound notes. Likely she'd thought there would be something in it for her if Daniel married the girl which was why she'd been for the match, or at least hadn't discour-aged it. But a bird in the hand was worth two in the bush. That was the way to play this. 'Let me make myself plain, Mrs Craggs. As I say, I've nothing against your niece but Daniel's mother has got her heart set on him marrying the daughter of a friend of hers, you know how these things work. If Daniel didn't see eye to eye with her on this she'd be at me to cut him off without a penny. That's how strongly she feels. And that wouldn't benefit any of us. Now if you could see your way clear to guiding Hope in a certain direc-tion, persuading her to see sense, you'd be doing both of the young people a favour.'

Jinny still hadn't moved or spoken, her eyes hard on his face.

Abe reached into his pocket. 'I was thinking a shorthand and typing course wouldn't be cheap and then there'd be your inconvenience and all . . .' He held out a roll of notes secured with an elastic band. 'This'd see you through and with plenty to spare.'

'*Get out.*'

'What?'

'Get out of my house, Mr Fallow, unless you want to feel that money shoved where the sun don't shine.' Jinny took a threatening step forward and such was her demeanour that Abe found himself backing away.

Unable to believe that he had misread the situation so badly, he paused at the kitchen door. 'You're making a big mistake,' he tried again. 'There's twenty pounds here. Take it.'

'I'd as soon cut me own throat,' Jinny said with dangerous quiet. 'You think you can swan in here actin' the big man because you've done all right for yourself? Well, let me tell you, you're scum in my book. I've always said you can't make a silk purse out of a sow's ear an' you're the livin' proof.'

Abe's face was suffused with colour as he swung round and walked into the hall. He opened the front door, stuffed the roll of notes into his pocket and stepped down into the street.

Jinny had followed him to the doorstep where she now called after him, 'I'll say nowt about this but only to spare my lass's feelin's. Want stringin' up by the nearest lamp post, you do!' And with that she banged the door.

Dear gussy! Abe looked neither to right nor left as he strode down the street, his ears burning. What an old harridan, going for him like that. Anyone would think he'd suggested something obscene rather than offering the daft old biddy twenty odd pounds. That'd be a good few months' dole money for her man and they weren't exactly living in clover from what he could see.

He crossed over the road into Prospect Row, inadvertently stepping into some foul rotting mess in the gutter as he did so. As the stench rose up into his nostrils, his temper went up another notch. Animals! The folk round here lived like animals and there was her daring to look down her nose at him. Well, she'd rue the day. Signs were the Depression would get worse before it got better.

On reaching the car he opened the door and flung himself into the driver's seat. Instead of starting the engine immediately, however, he sat for a moment, his eyes closed. Hope's aunt was a tartar but she loved that little lass, no doubt about it.

He breathed in and out a few times, still with his eyes shut as his mind replayed the last ten minutes. There had been an element to Hope's aunt that reminded him of his own mother although she'd been a little wisp of a woman, barely four foot ten and as thin as a rake.

Abe rested his elbows on the steering wheel, massaging his temples with the three middle fingers of each hand. His mam had had a hell of a lot to put up with, what with his da's drinking and having a bairn regular as clockwork every year, but she'd had the same fierce moral code, the same innate vitality as that old woman back there. He hadn't cried a tear when his da had copped it, and as far as his brothers and sisters were concerned he didn't give a damn – nor they for him – but his mam had been different. He'd grieved for her when the fever had taken her just after him and Emily had wed. Daft, but he still grieved for her. And he knew Annie felt the same. His mam had been more of a mother to Annie than her own; practically lived at their house, Annie had, and even when his mam had been hard pressed to put a slice of bread and dripping in front of them, she'd seen to it Annie had the same. Funny, but his mam never really took to Emily although she'd never said. But he'd known.

He sat a few moments more and as his anger cooled he found himself bitterly regretting the visit to Hope's aunt's house. Annie had been against it; he should have listened to her. She wasn't often wrong, Annie. And Emily would go barmy if she found out he'd been in these quarters. Not that she'd have minded if he'd been successful, of course. His mouth twisted. But if she knew he'd been sent away with a flea in his ear by the likes of Mrs Craggs, she'd be mortified.

He sat up straight. At odd times, like now, his thoughts regarding his wife were not what he would wish them to be. He had done his own bit of social climbing, he admitted it, and if anyone had called him an upstart he'd have agreed with them and added that he wasn't about to apologise for the fact either, but Emily . . . He frowned, shaking his head as though to dislodge his thoughts.

Oh, to hell with it! What was he sitting here for when there were a host of matters waiting for his attention at the works? Time was money. He started the engine, suddenly anxious to get back to the office where he was in control and what he said was law.

It was as he was about to turn the corner into High Street East and stopped to let a young mother with a baby in a perambulator cross the road that his car door was jerked open. Startled into stalling the engine, his head shot round to meet that of a youngish man peering into the car.

'Fancy seeing you here, Abe.' Jim Clark didn't smile. 'Slumming it, are you?'

'Hello, Jim.' Abe's gaze moved from him to his companion. He was a man who would have made two of most men but he wasn't fat, just big and solid. His nose was flattened and his hands were like great hams. He looked like a prize fighter. Maybe he was. Forcing a nonchalant note into his voice, Abe said, 'How goes it?'

'Not too well, Abe, but then you know that, don't you?'

'No, no, I didn't know that, Jim.' He wasn't about to discuss Clark and Son folding, not with that gorilla standing there. 'Look, I've got an appointment.' He started the engine again.

'Oh aye? Appointment, is it?'

The man with a face like a battered pluck positioned himself just in front of the bonnet. Short of running over him, Abe was going nowhere. His lower jaw moved from one side to the other before he said, 'Something wrong, Jim?'

'Plenty.' Jim Clark's eyes were as hard as bullets. 'For your information – as if you didn't know – we went to the wall last week. My da started about the same time as you, didn't he? Blood, sweat and tears, that's been his lot most of his life. And all for nowt. The business, the house, the cars all gone. We were lucky to keep the clothes on our backs the way the vultures came flocking.'

'I'm sorry.'

'Aye, I bet you are.'

Warning himself to go steady and not to react, Abe said, 'It's happening all over the hockey. Damn government. Couldn't run a bairn's Sunday school outing, let alone the country.'

'You blame the government, do you?' Jim's tone was almost conversational. 'Me, I see it a sight nearer home.'

When Abe made no reply to this, Jim said, 'Just come from the hospital, me da was took bad last night. Heart attack, the doctor called it. Me, I call it a broken heart. Same thing in a way, I suppose. What do you think?'

Abe swallowed. If he had to, he'd drive straight over the big fellow and answer to the law later.

'You've got both your sons working with you now, I hear.'

Abe's chin jerked. 'What does that mean?'

'Mean? Nowt. Except it's nice to have family, close family. Mean a lot to you, do they? No doubt you'll set the young 'un up like you did Cecil.'

Not for the world would Abe have betrayed the sickly feeling in the pit of his stomach. Instead he shrugged. 'Can't rightly say with how things are.'

'Oh, I'm sure you will. All things come to them that wait, isn't that what they say? It pays to bide your time, wait for the right opportunity.'

They weren't talking about him seeing Daniel all right. Abe revved the engine, rage replacing fear. 'Aye, mebbe, but it's up to me. One thing I'll say, Jim. I look after me own and I can be as nasty as the next fella when I have to be. Know what I mean?'

'I do, Abe. Never doubted it.' They stared at each other, eyes narrowed. 'But I'm keeping you,' Jim added. 'Didn't you say you've got an appointment?' He nodded to the big man who stepped onto the pavement, his long arms hanging by his sides. 'Give my regards to Cecil and your other lad. What's his name now?'

'Daniel.'

'Aye, that's right. Daniel. University-educated, I hear. You must be right proud of him.' He slammed the door shut on the last word and stepped back but continued to keep his eyes fixed on Abe's.

For a moment Abe just sat there, stunned by what had happened and the unexpectedness of it. Then his foot came down hard on the accelerator and the car shot forward round the corner into High Street East, narrowly missing a couple of pigeons pecking at something in the middle of the road.

That arrogant young pup! As Abe drove he was grinding his teeth. Threatening him like that. If it hadn't been for the big ape, he'd have given Jim what for. Virtually accusing him of being responsible for the old man's heart attack! If all that had been between them and the knacker's yard was that tender for Randall's job, they'd been finished anyway. But it bore out what he'd said about Jim Clark and the sorts he mixed with, wrong 'uns the lot of them. But forewarned was forearmed. He'd keep his wits about him and tell Cecil to do the same. Daniel was a different kettle of fish. He'd have to think carefully about what he said to Daniel. Perhaps something along the lines of an old employee who'd been sacked for having light fingers and now bore them all a grudge might do it. Daniel wouldn't press him for details, he wasn't like that, and since he'd been courting Hope he had his head in the clouds most of the time anyway.

The thought brought Abe back to the problem that was giving him sleepless nights and again he ground his teeth, his bushy brows meeting in a ferocious frown. Emily thought Daniel would jump at the chance to tour France and Italy for a few months but he wasn't so sure. That little minx had got her claws deep into him, no doubt about that, he fair worshipped the ground she walked on, but he wasn't about to stand by and watch his lad make the biggest mistake of his life. By hook or by crook he'd bring an end to it or his name wasn't Abe Fallow.

He nodded to the thought, his mouth grim. And it was like that, glaring through the windscreen, that he drove the rest of the way to the engineering works on the far west of the town.

Chapter 9

Hope averted her gaze from the groups of men standing by the engine sheds and goods station near Hudson Docks. She heard her Uncle George call out a greeting to a few who must have raised their hands to him but she kept her head bent. She knew the men would continue to stand where they were for the best part of the day, come rain, hail or snow, hoping and praying they'd get at least one shift but knowing the odds were stacked against them. The looks on their faces always made her want to cry.

'All right, hinny?' Her aunt's voice brought her head up and she nodded as the three of them continued to walk along the grey street. This was her wedding day, she was on her way to marry Daniel and yet she didn't feel at all like she had expected to. Nothing seemed real.

Her aunt's voice came again. 'You're still sure about what you're doin'?' Jinny asked softly. 'It's not too late to change your mind, lass.'

'I'm sure.' The last ten days had seemed like a lifetime but she'd never once doubted she wanted to be Daniel's wife, only that it would happen. But here she was with her aunt and uncle, all of them in their Sunday best and looking unusually smart for a weekday on their way to meet Daniel outside the registry office. And when she emerged she'd be a married woman, returning home not to the house in Moorgate Street but to the couple of rooms she and Daniel were renting in a two-up, two-down terraced house in Northumberland Street near Central Station.

No one spoke again until they were almost at the town hall in Fawcett Street in the heart of town. Then, just before she caught sight of Daniel waiting on the pavement, her aunt said, 'Your mam'd be proud of you the day, lass. Right proud. You look bonny, doesn't she, George?'

'Aye.' Her uncle turned his weather-beaten face to smile at her. 'Daniel's a lucky man.'

The lump in her throat was threatening to choke her and her voice held a slight tremor as she said, 'Thank you for all you've done for me,' before kissing each of them on the cheek. The unusual demonstration of affection had her uncle clearing his throat several times and her aunt's eyes misty.

And then Daniel was coming towards her, his hands outstretched and his eyes full of love, and now, for the first time since she had woken up, everything was real, wonderfully, shiningly real.

He kissed her, careless of her aunt and uncle and the passers-by, before murmuring, 'How do you feel?'

'Giddy, happy, funny.' She smiled at him. 'How about you?'

'The same.' And then he turned to her aunt and uncle. He shook her uncle's hand and smiled at her aunt. 'I'm so glad you could share this with us. My sister, Bernice, would have liked to be here but it wasn't possible. She wants to buy the wedding breakfast though and has booked a table for four at Binn's. Is that all right?'

'Aye, aye, lad.' George rubbed his nose, obviously taken aback. 'But we didn't expect nothin' like that, did we, lass?' he said to his wife who made the appropriate response.

'This is it then.' Daniel took Hope's hand, his grip firm and strong. 'Ready?'

'More than ready.'

And the four of them went inside.

'I can't believe your sister ordered champagne for us.' Hope sipped at her glass again, wrinkling her nose as the bubbles tickled her nostrils. 'And a three-course meal and everything. It's so kind of her, Daniel.'

Daniel squeezed her hand in answer. In truth he didn't want to think about Bernice right now. It would bring the concern he felt for his sister since she'd opened up a little to him to the forefront of his mind, and this was a special time. He raised his glass, keeping hold of Hope's fingers as he said, 'I want to propose a toast to the most beautiful bride in the world. And to thank her for taking me on. To my wife, Mrs Fallow.'

Hope's eyes were starry as she looked at him and when her uncle made a stammering stab at a speech too, saying how much he and Jinny would miss her, the lump in her throat was back. It was left to Jinny to bring them back down to earth.

'Aye, well, I can agree with that but now me an' George'll have a bedroom to sleep in for the first time in years, don't think you're comin' back, hinny. But when you visit we can entertain you in style in the front room, what do you think about that? Me best bone china an' doilies. There'll be no stoppin' us now.'

They all laughed as they were meant to but Hope's laughter was forced. Her aunt's words had brought back the memory of the humiliating afternoon at Daniel's house as well as reminding her of the huge divide between their two families. Her aunt and uncle had slept in the small front room ever since she could remember, the two bedrooms being occupied by their children. Their brass bed could now be moved upstairs – Constance had been assigned a put-u-up in the kitchen for the foreseeable future – but the front room was still shabby. For years her aunt and uncle had struggled to bring up nine children, keeping them clothed and fed and never a word of complaint. But the faded curtains at the front-room window which had long since been bleached into holes by the sun, and the moth-eaten horsehair suite over which Aunt Jinny and Uncle George had had to climb to reach their bed, told their own story. A story of sacrifice and dogged determination.

Hope had never loved them so much as in this moment. And Daniel's family dared to look down on such folk. Suddenly the terrifying prospect of facing his parents later that day lost some of its power. They were upstarts. Not Daniel and Bernice of course, but the rest of them. She would tell Abe Fallow so if he started bullying them, Hope decided through a haze of champagne bubbles.

The dinner was wonderful. When two bottles of very good wine followed the champagne, the meal became one of unrestrained hilarity which was something none of them had expected in the circumstances.

Three hours later they were all standing on the pavement outside the restaurant. George and Jinny, who had consumed most of the wine between them, were flushed and smiling as they made their goodbyes and caught a tram. Daniel, too, had more colour than usual although Hope didn't think he'd had more than one glass of wine after the champagne.

As they began to walk along Fawcett Street, Hope felt she had been given the reason for his glow when he leant towards her and murmured, 'The note I left on my father's desk at the office first thing said I wouldn't be home until late this evening. It's now,' he consulted his wristwatch, 'only three o'clock and we're close to our new home. Shall we have a cup of tea before we go and tell them we're married and I get my things?'

It wasn't a cup of tea he had in mind. Shyly now and thrilled to bits by the fact that he had referred to the two rooms and tiny cupboard of a scullery as their home, Hope nodded. She wanted to become Daniel's wife in every sense of the word; they would be really married then. Their limited lovemaking thus far had been pleasurable, but she knew there was much more to the physical side of love between a man and a woman. She wasn't sure what was entailed, her aunt had never discussed such matters with any of them, but from listening to the older women at the laundry chatting amongst themselves, she had gathered a little of what went on and she was nervous about it. Nervous but not frightened. Daniel loved her and she him and she wanted to belong to him, mind, soul and body.

Hand in hand they walked to the house in Northumberland Street. They were occupying the ground floor, the first floor being the home of two middle-aged sisters who worked at the pickling factory in the East End. The shared privy and wash house were situated in the tiny backyard, along with an outside tap which provided water for the house's residents.

After securing their future home and paying the initial month's rent five days ago, they had spent two evenings cleaning the two rooms from top to bottom. When Hope was satisfied with the state of the floors and especially the black-leaded range in the kitchen-cum-sitting room, they had scoured the local second-hand shops for essential items of furniture. The kitchen now contained a small square eating table with oilcloth and two wooden forms which fitted underneath it, along with a pair of flock stuffed armchairs which were remarkably comfy if a little battered. Either side of the range were built-in cupboards and they had bought pots and pans, a big iron kettle and other bits and pieces, including a dented tin bath which had seen better days. When turned on its end it fitted in the tiny scullery. It made getting to the deep stone sink something of a squeeze but there was no other place for it. A bright and new looking clippy mat in front of the range had completed their purchases for the kitchen and added a touch of colour and cosiness to the room.

In the bedroom, a double bed stood on bare floorboards along with a rather fine wardrobe. Daniel had put his foot down about the bed. Although he had seen the wisdom of shopping for second-hand furniture and had accepted Hope's argument that his account at the bank was going to be severely depleted as it was, he had flatly refused to start off married life in anything but a new bed. Sheets, blankets, pillowcases and an eiderdown from the Old Market had raised no objection, but the bed and mattress had had to be new.

Inside the house, Daniel pulled Hope into his arms in the

hall, kissing her in a way he had never done before. They were alone, the two sisters had told them they left every morning at seven o'clock and returned home after six, but in spite of that Hope couldn't relax. Now the time was here, she suddenly realised she was more apprehensive than she had thought. For the life of her she couldn't kiss him back as though she meant it.

'I love you. Do you know that, Mrs Fallow?' He raised his head and she was looking into his eyes, eyes that were glowing with love and need of her. 'You know about those girls at university but they didn't mean a thing. Nothing and no one has ever meant a thing before you. You do believe that?'

'Aye, yes I do.' She didn't know how to explain. Then she decided to just say it. 'I suppose I'm a bit nervous, that's all. I've . . . never done this before.'

'I know, sweetheart, I know.' He pulled her closer again but this time when he kissed her it was gently passionate, more like she was used to, the almost violent urgency gone.

Gradually Hope's taut nerves began to uncurl as the petals of a flower uncurl to the warmth of the sun. When after a few minutes he took her hand and opened the bedroom door, leading her in, she went willingly. In the bedroom, Daniel walked across and closed the thin curtains over the yellowing nets. The bedroom and kitchen curtains had been here when they had taken the rooms and had seen better days but Hope had refused to replace them, saying they would do for the moment.

Hope remained standing exactly where he had left her. Daniel went to her and helped her off with her coat and hat. 'Let's get into bed,' he said very softly. 'I want to hold you properly.'

Hope nodded. Daniel sat down on the edge of the bed which they had made up the night before with the freshly laundered bed linen. She watched him take off his shoes and socks with a casualness she just couldn't match. When he unknotted his tie and began to undo the buttons of his shirt, she too began to disrobe but with her back to him. The thinness of the cheap curtains meant the room was still almost as light as before he had drawn them, and Hope had never felt so embarrassed in the whole of her life. She somehow had never imagined they would do it in the daytime.

She and Daniel had brought all of her things to the house the evening before; they had barely filled two big cloth bags. Now she opened the wardrobe door and hung her coat and dress beside her other clothes, using the door as a shield as she wriggled out of her underclothes, leaving her shift on as a kind of nightdress. It was utterly beyond her to walk across to the bed naked.

She heard the bedsprings creak and knew Daniel had climbed into bed. Her stomach flipped. She found herself wishing Daniel hadn't told her about the two girls at university. She knew he had been determined to have no secrets between them and she appreciated that, she did really, but what if he compared her to those girls, who were bound to have been beautiful as well as intellectual, and found her lacking? She was ordinary and Daniel . . . well, he was anything but ordinary.

'Hope?'

His voice brought her from behind the wardrobe door and when she walked across to the bed in her shift, he made no comment, merely smiled and flung back the covers on her side so she could get in. As he pulled her down to lie beside him, she didn't actively resist him but her limbs were stiff. He put his arms round her so that her face was resting against the rough hair of his chest, his chin on her hair. He began to stroke her back with the tips of his fingers, every so often dropping little kisses on her forehead.

It was a while before he said, 'Shall we take your petticoat off now?' and when she dumbly acquiesced, he helped her pull it over her head, dropping it on the floor on his side of the bed. He began to caress her skin from her smooth shoulders to the small of her back. Minutes ticked by, and then the kisses on her forehead moved down to her mouth; they were still without any urgency but pleasurable. Very pleasurable.

Her eyes shut and her breathing deepening, Hope turned into him, beginning to kiss him back as his hands and mouth brought sensations hitherto unknown to her. She could feel his heart slamming against the wall of his chest and knew he was enjoying what they were doing by the little guttural noises in his throat. Her confidence rose and she stroked her hands up and down his back. He groaned softly.

'I love you, my sweet wife.'

She opened her eyes and smiled into the grey eyes which were waiting for her. 'I love you too.'

'Do you trust me? I want to give you pleasure, Hope, and I won't hurt you. Will you let me please you?'

She nodded, not really understanding what she was agreeing to but knowing Daniel loved her and that was enough. It would always be enough.

'I'm the luckiest man in the world.'

As the tram clunked and clattered its way towards Ryhope

Road, Hope's fingers tightened round Daniel's. They were sitting very close together, heads touching, and she wished with all her heart they didn't have to go and see his family tonight. Not after what they had shared together that afternoon. She kept blushing when she thought of what he had done and the pleasure it had called forth which she'd been unable to hide. Now they were one, like the Bible said, and she found she loved him more deeply because of it. That and his exquisite tenderness and the things he had said, beautiful, wonderful things, things she'd treasure for ever in her heart. But in a few minutes they would face his parents and everything would be spoilt. She knew it.

Daniel said nothing more until they were standing outside the house, hands entwined. Then he looked down at her. 'Let me deal with this. All right? We've done nothing wrong and we are legally married. End of story.'

Except it wasn't. Hope could see the tension Daniel was trying to hide. She found herself praying Abe would meet them halfway, for Daniel's sake. Emily and the others didn't matter so much, not to Daniel, but although she hated to admit it, she knew Daniel's father had a special place in his heart. If Abe would just let Daniel know he still loved him whatever he had done, that would be enough. They had faced the fact that it would be impossible for Daniel to continue working with his father and Cecil; they would manage on her sixteen shillings a week until Daniel found something. Daniel hated the office anyway; he said he didn't fit in and made countless mistakes and the only reason he was still there was because he was the boss's son. For her part, she would prefer to struggle for the whole of her life rather than for Daniel to be dependent on Abe Fallow.

Annie answered Daniel's knock. Her eyes widened at the

sight of Hope but she made no comment on her presence. She said simply, 'You lost your key or something?'

'I left it in my bedroom this morning.'

'Forget your head, you would, if it wasn't screwed on.'

Annie stood aside for them to enter the house and as Daniel passed her, he said, 'I left it on purpose. I shan't be needing it after tonight.'

Annie wasn't listening. Speaking directly to Hope, her voice low, she said, 'Don't take this the wrong way, lass, but it's not the best night in the world for you to come. There's been some bad news and Daniel's da's all of a two an' eight.'

'Bad news?' Daniel's voice brought Annie's gaze to him.

'Oh, no one in the family, lad, it's not that, but Maurice Randall's met with a nasty accident. Well, not an accident as such, according to what's being said. The law seem to think it was deliberate but meself I can't see it. I mean, who'd do a wicked thing like that?'

'Annie.' Daniel put his hands on the housekeeper's shoulders, stilling her gabble. 'What's happened?'

Annie took a deep breath. 'They found Maurice Randall face down in the water near the fish quay this morning. At first they thought it was some old drunk who'd had a skinful and lost his footing but it weren't. It was Maurice.' Annie's voice quivered. 'Him and his wife were only round here for dinner a few weeks back an' all.'

'All right, all right, don't upset yourself.' Daniel looked at Hope. 'We'll still have to tell them. Are you ready?'

She nodded, dreading what was to come.

'Annie, don't disappear.' As the housekeeper made to return to the kitchen, Daniel caught hold of her arm. 'I want you to hear this too, you're family.'

Annie smiled although her eyes were anxious. They could almost hear her thinking, what now?

Daniel entered the drawing room with his arm round Hope's waist, Annie following them. He saw immediately that his father was indeed in a 'two and eight', for instead of being stretched out in his favourite armchair with his pipe or standing with his back to the fire while he puffed smoke rings, something which irritated his mother beyond measure, he was pacing the floor. His mother was sitting with her petit point on her knee. Daniel had always suspected she had no real inclination towards embroidery but it was a pastime of the more refined, genteel lady and therefore she pursued it.

'About time.' Abe glared at his son, ignoring Hope. 'Where the hell have you been all day? I'm not running some sort of club where you can pop along when you feel like it, you know. In case you hadn't realised, it's a business we're about.'

'Hope and I have got something to tell you.'

The manner in which Daniel spoke must have alerted his mother to the fact that whatever this something was, they weren't going to like it. Looking straight at Annie, Emily said dismissively, 'Thank you, Annie.'

'No, I asked Annie to be here.' Daniel was often incensed by his mother's high-handed treatment of her childhood friend, and this came across in his voice when he added, 'She's part of this family, a big part of it as far as I'm concerned.'

'Well?' Abe had stopped his pacing. He too had sensed trouble. 'What's going on?'

'You all know how Hope and I feel about each other and that's not going to change, not now, not ever.' Daniel's arm tightened round Hope's waist. 'I hoped you'd see things from our point of view but that clearly was never going to happen. A few days ago I asked Hope to do me the honour of becoming my wife and she said yes.'

There was a moment's silence and then Emily said cuttingly, 'That's ridiculous, Daniel. You have only known each other for a short while.'

'I thought that's what you'd say.' The bitterness in his voice was apparent to all of them. Looking directly at his father now, Daniel said slowly and clearly, 'Hope and I got married this morning and before you ask, her aunt and uncle knew about it and gave their permission. In fact they were our witnesses. We're legally husband and wife and there is nothing you and Mother can do about it.'

Annie's gasp behind them mirrored Emily's reaction; both women were shocked into speechlessness. Not so Abe. Emitting the sort of base oath which normally would have brought his wife's wrath down upon his head, he advanced across the room until he was standing in front of them.

Daniel was ramrod straight and so was Hope, but whereas just a few minutes ago she had been hoping and praying for some kind of reconciliation, she now silently beseeched Daniel to stand up to his father – don't let him think he can frighten you, she thought. Be strong.

'You young fool.' Abe's voice was a growl and he was speaking only to Daniel. Hope might as well not have been there. 'Throwing your life away before it's barely begun. Can't you see what she's after?'

'Careful, Father.' Daniel's voice was low but the tone and the fact that he had not used the warm colloquial Da was a warning. One which Abe chose to ignore.

'Careful? Careful you say? My son comes and tells me he's

up and wed an' me not knowing a monkey's cuss about it and *you* tell *me* to be careful?'

'You'll live to regret this day.' Emily had found her voice. She was on her feet, her face as white as a sheet, and she fairly spat the words. 'And when you do, you will have no one to blame but yourself. We gave you everything, *everything*, and this is the way you repay us, by taking up with some little chit who's laughing up her sleeve at us.'

'Where did you get married?' Abe cut across his wife's voice. 'Not at Holy Trinity?'

'At the registry office.'

Emily collapsed back into her chair. 'The registry office? Holy Mary, mother of God, the registry office. We won't be able to hold up our heads once this gets about. She's in the family way, I suppose.'

'No, I am not.' Hope raised her chin, her breathing sharp. 'We married because we wanted to, not because we had to, Mrs Fallow. We love each other and we want to be together.'

'Don't explain yourself, not to her.' Daniel's expression was livid. Thrusting a piece of paper at his father, he said, 'We're leaving now and we won't be coming back. You can send a note to this address telling me when I can pick up my clothes and personal belongings.'

'You're going? Just like that?' Abe's face was a study in surprise but overlying it was rage, black rage. 'You'd really walk out on this note?'

'I didn't want it to be like this but I'm not staying where my wife isn't welcome.'

'Wife! For crying out loud, lad, you're still wet behind the ears. *Think*, think what you're doing because if you leave now you leave more than just this house. Don't think you can walk into work tomorrow as if nothing's happened because it don't pan out like that. You'll be joining the dole queue, that's what you'll be doing, and married life on bread and scrape might not appear so attractive in a few months' time. And you'll get nowt from me, do you hear me? Nowt.'

'Fine, if that's the way you want it.'

'And you. You say you love him and yet you're prepared to stand back and let him ruin his life?' Abe turned his attack on Hope. 'He's no easy meal ticket, let me make that plain. You two'll be on your own and the way things are he's got as much hope of getting a job as a snowball in hell.'

'I have a job, Mr Fallow, and we've already worked out we can manage perfectly well while Daniel looks for something.' Hope was shaking but this did not come across in her voice which was surprisingly firm and clear. 'We don't want a penny of your money, we never did.'

'Ha! If I believed that I'd be dancing with the fairies.'

'Believe it or not, it's up to you, but it's the truth. All we wanted was your understanding of how we feel. Not necessarily your approval even.'

'Come on, we're leaving.' Daniel turned her round and as Annie stepped back to let them pass, her hand at her mouth, he said brusquely, 'Goodbye, Annie.'

Outside the house they walked swiftly down the drive without speaking, but after they had been walking along the pavement for a few moments, Daniel stopped and took her hands. 'I'm sorry, sweetheart. I would have liked to spare you that.'

'No, no, I'm sorry for you.' And she was, so much. At the same time, a tiny part of her was glad his parents had severed all ties, which made her feel all the more guilty.

'We'll show them, eh?' He hugged her to him.

'Perhaps they'll come round.'

'Coming round wouldn't be enough, not after what's been said.'

They stared at each other for a moment. Then Hope said very softly, 'Let's go home, shall we?'

PART TWO

1933 – Sticky Webs

Chapter 10

'I hate that place, I can't stand it. I've had enough, Hope. I'll go barmy if I have to change another bed where some couple's frolicked the night before and left the stains to prove it.'

'Oh, Constance.' Hope's nose wrinkled with distaste.

'For goodness sake! Come down off your high horse. You've been married months and you're pregnant, you know what it's all about.'

And so did Constance, and her only fifteen. Hope stared at her sister. Constance had changed radically in the last twelve months or so. Not just in her appearance, although the buxom girl in front of her could easily have passed for going on twenty, but the real difference was in Constance's manner. Hope knew one or two of the girls Constance worked with were no better than they should be because her sister had related a few of their exploits when she'd first started at the Grand, but there were plenty of nice lasses too. Unfortunately Constance seemed to gravitate to the dubious element and Hope knew their Aunt Jinny was worried sick about her younger niece. Constance was staying out later and later at night despite the rows it caused, and although Jinny had never said, Hope suspected her sister didn't cough up much of her wage to their aunt despite the dire straits the family were in.

Quietly now, Hope said, 'The Grand pays well compared to some and with jobs so scarce you'd be best staying put.'

'Oh you.' Constance tossed her pretty head impatiently. She took a gulp of her tea before she said, 'It's all right for you, you've got Daniel to come home to. All I've got in life is clearing up after everyone all day and being treated like dirt half the time, and then Aunt Jinny's come evening. And the lads are such numbskulls. Ten minutes of talking to them and I want to scream. Betty Kirby said her mam wouldn't mind me moving in there and sharing Betty's room as long as I paid my share, and I might just do that.'

According to Constance, Betty Kirby had a different lad for every day of the week. Hope kept her eyes on her sister's petulant face as she said, 'But Aunt Jinny moved everything around so you could have the front room at night when you said you wanted some privacy and hated the kitchen. What'll she do without your bit coming in each week?'

'She'll manage, she always does.'

'But with Uncle George and the lads all laid off now, can't you wait till things get a bit better?'

'Huh, and when's that going to be?' Constance finished her cup of tea and stood up. The sisters had been sitting at Hope's kitchen table, and with the room as spick and span as always and a shaft of Saturday afternoon sunshine lighting up the delicate pink flowers of the cyclamen standing on the window sill, the kitchen appeared bright and homely. Perhaps it was this that caused Constance to say again, 'It's all right for you, our Hope.'

All right for her. Hope bit her tongue as she watched her sister pulling on her hat and coat. Constance knew full well she loathed her job at the laundry and that since becoming pregnant three months ago the smells – which ranged from a bit of a whiff to linen which stank to high heaven – had the power to make her physically sick. Not only that, but all Daniel's efforts to secure employment had come to nothing and they were still managing on her wage alone. His university degree looked good on paper but had proved virtually useless for the couple of trainee architect positions he had applied for. Realising that dream wasn't practical in the current climate when fully qualified architects were being forced to take junior positions, he had attempted to get into journalism, with the same result. An interview for an industrial design position had come to nothing, as had a tentative inquiry into the up-and-coming field of broadcasting. For every job there were hordes of desperate applicants, all willing to work for a subsistence income. And now she was expecting a baby and they thought they had been so careful.

'Ta-ra then, lass.' Constance put her hat on and fluffed her carefully styled curls into place round her face. Her hair had got lighter and lighter over the last six months and Hope was sure she was bleaching it with hydrogen peroxide in an effort to look more like her idol, Jean Harlow, although for some reason Constance wouldn't admit to it. 'I'll call round about the same time next Saturday, shall I?'

Hope nodded. 'And don't give your notice in at the Grand until you've got somewhere better, will you?'

Constance didn't answer this. 'Tell Daniel I'm sorry I missed him. He's late back from this walk of his, isn't he? It'll be getting dark in half an hour now the nights are dropping in.'

'He likes walking, we both do, but at the moment I'm not up to it.' Not for the world would Hope have admitted to her sister that Daniel would be hanging around at the Old Market waiting for the prices to drop, because she knew he wouldn't want her to. It was this same pride that kept him from applying for the dole, although they weren't sure he would get anything anyway with her working, and if he did, petty officialdom would soon find a way to withdraw it. Only the day before, the public assistance men had called at Mrs Potts over the road after a nosy neighbour had reported Mr Potts wearing a new cap. They had been in the house ages, apparently inquiring how such ostentation could be afforded and why it was that the brood of little Potts all looked so healthy. Now the Potts' dole was to be trimmed and Mrs Potts was beside herself with worry. And all over a cap Mr Potts had been given by his brother.

When Constance had left, Hope stood at the kitchen window looking out into the mean little backyard for some time, one hand resting on her belly which was already showing a definite swell. What were they going to do? How would they manage with a baby if Daniel didn't find work soon? But they would, somehow they would. God willing, she could work right up until the time the baby was due and her Aunt Jinny had said she'd look after it during the day when she went back to work. It wasn't what she'd have chosen, leaving the baby, but needs must. And she'd do anything, *anything* rather than see Daniel caught up working for his father again.

Resisting the temptation to sit down for a few minutes more, Hope forced herself to begin preparing the dumplings she was going to add to the mutton stew she had made with some scrag ends. Since she had fallen for the baby she was tired all the time, a deep, leaden tiredness she'd never experienced before, but as much as she could she hid this from Daniel, knowing how bad he felt about her having to work in her condition.

She popped the dumplings into the stew and cleared away the remaining flour and suet before washing her hands in the scullery.

The September twilight was deepening, the last of the weak sunshine had gone when she went back into the kitchen. Now she did allow herself to sit in one of the comfy old armchairs in front of the range. She didn't light the gas, economy dictated this was only done when it became absolutely necessary, besides which she liked staring into the red glow of the fire in the gathering shadows. She rarely had time to just sit and think, but when she did, warm thoughts of the baby – which she couldn't help being thrilled about despite the financial problems it would bring – vied with agitation regarding her father-in-law.

If only Abe had continued being awkward and hostile she'd have felt better, she admitted guiltily, but just days after their marriage there had been a knock at the front door one evening. There he had stood, olive branch in hand. Daniel had melted in the face of his father's contrition and since then Abe had become a regular visitor to their two little rooms. He always came alone, except once at Christmas when Annie had accompanied him, weighed down with parcels for the two of them. Emily had never once paid a call, although to be fair when they had received an invitation to Abe's New Year's Eve party and gone to the house, she had been civil.

By, that had been a cheerless night, Hope reflected, settling herself further into the chair as her eyelids began to droop. There had been plenty of food and drink, it hadn't been that, but it had been obvious Cecil and Gwendoline were at loggerheads for some reason, and Bernice and Rupert were barely speaking as usual. Rosaleen had been in a sulk all evening because Abe had refused to let her attend an all-night party one of the tennis club crowd was throwing, maintaining she was too young at sixteen, something he and Emily had disagreed about which had caused problems between them. The atmosphere had been so thick you could have cut it with a knife. Hope hadn't known any of the friends and business acquaintances there, but it was clear they were aware of the reason Daniel no longer worked for his father and this hadn't made for easy conversation. All evening she'd longed for her aunt's New Year's do when friends and the neighbours called round, never empty-handed but bringing a bottle of home-made beer or wine, or a plate of egg and ham pie or pickled onions for the table. Dear old Mr McCabe from three doors down always left the throng before midnight, armed with coal, bread and a bottle, and once the ships' hooters and church bells announced the beginning of the new year, Mr McCabe would arrive knocking on the door on the twelfth chime of the clock to fulfil his first-foot duty. It was a riotous time, like no other, everyone kissing and hugging and laughing. Not at all like the cool, stiff celebrations at Daniel's parents' house. She had even found herself feeling sorry for them at one point . . .

She must have fallen asleep because when the knock came at the front door, she jerked to life so suddenly her heart raced. Feeling distinctly light-headed, Hope made her way into the hall. When she opened the door she saw Abe standing on the step.

'Hello, lass.' He smiled, his rough-hewn face mellowing enough to carry more than a passing resemblance to Daniel's. 'You all right? You look a bit peaky.'

'I'm fine.' She tried to marshal her thoughts through the giddiness. 'Daniel's out, he's been for a walk but he should be back any minute. Come on in,' she added, stepping backwards as she spoke. 'I'll make some tea.'

'Thanks, lass. It's fair perishing the night. It might only be September but the signs are we're in for a rough winter this year.'

Take deep breaths, you'll be all right, Hope told herself. You've just got up too quickly. As Abe passed her and she closed the door, she hung on to the latch a moment longer. She felt funny, odd, but she couldn't let him see. They had told her aunt and uncle and Constance about the baby but had decided not to let on to Daniel's family for the time being. She knew Daniel was hoping he would pick up work of some kind before he had to give them the news.

'Anything wrong, Hope?' As she turned to face Abe she saw he was looking at her intently.

Hope tried to speak through the gathering blackness but it was beyond her. As the rushing in her head took over, she was aware of a sudden movement from her father-in-law and then . . . nothing.

'. . . get a doctor. Who do you use?'

'Preston. He's off the New Durham Road. I think the address is—'

'Daniel?' The effort to form words was enormous but as

she struggled out of unconsciousness she reached out to the familiar voice.

'Hope. Hope, darling. Lie still, you fainted.'

As her eyes focused, Hope became aware she was lying on their bed, the eiderdown on top of her, and Daniel was bending over her, his face ashen. 'I'm all right.' She needed to reassure him. 'Really, I'm all right.'

'I'll go and get the doctor,' Abe said.

'No.' Hope's fingers closed tightly round Daniel's. 'I don't want the doctor.' They couldn't afford it. 'You know what it is.'

She saw comprehension dawn in her husband's eyes; he clearly hadn't put two and two together. 'Is it normal then?' he asked softly as he helped her to sit up. 'This fainting?'

She nodded. 'Aunt Jinny said it might happen, it did with her apparently about this stage.' She glanced at her father-in-law who was standing at the end of the bed. It was no use prevaricating, she could see from the look on his face he had guessed. 'I'm expecting a baby,' she said quietly.

In view of everything that had gone before, she hadn't known what to expect when she and Daniel broke the news to his parents, but not for one minute had she anticipated the transparent delight that was now splitting Abe's face in a huge grin. 'Well, blow me.' He shook his head. 'A bairn.' Clapping Daniel on the back, he said, 'Congratulations. Congratulations to the pair of you. When's it due?'

'February time or thereabouts.' Daniel was grinning too, clearly pleased by his father's reaction.

'Well, you make sure you look after yourself, lass.' Abe looked at Hope's pale face. 'The doctor happy with you, is he?'

Hope hesitated and it was Daniel who said, 'We haven't been to the doctor yet.'

Abe's eyes narrowed but before he could speak, Hope said hastily, 'We just haven't had the time, have we, Daniel? But there's no rush, I'm young and healthy and I feel fine.' Then realising this sounded a bit silly in view of the circumstances, she added, 'Usually, that is.'

An awkward silence followed, and when Hope went to lift the eiderdown, Daniel's hand covered hers. 'You stay where you are,' he said softly, 'and I'll bring you a cup of tea in a minute. Just shut your eyes and rest a while, all right?'

If it wasn't for the fact she still felt quite odd, Hope would have protested. Daniel returned with a steaming cup of tea a few minutes later. After handing the tea to her, he sat down on the edge of the bed, his smoky grey eyes on her face. 'I ought to have insisted you go to the doctor when we first suspected you might be expecting a baby, the money doesn't matter,' he said very quietly.

This was his father talking and of course money didn't matter to Abe, he had plenty of it. Telling herself she had to go carefully because she'd long since recognised there was a strong stubborn streak running through her husband's mild nature, Hope smiled. 'There was no need but if you insist of course we'll go.' She flicked his nose playfully. 'Don't look so worried. I'm quite well, I really am, Daniel. Fit as a fiddle.'

He straightened his back, attempting a smile, but his face was strained when he said, 'Of course you are.'

Oh, why had his father had to come right at such a crucial time? When she was alone again, Daniel having flatly forbidden her to stir from where she was for the rest of the day, Hope brooded on what was being said in the kitchen. For all his congratulations she didn't trust Abe any further than she could throw him. It wasn't just that he was devious and persistent although he was, he certainly was; it was that rugged charm he could turn on and off like a tap which was the real problem. How many times had she sat in the kitchen with Abe and Daniel since her marriage and listened to the pair of them talk, thinking how her father-in-law could make you believe black was white? Countless times. Despite all his faults he had something which made folk warm to him and he knew it. Knew it and used it.

When Daniel came to take away her empty cup, he persuaded her to lie down again. But when he left the room, Hope sat up abruptly. She couldn't lie here another moment wondering what was being said. Whether Daniel liked it or not, she had to join them.

She had actually got her feet on the floor when she heard the kitchen door open and voices in the hall. Yanking the eider-down over her again, she slid down into the bed and waited for Daniel to come in. The front door opened and shut. A moment later Daniel poked his head round the bedroom door. 'I've just made another pot of tea. Shall I bring you a cup?'

'If you bring yours in here too.'

When he joined her she was sitting up in bed and without any preamble she said, 'Please don't let your da unsettle you. I'm fine and I promise we'll go and see the doctor tomorrow. How's that?'

'It's not just today, Hope. You shouldn't be working in that damn laundry, lifting and stretching and doing goodness knows what while I sit twiddling my thumbs.'

'You don't twiddle your thumbs. No one could have looked for work harder than you.'

'It hasn't been hard enough. I'm not prepared to have our child brought here, to two miserable rooms and with us living hand to mouth. We can't go on the way we are. It's grossly unfair on you.'

'No, no it isn't.' She reached out to him but although he took her in his arms, his body was stiff. 'There are lots of folk worse off than us,' Hope said. 'Look at the Potts—'

'I don't want to look at the Potts.' Then he gentled his voice and said, 'I'm not interested in the Potts or anyone else, only you. You and the baby. We have to be realistic, Hope. The state the country's in I'm not going to get a job for months, possibly years. You know as well as I do that there are hundreds of young men in their twenties round these parts who have never had a job at all and see no possibility of getting one either.'

'You're different.' Hope clung to him, willing him to believe it.

'Da's offered me a job but on a permanent footing this time, nine to five, like Cecil. I told him we would have to talk it through first but that I was interested.'

Daniel's voice was so flat that for a moment the content of the words didn't reach Hope's mind but seemingly hung in the air while she grappled with them. 'No.' Her hand went to her throat and she grasped the skin there. 'You hated it before, you know you did.' She had known this would happen. Ever since she had become pregnant, this had been her secret fear. If Daniel went back to work for his father, it would be the end of something precious, something she couldn't put a name to but which was tied up with the two of them belonging only to each other. 'Please, Daniel, I don't want you to. I can work for months yet and you could find a job next week or the next. Don't make any decisions yet. Promise me.'

'Hope, be practical. It would mean a steady wage, we could take a mortgage on a little house—'

'Promise me.'

'I promise I'll do nothing until we've seen the doctor. All right? I want you checked over and, depending on what he says, we'll talk then.'

Hope nodded, relief flooding her. She was young and healthy and the faint had been nothing untoward. Her Aunt Jinny had said she had fainted with each one of hers just after the three-month stage. Something to do with the baby turning, her aunt had maintained. 'We'll go and see him tomorrow.' She curved into Daniel, needing the closeness. 'And I'm feeling hungry, Mr Fallow, so once we've drunk our tea I'm getting up out of this bed and seeing to the dinner. I don't trust you not to drop it all over the floor or something.'

'Cheeky baggage.'

Daniel smiled, but Hope could detect the shadow in his eyes which hadn't been there before his father had called. Why couldn't Abe Fallow stay out of their affairs? She lowered her head, her teeth biting into the soft flesh of her lower lip. But perhaps Daniel's father was genuinely trying to help. To take the burden of their financial difficulties off his son's shoulders. Already she was feeling overwhelmingly protective of the new life growing inside her. Maybe this was a reflection of how her father-in-law felt.

Don't weaken. The warning came unbidden but strongly and Hope mentally nodded to it. She must not compare how she felt about her baby with Abe's desire to control every aspect of his family. It was different, very different. Look at poor Bernice.

'We'll go and see the doctor tomorrow,' she repeated. 'And everything will be all right. I know it will.'

'Twins? It can't be.'

'I think it highly likely, Mrs Fallow. Either that or you have a baby elephant in there.' Dr Preston smiled at his little joke. 'Do twins run in yours or your husband's family by any chance?'

'I don't think so.' She stared at the doctor. Twins. Two mouths to feed, two sets of clothes, two *everything*. And how long could she work? Myra Gibson had had twins and she remembered her Aunt Jinny commenting that their neighbour had been as big as a house at the end.

In something of a daze she left the doctor's office and joined Daniel in the waiting room. 'What is it?' He was frightened by the look on her face. 'What's wrong?'

'Nothing, nothing.' Acutely embarrassed by the interested glances of the other patients waiting in the small brown painted room, she left the surgery without even speaking to the doctor's receptionist, Daniel just behind her.

Outside, he took her arm. 'What is it?' he asked again.

Hope stared at him. In a few short words she was going to bind them to his father for ever. Because that was what would happen. She knew once Daniel heard they were expecting twins he would take the job with Abe and nothing she could say would be able to persuade him otherwise. Daniel's father had won. Without having to lift a finger, he'd won.

This particular battle but not the war. As the thought came, her small chin lifted. Daniel was accepting a job from his father, that was all, and she would make sure it was all. There would be no borrowing money from Abe as Cecil had done for his big house and expensive furniture. They would cut their cloth according to their weekly income and she would stand firm on this whatever her father-in-law said. No interest-free loans, no handouts, no tentacles wrapping themselves round them until they had to ask Abe permission to breathe. In the last year of getting to know her father-in-law she didn't doubt he genuinely wanted the best for his children, but mixed in with that was the iron control he endeavoured to exert in every area of their lives. It was relentless, implacable and all in the name of love. Abe's kind of love.

Hope took a deep breath and placed her fingers over Daniel's hand where it was holding her arm. Forcing a smile, she said, 'Brace yourself. I've got something to tell you . . .'

Chapter 11

'What do you mean, Daniel won't accept a loan? That house near Hendon Burn is perfect for him and we know several very nice families in the district. You must make him take it, Abe, and that's the end of the matter.'

'I can't force them to do what they don't want to do, Emily.'

'Of course you can.' Emily glared at her husband, putting down her needlework and leaning forward in her chair, her body stiff. 'I won't have a son of mine living in squalor, I tell you. It was different when people thought we had fallen out and virtually cut them off, but now Daniel is working for you his home reflects on us. Surely you can see that?'

Abe looked at his wife. She was as pretty as a picture sitting there, no one would guess she had borne four children. She didn't look a day over thirty in the mellow glow from the pink standard lamp behind her and the subdued lighting hid every trace of the few grey hairs which had begun to appear in the still thick, rich brown hair. He had noticed they rarely made use of the full lighting these days. Clearing his throat, he said gruffly, 'Don't go on, woman, and I don't want you mentioning the matter to Daniel either. It'll only make him dig his heels in even more.'

Emily picked up her needlework and stabbed at it a few times. 'He wasn't like that before he met her and I'm sure she's behind this. Daniel wouldn't have thought twice about letting us help him if he was married to someone else. Cecil was only too pleased to be able to provide Gwendoline with the sort of house she was accustomed to, but of course, I was forgetting.' She looked up and for once she didn't appear so comely. 'That little slut is used to filth and degradation.'

Dear gussy, he'd had enough of this. After the sort of day he'd had he ought to be able to come home to peace and quiet. 'If you had come with me to visit them like I asked, you'd know Hope keeps those two rooms spotless,' Abe said shortly. 'I'm going to see when dinner'll be ready.'

He could feel the waves of anger coming off Emily as he left the drawing room but for once he didn't feel inclined to pet and coax her out of her mood. In fact he was feeling less and less inclined these days. Frowning to himself, Abe made his way to the kitchen.

Annie turned from the range as he entered, her eyebrows raised inquiringly. 'What's the matter?'

'Why should anything be the matter?'

'Because you've a face like a wet weekend, that's why.'

Abe grinned, flinging himself into one of the hard-backed chairs at the table. He raked his hand through his wiry hair. She was a card, was Annie, but he'd say one thing for her, she called a spade a spade and he liked that. He'd found few women as straightforward as Annie, although he rather suspected Daniel's little lass might be of the same mould. Of course the two of them couldn't be further apart in looks, although Annie had never seemed bothered she'd been at the back of the queue when God had dished out pretty faces. Mind, it was a funny thing, when he was with her like this, just the two of them, he forgot how she looked. Strange that. Or maybe not so strange when he thought about it because he enjoyed her company, it was as simple as that. Even as bairns they'd struck sparks off each other and his mam, bless her soul, had liked nothing better than when he and Annie were getting in sly digs at each other. Laughed fit to burst, she had. 'If you two ever wed it wouldn't be a quiet house but you'd never be bored, I'll say that,' had been her favourite shot at them.

Abe shifted in his chair, suddenly uncomfortable with his thoughts. 'Daniel's adamant they won't accept a penny towards a decent house,' he said flatly, 'even though it'd be a loan.'

Annie didn't answer this directly. Instead she reached into a cupboard and brought out the whisky bottle and small glass she kept there for Abe's visits to her small domain. She placed them in front of him and turned back to stirring the soup.

'Well?' Abe had drunk one glass straight down and poured himself another before he spoke. 'Don't tell me you haven't got an opinion about it.'

'I won't.' Annie lifted the saucepan onto the steel hotplate at the side of the range and then joined him at the table. 'But it's likely one you don't want to hear.'

'That's never stopped you before.' Abe smiled. The whisky had burnt a pleasing path down into his stomach.

'Then I think you ought to be proud the pair of them are determined to make their own way without holding out their hands, even if it does make them less beholden to you.'

Abe's jaw tightened, his pleasant expression gone. 'What does that mean?'

Annie didn't lower her gaze but surveyed him from unblinking black eyes. Her voice was softer, though, when she said, 'Cecil doesn't wipe his nose unless you give him permission and you know it, and for all her tantrums Rosaleen does exactly what you say.' She didn't mention Bernice. Annie had her own opinon there too, especially about Bernice's husband.

'Rosaleen's a bit lass and a daft one at that,' Abe said. 'She needs a firm hand, especially the way her mother is with her. And Cecil is me second-in-command at the works, I can't be fairer than that, damn it.'

Annie did not answer but continued to stare at him, her expression quizzical.

Irritably now, Abe growled, 'Cecil's always needed guidance, you know how he is. Daniel's a different kettle of fish for all his quiet manner. He's more like me an' thinks for himself although Emily can't see it. She thinks the lass has changed him.'

'If she has, it's for the better.'

'Oh aye, I know you're for her. She could break the family up for good an' all and you'd still be for her.'

Annie sat forward in her chair. Her voice quiet, she said, 'I tell you something, Abe. I regretted my part in letting Father McHaffie loose on her that day. It wasn't right.'

Talking about Father McHaffie as if he was a pit bull terrier would have made Abe smile in other circumstances. 'Well, it didn't have any effect so I wouldn't lose sleep over it.' He finished the glass of whisky before rubbing the skin of his brow hard enough to make it bright red. 'I've had a devil of a day, lass. We was broken into again last night. I'm going to have to think about getting a couple of nightwatchmen in at this rate.'

'Much harm done?'

'Enough.' But the excrement all over the office had been the final straw. The message had been as clear as if Jim Clark was standing in front of him.

'And you still think it's him, the Clark lad?'

Abe nodded.

'You ought to tell Emily, you know, put her in the picture. You can't always keep anything bad from her.'

'She'd drive me mad, lass, she's not like you. She can't handle unpleasantness.'

'She's your wife, Abe.'

'Aye, I know.' He did not ask himself why he could discuss anything under the sun with the woman in front of him, whereas with his wife of twenty-nine years the conversation was, and always had been, superficial, but he knew it wasn't right.

He got to his feet. 'I'm going to have a bath afore dinner. How long till it's ready?'

'Half an hour.'

He nodded, leaving the kitchen without another word and making his way upstairs. He had thought it would be all plain sailing now Daniel had agreed to work for him again but this wasn't proving the case. Although he wouldn't admit it to a soul, he agreed with Emily in principle – Hope was behind his son's refusal to borrow some cash for a nice house and furniture. They'd certainly been proved wrong in thinking she was a little minx with an eye to the main chance, he told himself grimly, opening the door to the master bedroom. He could have handled that better, that was language he understood. But this refusal to take anything from him was damn insulting, that's what it was. If a father couldn't help his own son, it was a poor lookout.

In the bath Abe sat scowling at the water, his mind a million miles away. What with Daniel being awkward, Cecil sulking because he'd brought Dan back into the business, Rosaleen running around with a crowd that for all their money and connections hadn't got a brain cell between them and now Emily playing up, he'd had enough. Where would the lot of them be if it wasn't for him, that's what he'd like to know.

He shut his eyes and leant back against the cold rim of the bath. It was only then he admitted to himself that the main reason he didn't know which end of him was up was a direct result of the break-in the night before. It was all very well for the constable to say such incidents were becoming more common with the Depression biting, but last night's work wasn't down to some poor devil at his wits' end. It was a reminder from Jim Clark he'd got a long memory . . .

Abe sat up abruptly, causing the bath water to slosh on the floor. What was he doing letting Jim put the wind up him? He'd be damned if he'd let that little nowt intimidate him. If they tried any monkey business with him they'd find they'd bitten off more than they could chew. He'd held his hand to date, but now was perhaps the time to call in a favour and the blokes he had in mind were every bit as hard as Jim's crew.

He washed himself thoroughly with the carbolic soap he favoured and insisted on having despite Emily's attempts to educate him to the scented variety, then leant back in the water again.

He'd have a word with Edwin Mullen and his brother tomorrow. The three of them had earned a copper here and there since they'd been bairns of five or six, taking chances sometimes and running errands for some of the ne'er-do-wells plying their dubious trades down at the docks. Edwin's da had been like his, good for nothing and willing to let his family starve as long as he had his beer and baccy. Times were if he and Ed hadn't put food on their tables their families would have gone to bed hungry, but whereas he had used his native wit and cunning to start his own business, Edwin and Vincent had gone down a darker path.

The pair of them had got into trouble with the law a few years back, resulting in them being sent down for a stretch. When he'd heard, he had made sure their old mam had enough for the rent and food until they were out. He had done it because he liked the old lady, she had been a great friend of his mother's, but he'd also known that the brothers worshipped the ground their mam walked on, so it wouldn't do him any harm. Having pals in low places was sometimes as beneficial as having them in high.

Abe heaved himself out of the water and reached for one of the big fluffy towels. A little word in Jim's shell-like from Edwin and Vincent would hammer home the message that enough was enough. Jim had had his pound of flesh out of Maurice's hide when all was said and done.

Feeling a mite happier now he'd come to the decision he had been putting off for some time, Abe dressed quickly. He donned a fresh shirt and trousers because he knew it would please Emily. She had a thing about changing for dinner although he considered it a waste of time. It was the same thinking that had made her insist he join the Gentlemen's Club in town as soon as he could, along with umpteen other organisations. To her credit, though, he'd made some useful business contacts out of them places.

He went downstairs just as Annie announced dinner was ready. Emily exited the drawing room and swept past him, her face stiff and her mouth pulled tight. He stared after her, knowing she had worked herself up into one of her icy rages and that he was too weary of it all to coax her round. Walking after her, he thought, you're getting old, m'lad.

No, no, it wasn't that. Immediately he baulked at the notion. At fifty, he was as virile as ever. Damn it, he'd still like it every night if Emily were willing instead of the once a week she allowed but as he'd got older he'd realised the satisfaction of his bodily needs wasn't enough. A man needed mental stimulation from the woman in his life, intelligent conversation, wit, someone to laugh with. How he would have managed without his visits to the kitchen he didn't know. He was more at ease in Annie's company than he'd ever been with Emily, or any of his family come to that.

The feeling of unease which had come over him several times lately once again made itself known, and he mentally shook himself. He needed a good dinner and a couple of glasses of wine, that would sort him out, he told himself, entering the dining room and sitting down without glancing at his wife. And maybe a brandy or two to follow. And tomorrow he'd have another word with Daniel about the house near Hendon Burn, talk some sense into him. With a couple of bairns on the way they needed something a darn sight better than the two-up, two-down rabbit hutches they'd been looking at the last week or so, whatever Hope said to the contrary. He wasn't going to let a slip of a lass get the better of him, was he?

No, he damn well wasn't.

'I think this is the one.'

'And I think you're right, Mrs Fallow.' Daniel smiled at Hope as she turned to him, her eyes shining.

'Really? You like it too?'

He sensed the touch of anxiety beneath the surface of the question and knew she was worrying he was regretting turning down his father's loan, even though wild horses couldn't have dragged it from her. Several times in the past few weeks since he had started working for his father again, Hope had made some reference to the luxury he had been used to before they had married. He knew who had unsettled her. At first he hadn't cottoned on to what his da was doing when he called round on the odd evening, but then something had alerted him to the fact that the casual remarks his da made about the bath he'd just had, or their gardener cutting the lawns, or the peace and quiet he enjoyed in his study – 'Every man should have a bolthole in his home to call his own, don't you agree, eh?' – had all been aimed at Hope. The next morning at work when it was just the two of them he had set his father straight, and in spite of his da's blustering he knew he wouldn't be up to more tricks, but the damage had been done.

Daniel took Hope in his arms, holding her as close as her protruding stomach would allow. 'I love it,' he said firmly, 'and the fact that we're buying it and not renting will make it truly ours. Just one thing though, I want to decorate before we move in. Just a lick of paint and some new wallpaper but we might as well do it while the house is empty.'

Hope nodded. The little terraced house in Frederick Street was identical to hundreds of other two-up, two-down dwellings, but the fact that Mowbray Park was a stone's throw away once you'd crossed over Borough Road made it more attractive than the others they'd looked at. A lot more attractive than the one at the back of the gasworks where the air had been thick with fumes of burning coke. And she would make it bonny for Daniel, so bonny even his da wouldn't be able to pick fault with it. She had left off work the week before at Daniel's insistence so she now had plenty of time to scour the second-hand shops during the day with her Aunt Jinny and look for bargains.

The five per cent deposit the building society required was low due to the slump, but it had still taken every penny of their nest egg. She was so glad they hadn't touched the residue of Daniel's money during the last twelve months, it had been worth all the scrimping and making do on her wage not to have to ask Daniel's father for the deposit. Daniel's current wage meant they could pay the mortgage and all the bills each week and still have enough left over for food and coal, but they would need to be thrifty if they wanted to decorate and maybe pick up a three-piece suite from somewhere.

They were standing in the front room of the property; the estate agent who had let them in a few minutes before was sitting in his car outside. The dark brown paintwork and dull wallpaper made the limited space appear even smaller, and the two bedrooms upstairs were equally drab. The kitchen was the largest room in the house and had a tiny scullery through which the small backyard was accessed. This held a privy but no wash house although there was a huge mangle in the yard which apparently went with the sale. But although gloomy, everything was clean. Spotlessly so. The elderly schoolmistress who had occupied the house all her life, having been born there, had been a stickler for cleanliness, according to the estate agent.

'So this is the one, yes? You're absolutely sure?' Daniel asked, tucking her scarf more firmly round her neck as he spoke. The bitter October chill had permeated the empty house and the temperature inside was only a degree or two warmer than in the street.

'Quite sure.' And then Hope froze, a look of wonder spreading over her face. 'Daniel, I felt it. I mean them. They moved.' She put her hands to the mound of her stomach. 'I felt a kind of fluttering.'

Daniel grinned and put his hands over hers. 'That's it then, the seal of approval. They must know they're in their new home.'

'They're alive, Daniel. Our babies.' Hope was totally unprepared for the flood of fierce maternal love the first movements of her babies caused. Tremulously, she said, 'We're going to be happy here, I know it.'

She would make it so. It didn't matter that Daniel's parents disapproved of her, or that when they'd gone to dinner last week his mother had seemed determined to make her feel like an interloper. Nothing mattered but Daniel and the babies. She was going to be the best wife and mother in the world and make Abe and Emily eat their words.

She flung her arms round Daniel's neck, and now there was laughter in her voice when she said, 'An Englishman's home is his castle, isn't that what they say? Well, this is *our* little castle and I'm going to make it so bonny we'll be the envy of everyone, how about that?'

'I believe it.' Relieved her mood had changed, Daniel whisked her up into his arms despite her protests, saying, 'I didn't carry you over the threshold but I'm going to carry you back out now and that's just as good, so stop your wriggling unless you want me to drop you.'

And it was like that, with Daniel holding her against his heart, that they left the house and stepped into the windswept street.

Chapter 12

'You've done too much, I knew you would. You're exhausted, admit it.'

'Of course I'm a bit tired. So would you be if you were carrying two babies in your stomach.'

Hope and Daniel were standing arm in arm on the step of their home watching Jinny and George and the three lads still living at home walk away down the frosty street. It was the clearest of nights, stars twinkling overhead and the air so sharp it cut like a knife. Once the five turned at the corner of Frederick Street and waved goodbye, Daniel drew Hope into the hall.

There, as though there had been no break in the conversation, Hope said, 'But I promise I didn't do too much. How could I when you wouldn't let me lift a finger? Aunt Jinny dished up the dinner and you did all the washing and drying up, you even helped her with the sandwiches for tea.' Hope's voice was soft. She knew it was unthinkable for her uncle and cousins to have done what Daniel had done, they would have regarded it as a slur on their manhood. Hope had had a word with the manageress at the laundry before she left, knowing the woman had always had a regard for her, with the result that her aunt had secured the position, but even though Jinny did a full day's work, she came home to four men sitting on their backsides without a spot of housework done or the dinner prepared. That was 'women's work'.

'I still think it was too much.'

'Don't fuss.' Hope touched his face, her eyes loving him. 'Come on, let's sit in the front room a while before we go to bed.' It was rare they lit a fire in there, it was a waste of fuel they could ill afford, but today, Christmas Day, was different. This was what had prompted Hope to invite her aunt and uncle and three cousins round, knowing all her aunt had for Christmas dinner was a watery rabbit stew. Daniel had been despatched to shop late at the Old Market the night before. He had managed to pick up an enormous chicken for a fraction of its price as the stallholders packed up, along with a box of vegetables and potatoes and a stone bag of fruit. He'd arrived home just as the clock had chimed midnight, frozen but as pleased as punch with his bargains. Hope had marvelled – as she often did – at the remarkable lack of side to the man she had married. What her mother-in-law would have thought to such activities was another matter.

Daniel sat with his arm round her shoulders on the sofa and they stared into the red glow of the flickering fire, content to sit quietly. The paper chains linked into all four corners of the ceiling and the small Christmas tree with its handmade decorations were bright and cheering, as were the loose covers Hope had made to cover the shabby three-piece suite they had bought on moving into the house. Apart from a square of carpet which showed a border of bare floorboards and a bookcase holding the books Daniel had brought with him from his parents' house when they married, the room held nothing more, but the atmosphere was one of peace and cosiness. This pervaded the whole house, so much so that most visitors remarked on it.

'I wish Constance had come,' Hope said after a while. 'I don't like her living at the Kirbys, especially after that trouble last month with Betty's brothers.'

Daniel said nothing to this because there was no comfort he could give her. Frank and Lonnie Kirby had been caught thieving from the docks and given a prison sentence, and the case had left a question mark over certain other shady practices the brothers were suspected of being involved in but for which there was no proof. Hope had renewed her efforts to persuade her sister to come and live with them but Constance would have none of it. She and Betty were best friends, she maintained, and Betty's parents were lovely, didn't her mother treat her like a second daughter? Constance had been equally determined to spend Christmas with the Kirby family, refusing to even pop round on Christmas Day afternoon to say hello to her aunt and uncle whom she hadn't seen for weeks and weeks.

'Constance has changed, Daniel, the last little while since she's been at Betty's.' Hope spoke out the worry and unease which had grown stronger week by week. 'Sometimes I think I barely know her any more. And that Lonnie, I'm sure there's something going on between them.'

'Constance and Lonnie Kirby?' The question was full of disbelief. 'Surely not. He's double her age for one thing, Constance is still little more than a bairn.'

'Exactly. Before the court case, Constance was always mentioning him, saying how smart he was and that he had plenty of money to throw around.'

'Did you ask her if she was seeing him?'

Hope nodded. 'She denied it.'

'There you are then.'

'I don't believe her.'

'Dear gussy.' The saying was one of Abe's and spoken in the same deep tone he would have used. Raking back his hair, Daniel peered into her face. 'Look, don't you worry yourself sick about it, you can't do anything. Your aunt and uncle let Constance go to Betty's, it's out of your hands. Have another word with her about him the next time she calls round by all means, but you've more than enough to think about what with the babies and all. Bernice and Rupert want to bring the cribs round tomorrow, by the way, I was supposed to tell you.' Daniel grimaced apologetically. 'Bernice rang me at the office on Christmas Eve morning. It's all right, isn't it?'

'Of course it is.' Hope smiled but her heart sank. She had been looking forward to a quiet Boxing Day with Daniel, and Bernice and Rupert were one of the last couples she'd choose to see. Bernice was so very quiet and self-contained and Rupert she found utterly repulsive. He had a way of looking at her sometimes which made her flesh creep. Since she and Daniel had wed they had only seen Bernice and Rupert a couple of times and both occasions had been at Daniel's parents' house. Now they would be entertaining them here and it would be just the four of them. But it had been kind of Bernice to buy the cribs for the babies, and not just the cribs apparently, but sheets and blankets too. Hope had been expecting to cut down a sheet and blanket from the

Old Market and hem them round. Forcing a brightness into her voice she didn't feel, she said, 'What time are they coming?'

'After lunch. They'll only want a cup of tea, nothing more.'

She couldn't just give them a cup of tea, not when they were bringing such expensive gifts for the babies. There was the remains of the Christmas cake from tea today and she could bake some teacakes and scones tomorrow morning, that would have to do. A mental picture of the loaded tea trolley at Abe's place came into her mind; no doubt Bernice and Rupert provided similar for their guests. She knew their house on the outskirts of Hendon was every bit as grand as Abe's.

Suddenly the tiredness she had been endeavouring to keep at bay for the last hour or two became overwhelming, the dull ache in the small of her back making itself felt with renewed vigour. Close to tears and not really knowing why, Hope said in a small voice, 'Shall we go to bed now?' and for once she couldn't laugh and make light of her shape when Daniel had to help her up from the sofa. She felt enormous, absolutely enormous, and the flowing tent-like dress she had made herself with the small sewing machine they'd bought shortly after moving into the house barely fitted her now. How on earth was she going to last another six weeks or so until the babies were due? She waddled rather than walked now as it was. And she still had the curtains to make for both bedrooms – they'd had an old sheet hooked up since they'd moved in – and she barely had enough baby clothes for one infant, let alone two.

'What is it?' Once he had her on her feet Daniel kept her in his arms. 'What's the matter?'

'I feel big and ugly and I can't do half of what I want to—'

He cut her short by kissing her, hard. 'You're beautiful,' he said softly, 'and I'm the luckiest man alive. I catch myself looking at other men and feeling sorry for them, do you know that? Because whoever they're going home to, it isn't you.'

'Oh, Daniel.' Her taut muscles slackened. What did it matter that she was like some lumbering elephant? He didn't see her like that. And what odds tea trolleys and curtains and baby clothes? Nothing mattered except Daniel. A good night's sleep and she would be as right as rain in the morning, ready to do a bit of baking and then make Bernice and Rupert welcome for an hour or two. She smiled at him, wondering at how a few words could transform her mood into one of intense and grateful happiness. She was fickle, that's what she was, she told herself silently. And as daft as a brush into the bargain. Touching Daniel's stubbly jaw with the palm of her hand, she said softly, 'I love you, Mr Fallow.'

'Likewise, Mrs Fallow.'

In spite of her exhaustion, Hope found she couldn't sleep once she was in bed. She catnapped until the early hours when the backache became more persistent. Once it grew light, she slid quietly from under the covers and pulled on her thick dressing gown and slippers. She shivered in the icy air as she crept downstairs to the warmth of the kitchen to make herself a pot of tea.

Daniel had banked down the fire in the range the night before with damp slack and cinders she'd bought from one of the out-of-work miners who came round the doors selling barrow loads. Hope always took a supply if she could, handing over a shilling and sometimes a shive of bread and jam or a piece of sly cake if she'd been baking. Daniel had gently warned her she would be known as an easy touch but the sheer desperation in the once proud faces got to her every time.

It didn't take long for the fire to flare up, and once Hope had made the tea she sat in one of the two armchairs positioned in front of the range, her slippered feet on the clippy mat.

By the time Daniel came downstairs an hour later she had their porridge on the go and a batch of teacakes for the afternoon in the oven. The backache was still there, worse if anything, but she made light of it to Daniel, knowing he would put Bernice and Rupert off if she admitted she didn't feel too good. Bernice had been so generous, first with the wedding breakfast and now the cribs, and Hope didn't want her sister-in-law to think she wasn't welcome.

At two o'clock the fire in the front room had been lit and everything was ready, although by now Hope was wondering if she had caught a chill. She felt odd, slightly queasy and muzzy-headed and the backache had become vicious at times, although at others it was quite bearable. Wishing she had been honest with Daniel earlier, Hope decided to get through the afternoon with their guests as best she could and then admit to Daniel she was feeling unwell and go to bed early.

The knock at the front door coincided with a giant vice taking hold of her belly and squeezing until she felt she couldn't breathe. She heard Daniel open the front door and then voices but for the life of her she couldn't move from beside the table where she'd been fiddling with the napkins. She knew she ought to walk through into the hall and join the others in the front room but it was beyond her. And then, mercifully, the pain died away, leaving her forehead damp and her legs shaking as she clung onto the table.

'Hope?' She opened her eyes to see Daniel in the doorway, the smile on his face dying as he took in her posture. 'Darling, what is it?' he asked as he sprang across the room to her.

'I don't know.'

'You look ill, sit down for a minute.'

She sat down, more because of the feeling of nausea than anything else. Perhaps it wasn't a chill after all, maybe she had eaten something that had disagreed with her.

'Here.' As Daniel handed her a glass of water the pain in her stomach came again, building in intensity until she groaned out loud. It seemed to go on for ever. When at last it faded, Daniel was looking as bad as she felt.

Hope tried to smile reassuringly. 'I think I need to go and lie down for a bit. Can you explain to Bernice and Rupert and get them some tea?'

'It's just Bernice, Rupert's at his club and damn the tea.' Daniel raised her to her feet. 'Come on, sweetheart. Let's get you upstairs.'

They were halfway to the stairs when Hope had to stop. Bernice peered inquiringly round the front-room door but Hope found she couldn't even say hello. All she could do was clutch Daniel and pray the pain would go away. She was vaguely aware of Daniel and Bernice getting her up the stairs between them. Once she was lying on top of the bed, the pain began to ebb once more. 'I'm sorry about this, Bernice.' She smiled shakily. 'I think I've got a stomach upset.'

Daniel's sister sat down on the side of the bed and took Hope's hand. 'I think it's more likely the babies are coming,' she said very calmly. 'How long have you been having pains?'

'Not long.' Hope stared at her in alarm. 'I couldn't sleep last night and I had backache which has got worse today. I'm sure it's food poisoning or something like that.'

'Mother started with backache when she was having Rosaleen,' Bernice said quietly. 'I was just ten at the time but I remember the midwife saying it happens like that sometimes.'

'Oh.' Hope nodded. She felt embarrassed. It had needed Bernice who had never had a baby to tell her she was in labour.

Bernice glanced at her brother who had gone green round the gills. 'I think you had better fetch the doctor. I'll see to Hope,' she said matter-of-factly. 'My car's outside if you want to use it.'

Daniel shot off.

Another contraction came and went before Hope got undressed and into her nightdress with her sister-in-law's help. It was only fifteen minutes or so before Daniel was back with the doctor. Hope had had more contractions by then and they were strong ones.

Dr Preston was a no-nonsense middle-aged man, and after examining his patient he straightened, glancing round at the empty fireplace and the layer of ice coating the inside of the sash window. Frowning, he said, 'She can't have the babies here, it's far too cold. We need to move her downstairs and fast.'

'There's a fire in the front room and she could lie on the sofa,' Daniel said quickly.

'That'll do.' The doctor's voice was so low only Daniel could hear him when he muttered, 'With the bairns being so early I would have preferred to get her into the infirmary but that's out of the question now. We haven't time.' He turned to Bernice and raised his voice. 'I shall need your help, young lady.' His eyes moved over the extremely well-dressed woman who didn't look as if she had done a day's work in her life. 'My midwife is with family in South Shields over Christmas. Tell me, are you squeamish?'

Bernice looked him straight in the eye, her voice cool when she said, 'No, doctor. I am not squeamish.'

'Good. Put plenty of water on to boil and find some towels and old sheets, sacking will do if there's nothing else. Daniel, help me get Hope downstairs and then pop to Dr Ramshaw's in Corporation Road. Tell him I have need of his midwife. You may have to go and fetch the woman if she's available.'

Once Hope was lying on the sofa, the contractions started coming every two minutes. She felt panicky and frightened. Dr Preston was muttering orders to Bernice in between speaking to her, and the terrifying swiftness with which events unfolded combined with the excruciating pain made her feel she couldn't grasp control of what she was feeling. And more important than anything else, it was much too soon for her babies to be born.

She must have spoken her concern out loud because at one point Bernice bent over her and whispered, 'Don't worry, Hope, everything will be fine. Just do what the doctor says and all will be well.'

And then suddenly there was an overwhelming urge to push and a terrible burning sensation between her legs as an enormous pressure made itself felt. Almost as soon as it stopped, the urge was back again. She could hear Dr Preston saying, 'That's right, push, Hope, as hard as you can,' and if she'd had the strength she would have told him she couldn't

148

do anything else because her body was dictating things now.

By the time Daniel burst into the house twenty minutes later, without Dr Ramshaw's midwife who was apparently indisposed courtesy of a riotous Christmas party the day before, it was all over. He stared at Hope lying propped up on the sofa with the eiderdown from their bed over her, then his gaze moved in wonder to the two tiny infants cuddled against her body, swathed in blankets from Bernice's cribs. Each crib had been full of blankets and nappies and baby clothes; Bernice had thought of everything and it couldn't have been more welcome.

'You have a beautiful son and daughter, Daniel.' Dr Preston was beaming and Daniel could see that both women had been crying. 'They are very small and will need to be kept very warm day and night for the next few weeks, but both are healthy and remarkably vocal, or they were up until a minute or so ago. Now they're having a well-deserved sleep.'

Daniel's gaze moved back to Hope and her eyes were waiting for him. She smiled up at her husband as the tears rolled down his cheeks. 'I love you,' she whispered, 'and our babies.'

Bernice and Dr Preston quietly left the room as Daniel walked across to the sofa and fell to his knees, gathering his family into his arms.

Chapter 13

Over the next weeks Hope began to suspect that with the arrival of the twins her home had become a beacon for certain folk. Bernice's company she welcomed and relied on. From the very first, Daniel's sister had come every morning and stayed until Daniel got home from work, and she had been glad to help wherever she could. The babies only slept for half an hour at a time in the first month and needed almost constant feeding. Without Bernice on hand during this difficult period Hope didn't know how she would have coped. Even now, at the beginning of March, Hope counted herself fortunate if she had more than an hour's sleep between feeds during the night.

A bond had been forged between Hope and Bernice on the day of the twins' birth and as Hope got to know her sister-in-law better, she discovered a kind and warm-natured woman under the stiff and cool front Bernice presented to the world. Once, when the two women were sitting together on a snowy February afternoon, Bernice mentioned that she, too, had once loved a man but that her father had put an end to the affair and manipulated her into a marriage which was not a happy one. Beyond this Bernice did not elaborate and Hope did not press her.

Jinny called in most nights on her way home from work and to Hope's surprise her sister-in-law and aunt got on like a house on fire. The two women were so very different she hadn't expected that. Jinny always left the house with a bag of dirty washing tucked under her arm. She would return with it the next day, washed and ironed, the manageress at the laundry turning a blind eye to what Jinny was about. Hope's aunt adored the twins as much as Bernice did and the two were never happier than when they were holding one or the other of the infants in their arms.

Cecil and Gwendoline had visited just once, accompanied by Rosaleen who made no effort to hide her boredom after ten minutes or so. Annie had formed the habit of calling on a Saturday afternoon. This was her official time off although Daniel had told Hope that to his knowledge she had never made use of it before. She always arrived carrying a cavernous cloth bag containing cakes and buns or a couple of freshly baked loaves, a ham and egg pie or a cooked piece of pork. Hope knew how pleased Daniel was by Annie's visits. His mother displayed no interest in calling to see the babies and Annie's acceptance of them as a family did much to ease his disappointment at his mother's coldness. And if Emily wasn't affected or excited by the twins' birth, Abe more than made up for her lack of enthusiasm.

He had called round the day after they were born with an enormous bouquet of flowers for Hope and a bottle of the finest brandy for Daniel to toast their arrival, and the next

day he had placed an order with the local coalman for a sufficient supply of coal to be delivered each week to make sure
the little house was as warm as toast. He had formed the
habit of giving Daniel a lift home from work each evening,
often staying an hour or more for a cup of tea, during which
time he would sit in the kitchen, gently rocking one of the
babies in their crib or cradling one or the other of them in
the crook of his arm. It was all very pleasant and cosy – too
cosy, Hope felt. Week by week Abe was insidiously working
himself into the fabric of their lives and the old closeness
Daniel and his father had enjoyed before she'd come along
was now stronger than ever.

It wasn't that she was jealous of their affinity, she tried to
reassure herself when the frequent guilt about the way she
was feeling reared its head. Abe was Daniel's father and the
twins' grandfather after all, he was also good company and
funny and obviously concerned about their welfare, but . . .

Here Hope always felt more guilty because try as she
might, she couldn't rid herself of the conviction that Abe's
behaviour was partly a means to an end. Everything was
hunky-dory both businesswise and socially; Daniel was back
working for Abe and he had a foot in the door of their
domestic life. Daniel looked up to his father, respected him,
listened to his advice, advice she suspected would always be
weighted on the side of what Abe ultimately wanted rather
than what was best for her and Daniel and the twins. But
perhaps she was just being bitchy and nasty. Maybe she was
doing the thing she hated most about people and holding a
grudge. But how could you force yourself to relax and trust
someone when every instinct in your body was telling you
not to?

And so the tussle in her mind would go on until she wearied of it and put it on hold until the next time.

And then, a week into a March rife with driving snow and bitter winds, Hope had a visit from her sister, which led to a row between herself and Daniel of momentuous proportions.

Constance's visit started innocently enough. On the other occasions she had called since the twins' birth Bernice had always been present, but Daniel's sister was confined to bed with a migraine and so for once the two of them were alone.

The kitchen was warm and cosy and redolent with the smell of freshly baked bread, the whirling snowflakes outside the window making it all the more snug. The two sisters drank tea and chatted. Constance had finally left the Grand Hotel and started work at the Co-op in Hendon Road just after Christmas, a job she loved, and she was full of stories about the women who frequented the establishment. Hope had just fed Jack and Betsy and settled them in their cribs when Constance arrived, so she could give her sister her full attention.

As Constance regaled her with the exploits of a certain Mrs O'Leary and her nine children who descended on the shop on 'divi day' like a swarm of locusts, her blouse fell away from her wrist, revealing a massive black bruise.

'Constance, whatever have you done?' As Hope caught her sister's arm for a better look, she noticed other bruises marking the pale flesh.

'I caught my arm in the door at work.' Constance pulled away, flushing hotly. 'It's nowt.'

Hope would have left the matter there and taken her sister's words at face value but for something in Constance's manner.

She watched Constance fumbling to do up the button of her cuff. 'Did you have it looked at? How did it happen?'

Constance didn't raise her head from the cuff as she said, 'Things like that happen all the time, it's a busy shop. Don't fuss, our Hope.'

'But you did have it looked at?'

'Aye, aye, course I did.'

'By a doctor?'

'Aye, I've said, haven't I?'

Hope's stomach was churning. Quietly, she said, 'How did it really happen, Constance? It wasn't at work, was it?'

'What do you mean? Course it was. How many times—' And then with an abruptness which took Hope completely by surprise, Constance burst into tears.

Horrified, Hope left her chair and knelt down by her sister. She put her arm round Constance's shaking shoulders. Someone had hurt her, she felt it in her bones, but who? And then the answer came. Her Aunt Jinny had told her the Kirby brothers had been released three weeks ago. Flatly, she said, 'It was Lonnie, wasn't it? Lonnie Kirby. He did this to you.'

Even as she spoke she prayed she was wrong. Perhaps Constance had had something fall on her in the shop, something expensive that had broken and she hadn't dared say anything about it. Something, *anything* other than it being Lonnie Kirby. But when Constance said nothing and cried all the harder, Hope knew she had been right.

It took a while for Constance to calm down and all the time Hope's mind was racing. Eventually, when her sister's crying had settled to the odd hiccuping sob, she said, 'Tell me, Constance.'

'He . . . he didn't mean it, not really. He never does. It's because he loves me so much.' Constance rubbed at her nose with the back of her hand. 'Someone told him I'd been making on with another lad when he was inside but I hadn't, Hope. I promise I hadn't. I wouldn't do that, not to Lonnie.'

Oh Constance. Hope's heart sank to her boots. She poured Constance another cup of tea and handed it to her, waiting until she had had a few sips before she said, 'He's done this sort of thing before then?'

'Only when he thinks I've been giving someone the eye or another lad talks to me too much, things like that. He can be so jealous but it's only because he loves me.'

Hope stared at her sister. 'Love doesn't want to hurt the beloved, Constance. Don't you see that? And it's not as if Lonnie is a fifteen- or sixteen-year-old lad, still wet behind the ears. He's a full-grown man and as such should be able to control his temper, besides which even if you were carrying on with someone else he shouldn't hurt you.'

'I don't carry on, not ever. I wouldn't. I . . . I love him. And he's so good to me most of the time, Hope. We go out dancing and to the picture houses and he buys me things, anything I want. He can be so nice, honest he can. His . . . mam says he's always had a bit of a temper, right from a bairn. She reckons he gets it from his da.'

'His mother knows he's been hitting you?'

Constance nodded.

'Then can't she do something?'

'She won't get involved. She doesn't believe in coming between a couple.'

This was getting worse. Quietly, Hope said, 'Have you been with him, Constance? Properly?'

Constance turned her head away and sat gazing into the

fire. Her voice had a flat, far-away sound when she said, 'Aye, I have, and I don't regret it, all right? I love him and we're going to get married one day.'

Hope was aghast. Even if Constance had given herself to Lonnie Kirby, she did so hope it didn't lead to marriage. 'Please leave Betty's mam's place and come and stay here, at least for a while. It will give you time to think, if nothing else.'

'I don't need to think about me and Lonnie.' A defiant note had crept into Constance's voice. 'I've told you, I love him and he loves me.'

Hope did not question this statement, she knew it would do no good. Instead she nodded and gentled her voice further. 'All right, you love each other, but that doesn't mean you can't stay with us, does it? You could say to Betty's mam I need help with the twins for a bit, something like that, if you're worried she'd be offended.' And when Constance said nothing, she added, 'Please, lass, please come. And if Lonnie . . . lost his temper again while you were with us, Daniel could have a talk with him.'

Constance looked at Hope for a long moment now, her mouth tightening. 'Daniel.' It was said with contempt. 'You think the Fallows are so wonderful, don't you, our Hope? Pillars of society and all that.'

'I think Daniel's wonderful but then I would, wouldn't I? He's my husband.' Hope forced herself to show no emotion. This was the other side of Constance, the side that attacked as a defence. Her sister had always been the same.

'But you look down your nose at Lonnie and the rest of them just because Lonnie and Frank got put away.'

'It's not like that and you know it, Constance. I'm concerned for you, I admit it, and I think I've got every reason to be. You don't want to be with a man who knocks you about surely? You're young and pretty, you'd soon get another lad—'

'You think Lonnie's not good enough, you always have, even before today. I'm not daft, Hope. I can read you like a book.'

She wasn't going to rise to this. Looking steadily at her sister, Hope said, 'I'm not going to quarrel with you.'

'Lonnie and Frank might have got put away but that was only because they got caught. There's lots of folk who sail close to the wind and don't get caught, and for worse things than thieving. Your wonderful Fallows, for instance.'

Hope's heart began thumping against her ribs, knocking so hard she felt sick. She knew she was going to hear something she didn't want to hear. 'I don't know what you're talking about.'

'No, I don't suppose you do.' And then, as one of the babies made a little mewing sound, Constance's gaze left her sister and rested on the infant. Biting her lip, she said, 'Aw, forget it.'

'Forget it?' Constance rose from her seat and Hope stood up too. 'You can't say something like that and then tell me to forget it. I want to know what you mean.'

'I don't mean anything. Like I said, forget it.'

'It's something Lonnie's told you, isn't it? What's he been saying, Constance?'

'Nothing.'

'If you don't tell me I swear I'll go and see Lonnie myself and ask him.'

'No, you can't do that.' Fearfully, Constance reached out and clutched Hope's arm. 'He'd go mad. Please, Hope.'

'Then tell me.'

'I should never have said anything.'

'But you did.' Hope steeled herself against the plea in her sister's voice.

Realising Hope wasn't going to take no for an answer, some of Constance's previous bravado came to the fore. 'Well, don't blame me, it's you who's forced the issue. Among some of the lads in the East End it's well known your father-in-law's on the fiddle, and not in a small way. Bribes, threats, persuasion of a more physical kind, he's not averse to any of it. And if anyone gets in his way, like Jim Clark for instance, he has some of his bully boys teach them a lesson.'

Hope was transfixed by Constance's words. She couldn't believe her ears. 'He's lying,' she managed at last. 'Lonnie's lying.'

'He is not.' Constance's indignation would have been amusing in any other circumstances considering the man she was defending had come out of prison just a couple of weeks before. 'He's got no axe to grind, now has he? He knows Jim, he knows quite a few blokes . . .'

Constance paused for a moment as if wondering if she was saying too much, and in that moment Hope believed she was telling the truth. Impossible though it seemed, she was telling the truth.

'Anyway,' Constance went on, 'Jim was yapping on about Daniel's da. It appears Jim crossed him in some way, Lonnie didn't say how, and the next thing your father-in-law has the Mullen brothers work him over.'

'The Mullen brothers?' Hope said faintly. Constance had said it as though she should know who they were, as though everyone knew who they were.

Constance nodded. 'If Daniel's da wasn't into everything Jim said he was, how did he know the Mullen brothers and why would he get them to shut Jim's mouth? Lonnie said he hadn't believed Jim up to that point but once the Mullens were involved . . .'

Hope had the weird feeling everything solid in her world had shifted. It wasn't just the awful things she was hearing but the way Constance was telling them, as though her sister was totally conversant with this dark, secret world she was talking about. Betsy had begun to whimper fretfully and Hope lifted the little mite out of her crib and held her daughter close to her breast. Breathing in the warm baby smell, she shut her eyes for a moment. Then she opened them and stared hard at Constance. 'Daniel doesn't know about all this,' she said forcefully. 'I know he doesn't.'

Constance shrugged. 'According to Jim it's a family business, in more ways than one.'

'Daniel wouldn't be involved in anything illegal, let alone hurting someone. He's the gentlest soul on earth,' Hope said fiercely.

'Aye, well, I'm not saying anything against Daniel, lass. You're his wife and you'd know best.' Constance was hastily pulling on her hat and coat, clearly anxious to be gone. 'But perhaps it's better you know about Daniel's da in the long run, eh? Forewarned is forearmed. Look, I've got to be going and thanks for the offer of me staying. I'm . . . I'm sorry if I've upset you but don't let on to Lonnie if you ever see him, will you?'

'I'm not likely to see him,' said Hope, stony-faced.

Constance stared at her before nodding her head slowly. 'If that's the way you want to take it . . .'

Part of Hope wanted to reach out and take Constance's arm and stop them parting like this. Constance was her sister, after all, and she was mixed up with a man who was violent and no good. But the other part of Hope, the part that was reeling from shock and hurt and a hundred other emotions she couldn't have put a name to, hated her sister at this moment. And so she remained stiff and still as Constance flounced out of the house.

Immediately the door closed, she regretted it. This, added to the impact of Constance's revelations, had her nerves jangling and her head aching by the time Daniel came home.

'It's coming down thicker than ever.' Daniel entered the house by the scullery, stamping the snow off his shoes and shaking his coat. He hung it on one of the pegs on the wall before he came through to the kitchen. Following his normal routine, he peered at the twins in their cribs before coming to where Hope stood at the range. He took her in his arms and said softly, 'Good day?'

On a scale of one to ten it was minus a hundred. Hope said by way of answer, avoiding his kiss in the process, 'Constance came round.'

'Oh aye?' Daniel's eyes narrowed at her coolness.

'Your da not with you the night?' She had been planning to confront Abe with what Constance had alleged the moment her father-in-law walked in the house.

Daniel let go of her and stepped back a pace, his eyes tight on her face. 'Da and Cecil had someone to see earlier so I closed the office.'

Hope nodded. 'Wasn't the Mullen brothers by any chance, was it?'

'They've gone to Silksworth to see Edmund Osborne about

some work, as I understand it. Who are the Mullen brothers?'

'You don't know them?' asked Hope, watching him closely. Ever since Constance had gone she had been tormented by the thought that it was Abe's shenanigans that had put Daniel off working for his father when she had first met him, rather than that he didn't feel suited to the job. If this was so, his decision to work for Abe again virtually amounted to his giving his support to the shady dealings.

'Should I?'

'According to Constance, yes.'

'OK, Hope, what is this all about?' Daniel asked tersely. 'Constance has obviously been round and said something to upset you but I fail to see how I'm involved.' He took her arm, pushing her down into one of the shabby armchairs and then sitting down himself in the other one. Leaning forward with his hands on his knees, he said, 'Start at the beginning and let's have it all.'

'I'll get a cup of tea first.' Suddenly Hope felt she had been wrong. Of course Daniel didn't know anything about Jim Clark and the Mullen brothers and the rest of it. How could she have allowed herself to think so, even for a moment?

'The tea can wait.'

Hope stared into his face. She had handled this all wrong. Licking her lips, she said quietly, 'It appears Lonnie Kirby has been manhandling Constance, she was covered in bruises.'

Daniel blinked. Shaking his head, he said, 'He's scum, the lot of them are scum. The sooner she's out of there the better. Look, I'm sorry for Constance but how does Lonnie doing that tie in with my da and Cecil seeing Edmund Osborne, and why would you think I know these brothers?'

Taking a deep breath, Hope began to talk. It didn't take

long. By the time she had finished, Daniel's face was dark with rage. 'The man's lying,' he said grimly. 'I hope you told her that. My father is not some kind of crook, damn it, and he doesn't employ thugs and ruffians to beat people up. The whole thing is preposterous. And you actually thought I knew these Mullen brothers? That Da and Cecil and me were involved in some sort of conspiracy?'

'No, no I didn't.' Hope had never seen him look like he was looking now. The tender, gentle man she had married was gone and in his place was an angry stranger. 'I was confused, I didn't know what to think.'

'Oh, I think you did, Hope. I think you listened to Constance's prattle and had the three of us hung, drawn and quartered. For crying out loud, don't you know me at all? We've been married eighteen months, damn it. We have two babies. And yet on the word of a convicted criminal, who, incidentally, is ill-treating your sister, you decide I'm involved in hell knows what.'

'I'm sorry.' White-faced, Hope put her hand on his arm. 'I've said this all wrong.'

'My da started with nothing, you know that, and he nearly killed himself in the early days working day and night to build himself a business. Times were he was out of the house twenty hours in every twenty-four. Annie told me that. He worked hard, damn hard, and scum like Kirby who have never done a decent day's work in their life dare to blacken his good name. And you, believing it all.' He shook his head in disgust and stood up. 'You obviously don't know me, Hope, and I'm beginning to wonder if I know you.'

Hope looked up at him, appalled at what she had started. This morning she would have sworn on oath that she and

162

Daniel were as close as any couple could be, and now look at them. Why had she believed Constance? How could she have been so stupid? Throwing truth to the wind, she stood up and faced him. Her voice trembled slightly as she said, 'Don't be like this, Daniel, please. I didn't believe it, I swear it. Not about you.'

'But about my father and Cecil?'

She couldn't lie about them. 'I suppose I wasn't sure about your father and Cecil,' she admitted, 'but I don't really know them, do I? Oh, I know your da comes round here for an hour or so most nights since the twins have been born and he likes to be with them and you, that's obvious, but I still feel I'm in this family on sufferance, if you want to know.' Her chin rose slightly. 'I can't relax with him or any of them, except Bernice. She's the only one who makes me feel accepted for who I am rather than because I'm your wife.'

'So because they've made you feel this way you were eager to believe the worst of them?'

They both knew he was talking only about his father. Hope lost the feeling of guilt and anger took its place. 'In answer to that I can only repeat what you've just said, you obviously don't know me.'

Daniel ran a hand through his hair. 'Didn't it occur to you that Constance is jealous of you? I can see it every time she comes here and that's why she'd like to believe Kirby was telling the truth. As for him, no doubt he got wind of the fact we don't want Constance to have anything to do with him and he made up this story to get his own back.'

She hadn't thought of that. It was possible, more than possible. Hope nodded. 'I'm sorry, Daniel. I don't want to fall out over this. I'm sure your father has never been mixed up in anything untoward.'

'Oh, lass, come here.' When she was in his arms, he said quietly, 'I know it's been tough for you at times with them all and you've been good, more than good, but believe me when I say my da thinks the world of you now. At heart he's a grand man, Hope, and he would do anything for his family.'

'I know he would.' That was part of the problem.

'You're tired and it's no wonder, what with the babies needing feeding every two minutes or so. No one can think straight when they're tired.' Daniel glanced across at the twins and then tilted her chin up to him. 'It will get better, lass, I promise. Come the summer they'll be bigger and we can have the odd day out with them, take a picnic to the beach. You'd like that.'

She wanted to tell him she didn't mind being tied to the twins and the house, this was nothing to do with how tired she was, but he was trying to make everything all right and she didn't want to start the row off again. As it was, she knew things had been said this day which wouldn't be forgotten in a hurry, not least her accusations against Abe. She had told Daniel she was sure his father hadn't been mixed up in anything shady but did she believe it? In the depths of her?

The answer made her heart thud hard. Abe saw the business as the be all and end all, it provided for the family and if he had to take short cuts or go outside the law to make it prosper, then he probably would.

With her head resting against Daniel's chest and his arms tightly round her, Hope gazed over at the sleeping babies again. She wished Constance hadn't come here today. She wished she could go back in time to yesterday when all she had to worry about was getting enough sleep. Most of all she wished Daniel didn't work for his father. Daniel was gentle and trusting and he loved his father. It blinded him. If Abe was mixed up in anything – and he might not be – then by association Daniel might be put in danger. This world of people being beaten up and hurt, of dodgy dealings and bribes and thugs like the Mullen brothers was like a film showing at one of the picture houses. But she wasn't sitting comfortably in a one-and-ninepenny seat watching a flickering screen. This was real.

'Hope?' Daniel held her slightly away from him and looked down into her face. 'I love you, you know that.' Smoothing a wisp of silky hair from her brow, his mouth kissed where his fingers had touched.

'I love you.' And she did, so very much, which made this all the more scary.

'No more listening to Constance's stories, all right?' He kissed the tip of her nose. 'I'll have a word with that young lady when I see her next and put her right. And I shan't be chary about telling her what I think about Lonnie Kirby either. The sooner she sees him for what he is, the better. There would be ructions if Da caught wind of what she's been saying.'

Hope nodded but said nothing. Daniel folded her against him once more and they continued to stand in the warmth and quiet of the kitchen, only the occasional hiss and spit from the fire and the odd snuffling sound from one of the sleeping infants disturbing the peace. But Hope felt anything but peaceful inside. She'd come face to face with the dark and seamy side of life today, and through her own sister of all people. There was Constance determined to stay with a man who was physically ill-treating her, a man who wasn't just a convicted thief but apparently deeply entrenched in the criminal world, added to which was the possibility her father-in-law and maybe Cecil too were of the same ilk but just covered it up better. And she couldn't share her misgivings with the person closest in all the world to her. She didn't think she had ever felt quite so alone.

PART THREE

1936 – A Taste of Things to Come

Chapter 14

'You're not serious?'

'I am actually.' Hope faced her husband, hands on hips and mouth firm.

'But . . .' Daniel appeared lost for words. 'You mean to say you would sell round the streets?'

'And from the front room.'

'But what about the twins?'

'They would come with me when I go out of course. They can sit on the front of the barrow if they get tired. But I want to give this a try, Daniel. I've been racking my brains to come up with something and this is perfect. I'd enjoy making the toffee apples and stickjaw and ice cream for a start, and I've already contacted a couple of farmers out Silksworth way who will let me buy their apples cheap as long as I take a certain number and take them away myself. We can store them on wooden racks hung from the ceiling in the bedrooms and use them all year.'

'This woman who is going to sell you the barrow, if her

ice cream sells so well, why isn't she continuing with it herself?'

'She's Italian and her husband has just died. She's taking the children and going back to her family in Italy. But she's giving me the recipe for her special ice cream as well and it's wonderful. But I want to do more than ice cream and that's why I thought of the bags of stickjaw and toffee apples. I can make them cheap and sell them for a good profit, I know I can.'

Daniel stared at his wife. 'You never cease to amaze me,' he said slowly, but it was without reproof.

Hope grinned. 'Then you wouldn't mind if I gave it a go? It would work perfectly, Daniel, you do see that? I can still run the home and look after the twins as usual, but hopefully I'll be making some money too. Perhaps even enough so we can start saving a little. It would be nice to think about moving somewhere bigger one day.' She had been pouring two cups of tea as she spoke and now she handed one to Daniel. He was sitting at the kitchen table having just got in from work.

Daniel took several sips of his tea before he said, 'If you do this, it is on the understanding you stop immediately it gets too much for you. Promise me, Hope.'

'I promise.' But she wouldn't let it get too much. She would make this succeed whatever the cost. She had spoken about saving but they both knew it would be a while before they could think about that. They were three months behind with the mortgage and other bills were pressing. The Depression was biting everybody hard; there were increasingly bitter hunger marches and frequent riots sweeping the country. With two growing children to clothe and feed they had found Daniel's wage didn't stretch as far as they had hoped, despite all Hope's scrimping and robbing Peter to pay Paul.

Hope was determined not to go cap in hand to Daniel's father. It was what Abe expected, she could see it in his eyes every time he called round, but she would rather die first.

All her fears of two years ago had proved groundless to date, Hope admitted to herself as she bustled about setting the table for tea. But that did not necessarily mean Lonnie Kirby had been lying. One thing was for sure, she had enough to worry about with the recession and making ends meet, without speculating on ifs and maybes.

She placed a plate of bread and butter and a small dish of homemade blackberry jam on the table, along with a freshly baked seed cake, then went through to the scullery and opened the back door into the yard. Jack and Betsy were sitting in the evening sunshine stroking their pet rabbit whose hutch almost filled the space next to the privy. 'Come on, you two, put him back now,' she called. 'Tea's ready. Come and wash your hands.'

'One minute more, Mam?' This was from Jack who always tried to prolong the time with the rabbit, but at Hope's shake of her head he duly stood up and lifted the rabbit into its box, fastening the door before he followed Betsy into the scullery.

'Good lad.' Hope patted the child's head as he washed his hands, they had had some battles recently about his delaying tactics. Hope loved both her children passionately and their mop of fair curls, dark brown eyes and full rosebud lips made everyone remark, 'By, if ever a pair of bairns took after their mam, these do,' but in nature she felt her son grew more like his grandfather every day. There was a single-mindedness about Jack when he wanted something, an indomitability which went far beyond the self-will and tantrums of the average child and made him a handful, to put it mildly. From the moment the little boy had begun to toddle he had kept her on her toes, but such was his charm that he often wriggled out of trouble, especially if his grandfather had anything to do with it. Abe fair worshipped the boy.

Hope dried Betsy's hands for her and kissed her daughter's little button nose, then sent the child through to her father. She waited for Jack to finish washing his hands. He did it thoroughly, as he did everything, and without letting her help him in any way. His fierce independence was another thing that reminded her of Abe. Jack's similarity to his grandfather, along with the self-evident bond between the two, had given Hope plenty of sleepless nights in the last little while. It had also caused a few ructions within the family. Abe spent the same amount of money on Cecil's son, Edward, at Christmas and birthdays as he did on Jack and Betsy, but it was obvious Abe had no real interest in his eldest grandson and Cecil resented it bitterly. Family occasions had become minefields for Hope as she continually tried to diffuse situations and pour oil on troubled waters – waters which Abe himself refused to acknowledge existed.

'Nonsense, lass,' he said when Hope had first broached the subject of favouritism with him just after the twins' second birthday. 'It's not in my nature to make fish of one and meat of another. They're just different personalities, that's all, and I treat 'em according to how they are, the little lassie too. Don't worry about Edward, now then. And you want to see how Gwendoline's mam and da spoil the lad. Daft they are with him, buying him this, that and the other. They've already put his name down for a preparatory school that's costing a packet and marked out a public school to follow.'

Hope hadn't been talking about money and public schools. She had stared at her father-in-law and knew he would never understand in a month of Sundays that he was deeply hurting his eldest son. But that was Abe all over, he only saw what he wanted to see. He seemed completely unaware that Bernice could barely stand the sight of him after he had sent her young man away and married her off to Rupert, or that in the last year or so Rosaleen had become adept at telling him only what she knew he wanted to hear. Hope and Daniel were worried about Rosaleen for much the same reason they were concerned for Constance. The hooray Henrys at the tennis club were a wild lot and not particularly pleasant. Apart from the obvious difference in wealth, she and Daniel felt there was little to choose between Rosaleen's set and the dubious element Constance mixed with.

'Finished, Mam.'

Hope became aware Jack was holding out his hands for inspection. She smiled at him and he trotted through to the kitchen and climbed onto his chair at the table. As Hope poured a beakerful of milk for each of the children and tea for her and Daniel, she listened to Jack chattering away to his father. It was hard to believe he was only two and a half, his vocabulary was extensive and he used quite grown-up words in their correct sense. Betsy was way behind him in her speech and often seemed content to let Jack speak for her, which Hope didn't think was a good thing. Bernice was always telling her not to worry about it but then Betsy couldn't do any wrong as far as her aunt was concerned. If Jack was Abe's favourite, then Betsy was certainly Bernice's.

The thought of her father-in-law brought Hope's eyes narrowing. How would Abe take the news that she intended to make and sell the ice cream and so on? And then she mentally shook her head at herself. Why ask the road you know? He would be like a bear with a sore head until he got used to the idea.

Had this occurred to Daniel? She listened to her husband gravely explaining to his son why their rabbit wasn't having babies like Barnaby Hammon's next door but was just getting fat due to Jack putting extra titbits in his cage. If Daniel had thought about Abe's reaction, Hope knew he wouldn't mention it. Since their argument about Daniel's father two years ago, Abe had been something of a forbidden subject. Hope did not like this but felt powerless to change the situation because had Daniel challenged her on Abe's credibility, she could not have given him the reply she knew he would want to hear. For that reason she had decided to let sleeping dogs lie.

Well, whatever Abe said about her venture, she was going to do it, Hope silently resolved. And once she had earned enough to pay off their present debts, she would start to save. She didn't intend that they would stay in Frederick Street all their lives, but when they moved to somewhere better it would be because she and Daniel had made it happen, not because Abe Fallow had lent them the money and bound them to him for ever and a day.

It was the following weekend before Hope learnt exactly what Abe thought about her new undertaking. Of late, Abe had taken to buying tickets for himself, Daniel and Cecil at Roker Park on a Saturday afternoon. Sunderland AFC had been First Division runners-up in the previous two years and were enjoying great popularity and success, and for most men in the town football was the main topic of conversation. For the thousands of unemployed, revelling in their team's glory took them out of their desperate circumstances and made them feel like men again, for a while at least. Abe would normally drop Daniel off home after the match and stay for a cup of tea and a slice of cake. Then he and Annie, who still regularly visited on Saturdays, would leave together. If Bernice called in on a Saturday, she always made sure she was gone long before her father was due to arrive.

Hope had just made a fresh pot of tea and set the table with the fruit cake and bilberry tarts Annie had brought when she heard the men talking to the twins who were playing with the rabbit in the backyard.

Over the last two years Hope had found she liked Annie; in fact more than liked her. She had a warm affection for Abe's housekeeper just as she had for Bernice. There was a wealth of kindness in Annie which equalled that of Daniel's sister, and the older woman had a strong maternal streak which was very evident in her dealings with the twins. Hope now understood why her husband loved Annie in a way he never had his own mother. In spite of this, however, Hope was always very careful how much she said to Annie, knowing the housekeeper's deep loyalty to Daniel's parents.

'Good match?' Annie asked as Abe entered the kitchen with Jack and Betsy perched on each arm.

'Aye, they were on form all right.' As Daniel followed his father into the room, Abe added to Hope, 'That fruit cake looks good, lass, and me tongue's fair stuck to the roof of me mouth.'

'Come and sit down then.' Hope smiled at them before saying to the children, 'Have you two washed your hands?'

'We couldn't.' Jack as ever was ready with an answer. 'Granda carried us in.'

'Well, you can now. Go on, before you have a slice of cake. I've told you before that when you stroke Nugget you have to wash your hands before you eat or drink.'

'Aw, Mam.'

'Don't aw Mam me.' Betsy had already turned and trotted into the scullery but Jack was still standing where Abe had placed him, a mutinuous set to his mouth. Hope knew the signs; there was about to be yet another battle of wills between them, something she preferred to avoid in front of Abe. She used a ploy which never failed to have the desired result. 'Your sister will be ready before you if you don't get a move on.'

As Jack scurried into the scullery, Abe grinned. 'He's a lad, isn't he?' he said to Daniel. 'He'll go far, that one. You mark my words.'

Hope ignored this. When the twins were back and they were all seated round the table, she poured out the tea and the children's milk, placing a bilberry tart in front of Jack and Betsy but leaving the adults to help themselves. They fell into the easy conversation they often enjoyed at such times and, as she had done on many occasions, Hope thought what a pity it was that Annie wasn't Abe's wife. Everything would be so much easier, for Daniel as much as for her.

As though he had read her thoughts, Daniel said, 'Where's Mother this afternoon? With Gwendoline and Edward as usual?'

Abe, his mouth full of fruit cake, nodded, swallowing before he said, 'They've taken the bairn to Gwendoline's mam an' da's. I understand Cecil's getting his own tea.'

Hope and Daniel exchanged a glance. Gwendoline was spending more and more time at her parents. From what they could gather, Cecil regularly came home to an empty house in the evenings.

An uncomfortable little pause followed, a pause that Abe and the children seemed unaware of. Annie, in an obvious attempt to steer the conversation into safer waters, said brightly, 'I see you've got a nice big basketful of apples in the scullery, Hope. Get them cheap, did you?'

Hope was aware of two things at once. One, Daniel's head shooting up and a look of what she could only describe as apprehension on his face, and two, Abe's unconcerned expression as he munched on his cake. This told her that Daniel had not broached the matter of her little enterprise with his father.

She stared at her husband for a moment. Then she turned to Annie and said quietly, 'They're a sample of what Tollett's farm can let me have.'

'A sample?' Annie's brow wrinkled. 'I don't follow you, lass.'

'I'm going to try making ice cream and toffee apples to sell,' Hope said clearly, 'and perhaps barley sugar sticks and stickjaw.'

'To sell?' Abe had stopped eating. 'Sell where?'

'From the front room here and round the streets.' Hope took a sip of her tea as though she was unaware of her father-in-law's face darkening. 'An Italian lady I know has recently decided to go back to Italy and I'm buying her barrow and other stuff for a fraction of what they're worth. She's put me in touch with a butcher who has ice delivered to his shop, and I can get a block to grind up in the little machine she's giving me. She's given me her own recipe and it's beautiful ice cream. With the toffee apples and other things I think I'll do really well.'

'Round the streets?' It was as though Abe hadn't heard anything else. 'You're not thinking of hawking round the streets like the rag and bone man?'

'Other people sell round the streets besides the rag and bone man.'

'Aye, tinkers an' fishwives an' the like. Not respectable married women with a man in work and bairns to take care of.'

'Hold your horses, Da.' Daniel entered the conversation for the first time. 'This is between me and Hope and I'm happy for her to try her hand at this.'

'Then you're stark staring barmy, lad.' The note in Abe's voice caused the twins to stop eating, and as Betsy slid off her chair and sidled to Hope's side, Jack's bright gaze flashed from one grown-up face to the next.

'I don't think so.' Daniel's mouth was grim. 'But even if I were, this is still none of your business.'

'The hell it's not. What you do, what any of you do reflects on the family name and on me and the business. Damn it, boy, you're not stupid. Surely you can see that? There's no need for her to make us a laughing stock. You're in work, you don't want for nowt.'

'We need some extra money coming in.' Hope could feel Betsy shaking and it made her angry. 'Whatever you say, this is the perfect solution. I can keep the bairns with me and still earn something.'

'I forbid it.' Abe rose to his feet, his face like thunder. 'You're not dragging my grandchildren round the streets like one of the old gipsy women you see with umpteen filthy brats hanging on their skirts.'

'I won't be dragging them anywhere. Daniel is going to make me a little seat to fix on the barrel so they'll only have to walk if they want to.' She had thought of this the day before but hadn't mentioned it till now. She glanced at Daniel, looking for his support.

He gave it. 'Hope is a wonderful mother,' he said forcefully. 'She always puts the children first, that goes without saying. And I'm sorry, Da, but like I said, this is between me and Hope. No one else.'

Abe turned from his son to look at Hope. 'You say you need the money, so where did you find the wherewithal to buy this barrow an' all, eh? The Italians are a canny bunch, you can't tell me she's given you it on a promise.'

For a second the truth hovered on Hope's lips and the temptation to fling the fact that Bernice was lending them the cash into Abe's face was strong. But she didn't want to put Bernice in a difficult position. After a short pause, she said, 'We have paid Mrs Morrosini what she asked for. I don't think there is any need to say more than that.'

'Huh.' Abe was standing like a bull elephant preparing to charge, aggression in every line of his thick body. 'Well, if you take my advice you'll tell her you've changed your mind.' The tone of his voice rather than the words used made this an order.

'I've no intention of doing that.'

'Now look here.' Abe's furious gaze took in Daniel as well as Hope. 'I'm telling you I won't have a member of this family trundling round the streets knocking on doors and associating with every Tom, Dick and Harry. It's little more than begging.'

Hope's temper had been on a hairspring and it finally snapped. All the slights she had endured since Daniel had first introduced her to his family came to the fore, and nothing on earth could have stopped her from saying what came next. She stood up and faced Abe across the table, her hand on Betsy's head and her face burning. 'Don't be so ridiculous. You're talking absolute rubbish to try and get your own way and you know it. I'll be doing an honest day's work and getting honest money for it, and that's more than can be said for some people.'

Abe's eyes narrowed. 'Meaning?'

'I think it would be better if we left now.' Annie's intervention surprised them all and as Abe swung round to look at her, she added, 'You've had your say so leave it at that. All right?'

For a moment Abe's jaw worked as though the words on his tongue were fighting to emerge. Then he turned on his heel and walked out of the kitchen without glancing at Daniel or Hope.

'I'd better go with him.' Annie was pulling on her coat and hat as she spoke. 'He gets himself in a right tear I know but he thinks the world of you two and the bairns. You do know that?'

This last was to Hope but as she couldn't give the answer Annie wanted, she said nothing. Abe might indeed think the world of Daniel and the twins, but as for her . . .

'I'll talk to him.' There was an appeal in Annie's voice. She stepped forward and touched Hope's arm before hurrying after Abe.

The silence in the kitchen was broken by Jack saying, 'Is Granda coming back?'

'Not today,' said Daniel, his eyes on his wife.

'Can I have his bit of cake then?'

'What?' Daniel glanced at his son.

'Granda's cake, he's left some of it.' Jack pursed his lips and looked at Hope. 'That's naughty, isn't it, Mam, to leave your cake? An' he was shouting an' all.'

'Granda wasn't shouting,' Hope answered flatly as she lifted Betsy back onto her seat. 'He was just talking loudly.'

'If I talk loudly like that you sit me on the naughty stool.'

Hope stared into the bright little face looking up at her and she didn't know if she wanted to laugh or cry. In the event, she did neither. Instead she reached out and placed Abe's plate with its morsel of cake in front of her son before saying to Daniel, 'Can I get you another cup of tea?'

'Thank you.' His voice was stiff.

Daniel hadn't liked her saying that bit about an honest day's work being more than some people did and she could understand that although she hadn't actually accused his father of anything. It had been up to Abe the way he took it. He needn't have assumed it was directed at him.

Hope's mind was racing as she poured a cup of tea for Daniel. The suddenness of the confrontation with Abe and the significance of the look on his face when she'd said what she had made her stomach turn over. There had been something more than anger at what she was proposing to do at that point, she had seen it. She didn't know if it was wariness or surprise or fear or what, but there *had* been something.

As she handed Daniel the tea, he said very quietly, 'I thought we'd put that particular matter to bed some time ago, Hope.'

She stared at him but for the life of her she couldn't pretend she hadn't meant it that way because she had. She knew now she had believed every word Constance had said that day right from the start but for Daniel's sake she had tried to bury it, ignore it. And now Abe himself had confirmed all her fears without saying a word.

'Hope?'

'I'm sorry, Daniel, I don't want to believe it but . . .'

'You do,' he finished for her.

'Aye, yes, I do. Not about you, never that, but your da and Cecil, yes.'

'I see.' Daniel rubbed his hand around his face and there was a pause before he went on, 'I don't know what to say to you. I thought everything had been settled about this years ago. I'm disappointed you didn't say something if you've been harbouring such thoughts, Hope, but let me make it plain I'm not about to insult my father by putting such accusations to him. You're wrong and that's an end of it.'

'Mam?' Betsy reached across and tugged at Hope's sleeve for attention. 'More pease?'

'No more for now, pet.' Hope stood up and lifted Betsy from her chair. She said to Jack, 'You two go and play in the front room for a bit. Aunty Bernice brought some colouring books and pencils the other day. Why don't you see how nice you can colour in?'

'Betsy always scribbles everywhere,' Jack complained, but nevertheless he scrambled down from the table and took his sister's hand, and the two of them disappeared into the hall.

Hope turned back to Daniel, her stomach churning as she sat down. He might say this matter had been settled long ago but they both knew that wasn't true. Her suspicions about Abe just after the twins had been born had been between them ever since, a wedge in what had been a perfect marriage. A tiny wedge admittedly, but it had been there. 'Daniel, I know you love your da but can you honestly say hand on heart that you don't think there could possibly be a shred of truth in what Lonnie Kirby said? Can you?'

'Aye, I can,' he answered immediately. 'The man was trying to cause trouble because he knew we didn't want him seeing your sister.'

'I don't think Lonnie Kirby is the type to worry about what you or I think.'

'Oh, don't be so naive! He's controlled Constance from the moment they got together; of course he resented any influence we had on her. He knew full well we wouldn't approve of their relationship.'

Hope sat up straighter at his tone, her voice as sharp as his had been when she said, 'Well, you certainly finished any "influence" as you put it when you virtually banned her from this house.'

'I did not ban her. I told her she was welcome as long as she behaved herself and watched her tongue.'

'And you called Lonnie every name under the sun and threatened to go to the police and have him up for slander. You scared her to death, Daniel. You know you did. I've only seen her a few times in the last couple of years and that's been at Aunt Jinny's.'

'So what are you saying? Are you telling me you'd rather let Kirby get away with blackening my father's name, *all* of our names, and not say a word? You were the one who was so worried about her associating with Kirby in the first place, don't forget.'

'I'm not forgetting but your attitude just drove her into

his arms.' Her voice was too shrill and Hope knew she had to take control of herself. She bit her lower lip, shaking her head as she said, 'I don't want to quarrel over Constance, all that is history. I told you at the time I'd support you in what you felt you had to say and I have.'

'It sounds like it.'

This was getting them nowhere. Her face and body tight, Hope rose from her chair and began to clear the table. He wasn't even prepared to consider the possibility there might be a grain of truth in Lonnie Kirby's allegations, let alone speak to Abe about the matter. And she didn't understand that.

She took some of the tea things through to the scullery and stood for a moment looking out of the narrow window into the backyard.

It wasn't as if his father was a young skittish lass who would crumple and weep and wail at the thought of someone speaking harshly about them. The last thing anyone could accuse Abe of was being sensitive. But there it was, if Daniel wouldn't repeat Lonnie's accusations to his da she wasn't about to make him even if she could, which she doubted. She did so wish Annie hadn't interrupted them when she did, though. She had been about to blurt everything out and at least then it would have been in the open.

When Hope walked back into the kitchen, Daniel's chair was empty and she could hear him talking to the twins in the front room. She stood for a moment gazing at the remains of Annie's fruit cake. She had always felt sorry for Annie, her being unmarried and never even having stepped out with a lad as far as anyone knew, but at least she had been spared all the heartache and upset which went hand in hand with loving someone.

The thought brought a lump to her throat. She didn't want

to be at odds with Daniel and he was only standing up for his da, she knew that. It was his nature to be loyal to those he cared about and it was one of the things she loved about him. She wished now she'd never said anything and just let sleeping dogs lie. But she hadn't. And she couldn't pretend any more either, not now things had gone this far.

She gathered up the cake and put it in a tin, squeezing the rest of the tarts beside it. But then her hands went limp again as she heard laughter from the room next door, Daniel's deep voice mingling with that of the children.

Somehow they would have to find a way to agree to disagree about Abe and go on from there. It was the only way because she loved him too much for anything else to be an option. She was not going to let his father come between them, not any more than he had already anyway.

She raised her head, staring across the room. Far better to put all her energies into making a success of the ice-cream business, because one thing was for sure, she was definitely going to go ahead with it now, come hell or high water.

The urge to cry faded, her soft full mouth settling into a grimness alien to it.

She would show Abe Fallow. If she had been determined to make a go of the business before, that went double now. She would make the lot of them eat their words about her. Her Aunt Jinny always said that hard work never hurt anyone. She wasn't a hundred per cent sure if she believed that, she had seen too many poor souls in the East End working from dawn to dusk bringing up a family and taking in washing and a handful of other jobs besides to make ends meet. But she agreed with the principle at least. And she would work hard. As hard as she had to.

She nodded to herself, her eyes stormy as she muttered, 'Begging indeed. Cheeky hound.'

'I'm not saying I necessarily agree with it, just that you went too far, that's all. And what's more, you know you did. If you wanted to make sure Hope would go ahead with it, then you succeeded back there.'

'I can't speak me own mind now, is that it?'

'It's the way you go about it, you're . . .' Annie was lost for words to describe what Abe was.

'Look, I call a spade a spade, I always have done. I'm too long in the tooth to change my ways now, lass. And she'll cart them bairns round the streets selling ice cream or whatnot over my dead body, I tell you that straight.'

'Then you'll be six foot under shortly because Hope won't change her mind. She's too much like you for one thing.'

'What?'

'You might well look at me like that, Abe Fallow, but it's the truth and all the glaring in the world won't alter it. She is more like you than any of your bairns are and that's a fact. Stubborn as donkeys, the pair of you, and just as liable to dig your heels in if you think someone's trying to tell you what to do.' Annie settled further into her seat as she finished speaking and for a moment or two all was quiet in the car.

'I'm not allowing it.'

Abe had spoken so mulishly Annie could have smiled. Instead, her voice softer, she said, 'You can't prevent it. Get it into your head they are a married couple and capable of making decisions on their own. If Daniel's for it and Hope wants to do it, it's nothing to do with you.'

'He hasn't thought the implications through.'

'Whether he has or he hasn't, it's still nothing to do with you.'

'Damn and blast it, woman!' Abe thumped the steering wheel so hard Annie jumped. 'Why didn't they come to me if they were finding it hard to make ends meet? They know I'd see 'em right.'

'Because Daniel and Hope are not like Cecil, or Rosaleen for that matter, hands constantly stretched out like Oliver Twist,' Annie said tartly. 'And don't damn and blast me, Abe Fallow, not unless you want a clip round the ear. I don't presume to be a lady like Emily so I'm not above walloping you one.'

Abe groaned, pulling the car to a halt just past the synagogue in Toward Road and cutting the engine. He turned fully to face her. 'What am I going to do?' he muttered. 'I wouldn't mind her selling from their front room so much although that'll mean the house is never their own from morning till night, but round the streets . . .'

Annie stared into the ugly attractive face. She had watched this man rise from the depths of poverty to comparative affluence and wealth and knew him to be a shrewd and instinctive individual with an ability to sum people up quicker than most, yet he had never guessed how she felt about him. No, and never would, not if she had anything to do with it. For all his faults, and he had many, Abe didn't hold with folk larking on or looking at anyone else once they were wed. If he had an inkling of how she felt that would be the end of any visits to the kitchen or their car rides home on a Saturday afternoon. And they were all she lived for.

Keeping her face blank, she said, 'If you want to carry on seeing the bairns and being made welcome, you'll curb your tongue about this. You've said how you feel, you've left them in no doubt as to your opinion' – she allowed a certain acidic sarcasm to colour her words – 'so that's enough. Next time you call, take a bunch of flowers for Hope and say if things don't work out they can always come to you. And while we're on that subject,' she raised her eyebrows, 'you can't tell me you didn't know they were struggling. You could have given Daniel a rise months ago but you expected they'd come and ask for your help, didn't you?'

'What? I don't know what you're talking about.'

He was blustering and they both knew it. Annie sighed. He had been hoisted by his own petard.

'So you think I should stand back and let 'em get on with it?' Abe said after a second or two.

'I don't think you've any other choice.'

Abe stared at her for a moment and then swung round in his seat to stare out of the windscreen, his hands resting on the steering wheel. 'Do you know anything about what Rosaleen's getting up to?' he asked abruptly.

'What?' Taken aback by the sudden change of subject, Annie tried to marshal her thoughts.

'Me an' Emily have been having words about her for some time. She can pull the wool over her mam's eyes but not me. I've gone along with things so far for a peaceful life because Emily's got this hankering for the lass to marry one of them types she runs around with, but she came in the other night the worse for wear and it weren't the first time either. Now all right, at nearly twenty she's no bit lass but you know Rosaleen, Annie. She's not got the brains she was born with and no common sense either.'

No, because she had been spoilt rotten as a bairn, still was for that matter. The girl had never done a day's work in her life and that wasn't good for anybody. Swanning around at home all day painting her nails and the like and then staying out half the night. Emily had a lot to answer for with that one. Annie tilted her head at Abe. 'By worse for wear you mean she had been drinking too much?'

Abe didn't answer immediately. Then his words were slow as he said, 'I wish I did, lass. I wish I did.'

'I'm not with you.'

He turned his head and looked at her. 'She didn't know I'd still be up, it was gone three in the morning. I made out I'd been working on something that couldn't wait but the truth of it was I'd been waiting to . . .' He shook his grizzled head. Then said, 'I'd been waiting to catch her out, I suppose. I'm not as daft as I look, Annie. You know that. And lately there's been things that don't add up. I've got the idea that crowd she runs round with don't just drink themselves silly.'

Annie didn't have a clue what he meant and her expression must have revealed this because, impatiently now, Abe said, 'Drugs, woman. I'm talking about drugs.'

'Drugs?'

'Aye. The lot of them have got too much money. Talk about the idle rich. It was the worst day's work Rosaleen ever did getting mixed up with 'em, regardless of what Emily says.'

Emily couldn't see beyond the big houses and influential names.

'But Rosaleen doesn't have money to throw about,' Annie said, stunned and horrified by what he was suggesting. 'Not like the Stefford boys or Baxter's lot.' One of Rosaleen's

189

constant gripes was that *everyone* had a generous allowance these days apart from her.

'Aye, that's true enough, an' that's what I've been telling meself the last few months when I first started getting windy. But she's been seeing this Terence Stefford for a while now and for all his smarmy ways and calling me sir an' all that, I don't trust him any further than I could throw him. But you know what Emily is, they've got a title or two in the family and that makes 'em all right. By, lass, it's been a battle the last little while and to be fair I've got nothing more than a gut feeling to go on.'

Abe's gut feelings were usually right. 'What did Rosaleen say, this night you caught her?'

'It wasn't so much what she said as her manner. She was . . . bright, animated. Silly even. All keyed up and jumpy. Not like you'd expect at gone three in the morning and her having supposed to have been dancing all night.'

Annie felt sick. To combat the feeling that Abe was on to something, because to acknowledge it was terrifying, she said quietly, 'She was probably excited at having been with Terence, you know how young girls are, all starry-eyed and dreamy.'

Abe looked at her. A long look. It was enough to make Annie say, 'Oh, Abe. What are you going to do?'

He shrugged. 'Watch her like a hawk. Ask around. Get some people I know to whisper in a few ears but discreet like. If I'm wrong, and I pray to God I am, the last thing I want is for Andrew Stefford to come round accusing me of calling his son a druggie.'

'I'll keep my eyes open now you've said.'

'Thanks, Annie. I knew I could count on you.' Abe shook his head as he started the engine again. 'I tell you, lass, this having bairns isn't all it's cut out to be. You chose the right path sure enough.'

It hurt. Deeply. But Annie had long since stopped wondering how it was you could love someone and hate them at the same time.

Chapter 15

For the next twelve months or so Hope worked all the hours under the sun and gradually, by sheer determination, it began to really pay off. She made a name for herself for deliciously creamy ice cream, and the queue of customers with their glasses or cups or bowls ready for her to spoon in the ice cream grew each week.

She didn't mind walking miles to get a good crop of apples cheap from one or other of the farmers scattered about the outskirts of Sunderland, and the toffee apples, along with the bags of toffee and barley sugar sticks were a great hit with the children thereabouts.

Hope wasn't always as good a businesswoman as she could have been. She could never resist the appeal in the eyes of the one little bairn in a crowd of youngsters who didn't have any pennies. Many a toffee apple or bag of stickjaw was surreptitiously pushed into an eager little paw. But she was making money, and once she had repaid the loan to Bernice and cleared their debts, she began to save.

Some months were leaner than others but in May, with the coronation of George VI and the orders for ice cream for all the street parties in the town, she did particularly well. By the time the summer was over and the chill of winter was making itself felt with white frosts and icy raw winds, there was a tidy sum in rolled-up notes under the mattress of their bed. So much so that Hope finally gave in to Daniel's promptings that she open a bank account. She didn't quite know why she had resisted doing this for so long, although it might have had something to do with the fact that her Aunt Jinny had always declared that banks and building societies were out to swindle ordinary working folk out of their money wherever they could.

Whatever, when she emerged from the bank one cold December morning, the twins either side of her in little red coats and their small gloved hands in hers, she was glad she had finally taken the plunge. Everyone in the bank had been extremely helpful and the experience had been an enjoyable one. It was good to know her nest egg was secure. She and Daniel were expecting their third child at the end of March and she had slowed down a little of late and couldn't do as much as she would have liked. Once the baby was born, though – and the doctor had confirmed that this time there was only one – she intended to get back into the swing of things again. She was anxious that once the warmer months came no one poached her territory, which had been hard won. She knew Abe was hoping the new baby would mean the end of her little business, or at least taking the barrow round the streets, but she was determined this would not happen.

It began to snow as the three of them walked on, big fat

white flakes that suggested plenty more to come. To mark the occasion that she was now a woman of means, she had promised Jack and Betsy they would stop off at Binn's for a drink of pop and an iced bun but as she looked at the overcast sky she knew they shouldn't dally too long.

They had a lovely time in the restaurant, Jack chattering away nineteen to the dozen as usual and Betsy content to sit pressed into her mother's side as she watched all the comings and goings with wide eyes. It was nearly twelve o'clock when they left, and as they turned the corner into Frederick Street, the snow was coming down thicker than ever and the sky was as dark as though it was four o'clock in the afternoon.

Because of the near blizzard conditions, Hope didn't immediately notice the woman standing on her doorstep. It was Jack who pointed ahead and said, 'Mam? There's a lady knocking on our door.'

'Constance?'

Constance turned, giving Hope the shock of her life as she took in her sister's bruised and battered face. 'Oh, lass. I thought you weren't in.'

Tears began to flood from under the swollen eyelids as Hope reached Constance and took her into her arms. 'Oh, Constance, Constance, who's done this? What's happened?' she murmured, although her whole being was already crying out against Lonnie Kirby.

Constance had virtually collapsed on her but somehow Hope managed to insert the key in the front door and get her sister inside. The twins followed, with Jack silent for once. In the warmth of the kitchen Hope took off Constance's coat and hat as though her sister was a very small child, and received her second shock in as many minutes. Constance was expecting a baby. Hope did not comment on this, saying instead, 'Lass, you're soaked through. We must get you out of these wet things.'

Hope sent Jack and Betsy to play in their bedroom then followed them upstairs as quickly as her increased girth would allow. She scooped up some of her own clothes and hurried back downstairs to the kitchen. Constance was standing exactly where she had left her, silent tears still rolling down her face.

'Come on, lass, let's get you warm and dry and then I'll make us a cup of tea,' Hope said briskly, fighting back her own tears. When Constance made no move to begin undressing, Hope reached out and started to help her. By the time her sister was down to her bra and knickers, Hope was crying too. There were old and new bruises and weals all over Constance's arms and legs and back; even her swollen stomach showed the odd mark or two.

Constance still did not speak, but once Hope had dressed her in clean, dry clothes, she sank down in one of the armchairs in front of the fire, holding out her hands to the warmth.

Hope had put the kettle on the hob before she fetched the clothes and now she quickly mashed a pot of tea. Then she fetched a small bowl of water and drew up a chair close to her sister. It was as she began to gently clean the blood from the side of Constance's mouth that her sister spoke. 'He's thrown me out,' she said dully. 'On a day like this he's thrown me out.'

'Lonnie?'

Constance nodded, wincing as Hope cleaned a cut on her lip. 'He's been drinking for days. Usually I can read the signs and I get out to his mam's before he can start on me, but he woke me up this morning when he came in with a pal of his. He wanted me to . . .' Constance faltered for a moment, then carried on, 'Look after his pal but I'd told him I was having no more of that, not with the bairn.'

Hope felt sick. Constance couldn't mean what she thought she meant. Tentatively, she said, 'Look after?'

Constance looked at her.

'Oh, Constance.'

'Aye, I know, I'm the world's biggest fool.' Constance's eyes had dropped away from Hope's and now she wrung her hands over and over in her lap as she whispered, 'It didn't start until a month or so after I'd moved in with him. The first time he said a good friend of his needed some comfort because his wife had died and he was beside himself. I said no, I swear I did, Hope, and kept saying it for days, but he said if I really loved him I'd help his friend.'

'Oh, Constance.' It was the only thing she seemed able to say.

'Then once I'd done it, this pal came again, and . . .' Constance shrugged. 'Lonnie made it seem, well, not wrong. He waited a bit before he brought the others of course.' Her voice was bitter now.

'And the baby?'

Constance's head drooped further. 'It could be Lonnie's but . . . but it might not be. He says it isn't. When I knew I was expecting I got down on my knees and begged him to marry me but he said he wasn't taking on someone else's brat. He told me to get rid of it, he said he'd pay but I was too scared to go through with it. A girl I know died last year after having an abortion and they said you could hear her screams houses away. I . . . I took something Lonnie's mam gave me but it didn't work except I was on the privy all night and as sick as a dog.'

Hope's head was whirling and her face was tight with pain, although not the physical kind. Hope had never imagined she would seriously want to harm anyone but if Lonnie Kirby had been in front of her now she would have gone for him with anything that came to hand.

Turning her head slowly, Constance looked up at Hope. 'Do you hate me?'

'Of course I don't hate you, how can you ask such a thing?' Hope said fiercely. 'But I hate him. He's evil, Constance, through and through. To make you do that . . .' She took a deep breath. 'When's the baby due?'

'I'm not sure. The end of February, I think,' Constance said vaguely.

'Have you been to see a doctor?'

Constance shook her head, her voice little more than a whisper as she said, 'I couldn't. I'd have to say I'm not married. I . . . I haven't been out lately unless it was dark in case someone saw me and said anything to Aunt Jinny.' Her eyes, tear-filled and pleading, held on to Hope's.

'Constance, she'll have to know. You're going to have a baby, you can't keep it a secret.'

'And the rest?' Constance bent forward, bringing her face close to Hope's. Her hand came up and gripped Hope's wrist. 'What about the rest of it?'

Hope didn't know what to say. If her aunt had heard anything about Constance's goings-on she knew she would have mentioned it, but that wasn't to say she wouldn't hear something in the future. The East End was a tight-knit community and not much went on that wasn't public knowledge. People talked, it was natural, and let any of the old wives get hold of a juicy titbit and it went from back-yard to backyard like wildfire. The neighbours would have seen Lonnie bring men to the house but with any luck they would have assumed they were his pals and that was all. Hope felt sick and swallowed against the rising bile. 'I'll say nothing if that's what you mean.'

'Even to Daniel?' And when Hope hesitated, Constance moved her head in a desperate fashion. 'Please, Hope, don't tell him. It's bad enough I'm in the family way, if he knows the rest I'll kill myself. I mean it, I will. I'll throw myself off Wearmouth bridge or something.'

'Quiet, quiet.' Hope stroked Constance's hair back from her poor bruised face with her free hand, and when her sister loosened her hold on her wrist she gently cupped Constance's head and drew it to her breast. Constance's sobbing mounted and as Hope held her tight, an overpowering feeling of rage against Lonnie Kirby rose in her.

'He . . . he said he . . . would kill me if I . . . ever left,' Constance gasped.

'You didn't leave him, he threw you out.'

'But what if he comes looking for me?'

'He won't.' She would make sure of that. She would go and see this piece of scum and warn him if he came within a mile of her sister she would go to the police. And then, as she remembered how Constance had been in the past, she drew back a little so that her sister raised her head. 'Do you want him to come for you?' she asked softly. 'And tell me the truth, Constance.'

Constance shuddered. 'No. I've wanted to leave him ever since I moved in and he started all that but I was too frightened. And . . . and I didn't know if you'd talk to me if you knew about everything.'

Hope was overcome with emotion. 'You're my sister, my *sister*. How could I ever not talk to you? I don't care what you've done and it was him anyway, making you. You'll stay here with us. You'll be safe and we can have our babies together. I'm due the end of March. It will be all right, Constance, I promise. Stop crying now. There, pet.'

Constance was fast asleep in Betsy's bed when Daniel came home from work. Hope knew she would be eternally grateful to him when, after gravely listening to her explanation that Constance was pregnant with Lonnie Kirby's baby and had walked out on him after he'd beaten her once too often, her husband said, 'Of course she must come and live with us,' without a moment's hesitation.

'There's other things too.' Hope had told her sister she would have to say that much to Daniel to ease her conscience. 'Humiliating things, but Constance would prefer no one else to know but me. She's so ashamed, Daniel. He's treated her more badly than we could ever have imagined.'

Daniel looked at her, his grey eyes keen. 'I don't have to know it all,' he said softly, 'but I'm glad she confided in you. Are you sure she's really finished with Kirby this time?'

Hope nodded.

'Then somehow we'll work things out. Where is she going to sleep? I can't see us squeezing a bed into the front room.' They had already bundled the three-piece suite into one corner, the two chairs perched on the sofa, so that Hope had the main part of the room for her little business.

'I thought she could have Betsy's bed for the time being

and the twins will have to top and tail. They'll be all right, they sleep like little logs anyway and that way there will still be room for a crib at the side of Constance when the baby's born.'

They exchanged a rueful glance. They had only been congratulating themselves the night before that everything would be so much calmer and more under control when this child was born in March. Now the little house would be bursting at the seams.

But they would still be miles better off than her Aunt Jinny had been when she had raised her own children and two more besides, Hope thought in the next moment, and at least she wasn't expecting twins this time. That might have been a bit too much to handle. Throwing her arms round Daniel, she hugged him tight. 'Thank you,' she said softly. 'She really is at the end of herself, Daniel, and dreading what people will say when they find out she's having a bairn and not married. You know how cruel people can be.'

Hope didn't wake Constance when the evening meal was ready; sleep was the best medicine for her sister in her present state. Even when she put the twins to bed some time later, Constance slept on, curled on her side under the covers with her face to the wall as though she couldn't bear anyone looking at her even in her sleep. Hope stood for a long while once Jack and Betsy had drifted off, just staring down at the figure under the eiderdown. This was her baby sister and she loved her whatever had gone on in the past. She had missed her terribly the last couple of years and hated the fact that they were estranged, but she wouldn't have wished reconciliation to come at such a cost. When she thought about what Constance had gone through . . .

Don't. Don't think about it, she told herself in the next moment. Not now. Take it one minute at a time and save your strength for when you go and see Lonnie Kirby with Daniel and warn him to keep his distance. Daniel had actually forbidden her to accompany him when she had raised the subject but she was determined to work on him on that. She wanted to look this loathsome man in the face and let him know he didn't frighten her and that his days of controlling Constance were over.

Her chance to do this came sooner than she had anticipated. She and Daniel had just finished their mug of cocoa in front of the fire in the kitchen and were thinking about going to bed – it was clear that Constance would sleep through till morning now – when there was a knock at the front door.

Daniel's brow wrinkled. 'Who on earth is that at eleven at night?'

Hope didn't answer. She felt she knew who it was and in spite of her desire to tell Lonnie Kirby exactly what she thought of him, her stomach turned over. As Daniel rose from his armchair, she jumped to her feet and caught his arm. 'Be careful.'

'You think it's him?'

'Most likely. He's probably realised Constance isn't going to crawl home again like she's told me she's done in the past when he's acted like this.' Kirby would be worried one of his sources of income had finished because she was sure he had been accepting money from the men he brought to the house although Constance had apparently never seen any of it.

Daniel's jaw set. 'You stay in here. I'll see to him.'

Hope let him get as far as opening the front door before she came up behind him. No way was she letting Daniel confront a thug and violent bully like Lonnie Kirby without her being there. There was no knowing what this man would do.

'I want me wife.'

'What?'

Hope peered over Daniel's shoulder at the red, bloated face of the tall thickset man standing on the pavement. Lonnie Kirby wasn't the handsome figure he had once been. She had only caught a glimpse of him and his brother once or twice in the old days when she had been living in the East End, but Lonnie bore little resemblance to the flash but attractive man he had been then.

'I said I've come for me wife and don't tell me she isn't here because there was nowhere else for her to go besides me mam's and she's not there.'

'Constance isn't your wife.' Hope's voice was trembling as she spoke, not with fear but with hatred. 'And she's finished with you for good.'

'She's as near me wife as dammit and her place is with me.'

'I don't think so.' Daniel's arm had come out to prevent Hope pushing past him and now he turned his head to her and said, 'I told you to stay in the kitchen. I can deal with this.'

'Look, man, I don't want no trouble.' Lonnie's voice wasn't exactly placatory but the initial aggression had dampened. 'We had a row and I admit I lost me temper when I shouldn't but I'll make it up to her.'

'How will you do that?' Hope cut in again before Daniel

could speak. 'She's black and blue as a result of your fists. Can you take away her pain? You're God now, is that it?'

For a moment the somewhat bleary gaze narrowed on her face and two pinpoints of sheer black light glowed from under heavy lids. Hope blinked, her skin crawling. She had called this man evil earlier to Constance and she had been right.

Kirby's eyes switched to Daniel. 'She's coming home with me,' he said, speaking slowly and flatly. 'One way or another, she's coming home with me.'

'That's out of the question,' Daniel said firmly.

'And she doesn't have a home with you.' Hope wondered how Constance could have allowed this man to dominate her for so long. 'Whatever it is, it isn't that. You're filth, you know that, don't you? The worst sort of scum there is. Constance was a pure young girl when she met you and you've done your best to ruin her but you won't succeed. I'll see to that.'

Kirby ignored her but she'd caught him on the raw because his voice was a growl when he said to Daniel, 'I'm asking politely one more time and then I'm done asking. You going to let me see her or what?'

A slight movement behind her on the stairs caused Hope to turn her head and she saw Constance was crouched one or two treads from the top, her face as white as a sheet and her eyes wide with terror. She was out of Kirby's vision and Hope prayed her sister would have the sense to remain where she was.

'My wife has already told you Constance has no wish to see you and that's the end of the matter.' Whether Daniel had heard Constance too, Hope didn't know, but he closed the door a fraction as he spoke. 'I'd advise you to make yourself scarce.'

A mouthful of obscenities followed and Kirby put one of his thickly soled hobnailed boots over the threshold to prevent the door being shut. 'You pair of hypocrites, coming the holier than thou routine with me. I know all about you and your da so cut the flannel.'

'Whatever you think you know is a pack of lies.' Daniel's voice was icy now. 'You take one step into this house and I swear I'll take this further.'

'Oh aye?' Kirby was clearly unperturbed. 'If you're talking about the law then you might find I can tell 'em a pretty story or two about certain goings-on so I'd advise you to tread careful there. And if it's the Mullen brothers you've got in mind, I'm not Jim Clark. Just remember that. Jim's a light-weight compared to me and Frank.'

'You can threaten all you like.' Hope thought about Daniel's cricket bat which was in a box under the stairs and easily reachable. If Kirby tried to force his way in she could run for that. 'But you're not seeing Constance. She wants nothing more to do with you and I don't care what you might say to the police, get that through your head. My sister is far more important. She's told me everything, *everything*, and you're not touching her again and neither is anyone else.'

They glared at each other for a moment which seemed to expand and stretch, hatred in both pairs of eyes. 'You wouldn't want me to shop him and the rest of them.' Kirby jerked his thumb at Daniel. 'Nice pickle you an' the bairns would be in then in spite of this little number you've got running. Ice cream and toffee apples don't keep a family from the work-house.'

So he knew about her enterprise. She'd bet there wasn't much that got past Lonnie Kirby and his cronies. Her face was hard, her voice equally so as she rapped out, 'Try me, just try me. You're not capable of loving anyone so you wouldn't understand but I'll do whatever it takes to make sure Constance is free of you.'

His tongue drew a quick line over his upper lip. He was less sure of himself now. Hope suspected that his stretch in jail had been unpleasant enough for him not to want to return. He stared at her as though trying to work out if she meant what she said. Then he gave a sneering laugh which didn't quite come off. 'You want to keep her and her flyblow? Then be my guest. It'll save me having to feed 'em. She'd gone off the boil anyway, your precious sister, even before she got her belly full. The punters were beginning to complain. There's ten, twenty more where she came from and young and fresh with it.'

'What?' As the import of Kirby's words hit Daniel, he turned to look at Hope and saw her face. With a sound that was somewhere between a growl and a cry his fist shot out and caught Kirby totally unawares, causing him to stumble back and then sprawl into the road. Hope didn't wait to see him right himself, she wheeled round and ran to the cupboard under the stairs, grabbed the cricket bat and thrust it into Daniel's hand just as Kirby came at him like a charging bull elephant.

'I'll use it.' As Daniel held the bat in front of him Kirby checked himself. He wasn't badly hurt, his bulk and compacted muscle would make two of Daniel but no doubt his pride was injured. 'And you come anywhere near Constance again and you'll regret it, you have my word on that.'

'You arrogant young pup.' Kirby was panting, more from rage than anything else. 'You think you can threaten me? I'll see my day with you, you see if I don't, and them pitbulls your father gets to do his dirty work will find they've bitten off more than they can chew if they come for me. You can tell the Mullens that from me, all right? And as for you,' his malevolent gaze fastened on Hope, 'I wouldn't touch your sister with a bargepole, not if she paid me in sovereigns. I'm picky, see? But there's many an accident happens on a dark night so think on that.'

He was backing away from the doorstep but Hope was too busy holding on to Daniel who had tried to leap after him to bother with Kirby. 'No, Daniel, no more,' she said, twisting herself round so she was between him and the retreating man. 'He's not worth it.' In spite of the cricket bat she wouldn't rate Daniel's chances if he went head to head against Kirby who was built like a brick outhouse. 'Please, Daniel, leave him. Please.'

Within seconds Kirby's dark bulk was lost in the snowy night. Suddenly Daniel relaxed, his arms falling to his sides and the cricket bat loose in his fingers. Now that the danger was past, all the fight seeped out of Hope. She felt funny, a sickly odd feeling and her hands on Daniel were clinging now rather than restraining. She made a little sound in her throat. He looked down at her and she heard him swear softly, then she was being lifted up and carried and she heard him shouting for Constance.

The next thing she knew she was emerging from a whirling void to find herself cradled in Daniel's arms. He was sitting in one of the old armchairs in front of the range, holding her on his lap, and Constance was dabbing at her forehead with a cold flannel.

'It's all right, you're fine.' As Hope's eyes focused on her husband's face, she saw he was as white as a sheet. 'You fainted, that's all.'

Hope nodded to let him know she understood. Speech was beyond her right at this moment.

'I'm so sorry, lass.' Constance had sat down in the other armchair and they could see she was trembling. 'I never thought Lonnie'd come here.'

'How could you stay with a man who treated you like that?' Daniel was staring at Constance as though he didn't know her which was exactly how he felt. 'You should have left years ago.'

'I know that. If anyone knows that, I do, but . . . you don't know him. You don't know what he's capable of.'

'I've got a damn good idea.' Daniel stood up with Hope in his arms and placed her in the armchair. 'I'll make some tea. I think we could all do with a cup.'

'Daniel, about what he said, what . . . what I've been doing. You won't tell anyone?' Constance's cheeks were flaming.

Daniel took a deep breath. 'No, Constance, I won't tell anyone.'

'Thank you.' She bowed her head.

Daniel and Hope exchanged a glance, and Hope mouthed her thanks too. Daniel put out his hand and touched her cheek. The caress told her everything was all right between them but she knew her husband well enough to see he was rocked to his foundations and the revelations about Constance's goings-on were only part of it. No one could have failed to see that Lonnie Kirby was telling the truth tonight when he spoke about Abe and the Mullen brothers.

Hope watched Daniel as he made the tea but he did not meet her gaze again. How would he handle things with his da? She didn't know, but she did know she was going to leave it to him, for better or worse. She had enough on her plate, what with being pregnant and coping with the twins and trying to carry on the business as best she could, and now there was Constance too. Why, when everything seemed to be going along on oiled wheels, did something always happen to throw a spanner in the works?

Chapter 16

'You've done *what*?'

'Hope and I have taken Constance in. She's in the family way and has nowhere else to go.'

Abe took off the glasses he needed for close work these days, peering up at his son who was standing in front of his desk. It was ten to nine in the morning, and while Daniel was a few minutes early, Abe had been in the office since just after seven. This was not unusual.

Abe glanced through the glass panelling which allowed him to view the occupants of the outer office. This was where his secretary and three office girls, along with Cecil and Daniel, worked. The accounts office which harboured four more employees and the personnel office were much smaller rooms either side of this. Cecil was sitting at his desk staring at them, no doubt wondering what was being said. He, too, had been at work since seven. That way father and son got any confidential matters put to bed before anyone else arrived.

Turning his eyes on Daniel again, Abe said, 'Sit down.'

Daniel sat. This was not going to be an easy conversation for all sorts of reasons and he had no wish to antagonise his father unnecessarily. He intended to get to the bottom of the matter which had been between him and Hope since just after the twins were born. There was no doubt Lonnie Kirby had been telling the truth as he knew it about his father and these Mullen brothers last night, and Daniel felt foolish and angry and disappointed and upset and a thousand more emotions besides. In fact he didn't know how he felt except that he had been mad, stark staring mad not to mention the accusations to his father before this, if only because it had affected his marriage. He had made a promise to himself during the long sleepless night that he'd speak to his father today, and he would.

Before he could say any more, however, Abe put the palms of his hands on his desk and leant forward. 'You aren't going to like this but I'm saying it nonetheless. You'll be making a rod for your own back if you let that sister of Hope's get her feet under the table. And what about the neighbours an' all? They'll have a field day, you know they will. The mud will be flung in all directions and you and Hope and even the bairns will find it'll stick to you. That's how it works. It shouldn't but it does. Is it the same fella she's been knocking around with for years?'

Daniel nodded. His father knew little of Constance's circumstances, he'd never been interested before this moment. Carefully, and with his eyes tight on his father's face, Daniel said, 'His name is Lonnie Kirby.'

The tough old face didn't change expression by so much as the flicker of an eyelash. Clearly the name meant nothing to his da. 'So they've been courting for donkey's an' he's still not prepared to wed her, even with a bairn on the way? Something stinks, lad, an' it's not a barrel of fish neither.'

'Constance wouldn't want to marry him now after their last barney. She . . . she doesn't think he's the right one for her.'

The keen eyes narrowed. 'Took her long enough to come to that conclusion, didn't it? It would have been a darn sight better before she had a bun in the oven.'

Daniel shrugged. He had to be careful what he said. He had promised Constance. He knew his father wouldn't like it but in an effort to make the situation sound feasible, he said, 'We understand she moved in with him a little while ago and since then he's turned a bit rough with her.'

'Moved in . . .' Abe leant back in his seat. 'Lad, the lass is a bad 'un whether she's Hope's sister or not. You know as well as I do that a decent lass wouldn't countenance such a thing whatever she thought of the man concerned.'

'She's not bad. Gullible, but not bad.'

'I've heard it dressed up all ways but it boils down to the same thing. And the gossip'll be fierce. There's enough already what with Hope pushing that barrel round the streets. It hasn't gone unnoticed.'

'Of course it hasn't gone unnoticed. The amount of money she earns testifies to that as well as the quality of what she makes. She's doing well, really well, and all by her own efforts.'

'All right, all right, keep your hair on. I admit she's got a bit about her and she's a worker, there's none could say different.' Abe changed tack, warned by the look on his son's face. 'But this with Constance is different. You'll be sending out the message you approve of what she's done if you take her in and it'll re-bound on you all. You're not to do it, lad. Let her find somewhere else.'

'There is nowhere else, except the workhouse.'

'Aye, well, perhaps that would be a sharp short lesson.'

Daniel stared at his father. He loved this man, he had idolised him from a small child. 'You don't mean that.'

'Rather than you landing yourself with two more mouths to feed in due time? Aye, I do, lad. Because let's have one thing clear, you won't get rid of her or the bairn in a hurry. They'll be with you for good unless she can fool some poor sop into taking her, which I doubt, not with the evidence of her fall from grace bang smack in front of him. It's one thing for a man to shut his eyes and his ears to what's gone on before if he's besotted with a lass, but a bairn can't be ignored so easily.'

'You're worried the scandal will reflect on you and the rest of the family.'

Abe drew in a deep breath before he replied. Then he nodded slowly. 'To a certain extent, aye, I am. The leading lights in the town can't be seen to look the other way regarding things like this and word soon gets around. Now you know and I know that most of them are psalm-singing hypocrites. It's all right to have a mistress tucked away somewhere or to have fathered umpteen bairns on the wrong side of the blanket as long as you don't broadcast the fact. Once it gets into the public arena, that's a different story. Fifteen years ago our main rival was Armstrong and Grant and then Grant's son was had up for lewd behaviour in Mowbray Park. The phone stopped ringing, contracts died or were cancelled. Within twelve months they were bankrupt.'

'We shall make Constance and her child welcome for as long as they want to stay.'

Abe closed his eyes; then, opening them again, he picked up his glasses. 'Don't say I didn't warn you.'

'I won't.'

'Just remember that reputation and character are different things. You can have the best there is of the latter but if the former is tarnished, albeit unfairly, it can ruin a man.'

It was the perfect opening. Daniel drew breath to speak – and the telephone on his father's desk rang. Abe picked up the receiver and waved at him to be quiet.

'What do you mean, she's sold them?' he said after a moment or two, the tone of his voice causing Daniel to sit up straighter. 'They're not hers to sell.'

Daniel watched his father's face begin to colour, turning redder and redder before he snarled, 'Keep her there, do whatever you have to do but keep her there. This is what comes of letting her have all her own way and it's no good moaning and wailing about it now. The horse has long since bolted. I'm coming home.'

'Da?' As his father slammed down the receiver with enough force to cause everyone in the outer office to raise their heads, Daniel said, 'What's wrong? Is it Rosaleen?'

Abe didn't answer this. What he did say was, 'I'm going home and I might not be back today. You and Cecil will have to hold the fort.' He stood up and walked over to the coat-stand in a corner of the room. He pulled on his hat and coat, his face like thunder. 'Give her enough rope and she'll hang herself, I've been saying that to your mother for years but would she listen? Would she heck. If Rosaleen wanted something, Rosaleen had to have it regardless. She's ruined the girl, that's what she's done.'

'What's happened?'

Again his father didn't answer. He marched to the door and flung it open. 'Cecil, get in here.'

'What's up?' Once in the office and with the door shut, Cecil's eyes went from his father's face to Daniel's and then back to Abe's.

'I haven't got time to explain now but I have to get home. You and Daniel'll have to deal with things here between you. That union meeting on the shop floor at lunchtime, watch how they are afterwards. McArthur's been stirring them all up on the sly but if there's any talk of a strike you tell 'em we'll sack the lot of them because there's a hundred for every one of their jobs. All right? Put the fear of God into them. And Routledge's delivery has to go today come hell or high water. Tell Finlay I expect the month's accounts on my desk first thing tomorrow and check the post for Hedley's cheque. His girl was supposed to be sending it yesterday.'

Abe fired off his orders while sorting papers on his desk. He put a wad in his bottom drawer and then locked it and pocketed the key.

When he had finished speaking, he turned, looked at them both and said irritably, 'Well?'

'Is Rosaleen all right?' Daniel asked tentatively.

'No, she's damn well not all right.'

It was the only answer they got before he pushed past them and marched out of the offices, looking to neither right nor left.

'What was all that about?' Cecil asked.

Daniel shrugged. 'Your guess is as good as mine.'

'You two were talking pretty intently before the phone rang.'

'That was something else.' Daniel hesitated. He supposed

he might as well tell Cecil now, he'd find out in the next day or two anyway. 'Constance is staying with us. She's expecting a baby. She turned up on the doorstep last night having walked out on the bloke she was living with.'

Cecil gave a low whistle. 'Blimey.'

'I didn't get a chance to tell him the rest of it. The man concerned paid us a visit at eleven o'clock last night, shouting the odds and carrying on. He's been knocking Constance about so there's no way she's going back to him but it took him a while to accept that and things got nasty. Apparently he's a pal of Jim Clark's.'

Cecil stared at him. His voice was flat as he said, 'Jim Clark, eh?'

'And this Lonnie, Constance's bloke as was, had plenty to say about Da and the rest of us. He mentioned the Mullen brothers.' Daniel waited. If their father was involved in anything at all then Cecil was party to it, that much was for sure.

Cecil continued to stare at him. There was a long silence before Cecil said, 'What do you want me to say?'

'The truth.'

'You sure about that?'

'What does that mean?'

'It means, little brother, are you sure you wouldn't be more comfortable continuing to bury your head in the sand?'

The venom in Cecil's voice shocked Daniel more than the implication of his words, possibly because he had already faced the fact that his father and brother were guilty of something. It was how much they were guilty of he wasn't sure about.

Cecil bent close to him, one arm going round his shoulders

so that to any onlookers in the outer office it would appear they were having a friendly heart to heart.

'You make me sick, do you know that? For years you've made me sick,' Cecil said quietly. 'There's no one like you as far as the old man's concerned and yet what are you? A nowt. I was the one who left school and got stuck into the business, working my socks off day and night trying to please him and putting up with all sorts. You haven't got half my brains and gumption and yet everything always falls into your lap.'

Daniel drew back, forcing Cecil's arm to drop away. He was stunned with the depth of hatred his brother was revealing and the quietness of his voice made it worse somehow. This wasn't a hatred born of the anger and rage of the moment but something enduring.

'You haven't done too badly out of it all.' It was all Daniel could think of to say.

'You mean the house and the car?' Cecil smiled bitterly. 'But they aren't mine, are they? They're his.'

'It was up to you whether you accepted Da's offer of a loan, same as it was up to me.'

'No, it wasn't. I had to keep Gwendoline in the manner to which she was accustomed. Both her parents and ours made that very plain.'

'Then you shouldn't have married her if you didn't want to go down that path.'

'You never said a truer word. I shouldn't have married her, Daniel, but like everything else, I did it to please him. But you don't understand that, do you? You've never had to try and earn a smile from him. And on top of everything else, Hope comes along, the love of your life. Because she is, isn't she, little brother? She's the love of your life. You two are supremely happy together in your cramped little house with its outside privy and few feet of backyard.'

Daniel truly didn't know what to say. He felt angry and affronted and deeply hurt, but the overriding emotion was pity for his brother. And pity was the last thing Cecil would accept from him. Keeping his voice steady, he said, 'We're not discussing me and Hope. Do you and Da know the Mullen brothers?'

'I know *of* them.'

'And Da?'

'They all grew up together.'

'Cecil,' Daniel's voice expressed his rising impatience, 'you know what I'm asking.'

Cecil's voice was even quieter when he said, 'Aye, I know, Daniel, so I'll ask you again. Are you sure you want this particular can of worms opened?'

'So there is something between Da and the Mullens? Did they work Jim Clark over on Da's orders?'

'You don't *order* blokes like the Mullens. Da called in a favour and asked them to warn Jim Clark and his cronies off our patch. They'd been taking liberties, breaking into the works at night and causing damage. They'd also threatened Da and the family.'

'This Jim Clark had a grievance then. Was it justified? Have you and Da been taking short cuts?'

'You ought to hear yourself.' The scorn in Cecil's voice acted on Daniel like the crack of a whip and brought him taut and tight-faced. 'You damn hypocrite. You've looked the other way for years, admit it. You've never been interested in knowing more than what was in front of your nose because it suited you that way. Da's done what he's had to do over the years, no more and no less. All right? And when you're up there on your sanctimonious, holier-than-thou high horse, don't forget you were damn glad there was a job here waiting for you when you and Hope were expecting the twins. Tried it on your own, didn't you, and but for the little lady at home you'd have been penniless. Admit it.'

The pity fled, replaced by a healthy dose of fury. 'At least I *did* try it on my own which is more than could be said of you. And while we're talking of hypocrites, don't forget that people who live in glass houses shouldn't throw stones.'

'And what does that mean?'

'You accepted the easy route, Cecil, *all* the way. Nice job as Da's second-in-command, cultured wife, beautiful home and the social acclaim that goes with all that.'

'The easy route?' Cecil exclaimed scornfully. 'You haven't got a clue, Daniel. I'll tell you something now that will make you laugh. If I'd gone to university, it wouldn't have been maths that would have interested me, or one of the science subjects or history. It would have been English literature. Shakespeare, the poets . . .' His voice tailed off and for a moment his expression was almost dreamy. 'But English liter-ature has no place in an engineering works, isn't that so?'

'If you had told him—'

'He wouldn't have understood. He wouldn't have *let* himself understand because that would have interfered with his plans for the development of the business.'

Daniel stared at his brother. For the first time he realised that Cecil understood their father far better than he did. Understood, loved and accepted him for exactly what he was.

The two brothers looked at each other for some moments, resentment and deep bitterness in Cecil's face and confusion and turmoil in Daniel's. A phone rang in the outer office, a door banged somewhere but it didn't intrude into their world.

'There is going to be a war, Daniel. You can't mistake the signs. Hitler and Mussolini joining forces, Franco tightening his grip on northern Spain. It's coming and it'll be a hundred, a thousand times worse than anything that's gone before. However bad things are now, they'll get worse, and that brings everything into perspective, don't you think? But they'll need engineering works in a war. So you just do your nice comfortable job and go home to your wife and bairns at night and don't rock the boat. Believe me, it'll be rocked soon enough. And when all's said and done, what choice do you have? Another bairn on the way and now Constance living with you and Hope and the twins. They'll all be looking to you, little brother.'

There was another long pause and when Daniel made no reply, Cecil said, 'You see? The easy route isn't always all it's cut out to be.'

Chapter 17

'Where is she?'

Abe entered the house with all the finesse of an enraged elephant. Emily, who met him in the hall, inclined her head towards the stairs. 'In her room.'

'Get her down here.'

'What are you going to say?'

'What I'm going to say should have been said a long while ago.'

'Abe—'

'No. Enough, Emily. No more. I'm not having the begging and pleading for me to go easy. That jewellery was expensive, it set me back a tidy sum, I can tell you, and I'm not complaining. Not when it was for you on your birthday. But for her to take it and sell it . . . I want an explanation and it had better be a good one, I tell you. But I can't think of anything she could say that would justify her actions, so prepare yourself.'

Emily was chalk-white and she still didn't move from her

position at the foot of the stairs. 'At least she admitted she'd taken it.'

'And that's to her credit?' Abe shook his head. 'Where are your brains, lass? There's something going on with our Rosaleen and I'm determined to get to the bottom of it. She's been different the last few months and you know it.'

Emily, her hand to her mouth, said, 'She's a young woman, Abe.'

'A young woman who does damn all, has a more than adequate allowance and has now taken to stealing off her own mam and da? Can you hear yourself, woman?'

Annie had appeared from the kitchen during this exchange, standing silently to one side. As Abe glanced at her, she said, 'She came in sort of dopey earlier, then she started to play up.'

'Play up?'

Annie glanced at Emily but when she said nothing, Annie cleared her throat. 'She . . . took off her clothes, said she was too hot. And she was laughing.' Annie shook her head, leaving Abe in no doubt as to what the laughter had been like.

'And when did you find the necklace and earrings gone?' Abe's eyes returned to his wife.

Emily stared at him for a long moment. 'I went to check my jewellery when I saw the state of her.'

She knew. It was like a thunderclap in Abe's head. All this time when he had been tearing himself apart with his suspicions and not daring to voice them to Emily for fear of what it would do to her, she'd known. Suddenly all the doubts he'd had about whether he was right about Rosaleen were gone, his worst fears confirmed by the look on his wife's face. 'Why didn't you say?' There was none of the usual force in his voice. 'Why in the name of all the saints didn't you say?'

She didn't answer him, just stared mutely into his eyes. 'Emily?'

At last she said, 'I think it started at one of the parties Terence took her to. They all do it, it's the done thing in their set, it doesn't mean anything.'

Abe's bewildered glance moved to Annie but she was now staring at the floor.

'How long?'

'What?'

'How long has she been at it?' Abe barked, making both women jump.

'I don't know.' Emily clutched the front of her dress. 'I mean we haven't actually discussed it or anything, but like you said, she's been different. But Terence and her are much closer, Abe. I know he's going to ask her to marry him. I feel it in my bones.'

'Is anything else missing?'

Emily lowered her head. 'There's been the odd thing but nothing as expensive as the emerald and diamond set.'

He could hardly believe this was happening. Abe rubbed his hand across his eyes and made to go up the stairs.

But Emily remained where she was, barring his way. 'Where are you going?'

He didn't answer. He pushed her out of the way with the flat of his hand and began to climb the stairs. He was aware that it was Annie and not his wife who was following him.

When he entered Rosaleen's bedroom she was lying on top of the bedclothes in her bra and knickers, her eyes wide open and fixed on the ceiling.

'Rosaleen?' His voice was loud.

There was no reaction at all from the girl on the bed.

'*Rosaleen.*' He walked over to the bed and shook her arm. 'Sit up. I want to talk to you.'

She turned her head, her voice thick and soft. 'Hello, Da.'

'Sit up.' He hauled her up so sharply he heard her neck crack. When she was propped against the headboard, a silly look on her face, he said, 'What have you taken?'

'Taken?'

'I know you've sold your mother's jewellery to buy drugs, Rosaleen. It's no use pretending. What have you taken?'

'I can't tell. It's a secret.' She giggled, her hand going over her mouth as she slipped down the bed again. 'I can fly, over the moon and back again.'

'Should I call the doctor?' Annie had come to stand beside him. 'She's never been like this, Abe.'

'No.' Abe turned, looking round the room. 'Watch her while I see if there's anything here.'

It took him no more than a minute to find the stash of little packets of white powder in Rosaleen's chest of drawers. His face was grey when he showed them to Annie who silently nodded before pointing to Rosaleen's left arm. The smooth flesh was pockmarked.

Abe shut his eyes, his hand going to his brow. 'I'll kill that Stefford lad,' he hissed. 'I'll kill the lot of them.'

Rosaleen was wide-eyed and vacant, a smile on her lips as she hummed softly to herself. Annie bent and pulled the eiderdown up to her chin. 'It's no use talking like that, Abe. The last thing you want is to bring the law down on you. By all means have a word with Stefford's father and tip him the wink. You can bet he knows nothing of what his son's up to and he's in a better position than you to ferret out who's selling them this poison within their social circle. But our main concern has to be Rosaleen.'

Neither of them thought it strange that she had spoken in much the same way a mother would.

Abe groped his way across the room as though he was blind, sitting down so heavily on the flimsy pink dressing-table stool that Annie thought the thin legs might snap. 'I've given her everything.' He turned an agonised face on Annie. 'And this is the result. I tell you one thing, Annie. I don't pretend to hold with all Hope's got up to but I wish Rosaleen had just a bit of the lass's moral fibre. I do straight.'

There was a short, tense silence broken only by Rosaleen's monotous humming.

'What are you going to do?' Annie asked softly.

'Get her as far away from her mother and that lot as I can, for a start.'

'But where?' Annie sat down at the foot of the bed. 'She'll need supervision, Abe. Once they're on this sort of thing, it becomes a craving. If you send her on holiday, someone would have to go with her and watch her like a hawk twenty-four hours a day.'

'I wasn't thinking of a holiday,' Abe said grimly. 'You remember I've got a branch of the family on me mam's side in Scotland? Well, on the borders, they are. There's only a cousin and his wife left now as far as I know, they've a tuppenny-farthing farm in the middle of nowhere and live hand to mouth. I haven't heard from them in years, there's no phone and they don't have a car but if they're still alive and kicking they'd jump at the chance of some easy money and I'd pay 'em well.'

He stood up, the greyness fading and the old vitality coming back into his voice. 'Pack her things, lass. Plenty of warm clothes and boots and things, and you'd better make a bundle of warm bedding and her eiderdown. Likely it'll be enough to freeze the vitals.'

'You aren't taking her now?'

'That's exactly what I'm proposing to do, before her mam comes up with a hundred reasons not to.'

'But what if they're not there, this cousin and his wife? What'll you do then?'

'I'll cross that bridge when I come to it.'

Annie glanced down at the girl on the bed. 'She's quiet now,' she said, 'but she was like something possessed earlier. If she starts playing up in the car, how are you going to handle her? Would Emily come with you?'

'I doubt it.' Abe's tone made it clear that the idea didn't appeal.

'Well, if she doesn't, I will. How long are you intending to stay?'

'Damn it all, Annie, how many more questions? Look, pack enough for a day or two for me and you. For Rosaleen . . .' His gaze went to his youngest child and for a second a muscle in his jaw clenched and worked, then he turned and walked to the bedroom door. 'Pack everything she's got, within reason', he said over his shoulder. 'She'll be staying there some time.'

'Saints alive, Abe, is that it?' They had been following what was little more than a rough track of ridged snow for some miles after leaving the main road and more than once Annie had thought the car would get stuck. Luckily the track had wound through a large expanse of pine trees for most of this time, which had protected the road from the worst of the elements.

'Aye, that's it and from the smoke coming out of the chimney, it looks like someone's home at least.' Abe stopped the car and they stared through the windscreen at the small house in the distance and what looked to be a barn beside it.

Although Annie hadn't been aware of it they must have been travelling up a slight incline since leaving the main road because now, as they came out of the last of the pine trees, there was a steep drop in front of them to the valley where the house was nestling.

'We're going to have to walk it from here, I daren't risk trying to get the car down there.' Abe turned and glanced at Rosaleen who was fast asleep on the back seat, packed round with bedding. She had slept for the whole of the five-hour journey. 'We'll manage her between us and I'll come back for our things later.'

'But it's getting dark, and what if it's not your cousin down there? What if he's sold the place to someone else?'

'Then I'll pay 'em handsomely to put us up for the night and we'll be off in the morning. We can't spend the night in the car, lass,' he added reasonably.

The next hour was forever engraved on Annie's memory. When they woke Rosaleen, she realised for the first time what was happening and became hysterical. Abe had to slap her once hard across the face. They struggled through snow-drifts until finally, blue with cold, they were banging on the door of the farmhouse.

Abe's cousin and his wife turned out to be two thin, dour-looking individuals who nevertheless made them welcome enough. The house was small, poor small, and dirty into the bargain. There was just one large room downstairs, containing a table covered with oilcloth, four chairs and a long wooden settle and dresser. Another table held pots and pans and a washing-up bowl, with a tin bath beneath it against the far wall. A solid ladder led up to the first floor of the house. But the place was warm. A good fire was burning in the old black-leaded range and a kettle was simmering on the hob. When they'd had a cup of strong tea – they weren't offered sugar – it was quickly established they would have to leave the bedding and clothes where they were in the car until morning. The walk to the house had taken much longer than they had thought and it would be too dangerous to attempt a return journey in the dark.

Rosaleen said she felt ill and wanted to lie down, so she and Annie followed Flo up the ladder, leaving Abe to explain the situation to his cousin. Upstairs was also just one room. It held two large pallet beds, only one of which had bedclothes on it. 'The bairns used to sleep on the other one,' Flo told Annie and Rosaleen, nodding at the ancient bare mattress, 'but they've long since gone. Live in the town now, all five of 'em.' Annie glanced round the room, lit only by the flickering light of the oil lamp Flo was holding. There was no electricity or gas to the house, and no running water. Annie's gaze came to rest on Rosaleen's white face. Rosaleen had been used to the niceties of life from the moment she could crawl, she would never adapt to such primitive surroundings. Abe couldn't leave the lass here.

But it wouldn't be forever. Annie looked round again. And its isolation was perfect. Flo had already said they never saw a living soul from one month to the next in the winter, so there would be no worry that Rosaleen would make contact with the Stefford lad.

By the next morning it had all been decided. Abe, who had spent the night on the settle and could hardly move now without grunting with pain, fetched the bedding and clothes from the car with his cousin's help. He and Annie would stay for a couple of days until Rosaleen, who appeared to be sick, was feeling better. They all knew her shaking and vomiting was probably due to the substance she had been taking, but no one voiced this.

It took longer than two days and was the stuff of night-mares but eventually, after days and nights punctuated with Rosaleen's cries and moans of pain and Abe constantly muttering what he would do to Terence Stefford given half a chance, there came a time when Rosaleen was sleeping peacefully. With the rest of the household asleep, Abe and Annie sat in front of the flickering fire on the evening of the fifth day, too exhausted to move.

'There were times when I didn't think the lass would get through this,' Abe said quietly after a while.

'There were times when I didn't think *we* would.' Annie smiled at him but she was only half joking. Rosaleen had been in agony and it had been terrible to see.

'I tell you something, lass, there's no one in the world I'd rather have had with me to see this through than you.'

He had spoken so quietly that for a moment Annie didn't think she had heard right. She stared at him, not daring to speak in case she gave herself away. He had been talking about friendship, nothing else, she told herself silently.

'Have I embarrassed you?'

He was looking at her in a way that made her heart beat faster although the rugged face was just the same as normal. But it was his eyes. She didn't think she had seen such tenderness in his eyes before but it could be a trick of the moving shadows thrown out by the oil lamp and the fire. Trying to pull herself together and present the steady, no-nonsense individual he was used to, she said, 'Embarrass me? Of course not. That . . . that was a nice thing to say.' And then she added, because she knew it was the sort of thing he would expect from her, 'It's just unlike you to be complimentary, that's all.'

'Aye, that's true enough.' He shook his head slowly. 'I like to play the big fellow, don't I? Abe Fallow, who made it against all the odds. A rough diamond and all that.'

There was a long pause and when she made no reply he looked at her again and said, 'But I didn't feel like the big fellow watching my bairn go through hell, Annie. I should have followed my instincts long before this and done whatever was necessary to finish her liaison with Stefford and the rest of them. I felt in my guts something was badly wrong with Rosaleen but it was easier to go along with Emily than have her play up. But I can't blame Emily, she is what she is. The blame rests fairly and squarely on my shoulders.'

'That's not true.'

'Aye, it is.' He stared into her face, her sharp features mellowed and softened by the kindness of the dim light. Then he said softly, 'I missed the boat all them years ago, Annie. I went for what was right in front of me nose, for the tinsel and glitter of a pretty face because I was shallow then. Maybe I'm still shallow, I don't know. I'm certainly a fool because I could have tried for something – someone – much more precious. I might not have managed to win them, but if I had known then what I know now, I'd damn well have tried.'

The constriction in her throat made it impossible for her to speak.

'I'm going to ask this one thing and you don't have to answer,' he said after a full minute had ticked by. 'But I'd like to know, that's all. It won't alter the way we are and you know me well enough to understand I'd never presume on your friendship or do anything to dirty me wedding vows, but if I'd had me wits about me all them years ago, would I have stood a chance?'

She had dreamed of this moment. In the deep hidden recess of her heart wherein her love lay, she had allowed herself to imagine what it would be like if he told her he cared for her. And then the morning light would come and she would look in the mirror and reality banished the remnants of the dream. Till the next time.

She rose from the hard-backed chair abruptly and went to the old table which held the pots and pans. She bent and put her hands on it, looking down at her fingers gripping the wood. 'Aye, Abe, you'd have stood a chance.' You're my sun, moon and stars, the reason I breathe, the light of my life. You'd have stood a chance.

She heard the movement of his chair and then she felt his hands on her arms, turning her round. She saw the moisture in his eyes but she didn't realise she herself was crying until he drew out his handkerchief and gently wiped the tears from her face. Then he drew her against his chest, not speaking, not moving as he held her close to him for a long, long time.

When at last he let her go she knew he would not repeat what had happened or suggest anything more. But it didn't matter, it was enough. For this, she had allowed Emily to subjugate her all these years; she had heard their bedroom door close and lain awake for hours in bodily and mental torment; she had seen his children born and watched the gentleness in his big calloused hand as he had stroked downy heads; she had endured hell on earth. But it was her he had called precious.

Their leave-taking of Rosaleen the next day was traumatic for everyone. It soon became clear that Rosaleen had thought she would be able to talk her father round, and her despair at finding that Abe was resolute she stay with his cousin and wife at the isolated farmhouse was fierce.

'Please, Da, please.' She clung to Abe as he tried to walk out of the door. 'I swear I won't see Terence any more or take anything, I mean it.'

'You will, lass, unless you're far away from him. From the moment you got tangled up with that lot it was all downhill. I shall see his father and tell him what's what and make arrangements for you to go somewhere with your mother for a while. Somewhere nice. You'd like that, wouldn't you? It could be abroad if you like, Europe maybe.'

And then Rosaleen cut across everything she had said when she cried, 'I don't want to go to Europe or anywhere else. I love Terence, don't you understand that? And if you say anything to his da he won't want me any more. You'll make me the laughing stock of them all. Everyone does what I did, everyone.'

Abe's face hardened. He prised her fingers from his coat and led her to one of the hard-backed chairs. He pushed her down on it. 'Do you want to go through the last few days again, girl? Haven't you any sense? That stuff will kill you.'

'No it won't, Da, it won't. It's not like that.'

'That's exactly what it is like.'

'But I promise I won't do it again, all right? I mean it.'

'Rosaleen, listen to me.' Abe knelt down in front of the distraught girl, holding her shoulders and looking into her face which was streaming with tears. 'If Terence Stefford thought anything of you he wouldn't have introduced you to that muck. Face it, girl. Face it. He's no good. Oh, he might have enough money to buy and sell us ten times over but that's nowt, in my opinion. None of that lot have done a day's work in their lives, they live off their parents like damn parasites. Well, your days of running around with them are over.'

'You go, Abe, she'll be all right with us.' Flo touched his arm and motioned to where Annie was standing by the open door, her face white and troubled. 'Go on, you and Annie go now. This is only prolonging things.'

'If you say anything to Terence's father he'll cut Terence off without a penny, he's been threatening to do it for ages. And Terence will never forgive me, I know he won't. You'll ruin my life, Da.' Rosaleen had stopped crying and her voice was flat now.

'Your father's trying to save your life, lass, not ruin it,' said Annie from the doorway.

'You don't understand. None of you understand except Mam. She likes Terence, she wants me to marry him.'

'For crying out loud, Rosaleen.' Abe's patience had run thin. 'Do you really think that is going to happen? How long have you been seeing him? And has he ever talked of marriage? Once? Has he? He's not, and he's not likely to. His sort never do. When he weds it'll be a society match, a lass with a title likely as not because you can bet that's what his parents have got their eye on. I know old man Stefford and he wouldn't settle for less. The lad's a non-starter, lass. I've been telling your mother so for years.'

'I don't believe you.'

'Whether you do or you don't, it's fact. Now me an' Annie need to get back but I'll come for you as soon as everything's sorted. You'll feel better in a few days, more like your old self.' He straightened, wincing as his back muscles protested. 'Look, lass,' he said, his voice softer now, 'you've got your whole life in front of you. You're young and bonny and there'll be someone out there who'll bless the day you came across his path. But it won't be Terence Stefford. Resign yourself to that. It never would have been.'

He stood waiting for Rosaleen to speak but when she didn't he bent and kissed the top of her head. He could have been kissing a stone statue for all the response he got. He walked to the door and shook his cousin's hand. 'Thanks, man, for taking her.'

'Aw, don't be daft. We'd have done it for nowt but I won't pretend a bit extra won't be handy. We've had a bad year with one thing and another.'

Abe nodded. He suspected they'd had more than one bad year.

It was as he was about to follow Annie out of the house that Rosaleen spoke. 'If you leave me here I'll never forgive you, Da.' She stood up, her eyes meeting his. 'Never, do you hear me?'

'Aye, I hear you, lass.' There was a weariness in Abe's voice. This was her mother all over, twisting the emotional knife if the tears and tantrums didn't work. 'But I have to do what I know is right.'

'What you've decided is right.' Rosaleen was chalk-white but for two spots of colour burning across her cheekbones. 'You think you know what is right for all of us all the time. Mam, Cecil, Bernice, me; only Daniel has gone his own way and even then you've managed to rein him in. I've never liked Hope but I take my hat off to her for one thing, she stood up to you and that takes some doing.'

'If you say so, lass.'

Rosaleen stared at her father for a moment. Then, her voice and face changing, she said brokenly, 'Please don't leave me here, Da. Let *me* talk to Terence and tell him it's over. I will, I swear I will. I'll die if you speak to his father.'

For answer, Abe stepped out into the snowy day and closed the door quietly behind him.

It was only a barn owl out hunting for the night that saw the solitary figure slip out of the farmstead just before midnight. The big yellow eyes watched as it stumbled and slipped its way towards the river, the moonlit vista and drifts of sparkling snow making its progress easy to follow.

On the white river bank the figure stopped, remaining stationary for so long that the owl lost interest; he spread his great cream and brown wings and swooped off into the night with a screeching cry to warn would-be trespassers that this was *his* territory.

Rosaleen heard the sound. She tilted her head, looking up into the sky, but the owl was gone. All was quiet, deathly quiet.

She'd make him sorry for leaving her here. She turned her gaze to the swollen river, the icy water as black as ebony. And how could her mother agree to it? She'd thought her mam was on *her* side. That stinking filthy cottage back there with mice squeaking all night long and the privy at the end of the garden. How dare he, how *dare* he leave her with these awful people? But she'd show him, she'd show the lot of them. They'd regret treating her like this.

A snowflake drifted on the raw wind and landed on her face, mingling with the salt of her tears as she began to edge down the snow-encrusted bank towards the water. Her feet slipped from under her and she began to slide on her bottom, her hands scrabbling desperately at her sides, but the snow was too thick for her to grasp the grass beneath. And then she was in the water and under it, the coldness like nothing she'd experienced before.

Gasping and spluttering, her head emerged but already the current was taking her on. She tried to scream but her chest seemed paralysed by the icy cold and only the weakest of sounds emerged, the whimpering cry of 'Da' lost in the night.

Within a minute or so the splashing had ceased and the river was as it had been before. The owl returned, a dead mouse hanging from his talons. He settled on his favourite branch and proceeded to rip his meal apart, the great yellow eyes sweeping over the quiet countryside as the snow began to fall again.

Chapter 18

The day of Rosaleen's funeral was bitterly cold. The body was not found for some weeks, so the service did not take place until just after the New Year, on 3 January, the same day the country received the chilling news that all school-children were to be issued with gas masks.

It had been a sombre Christmas and New Year for the adults. Hope had made it her business to see that the grief and heartache touched Jack and Betsy as little as possible. For the children's sake they had celebrated Christmas as normally as they could, buying a small tree which the twins spent many happy hours making decorations for. On Christmas morning the twins had found their stockings at the end of their shared bed, complete with a fine model aeroplane for Jack and a sweetly dressed doll for Betsy, as well as the usual orange and apple and little bags of shiny new coins.

Constance offered to stay at home and look after Jack and Betsy so that Hope and Daniel could go to the funeral alone. Hope was exceedingly glad of this, the more so when Emily went hysterical at the graveside and had to be bodily restrained from throwing herself on top of the coffin after it was lowered into the ground.

All in all it was a white-faced and shaken company who assembled for the reception afterwards, which Bernice had arranged at her house. The house was full with family and friends and business colleagues of Abe's. Daniel found Hope a seat in an alcove out of the general throng and fetched her a plate of food. She had been too upset to eat anything before-hand but now, due to her advanced pregnancy, she was feeling faint and sick and knew she had to force something down.

By mid-afternoon most of the assembly had paid their respects and departed, and only the immediate family remained. Bernice had been at her mother's side all day but a short while before had persuaded Emily to take a pill and go and lie down in one of the spare bedrooms. Bernice came and sat by Hope's side on the sofa in the alcove.

'How is she now?' Hope asked. 'Your mam?'

'Sleeping.'

Hope nodded. Even a few minutes of sleep was some sort of opiate against the agony.

'The thing is, Rosaleen was always Mother's favourite,' Bernice murmured without the slightest trace of resentment. 'I think before she was born Mother had despaired of producing a child who didn't bear the Fallow stamp. She had high hopes of Rosaleen making a brilliant match with her looks and figure.'

'I still find it hard to believe she has actually gone.' Hope shook her head slightly. 'She was so full of life, so vivacious. And an accident seems worse than anything somehow, so random and pointless.'

Bernice cast a sidelong glance at her.

'What?'

Bernice shrugged her thin shoulders.

'But that was the result of the coroner's inquest surely? A verdict of accidental death?'

Again Bernice shrugged. 'What's a coroner's inquest when my father is involved,' she said, bitterness evident in her low voice. 'And do you and Daniel really believe their story that Rosaleen had agreed to stay on for a holiday with my father's cousins in Scotland?'

'Your parents said it was because of Terence. They'd had a row and Rosaleen was terribly upset. I know your father dashed home that day she went to Scotland because Daniel and Cecil were in the office when your mother phoned.'

'I know that,' Bernice said a little impatiently.

'So what are you saying?'

Bernice stared straight ahead for a moment, her angular figure held tense and stiff. Then with a little sigh she relaxed, turning to glance at Hope. 'I don't know. I don't know what I'm saying, I suppose, but something isn't right. It's not just that Mother is beside herself, that's only to be expected in the circumstances, but the way she is with my father . . . There's something. Perhaps rather than Terence being mean to Rosaleen, he asked her to marry him. My father can't stand Terence Stefford. Perhaps he whipped Rosaleen away against her will and these cousins agreed to hang on to her while Father sorted things out down here. He's very good at sorting things out.'

Hope's brow wrinkled. Gently, she said, 'You don't think you might be imagining things because of how your father behaved with you?'

'No. Yes. Oh, I don't know, possibly. I've a good mind to go and see Terence Stefford myself and ask him what went on before Rosaleen and Annie and Father took off. And don't you think that's a bit strange too? Annie going? Why not Mother? If Rosaleen had been upset about a quarrel with Terence, it would have been the most natural thing in the world for Mother to accompany her, but if Father was whisking her out of the way against her will, I can see Mother wanting to distance herself from that. She wouldn't have wanted to fall out with Rosaleen.'

'What does Rupert think?'

'Rupert?' It was scathing. 'He is the last person in the world I'd discuss this with. Father has had him in his back pocket ever since our marriage.' She stood up, smoothing down her crisp black dress. 'I'd better see about Mary serving everyone a cup of tea and slice of cake before they go. And don't look so worried. You're probably right and I'm putting two and two together and making ten. Perhaps Rosaleen was agreeable to staying in Scotland, perhaps she did go for a walk with Florence and slip off the river bank, perhaps Father's hand in all of this was perfectly innocent.'

But Bernice did not think so. Hope watched her sister-in-law as she walked away. And now neither did she. She rubbed her hand irritably across her brow. Nothing was ever straightforward in this family, but this was something apart. Rosaleen had had her whole life in front of her and to die like that, to be swept away knowing you were going to drown. It didn't bear thinking about.

Easing her shoes surreptitiously off her feet, Hope rubbed her swollen ankles one after the other. Standing for such a long time both at the church and graveside hadn't suited them.

As she glanced up again, she caught Daniel's eye. He was standing with Rupert but although he smiled at her he made no effort to leave his brother-in-law and come over. She had thought Lonnie Kirby's visit would make things better between them but if anything Daniel was more . . . What was he? She frowned to herself. Remote, guarded, wary, even defensive? She couldn't really put a name to it. But then sometimes, for hours at a time, he was the old Daniel. Of course it didn't help having Constance with them even though her sister was being as good as gold, but there was nothing she could do about that.

Suddenly, for no reason, Hope felt very alone. She looked round at the others, the old feeling that had dogged her since childhood – that of being on the outside of a family looking in – so strong she could taste it. Abe, who seemed to have aged ten years in the last month, was deep in conversation with Cecil, Annie was bent close to Gwendoline who had Edward on her lap, Daniel was still conversing with Rupert and Bernice was talking to her housekeeper. They seemed a closed unit, separate and functioning without her, and yet she knew if she and Daniel were right she wouldn't be feeling like this.

To occupy her hands, she forced her shoes onto her feet again, her swollen flesh objecting. Maybe, now the awfulness of the funeral was over, things would settle. Maybe Daniel would talk to her, confide in her like he had done when they had first met. Maybe, if Bernice didn't stir up more skeletons in Abe's cupboard, Daniel's father would cease to be a bone of contention between them.

And maybe there were too many maybes.

*　　*　　*

Across the other side of the drawing room, Daniel was aware of every fleeting expression on his wife's face, even as he talked to Rupert.

He ought to go and put his arm round her or hold her hand, she looked very young and small sitting there, in spite of her swollen stomach which proclaimed she was a woman. But then Hope was a curious mixture of strength and frailty, of vulnerability and blind, dogged determination.

'. . . and so I said to him, do you know who I am? I could buy and sell you ten times over so just watch your step.' Rupert was deep into a story of how he had bullied his way into a card game at some club or other and Daniel let him prattle on, his thoughts a million miles away from the bloated, perspiring individual in front of him.

Why hadn't he talked to her about the night Lonnie Kirby had come shouting the odds? He'd meant to, like he'd meant to have it out with his father, but after the conversation with Cecil everything had got muddled in his mind. It was still muddled; in fact he felt his mind was like a battlefield, love and hate, resentment and anger, shame and bitterness and recrimination all warring until he felt his brain would explode.

He should have walked out the day Cecil laid it on the line, but how could he? With Hope and the bairns and another one on the way, not to mention Constance and her bairn, he was trapped. It was all very well for Hope to take the moral high ground about his father's dealings with blokes like the Mullen brothers, but he couldn't afford such a luxury, not with umpteen mouths to feed. He was caught, like a rat in a trap, and although he knew it wasn't Hope's fault, his bitterness had grown the more he had thought about it. But for her he would still be living in blissful ignorance of any shady goings-on.

Aw, that wasn't fair. He felt the self-disgust rise, as it did a hundred times a day when his thoughts veered off down this path. He couldn't blame Hope for his cowardice, and that's what it boiled down to. He might excuse it by telling himself he couldn't cause his father more grief by walking out and causing a rift in the family – as it surely would – after Rosaleen's death, or that his first priority had to be keeping a roof over his family's head and food in their stomachs, but at bottom he knew he couldn't endure the shame and humiliation of the dole queues. Hell, when you saw the men on the street corners with their dead eyes and over-polished boots, it twisted your guts until you couldn't breathe.

And what had his father done, after all? Just the same as most men in his position most likely. Business was all about backhanders and short cuts, it wasn't what you knew but who you knew, and if Jim Clark hadn't opened his mouth too wide he wouldn't have been paid a visit by the Mullens.

Hark at yourself. He felt the colour flooding into his face almost as if his thoughts had been broadcast for everyone in the room to hear.

'You feeling all right, Daniel?'

Rupert was looking at him with some alarm and now Daniel loosened his shirt collar, his voice gruff as he said, 'It's hot in here, that's all.'

'I know what you mean. Bernice always keeps the place as hot as a greenhouse. She feels the cold, what with being so scrawny.' For a moment the two men stared at each other. Realising he'd put his foot in it, Rupert added, 'But she's always been on the slender side, isn't that right?'

Daniel stared into the moist face of Bernice's husband. He had never warmed to Rupert, not from the first time his father had invited him to dinner years ago, but now he realised he actively disliked him. 'Slender, yes,' he said stiffly. 'The sort of woman who can show a dress off to its best advantage.'

'Quite so, quite so.' Rupert nodded his balding head enthusiastically. 'I'm a lucky man, no doubt about that. No doubt about that at all. Now, if you'll excuse me I just wanted a brief word with your father . . .'

Nasty little individual. Daniel stood stony-faced as Rupert backed away. How on earth did Bernice put up with him? Whatever that other fellow had been like, he had to be head and shoulders above Rupert. Did she ever think of him? The man whom their father had considered not good enough for her?

He glanced to where Bernice was now sitting with Hope again, and as he did so the stark contrast between the two women caused him to look at his wife afresh. By, she was bonny. If ever a woman had more than her fair share of looks, Hope did. And pregnancy suited her. He felt himself harden, his body involuntarily responding to the memory of what Hope had looked like the last time they had made love, her rounded curves and soft flesh inviting. And she was generous with her love. Never once had she turned him away, not even in the early days with the twins when she was too tired to do more than put her arms round him and hold him tight as he had taken his pleasure.

He was a fool. His stomach clenched, his manhood shrivelling under the weight of his self-loathing. He was destroying the one thing in his life that had any real meaning. He had seen the question in those big brown eyes lately. She was wondering what was wrong with him and he didn't blame her.

But still he didn't make his way to the other side of the room.

Chapter 19

So what should she do now? Bernice stood quietly on the slushy pavement outside the tea room in Fawcett Street where she had been talking to Terence Stefford for the last half an hour. She hadn't enjoyed talking to him; she considered Terence a man of little real substance, the sort of individual who had no capacity for deeper feelings. It did not surprise her that Rosaleen had been in love with him though. Terence possessed a surface glamour, he was charming and certainly handsome enough to appeal to the ladies.

There had been no quarrel between Terence and her sister. Bernice began to walk on before spotting the approach of a taxi cab which she hailed with her furled umbrella. Which meant her father had been lying.

'Where to, miss?'

She stared at the taxi driver and it wasn't until she heard herself give the address of her parents' house that she realised the decision had been made. For once in her life she was going to challenge him. She drew back the cuff of her glove and glanced at the small gold wristwatch which had been a twenty-first birthday present from her parents. Five o'clock. That meant she would have some time alone with her mother before her father came home. Should she broach the subject of why they had seen fit to ship Rosaleen off and incarcerate her in the middle of nowhere? Or keep it for when he came home?

The decision was taken for her when she arrived at the house to find her mother was taking an afternoon nap.

'I'd prefer not to wake her if you don't mind,' Annie said apologetically after they had walked through to the drawing room where a huge fire was crackling in the grate. 'She had another bad night, by all accounts.'

Bernice nodded. 'No, no, don't wake her. It was Father I wanted to see anyway.' She saw Annie's gaze narrow and knew what the other woman was thinking. Normally she timed her visits to avoid seeing her father.

There was a brief moment of silence and then Annie said, 'Can I get you a warm drink, lass? Tea, coffee, hot chocolate? It's enough to freeze your lugs off out there.'

'No thank you. I've just had tea and toasted muffins actually.' And then Bernice looked Annie straight in the face as she added, 'With Terence Stefford.'

Annie stared at her. 'Terence Stefford? I didn't know you had any truck with him.'

'I don't, at least I haven't before.'

'So why did he want to see you?'

'He didn't. I asked him to meet me.'

'I see.' And then Annie shook her head. 'That was a silly thing to say. I don't see at all. Why would you want to meet Terence Stefford? As you've made a point of telling me about seeing him I don't feel backward about asking why.'

Bernice could have smiled if the circumstances had been different and she felt a rush of affection for the housekeeper who had been such a part of her growing up. She knew Daniel had always been Annie's favourite but she was also aware the housekeeper had a soft spot for her which certainly hadn't been there in her dealings with Cecil and Rosaleen, although she had cared for them all to the best of her ability. 'Same old Annie,' she murmured softly, the tone of her voice making it a compliment rather than a criticism. 'No beating about the bush.'

'Aye, well, you know me, lass.' Annie tilted her head as Bernice seated herself in an armchair which was pulled close to the fire and held out her hands to the blaze. 'I can't abide with going all round the houses.'

'Father said the reason he had taken Rosaleen to his cousin's house was because she was upset and wanted to get away after an argument with Terence.' Bernice looked at Annie for a moment before returning her gaze to the fire. 'That's not true, is it?'

'Says who?'

'Says Terence and he should know surely?'

'And you believe him? You'd believe a wastrel like Terence Stefford over your da?'

'Yes, I do, Annie. Terence has no reason to lie.'

'And your da does?'

Bernice did not reply to this but she stood up, turning to face Annie. 'Why did you accompany Father to Scotland instead of Mother,' she asked quietly, 'if not for the fact that

Mother would not have wanted to go if Rosaleen was being taken there against her will?'

'It wasn't like that.'

'I think it was. I think that once again Father has meddled in our lives and this time it has ended in tragedy. Not content with ruining my life and Cecil's too, if it comes to it, he's had to interfere once more.'

The bitterness hung in the air, made all the more apparent by Bernice's measured tones.

'Listen to me, Bernice.' Annie's voice was low and agitated. 'Whatever you think you know, you're wrong.'

'And was I wrong about Thomas Howard?' Bernice's cheeks were flushed, her sharp white nose standing out in contrast. She saw immediately Annie knew what she was referring to. 'My father sent him away by blackmailing him and threatening to force Thomas's mother and brothers and sisters into the workhouse. And then he saw to it I was married off to Rupert.' Her lips came back from her teeth. 'Thomas was ten times, twenty times the man Rupert is but my father in his wisdom decided he wasn't good enough. I'll never forgive him, never.'

'How long have you known?' Annie asked flatly.

'Years.' Bernice smiled a smile which wasn't a smile at all. 'And if you're thinking I've done nothing about it, you're right. Like Cecil I'm weak where my father is concerned. But now I *am* going to speak my mind and nothing on earth can stop me.'

'Your father made a big mistake about you and Thomas, lass. I told him so at the time but he thought he was doing the best for you.' And at Bernice's exclamation of disbelief, Annie added, 'He did, not that that excuses him, but you must believe me, Bernice, this with Rosaleen is different. There's things you don't know, things which made it essential she was got away from Terence Stefford and all his crowd.'

'Annie, you'd swear black was white for my parents. And that's laudable, up to a point.'

'I'm telling you the truth.' Annie's voice was still low but rough-sounding now. 'Terence had got her on drugs.'

Bernice's mouth opened but no sound came forth. After a moment or two, she said incredulously, 'And you believed my father when he said that?'

'All that set are taking 'em. Your da went to see Terence's father when we got back from Scotland, before we knew Rosaleen was . . . was missing, and the upshot of that was Terence was sent off to some clinic or other in Switzerland for a while.'

'I don't believe it.' Bernice thought back to her earlier conversation with Terence Stefford. 'He seemed quite all right this afternoon, perfectly normal.'

'I've just told you, he was sent away to sort himself out. Of course he seems normal now, probably did before, if it comes to it. Rosaleen seemed all right for most of the time.'

'Rosaleen wouldn't take drugs.' Bernice swallowed deeply before she went on, 'It's ludicrous to suggest such a thing. Father wanted to separate her from Terence for his own reasons—'

'And why would he do that?' Annie interrupted. 'Terence isn't like Thomas Howard, lass, surely you can see that? He's well-connected, he'll come into a small fortune as the only child when his mam an' da pop their clogs.'

'Father's never liked him.'

'Aye, I'll give you that, but only because he knew the lad was stringing Rosaleen along, but it wasn't until this latest that he took some action. Ask your mam if you don't believe me. She knows it all. She saw the marks on the lass's arm same as I did. Your da did what had to be done, Bernice. You ought to have seen him when we was up in Scotland and the lass was so bad. In a terrible state he was, blaming himself and all sorts but to my mind it's Terence Stefford who's at fault and your mam to some extent for encouraging the match even when she suspected things weren't right. Your da's got nothing to reproach himself for, nothing. He thought he'd left her well looked after but she slipped out of the house the night we came back here and . . . well, you know the rest. But he's not to blame. That's the honest truth. I wouldn't lie about a thing like this.'

There was a light dawning in Bernice's mind. Slowly, she said, 'I think you would. I think you would do whatever it took to protect my father, Annie.'

Seconds ticked by. It was clear to Bernice that Annie didn't know what to say. For her own part she was trying to take in the enormity of the realisation that had come upon her. It was more shocking, more incredible even than hearing that Rosaleen had been a drug addict, and yet, thinking about it, she supposed it shouldn't be. For years she had wondered why Annie tolerated their mother's cavalier treatment of her; she had put it down to them being the only family Annie had.

She had always felt something of a kinship with Annie, born of the two of them being as plain as pikestaffs with little to commend them. She had often mused that if she had been born into less privileged circumstances she might well have lived her life looking after other folk, especially if the folk in question were childhood friends. *But it wasn't friendship Annie felt for her father.*

Did he know? And then she immediately rejected the idea. Whatever her father's faults – and they were legion – he was, and always had been, devoted to her mother, and his ease with Annie was genuine. He wouldn't be like that if he knew Annie cared for him in *that* way, not with his fierce views on the sanctity of marriage.

Bernice cleared her throat. For the first time since entering the house she was well and truly out of her depth. She loved her mother, but she loved Annie too. It was Annie who had virtually brought her up, after all, and had always displayed more interest in her childhood hopes and fears than anyone else in the family.

She cleared her throat again. 'Are you sure about Rosaleen? About the drugs and Terence being responsible and everything?'

'I'm sure.' Annie raised her chin.

The action was defiant and at odds with the expression in the housekeeper's dark eyes, which reminded Bernice of a small whipped puppy. 'Then I have to believe you,' she said softly. She saw the tense shoulders relax.

'What are you going to do?'

Annie was inquiring about more than Rosaleen. Bernice stared at her. 'Nothing,' she said simply. 'It's none of my business.' And then she added, 'Why stir up a hornet's nest for no good reason? Nothing can bring Rosaleen back or alter what's happened. I'm content for everything to go on as before.'

Annie bowed her head. 'Thank you.'

'I'll go now before Father gets back or Mother comes down.' Bernice walked across the room and out into the hall where Annie fetched her hat and coat. They looked at each other for a moment. 'You could have met someone else, got married, had a family,' Bernice said, a catch in her voice, 'but selfishly I'm glad you didn't. But I'm sorry, Annie, you're worth a hundred of him. I know you won't like me saying it but that's how I feel.'

'I know.' Annie reached out and touched the arm of the tall thin woman in front of her. 'But you don't know him like I do, lass. Daft to say, perhaps, with you being his own flesh and blood, but true nonetheless.'

'All I know is that he did his utmost to ruin my life,' Bernice said in a fierce undertone, before turning abruptly and, her head down, opening the front door and leaving the house.

She walked swiftly down the drive and out onto the wide pavement of Ryhope Road, continuing at the same hurried pace until she slipped on a patch of ice and almost went headlong. The twist she made to save herself caused a sharp pain in her back which caused her to feel sick for a moment. She stood still, holding on to the iron railings bordering a front garden and biting at her lower lip until the pain gradually receded.

The conversation with Annie had brought up all the anguish and pain about Thomas she normally managed to keep under lock and key in the depths of her heart, but mixed with it was an old ache which had been with her since she was a small girl. Why didn't her father love her? Even if she wasn't the pretty, graceful daughter he'd obviously wanted, he should have loved her. He was her *father*.

After a while she brushed the tears from her face and began to walk on in the darkness. And if he couldn't love her, why had he been so cruel as to send away the only man who ever had? She hated him. She would always hate him.

She repeated the refrain over and over in her mind as she picked her way along the frozen pavements. As always, it brought the strength she needed and vanquished the momentary weakness. Never for a second did she allow herself to acknowledge that hate and love are sometimes only a heartbeat apart.

In spite of the treacherous pavements and the snowflakes drifting in the raw wind, Bernice made no attempt to catch a tram home. Rupert had taken to returning from the office earlier and earlier of late, which meant she was forced to endure his company before dinner for longer. Once the meal was over she always retired to her room but he had even attempted to stop her doing that once or twice, engaging her in pointless conversation until she could have screamed. She didn't understand why, after years of a domestic routine which suited them both, he should suddenly change tack, but she didn't like it. No doubt he thought he was being charming but she found his oily compliments about her dress or hair and his empty inquiries about how she had spent her day wearisome. She much preferred the cold silences of the past.

On reaching the attractive stone house set in its own grounds close to Barnes Park, Bernice paused at the beginning of the pebbled drive. The drawing-room lights were on and the curtains were closed, which meant Rupert's car was probably in the garage. No doubt he would be sitting in front of the fire with a glass of whisky in his hand. He usually got through several before dinner. Not that she minded that, he could drink himself to death for all she cared, but since he'd started coming home earlier and therefore drinking more, she'd found alcohol caused him to become tactile and she *did* mind the touch of his hand on her shoulder or arm.

She walked slowly up the drive. She inserted her key in the lock of the front door and entered the house. She had been hoping to slip upstairs without seeing Rupert but, quiet as she had been, he had heard her.

'Hello there.' He appeared at the door of the drawing room, whisky glass in hand. 'You're late, aren't you?'

'Late?' She eyed him coldly. Since that devastating day when she had discovered what she had married, she had found treating him with cool contempt was the best way to handle things.

Now, though, instead of shrugging indifferently and turning away, he said, 'Mrs Todd told me you left the house at three to meet someone in town for afternoon tea.'

'Yes, I did. Then I called at Mother's.'

'Who did you meet? Arabella Palmer I suppose. You're aware the only reason she keeps ringing is because her husband's windy about that new building programme he wants to implement. He's right to be, too. There is no way the council intends to grant him planning permission. Asked you about it, did she? Nice and casual over a cup of tea and cream cake?'

'I did not take tea with Arabella.'

'No?'

'No.' And then, because she did not have the slightest intention of telling him about Terence Stefford, she said, 'If you'll excuse me I want to change before dinner.'

He said nothing as she passed him and began to climb the stairs, but just before she reached the first landing, his voice came from the hall. 'Don't be too long, m'dear. I'll pour you a sherry.'

She paused for just the slightest moment and then carried on to her room, shutting the door behind her and locking it before she sank down on the small couch at the foot of the bed. Sherry? And telling her not to be too long? He played the devoted husband when they had guests, of course, but never without an audience. Mrs Todd he didn't bother about. Their housekeeper was merely a servant and therefore hardly a person, as far as Rupert was concerned.

She took her time over her toilette and when she finally made her way downstairs, she met Mrs Todd in the hall. 'Oh, madam. I was just coming to say dinner will be ready in five minutes.'

'Thank you, Mrs Todd.' Five minutes. She could stand it for five minutes and once they had eaten she would plead a headache.

Rupert looked up as she entered the room, his voice genial as he said, 'There you are. Come and sit by the fire and have your sherry.'

Bernice seated herself in the armchair opposite her husband without speaking. She took a sip of the sherry and then placed the glass back on the side table that Rupert had put by the chair. Her hands folded in her lap, she gazed into the fire, trying to distance herself from both the room and the man in it. Normally she managed this very well, she'd had years of practice after all, but since Rupert had changed his behaviour, letting her mind take her somewhere else had become difficult.

'How is your mother?'

He had allowed a minute or two to elapse and Bernice took another sip of her sherry before she said, 'She was taking an afternoon nap. Annie gave me to understand she'd had another bad night.'

'Only to be expected.' Rupert nodded as though he understood what Emily was feeling. 'The loss of a child, terrible thing. Terrible thing.'

She glanced at him for a moment. 'Yes, I would imagine so,' and then returned her gaze to the glowing fire.

'And of course she would feel it worse than your father. They say mother love is the most powerful force on earth. But at least she has you and Cecil and Daniel. That must be a comfort.'

Bernice did not reply to this. Rupert had little interest in anyone but himself. She didn't think for a second his sympathy was genuine.

'Yes, a powerful force to be sure,' he murmured after a moment or two. 'And one every woman should experience if she is able.'

Bernice stopped breathing. She remained perfectly still for a moment or two and then reached for her glass, keeping her face blank. She didn't look at Rupert although she knew he was watching her intently.

Mrs Todd chose that moment to tap on the drawing-room door and announce dinner was ready. To forestall Rupert taking her arm – as he'd done of recent days – Bernice rose swiftly to her feet and preceded him into the dining room.

Once they were sitting at either end of the long rectangular table, Mrs Todd served the soup and then left the room. Forcing herself to begin the meal as though nothing untoward had been said, Bernice struggled to bring her racing thoughts into order.

Could she have been mistaken? Could Rupert have merely been making an innocent observation about women in general? But no. Preposterous and incredible though it was, she knew it was to her he had been referring. All the last weeks had been leading up to this. Her stomach turned over and her heart beat so hard it threatened to jump out of her chest.

The meal seemed to go on for ever and Bernice knew she did not do justice to Mrs Todd's excellent food. Nevertheless, in an effort to give Rupert no clue as to how she was feeling, she managed to eat a little of everything. After Mrs Todd had brought in the coffee and brandy, Bernice pushed aside her napkin and rose to her feet. 'I'm rather tired,' she said flatly. 'If you'll excuse me . . .'

'Sit down for a minute, would you? I'd like to put something to you.'

She did not sit down. 'Yes?'

'It won't take long.' He waved at the chair behind her.

She sat down and forced herself to look him directly in the face. The full moist lips were smiling and there were crumbs from Mrs Todd's bread and butter pudding in his moustache. 'Well?' she said crisply. 'What is it?'

In spite of her tone the smile didn't falter. 'Although it may not have always seemed like it, I want you to know I have the greatest regard for you, Bernice.'

She raised her eyebrows but said nothing.

'I can see why you would doubt this in view of my little . . . indiscretions—'

'Would you get to the point, Rupert?' she said, her voice level and cool in spite of her churning stomach. 'I presume there *is* a point?'

He straightened in his seat, his chest out and shoulders back as he smoothed what was left of his hair either side of his ears. 'We're both Catholics, that's what I'm getting at, and as such believe marriage is for the procreation of children.'

She stared at him. 'You are joking of course. You only pay lip service to the faith.'

'Not at all.' His voice changed, becoming wheedling. 'Look, Bernice, we've been married over eight years and people expect certain things. It reflects on me, don't you see? People make comments about . . . about my prowess in that department.'

Slowly, she said, 'Who's made comments?'

'Some of the men at the club. I walked in on a conversation where I was the butt of a certain type of humour.'

And he wouldn't have liked that. She stared at him, finding it difficult to believe they were even having this conversation, let alone that he could think she would tolerate him touching her again. 'If you seriously think I would allow what you're suggesting then you must be mad. Your floozies will have to be enough for you.'

'I've stopped all that. I swear it.'

'I don't believe you, Rupert. Not in a hundred years. But even if you had changed your ways, I still wouldn't share your bed.'

'I want a son.' He thrust his head towards her now, his voice no longer cajoling. 'It's my right as a husband, damn it.'

'You have no rights, you forfeited them a long time ago and without a shred of remorse.' Bernice had risen to her feet, her face white but her voice strong. 'I entered this marriage determined to make it work but you lied to me from the beginning. And now, because you suddenly have the notion you would like a child, you think you can persuade me to comply? Think again.'

'I'll get Father McHaffie in. Do you want that? And you know what he would say. It is your duty to fulfil your wifely obligations—'

'*I have no obligations. Not to you.*' Her voice was like the crack of a whip and jerked Rupert out of his chair. He stood glaring at her and his lower jaw worked from one side to the other as she said, 'You get Father McHaffie here by all means but rest assured I shall inform him of our domestic arrangements and why they occurred. I think he would be very interested to know why I left your bed only months after we were wed. And I'd tell him, Rupert. Degrading and humiliating as it is, I would tell him everything. I'd keep nothing back.'

'And I'd tell him those days are over, that I've repented of my wicked ways.' There was a slight sneer on his lips now. 'There's nothing a priest likes more than a soul returning to the fold. You should know that, you listen to enough of his damn sermons every Sunday. Sitting there like a pious nun with your knees tightly together and your hands in your lap. A convent would have suited you down to the ground, you'd have been right at home with the rest of the ugly crows.'

'You really are a most repulsive man.' Her voice was controlled but the expression on her face showed her disgust loud and clear.

'And you're a dried-up stick of a woman. You ought to be down on your knees thanking me for taking you on because no one else would have, I tell you that. Your father saddled me with you and I've not had my money's worth out of the bargain, not by a long chalk. But that can be remedied.'

From somewhere Bernice dredged up the strength to remain straight and cold-faced. Not for the world would she reveal how much his barbs hurt. 'Don't threaten me, Rupert.' She raised her head. 'Not unless you want me to tell a divorce lawyer everything I know. It would make a pretty headline in the papers, don't you think?'

It was an empty threat but she prayed he wouldn't realise it. She just wanted to get away from the sight of him and to the safety of her room; she was inwardly reeling from the savagery of their fight which had erupted so swiftly.

When she turned and left the room, she half expected him to come after her. It wasn't until she was actually in her bedroom and had turned the key in the lock that her trembling increased to the point where her legs gave way. The storm of weeping which followed eased her somewhat but she was still shaking when she got undressed and into her nightdress. She slid under the covers and turned out the bedside lamp, only to lie awake for hours replaying the ugly scene over and over in her mind before finally drifting off into a troubled sleep.

When the hand came across her mouth and nose, cutting off her breath, Bernice thought for a moment she was still in the midst of a nightmare. And then hard fingers clawed at her nightdress and a crushing weight descended and she knew this was real.

'Thought you'd lock me out, didn't you?' Rupert's whisky-soaked breath was in her face. 'But I know the way your narrow little mind works. I thought you wouldn't listen to reason and so I had another key cut to this room a few days ago.'

She tried to struggle but he'd eased the bedclothes back before he had woken her and now he entered her immediately. Her scream of pain and terror was muffled by his hand and her body was pinned by his as he pounded her into the mattress, muttering vile oaths as he did so. It had been so long since she had slept with him that her body felt as if it was being torn in two but it was the horror of her absolute helplessness as she was being defiled that was worse than anything else.

And then he collapsed on her, grunting like a pig for a couple of seconds before rolling to the edge of the bed. 'You asked for that,' he said thickly. 'Treating me like some lackey or other you can dismiss at will. I'm your husband, your *husband*, and don't you forget it. There's going to be changes in this household. You'll give me a son and do your duty as a wife or so help me you'll wish you'd never been born.'

She couldn't move, couldn't speak. She wanted to. She wanted to leap up and tear and scratch at his face but she remained limp and drained of life in the middle of the bed.

And then the shadow that was his bulk stood up and moved across the room, stooping and picking something up from the chair by the door, presumably his dressing gown.

Even when the door had shut behind him and she was

alone again, Bernice couldn't move. It was only when she began to shake uncontrollably with a mixture of shock and cold that she managed to drag herself up from the covers, feeling the stickiness between her legs with revulsion. With her hand pressed tightly over her mouth she staggered to the washbasin set in an alcove. She ripped off her nightdress and began to scrub at her flesh with soap and the little nailbrush. She only stopped when her flesh was red raw but still she felt dirty.

Naked as the day she was born and frozen to the marrow, she stood with her arms wrapped round her waist as the tears came. Swaying back and forth, she moaned softly. If there was a consequence to this night, if she had been impregnated by his seed, she would kill herself. She would, she would.

The tears were dripping from her chin as she made her way to the bed. When she reached it she recoiled sharply as she caught a whiff of the sickly sweet cologne Rupert used. She stood for a moment, fighting nausea, and then groped her way to her wardrobe. She dressed in the dark. It took a long while, she was shivering so violently her stiff fingers made hard work of it, but eventually she was ready. She found her handbag and then walked to the door and opened it silently. The house was quiet. It would be some time before Mrs Todd rose at six o'clock.

In the hall she pulled on her hat and coat and left the house as silently as a mouse. She paused for a moment in the drive. It was still dark but the snow which blanketed everything reflected the light from the street lamps in the road beyond the drive. The air was bitingly cold but there was no wind. The snow beneath her feet was crisp and crackly. And it was clean. For a mad moment she had the urge to smother herself with it, to take great handfuls and rub it over her skin, in her hair, to fill herself with it and take away the ache between her legs.

Instead she continued stumbling on in the silent morning.

Chapter 20

'Bernice?' It was Hope who answered the knock at the door at just gone five o'clock. The habit she'd acquired after the twins were born of sleeping with one ear cocked had never quite left her, and now, with her pregnancy, she found she catnapped on and off all night. Daniel, on the other hand, slept like a log and so did her sister. She'd heard Constance's snores as she'd left the bedroom. She looked in amazement at the tall thin woman in front of her who made no effort to step over the threshold but stood leaning against the wall. Putting out her hand, Hope said, 'Come in, lass, come in. Whatever's brought you here this time of the morning?'

When Bernice still didn't move but continued to stare at her in an odd fashion, Hope physically pulled her into the hall, her voice concerned as she said, 'You're ill. Come into the kitchen and get warm, you must be frozen.'

'I didn't know where else to go.'

It was a whisper, and as they reached the kitchen, Hope let go of Bernice's arm and said, 'Give me your hat and coat and sit down in front of the fire. I'll put the kettle on.' She reached out and touched Bernice's arm again. 'You look awful, lass. Whatever's happened?'

Bernice sank down into one of the armchairs. 'I'm not going back.'

'Back home?'

Bernice inclined her head. 'I could stand it before but not now.'

Knowing something terrible had occurred, Hope drew the other armchair close and sat down, taking Bernice's icy hands in hers. 'Do you want to tell me?' she asked softly.

Again Bernice inclined her head, her eyes holding Hope's as she whispered, 'There . . . there's so much to say.'

'It's just the two of us and whatever it is, whatever's happened, you know I'm for you. Utterly and absolutely.'

Bernice's face quivered. Brokenly, she said, 'I'm so ashamed.'

'Don't be, not with me.' Hope hugged her close for a moment before settling in her own chair again. 'I know we're not related by blood but in every way I consider you my sister.'

Bernice bowed her head. As she began to speak, Hope sat stupefied, unable to believe her ears. Holding tight to her sister-in-law's hands, she murmured unintelligible sounds of comfort but as Bernice's words gathered pace and came tumbling out in no real order of events, Hope knew she must not interrupt the flow. Daniel's sister had held all this in too long and she needed to tell someone. The horror of the last few hours was only part of her suffering.

By the time Bernice had finished, both women were weeping and Bernice was again trembling from head to foot. The immense pity Hope felt for her was only matched by the rage burning inside her chest for Rupert and to a lesser extent Abe. It was clear Bernice's husband was twisted and warped, a pervert who relied on the unnatural to bring him pleasure, but if Abe hadn't interfered in her life, if he'd let Bernice have her Thomas, none of this would have happened.

Hope gently helped Bernice off with her outdoor things and gave her her own slippers to put on – her feet were soaked through and blue with cold from trudging through the snow and ice. Then she made a cup of tea. It was only when Bernice had drunk a cup laced with a measure of brandy from the bottle Abe had given Daniel at Christmas that Hope said quietly, 'Do you need to see a doctor?'

Bernice shook her head. 'I couldn't bear it. Anyway, what good would it do? Rupert is my husband. It's not as if I was attacked by a stranger.'

'But you don't intend to let him get away with this?'

Bernice shuddered, shaking her head as the tears seeped from her eyes. 'I want a divorce, I want to be free of him but how can I? Apart from the Church and Father McHaffie, my parents would never allow the scandal.'

'He raped you, Bernice. Not only that but you've endured years of misery after you found out about his adultery, and before that pain and degradation from the day you wed. He's abnormal and depraved and your parents must be told exactly how it was, the priest too.'

Bernice bowed her head. 'I couldn't, I couldn't, Hope.'

'You can and you must.' Hope put her arms round her, her voice soft as she said, 'I'll come with you if you like, I'll stay with you.'

'Would . . . would you tell him first?' Bernice looked at her, her face pitiful. 'Prepare him for when I see him?'

It was her father's reaction she was really worried about. As Hope stared at her sister-in-law her fury at Abe went up a notch. 'I'll do anything you want.'

'He'll blame me, they all will.'

'Not if I have anything to do with it,' Hope said grimly. There could well be blame slung about in all of this but she would see to it it reached the shoulders of those who were really responsible.

By the time Hope heard the others stirring, Bernice had eaten two slices of toast with another cup of tea and was dozing in the armchair in front of the fire. Once her sister-in-law had closed her eyes, Hope chewed over what they were going to do. Bernice wouldn't want to go to her parents' home and although she got on with Cecil and Gwendoline she wasn't particularly close to her brother or his wife. She would need someone to talk to over the next days and weeks, particularly if things got nasty as they were almost bound to do. She needed family. But if she stayed here, where on earth were they going to put her? There were going to be two babies joining the household in the very near future. It was going to be bedlam. But here was where she must stay and the front room was the only place left.

Daniel was the first down and as he walked into the kitchen his eyes opened wide at the sight of Bernice asleep in the armchair. Hope put her finger to her lips and motioned for him to go into the hall where she joined him, shutting the kitchen door carefully behind her.

'I heard her knocking about five,' she whispered, pulling him into the front room and again shutting the door. 'And prepare yourself, you won't like what I'm going to tell you. Things with Rupert were far worse than ever we suspected.

From the day they were wed he demanded unnatural things, horrible things, Daniel, and then a few months later she returned home unexpectedly and caught him with two prostitutes he'd brought to the house. After that they didn't sleep together again but then last night . . .'

'What?' Daniel's face was white. 'What did he do?'

'He told her at dinner he wanted a child, that she had to give him one. She refused. In the middle of the night he came to her room when she was asleep and . . .' Hope bit her lip, the look on Daniel's face was paining her, 'he forced her. He raped her, Daniel.'

'He . . .' It was clear Daniel could hardly take it in. Then, his face changing, he said, 'I'll kill him. The filthy swine, I'll kill him.'

'No, no.' She tried to hang on to him but he pushed into the hall and snatched his coat and hat from the pegs on the wall, disentangling her hands from him once again and opening the front door. 'Please, Daniel, don't do this.' She tried one more time. 'Wait a while. Let Cecil and your da come with you.' She hadn't expected he would fly off the handle like this. Perhaps she should have, she thought feverishly, but this was so unlike the calm, steady man she knew.

'They can do what they want but he's had this coming a long time and I'm not waiting, Hope.'

'This won't help anything, it'll make things worse.'

He wasn't listening and she stood on the doorstep, her dressing gown pulled over her swollen stomach, and watched him run down the frozen street as fast as the icy pavements allowed.

'What on earth is going on?' Constance appeared at the

top of the stairs, rubbing her eyes, Jack and Betsy behind her, just as Bernice opened the kitchen door.

Hope looked at them all. 'Bernice is staying for a bit, she's had an argument with Rupert and Daniel's gone to see him.'

'He's what?' Bernice put her hands over her mouth. 'Oh, Hope, you shouldn't have let him.'

'Believe me, I couldn't stop him.'

The children came scurrying down the stairs, Betsy making straight for her aunty, and as Hope watched Bernice bend and lift the little girl into her arms, it was all the confirmation she needed that Bernice had to stay with them. She just hoped Daniel didn't do anything silly, she thought distractedly. He wasn't a violent man, her Daniel, but the state he'd been in . . .

Coming swiftly to a decision, she said, 'I'm going to get dressed and pop to the post office to phone your father, Bernice. I don't like Daniel going to see Rupert alone.'

Bernice nodded. And then Betsy put her chubby little hands either side of her aunt's face and said, 'Your nose is red, Aunty Bernice, like mine goes when I've been crying.'

'I've a cold, that's all, darling,' Bernice said, hugging the child to her. 'Now, let's see about getting you dressed and then I'll get some breakfast for when Mam comes back from the post office.'

'I can dress myself.' Jack looked askance at his twin. 'But she *still* needs Mam to do her buttons.'

Constance followed Hope into her bedroom while Bernice supervised the twins. 'Big argument, was it?' she whispered.

'Big enough.' Hope divested herself of her dressing gown and nightdress and began to pull her clothes on. 'They haven't been getting on for some time.'

Constance nodded, then said, 'Still, being Catholics they have to make a go of it, don't they?'

'That's up to them.' She wasn't going to discuss Bernice's private affairs with Constance. It was up to her sister-in-law what she told folk.

'At least he cared enough about her to marry her.'

This was a theme Hope heard in one way or another a hundred times a day but this morning she hadn't the patience or the inclination to jolly Constance along. Reaching for her thick woollen dress with its full gathers under the bustline, she said abruptly, 'I have to go, Constance, but would you help Bernice with the twins please.'

Constance stared at her for a moment. Then she turned on her heel, leaving the room in what she fondly thought was a flounce. The effect was spoilt somewhat by her enormous stomach which made the flounce more of a duck waddle. Hope sighed. Constance had become more and more demanding as time went on; she just hoped her sister settled into motherhood when the baby was born. But she hadn't the time to worry about that now.

Hope left the house some minutes later. The air was so cold it made her gasp. She warned herself to tread carefully, the pavements were like glass and all she needed now was to break a leg or, worse, hurt the baby.

By the time she reached the post office it was half past eight and they were just opening. There was a small queue of people before her but none of them wanted to use the telephone situated in a small alcove away from the main counter. After getting a friendly postmistress to show her how to use the machine, Hope dialled the office number, knowing Abe would have left the house an hour or so before. Almost immediately Abe's voice barked down the line. He sounded so near, Hope almost dropped the receiver.

'It's Hope.' She kept her voice low although no one was near.

'Hope? What the dickens . . .'

She could imagine his face stretching. She would be the last person in the world he would expect to hear from. Cecil and Bernice had a telephone in each of their houses but she and Daniel could never aspire to such luxury. 'I'm telephoning from the post office,' she said quickly. 'Daniel has gone to see Rupert and I think he's going to fight him.'

'Fight him? Why on earth would Daniel want to fight Rupert? Have you lost your mind, girl?'

'*Listen to me please.*' It wasn't the tone in which to speak to your father-in-law but Hope didn't care. 'Bernice is with us, she arrived early this morning in a terrible state.' She glanced about her, then said quietly, 'Rupert attacked her last night.'

'*Attacked* her?'

When was he going to stop repeating everything she said? 'Aye, attacked her. He broke into her room in the middle of the night and . . .' she couldn't say rape, not here, 'and he forced her.'

There was silence, and then he bawled, 'Nonsense! I don't believe a word of it! The woman's clearly deranged. Rupert wouldn't—'

'*Rupert would.*' Hope wished she could shout back but she contented herself with fairly hissing, 'The wonderful councillor you foisted on your daughter is a sexual pervert of the worst kind. He put Bernice through hell on earth after they were married but then she found him with two prostitutes

271

he'd brought to the house one day and after that they had separate rooms. Now he's suddenly decided he wants a family and when Bernice refused, he . . . forced her.'

The silence lasted longer this time. Hope took the opportunity to glance about her again but everyone was seeing to their own business and the racket two little toddlers were making was deafening anyway. Hope watched as their harassed mother boxed both sets of ears, which didn't help the noise level one iota.

'You say Daniel's gone to the house?'

It didn't sound like Abe's voice. Remembering that it was only a few days since they had buried Rosaleen, Hope said more softly, 'Aye, he has, and I'm worried. He was so angry, beside himself. I don't know what he'll do.'

'I'll take Cecil and we'll go straight there.' This was more the decisive Abe she was used to, the broken sound in his voice before had unnerved her. 'You go back home, lass, and go careful while you're about it. It's treacherous underfoot.'

There was a click and then a buzzing in her ear. Hope stared at the receiver before replacing it slowly on its receptacle. Suddenly she felt all trembly.

It was over two hours later when Abe brought Daniel home. Cecil was no longer with them. Hope had been beside herself with worry and when the two men walked through the door, it took all her strength not to break down with tears of relief. Instead she said, 'Sit down. I've just made a pot of tea.'

They sat, both of them, like children being told what to do by their mother. It was Abe who spoke first. 'Where's Bernice?'

'She's sleeping in our bed.' Hope looked at Daniel as she

spoke. 'And Constance is lying down because she's had pains, and the twins are with Mrs McGuigan two doors down. Their cat's had kittens.' She didn't know why she added that last bit, it sounded silly, but she wanted to introduce some normality to take the awful look from their grim faces. 'How did you get on?' And then she caught sight of Daniel's bloodied knuckles and, her hand going to her mouth, she whispered, 'Oh, Daniel.'

'It's all right, it's all right.' He held out his arms and she went into them like a homing pigeon. 'I left him alive if that's what you're worried about although if Da and Cecil hadn't turned up it might have been a different story.'

Hope was now sitting on Daniel's knee and as her gaze went to her father-in-law, he answered the consternation in her eyes by saying, 'He saved me the job of beating him to a pulp, lass, an' that's the truth but I'm not having any of us sent down the line for murder, even if he deserves it.'

'But what if he goes to the police?'

'He won't,' Abe said grimly. Hope felt a little shiver down her spine, her thoughts immediately going to the Mullen brothers, but then he continued, 'He won't want it all getting out, take it from me. It'd be the end of him. There's plenty of good-living citizens in high places and Rupert likes to think of them as his friends, but a whiff of what he's been up to and he knows every one of 'em would cut him dead. No, he'll do what he's told. He'll give Bernice her divorce on whatever grounds she decides she wants and financially he'll pay through the nose. And he'll leave the town for good an' all.'

'Did he say that?' Hope turned to Daniel. 'Did he promise?'

'Aye, and a lot more besides. Our esteemed councillor wasn't such the big man this morning.'

Hope laid her face against his for a moment before standing up and walking over to the range where she took the big black teapot off the hot steel shelf. She brought it to the table and poured them all a cup of tea and then sat in a chair by Daniel's side, facing Abe. She wondered if he would bring up how she had spoken to him. She didn't regret it but she wondered now how she had dared.

Whether he would have or not she was never to know because the next moment a rustling sound brought their heads swinging to the doorway of the kitchen. 'I heard voices.' Bernice's cheeks were flaming and Hope knew what it had cost her reserved sister-in-law to face her father. Before Bernice had gone to lie down Hope had told her over and over again that there was no shame attached to her, that it was Rupert who should be feeling ashamed and self-abased but Bernice couldn't see it that way. And Hope could understand it. All Bernice had had over the last years was her dignity and fierce self-possession which she had used as a shield against most of the world. Rupert's barbarism had stripped even that from her.

'Oh, lass.' Abe's Adam's apple moved up and down as he swallowed. 'I'd like to see the blighter swing, I would straight. I trusted him with me little girl and this is what he does. I never knew, lass. Never in a million years.'

Bernice didn't move, she could have been turned to stone.

Abe stood up, his swallow audible to all of them. 'He'll pay for it, lass. I swear I'll make the scum pay in a hundred different ways.'

'Da.'

It was a small sound but enough for Abe to cover the distance between them in one bound. As Bernice broke into a storm of weeping, he cradled her to him, his tenderness such that Hope and Daniel felt they were intruding. Abe gently lifted his daughter into his arms as though she was the little girl he'd spoken of and carried her over to one of the armchairs where he sat with her held close. Hope and Daniel quickly left the room, both their faces wet.

Let it be a new beginning. Hope found she was praying as she followed Daniel up the stairs to their room. Let some good come out of this horrific thing.

Daniel sank down onto the bed, wincing as he did so. 'You're hurt?' Hope sat beside him, lifting one of his bruised hands and kissing it gently.

'He managed to get in a few punches,' Daniel admitted wryly.

'You shouldn't have gone like that.' He put his arm round her and she leant her head on his shoulder. 'I was so frightened.'

'You? Frightened?' Gently he turned her face to meet his. 'I don't believe it for a moment. You don't know what fear is.'

Oh yes she did. She had been experiencing it more and more of late when the change in him became more noticeable. She put her arms round him, holding him as close as her stomach would allow. 'I love you,' she said fiercely, speaking against the intangible something that was forcing them further and further apart. 'I love you so much.'

'And I love you.'

'I want—'

'What?'

'I want it to be like when we were first married.'

'You can't go back in time, Hope. We've got children now, responsibilities.'

She wasn't talking about those sorts of things and she was sure he knew that. But before she could say more, they both heard Constance cry out her name.

'The baby.' Hope stared at him. 'Oh no, not today. Not now. Please don't let it be that.'

But when she entered the other bedroom a few moments later and saw Constance half standing, half crouching, saying, 'My waters have broken, get some towels quick,' she knew that prayer at least was not going to be answered.

Constance's baby was born just before nine o'clock the following morning after a difficult and exhausting labour. It was a girl and she was a big baby, plump and bonny with a pair of lungs to match her size. Constance displayed no interest in her child after Hope and Beattie Lee, the midwife, had helped her wash and changed the bed linen, even going so far as to start crying and shouting for Beattie to take the baby away when the midwife tried to persuade the new mother to feed her little one.

'She'll come round after she's had a bit of a sleep,' Beattie assured Hope as she saw the midwife out. Beattie stroked the downy head of the baby in Hope's arms. 'Give this one a pap bottle with some boiled sweetened water for now.'

When Beattie had left, Hope took the baby through to the kitchen. Daniel had left for work some time before and now there was just Bernice and the twins sitting at the table, the children busy colouring their picture books, Betsy sitting on her aunt's lap as she scribbled.

The two women smiled at each other. Constance had become distressed every time Hope had tried to leave the bedroom and so the running of the household and care of the twins had fallen on Bernice's shoulders, but in spite of her recent trauma, Bernice had responded magnificently. In fact Hope thought looking after everyone had helped in some way because Bernice was definitely more her old self this morning.

'You look worn out.' Bernice stood up and took the sleeping baby from Hope. She placed her in one of the twins' old cribs which Daniel had got down from the roof before he'd left that morning. 'If you're not careful we'll have another new arrival.'

'Don't say that.' Hope smiled wearily. 'One is more than enough for now. Did you get any sleep?'

'Enough.' Bernice had spent the night dozing in one of the armchairs. When Abe had left the day before, she had told Hope and Daniel that she had agreed to go back to her parents' home for a while. 'Annie's got her work cut out looking after Mother at the moment,' she'd told them, 'and I can help there.' When Hope had protested, she'd added gently, 'There's no room here and kind as it was to suggest I take over the front room, you have your business to run. Besides which . . .' She had paused for a moment and then, smiling a tearful smile, said, 'Da wants me to stay with them.'

Hope had said nothing more after that.

Constance slept the rest of the morning and when Hope saw to the fire burning in the small black-leaded grate, she was careful not to wake her. When she had taken up a light lunch for her sister and made sure the bedroom was as warm as toast, though, she and Bernice brought the crib and Constance's daughter into the room.

'I don't want it in here.' Constance's expression changed

as she glanced at the baby in Hope's arms. 'Keep it downstairs.'

'She needs feeding, Constance,' said Hope quietly.

'So feed it yourself. Give it a bottle.'

'She needs her mother. Hold her for a while.'

'I'm not feeding it and I don't want to hold it.'

Hope glanced at Bernice and as her sister-in-law left the room, she sat down on the end of Constance's bed, still with the baby in her arms. 'Your baby is a she, Constance, not an it. A bonny little lassie. At least acknowledge that.'

'All right she's a girl. Satisfied?'

'Look, I know the birth was awful but if you'd just hold her and see how bonny she is—'

'For the last time, I don't want her in here and it's nowt to do with the birth. I don't like bairns, I never have. I only carried on with it because I thought Lonnie would change his mind about marrying me if I was expecting, otherwise I'd have gone to Gertie Price in the East End and took my chance even though I was scared to death. I thought his mam would help me change his mind, she always liked me, Lonnie's mam, but she wouldn't lift a finger except to give me the stuff that had me on the privy for days. But it was too late by then. I saw Gertie just before Lonnie threw me out and she said she didn't dare do it with me so far gone. That's what did for the girl I knew, apparently, having it done too late.'

Hope sat staring at her sister. This was her own flesh and blood and yet she didn't know her. Never in a hundred years would she have expected to hear what was coming out of Constance's mouth. As her niece stirred in her arms, Hope glanced down at the small sweet face and suddenly she was angry. 'This isn't about you, Constance.' She glared at her sister and thrust the baby onto her lap. The small arms flailed and then the baby began to cry lustily. 'You know as well as I do she'll need your milk and if you think everyone else is going to feed her and clean her, think again. I've got more than enough to do as it is.'

'Bernice can do it.' Constance looked at her sulkily. 'She likes bairns, look how she is with your two.'

'Bernice is going to her parents later on today, she won't be around.'

'I'm ill.'

'You're not ill. You're tired, aye, but you're not ill. You've had a baby, that's all. Thousands and thousands of women have babies in much worse conditions than you and they get on with things.'

'You're hard, our Hope.' Constance began to cry, fat tears rolling down her cheeks. 'And it's all right for you. You've got Daniel and this house and a good going-on. What about me? What's everyone going to say when they know I've had a bairn an' I'm not wed?' And then she glanced down at the child whose cries were even louder. 'Can't you shut her up?'

'She's hungry.' Her voice softer, Hope leant towards Constance and picked up the baby again. 'Feed her and I'll keep her downstairs for a day or two until you're feeling better. I'll put the crib back in the kitchen. How about that?'

Constance wiped her wet face with the back of her hand, sniffing loudly. 'I just have to feed her?'

'For now, aye. But she'll have to sleep in here at night.'

There was a long pause and then Constance opened the buttons of her nightdress, holding out her arms for the child. The tiny mouth fastened onto Constance's nipple without hesitation but Constance still continued to look down at her with something like distaste on her face.

'What are you going to call her?' Hope asked gently after a few moments.

Constance shrugged. 'I don't care.'

'Our mother's second name was Alice.' Betsy had been their mother's first name.

Constance shrugged again. 'Call her that if you want.'

'Alice Constance then.' Hope said nothing more until Constance handed the baby back to her. Then she smiled at her sister. 'Your milk will probably come in tomorrow or the next day. You'll feel better then.'

'Oh, Hope.' Constance's tone implied Hope was foolish to imagine she would change her mind about the child.

When Hope returned to the kitchen, Bernice raised her eyebrows inquiringly. 'She fed her.' Hope paused. 'On the condition the crib comes back down here for now.'

'I see.' Bernice nodded. 'I'll fetch it down.' And then she turned at the kitchen door, her voice low as she said, 'The world is definitely divided into those who take and those who give. I know Constance is your sister and you love her but be careful, Hope.'

Much later that night, in the privacy of their bed, Hope repeated Bernice's words to Daniel.

'She's right.' Daniel was lying so his body didn't touch hers, his eyes wide open in the darkness. It had been over a month since he had made love to her and when she had shyly made overtures to him a few days before, he had used the excuse that he was worried he'd hurt the baby. But it wasn't that. And it wasn't that he didn't find her attractive, he wanted her so much some nights he was as hard as a rock for hours and unable to sleep, even though he pretended to be fast off. He couldn't really put a name to what was stopping him except it was all tied up with him keeping his mouth shut about what he knew went on with his da and Cecil and the business. Which didn't make sense . . .

'Perhaps she'll grow to love Alice.'

He didn't want to quench the hope in her voice and so he said, 'Aye, perhaps.'

'When she's feeding her and holding her maybe. I mean, how could you not? And she's such a bonny little lassie and twice the size the twins were. It'll seem strange if this one is as big as Alice after Jack and Betsy.'

As Hope talked on, Daniel made all the appropriate noises at the right places but his mind was elsewhere. Now he'd had time to reflect, he wasn't proud of the events of the previous morning. Not that Rupert Hogarth didn't deserve the beating he'd given him, he did, and much worse. The man was scum, filth. And even if all this other wasn't constantly playing through in his head, he would probably have done exactly the same.

But that was the point – *he* knew his motive for giving his brother-in-law a hiding wasn't all to do with the way Rupert had treated Bernice. He'd tried to fool himself it was, but he wasn't going to start being a hypocrite on top of everything else. He had wanted to show Hope he was outraged, that he wasn't afraid of Rupert or any repercussions that might arise, that he was a man, in fact. The bile of self-disgust was acidic in his mouth. He'd wanted to prove he wasn't the weakling he knew himself to be.

'. . . where her Thomas has gone?'

'What?' He became aware Hope was waiting for an answer to a question he hadn't heard.

'I said do you think there might be someone who would know where Bernice's Thomas has gone? All we know is that his surname was Howard and that he moved away from Sunderland some time in nineteen twenty-nine.'

'Why would you want to know where he is?' Daniel asked flatly. 'No doubt the man is married by now with a wife and umpteen bairns.'

'He might not be.'

'Even if he's not, Bernice is still a married woman, Hope.'

'For the moment.'

Daniel moved slightly, shifting his position so that he could just see the white blur of her face in the darkness. 'Don't interfere in her life, Hope,' he said stiffly. 'She's had enough people doing that.'

There followed a silence, a hurt silence. One which Daniel made no attempt to break. He could hear Alice beginning to whimper in the other bedroom and then the creak of Constance's bed. She must have reached for Alice before the baby woke the twins. The four people in that room along with Hope and the child in her belly, his child, represented his world. They were stomachs to feed, bodies to clothe, feet to shod. They were what kept him working for his father and enduring the scorn in Cecil's eyes every time his brother glanced his way, and more and more they were beginning to feel like the tentacles of a giant squid snaking about him and holding him tight. He loathed himself for thinking this way but he couldn't help it, damn it.

'Goodnight.' He felt Hope's lips brush his cheek and then she turned on her side away from him as he muttered a reply.

He continued to lie still and tense as the minutes ticked by and eventually her steady, even breathing told him she was asleep. It was only then he let his limbs relax, stealthily putting his hands beneath his head. He continued to lie on his back in the darkness, staring blankly up at the ceiling.

Chapter 21

All through the first quarter of the year the newspapers were full of the rumblings of Adolf Hitler's doings; Britain's rapid rearmament programme and some cities carrying out mock wartime 'black-out' exercises did nothing to reassure the nervous. Normally Hope managed to shrug away the rumours of a second world war, she'd think about it if and when it actually happened, but by the time her third child was born at the end of March, she was as worried as the next citizen. Daniel and Abe and most of the men thereabouts were sure confrontation with the Nazis had to happen, and the thought of the menfolk in the family being called up to fight and her children being put in danger filled Hope with dread.

Considering how disturbed she had been in the latter half of her pregnancy, it was amazing how happy and placid her new daughter was. The birth had been quick and easy and although Grace Rosaleen hadn't weighed in as heavy as Constance's baby, she was a decent size and fed well. By the time the long-awaited summer arrived in a blaze of sunshine at the beginning of June, Hope had got stuck into her little business again and it was thriving. She had roped a reluctant Constance in to help her after making it clear to her sister a few weeks after Grace was born that Constance had to pull her weight in the household. She had discovered to her consternation that left to her own devices Constance would happily lie in bed all day, pleading one ailment after another. She had given Constance the benefit of the doubt at first, but after Grace was born and Hope found herself coping with two babies most of the time as well as the twins, she decided enough was enough. The ensuing row and Constance's resulting sulkiness didn't make for the best of working relationships but Hope was past caring.

Now it was the middle of a hot and sticky July and Hope was enjoying bumper sales of her ice cream. As she trudged the last few yards down the dusty back lane and opened the wooden gate leading into their little backyard, she was gasping for a long drink of cold water. She'd been out since midday and it was now getting on for five thirty, but she'd expressed enough breast milk to fill a pap bottle for Grace's feed while she was gone.

As Hope pushed the barrel into its place against the wall and squeezed past the rabbit hutch, she could hear both babies crying in the house. She frowned to herself. The last time this had happened she had found her sister taking a nap upstairs and Jack and Betsy in charge of the infants. Constance's defence that she had a headache just hadn't been good enough and for the first time for a long while Hope had lost her temper. After screaming at her sister that she was endangering the life of her own child as well as hers, she had pulled Constance out of bed and thrust her down the stairs to see to Alice. They had hardly spoken for a week after that.

Taking a deep breath in preparation for she knew not what, Hope opened the back door and walked into the house.

When Daniel entered the house at six o'clock he didn't immediately sense something was wrong. Jack and Betsy were feeding the rabbit in the backyard, Alice was fast asleep in her crib and Hope was nursing Grace at her breast where she sat in one of the armchairs.

'Heard the news?' he said, dropping a perfunctory kiss on the top of Hope's head before sitting down at the kitchen table and holding up the newspaper for her to see the headline. 'The government's ordered one thousand Spitfires. Now you can't tell me they're not expecting a war pretty soon.'

'Constance has gone.'

'Gone?' He lowered the paper. Hope's voice was strange. 'Gone where?'

'I don't know. She left us a note.' Hope nodded at a piece of paper propped against the milk jug and as Daniel reached for it, she added, 'Jack said she left as soon as I was gone at lunchtime so the twins were left here all alone with the babies. Alice and Grace were screaming their heads off when I walked in and the twins were at their wits' end, poor little mites. Anything could have happened, anything. I can't believe she was so irresponsible. The twins are practically babies themselves.'

Daniel took his eyes from his wife's face and glanced at the note in his hands. Constance's scrawl began abruptly with the words:

I'm sorry but I can't take any more. You know as well as I do I'm not cut out to be a mother, I hate everything about it, besides which I keep thinking of what Lonnie said about an accident on a dark night. You don't know him like I do and, believe me, it was no idle threat. I have to get away. I'm going to find work down south and I'll send money for Alice's keep, I promise. Try not to think too badly of me.

love, Constance.

P.S. I've took what I need for my train ticket and somewhere to stay for a bit from the month's takings. I've earned it.

'She cleared the tin.' Hope was referring to the somewhat battered Fry's biscuit tin on the kitchen mantelshelf where she kept the money from the business before banking it at the end of each month. And then she shook her head as Daniel raised his gaze from the note. 'Not that that matters, not a bit, but to leave Alice.' She glanced down at Grace nestled in her arms. 'How could she, Daniel? I just don't understand it.'

He did. He had noticed more than once that in spite of Constance's tears and sulks and manner, which bordered on the babyish at times, Hope's sister had a streak of pure granite running through her. She was a strange mixture, was Constance. The fact that she had played the whore for Kirby and then had a baby out of wedlock had left no real mark on her apart from a superficial shame which had evaporated in time. Perhaps it was best it had. Perhaps it didn't do to think too much. He was sending himself round the bend doing just that. Realising Hope was waiting for a response, he said, 'How will you cope, in the day, I mean? With the best will in the world I can't see you managing to carry on with the ice cream and toffee apples with four children under five to see to.'

She did not reply immediately but looked straight into his eyes, and her look made Daniel drop his gaze after a moment. He pretended to read through Constance's letter again. It was on the tip of his tongue to say, 'Aye, all right, I don't like you working in spite of it having got us out of the mire more than once,' but to do so would mean they would have to talk, really talk, and he wasn't about to open that can of worms. And what could he say anyway? I didn't expect it to mushroom like it has. You're earning too much now and that bank account is another wedge between us, giving you an independence you don't seem aware of at the moment but which one day will make you realise you don't really need me. I'm scared to death of losing you half the time and yet all I do is push you away.

She would think he was barmy and she would be right.

'I am aware I'll need to rethink things.' Hope's voice was stiff. 'But if you're asking if I'm prepared to see all the hard work of the last two years go down the drain, the answer is no, I'm not.'

She stood up and placed Grace in her crib. Her voice had changed when she said, 'There's an obvious solution to this, Daniel. We could run the business together. I've been meaning to put this to you for some time. It could work, I know it could. Even when Constance was here I couldn't keep up with the demand, and if we did it together, we could sell so much more. It would be ours, yours and mine.'

He stared at her. 'That's not an option.'

'Why? Why isn't it?'

'You started this business, it's yours.'

'Of course it's not. I did it for us, for us and the bairns. Everything I earn is for us all, like the money you earn at your job.'

'Oh, so you *have* remembered I have a job then?'

'Don't be like this.'

'I have a job and it's secure, Hope. This other,' he moved his hand in a manner that could have been termed scornful, 'could fold any moment.'

'No it couldn't.' She eyed him hotly. 'It's going from strength to strength and you know it.'

'I'm sorry, Hope, but I'm not prepared to risk our home on a whim and that is what it would boil down to if we couldn't pay the mortgage.'

'This isn't a whim. Listen to me, *please*. Just hear me out before you make a decision. I could easily sell ten times, twenty times the amount of ice cream I make, and that's just round the streets. I'm so limited here, what with the ice and time, everything, but if we moved to a bigger place, shop premises perhaps with living accommodation above, I could do so much more. We could still sell round the doors but the shop could have an area where people could sit down and eat if they didn't want to take their ice cream away. I could make sundaes and Knickerbocker Glories, things like that. I've built a good reputation over the last two years, Daniel. People like me and they like what I sell.'

She had it all worked out. This was no sudden notion. Daniel looked into the beautiful face staring at him so passionately and the feeling that she was slipping away from him, *had* slipped away, was strong. And it was his own fault. The old Hope, the Hope he had married would have shared this idea with him the minute she had thought of it.

And if she had, what would he have said? In answer to the accusing voice in his head, he said, 'There's a war coming, Hope. Everyone knows it. The only question is how soon. Ice cream won't matter if the world's turned upside down.'

'People will still want to eat.'

'Eat, aye, but not fancy ice cream and sweets.'

'So that's your answer?'

They stared at each other and then Daniel said quietly, 'We know that whatever happens, my job is secure as long as I'm working for my father.'

'Your father!'

'What's that supposed to mean?'

'He's always there, isn't he, in the background?'

'He's my father, Hope. Of course he's part of our lives.'

'I don't mean that and you know it. If he was just part of our life, like Aunt Jinny or Bernice or even Annie, it would be fine. But it's different with your da, it always has been. He . . .' she paused for an infinitesimal moment before taking a breath and saying steadily, 'He controls us. He controls *you.*'

So it had come out into the open at last. Daniel despised himself that it was Hope who had brought it out. Keeping a check on his voice, he said, 'I work for him, Hope. That's all.'

'That's not all.' She was twisting her hands as she spoke but still the words came. 'And I know in the past it would have been difficult for you to find a job, I understand that, but that's only part of the reason you don't want to rock the boat. You don't want to walk away from *him*, none of you do. Even after what he did to Bernice, she was still desperate for his approval, his love. I don't understand you all. I don't see why he's got such a hold on his children. It's like you're all scared to disappoint him by disagreeing with him, and it's not healthy. When we found out the truth from Lonnie Kirby and I wanted you to leave, you chose not to say anything to him because at bottom you knew I'd stay and love you whatever you did and that was better than incurring his displeasure like you did when we got married.'

'You think I consciously chose to put him before you?' Daniel asked incredulously.

'Yes. No. Oh, I don't know. I'm not saying this very well. All I know is Jack is following in your and Cecil and Bernice's footsteps. He worships your da, there's no one like him. And . . . and I don't think your da is the best person for our son to hero worship.'

'Now you're being ridiculous. Jack is only four and a half, of course he loves his granda and if you think I'm going to stop him seeing him, think again.'

'Of course I don't, I didn't say that, did I? And you might not believe this but I do actually like your da, it's impossible not to and—'

'You're right, I don't believe it.'

She moved impatiently. 'Now you're just trying to pick an argument to avoid what I'm really saying.'

He stared at her, perturbed in his mind that she could read him so easily when he didn't have a clue what made her tick. And all this because of Constance going. He could wring her flighty little neck.

'We could move from this house and work together, start again.' She took a step towards him, her voice soft now. 'We could try, couldn't we? It would be a family business. Later the bairns could come in with us when they left school if they wanted to.'

The risk was too great. They could lose everything, he'd seen it happen in business more than once since the Depression took hold. She didn't understand how it was. She was looking at this with rose-coloured glasses. 'We're already part of a family business,' he said flatly.

She turned from him and went to the kitchen window, and with her back to him, she said, 'No, Daniel. You are.'

'Me. Us. It's all the same, isn't it? We're man and wife.'

She swung round and looked at him in silence for some moments and then, as Betsy appeared in the scullery doorway saying please could Mam come and help because the rabbit had bit Jack on the finger when he had tried to put him back in the hutch, Hope took her daughter's hand and left the kitchen.

It was the next day and Hope and her Aunt Jinny were sitting in the kitchen drinking a glass of Hope's homemade lemonade, or at least Jinny was. Hope had been up and down answering the door to customers three times in as many minutes, and as she returned once again from the front room, Jinny said, 'It's no wonder you're as thin as a lath, lass. Your backside hasn't kissed that seat for more than ten seconds since I've been here. If it isn't one of the bairns it's someone at the door.'

Hope smiled although in truth she felt more like weeping. She hadn't slept all night and she suspected Daniel hadn't either although both of them had lain still and stiff, with their backs to each other, through the long hours of darkness.

And then Jinny asked the same question Daniel had put to her the evening before. 'How are you going to keep on

292

with the ice cream an' all with the bairns to see to and a house to run?'

'I'll manage, Aunt Jinny.'

'Aye, there's many said that who've ended up in the loony bin.' Jinny shook her head, glancing at Alice who was sitting chewing on a crust of bread in one half of the double-seated wooden high chair Daniel had cobbled together for the twins when they were babies. 'And that poor little mite, abandoned by her mam without so much as a by your leave. Wicked, I call it. An' I dare bet you won't see a penny for her keep, whatever Constance says.'

'Probably not. It doesn't matter anyway. She'll be brought up as our own until the day Constance wants her back.'

'I wouldn't hold your breath for that, hinny. You've got the bairn for good, take it from me. And I have to say she's a darn sight better off with you than Constance, that's for sure. As if it wasn't enough you had twins the first time round, it looks like history's repeated itself, so to speak.'

'It's easier than that, Aunt Jinny. At least Alice is that bit older than Grace and can sit up now.'

'I suppose we ought to be thankful Constance waited long enough to wean the bairn afore she skedaddled,' Jinny said grimly. 'I'm surprised she didn't expect you to have one either side like you did with the twins.'

'Well, if I'd had to, I would have.'

'Aye, I know that.' Jinny reached across and touched Hope's face with the side of her hand in a very rare gesture of affection. 'You've always been a canny lass. How two sisters from the same mam an' da could be so different beats me.'

Hope smiled but said nothing. The row with Daniel followed by a sleepless night had left her feeling raw and tired, and much as she loved her aunty, she wished she hadn't called in today on her way home from work. Daniel would be back soon and although she'd said nothing of their quarrel to her aunt, things would be uncomfortable.

'Now look, hinny, I've something to say.' Jinny had the air of one who had come to a decision. 'I can't stand by and see you turning cartwheels to be everything to everybody until you disappear up your own backside. I've had enough of the laundry, all that damp washing plays havoc with me arthritis, and with your uncle and the lads in work for the first time in years, I don't need to carry on there. That being the case, I'd far rather be here givin' you a hand.'

Hope stared at her aunt in surprise. She hadn't expected this. 'But no one really knows why the mines and shipyards are on full time again or how long it'll last. It might end tomorrow.'

'Aye, that's true enough, but you'd have to be pretty daft not to see it's got somethin' to do with Adolf Hitler, the old so an' so. And he's put the wind up our lot, look at all the gas masks that have been given out. They wouldn't do that lightly. I reckon we're in for a packet right enough.' And then Jinny flapped her hand, saying, 'Aw, don't look like that, hinny. Take no notice of me. All these rumours might come to nowt.'

But her aunt didn't think so. Hope's stomach turned over. Her Uncle George was the steadiest, most down-to-earth individual she'd ever met and her aunt always echoed his views. If he thought Germany would force a war on them, he was probably right.

'Anyway, whatever the likes of me an' you think about a war doesn't make a ha'porth of difference, lass. What will be, will be,' Jinny said with homespun philosophy. 'All I know is that for the first time in ten years me cupboard's overflowing and the rent book is clear. And so I say again, do you want me to lend a hand?'

Hope looked into the plump homely face and answered from the heart. 'There's nothing I'd like more.'

'Then so be it. Atween the two of us we'll do all right, hinny.'

Yes, they would. In spite of the cloud of despondency which had hovered over her all day, Hope felt a stirring of the excitement she'd felt the evening before when she had put her thoughts to Daniel. This morning she had been unable to see her way clear to even making a success of the little shop in the front room let alone continuing on her rounds, but suddenly her vision had cleared. She didn't want to do this without Daniel but if she had to, she would.

Jack and Betsy burst into the kitchen from the back lane where they had been playing with some of the neighbourhood children. As mucky as they were, Hope bent down and gathered the two small bodies against her, hugging them fiercely before letting them go to wash their hands and faces. She owed it to her children – and there were four of them now – to do all she could to secure their future and she felt in her bones her business could be more successful than ever she'd dreamed of two years ago. Her aunt's offer had come at just the right time and it was a sign. She would take it a day at a time, and put the ultimate plan of a shop with a flat above on hold for the next little while, but one day she *would* achieve it. And she wouldn't let Daniel or his da or even this war everyone was so sure would come stand in her way.

PART FOUR

1939   A Mad World

Chapter 22

'Jack? *Jack.*' Betsy tugged on her twin's arm. 'Why is Mam crying?'

'Ssh, they'll hear us an' I've told you why. On Sunday we went to war with Germany and now Da's going away to fight.'

Betsy frowned. 'But why is she *crying*? Everyone was cheering and shouting the other day when those soldiers marched through town.'

Jack looked at his twin. The two children were sitting huddled together halfway up the stairs, their attention riveted on the sounds emerging through the kitchen door which was slightly ajar. 'Because she will miss him of course,' he whispered, adding scathingly, 'You're so silly, Betsy.'

'I'm not silly,' Betsy answered as a matter of routine. Her brother called her that at least once every hour. She thought for a moment. 'Will she cry when we go to the country?'

Jack sighed with all the exasperation a five and a half-year-old feels at pointless questions from his sister. 'Course not. She's coming with us so why would she cry?'

Betsy shrugged. 'I dunno.'

He cast his eyes heavenwards. 'Mam's taking us and Alice and Grace to the country and we're all going to live there till the war's over. I've *told* you.'

Betsy was quiet for a moment. Then she said, 'Why does Da like the war better than the country?'

'Because there's no Germans to fight in the country.'

'Why?'

'Because there isn't. There's just cows and sheep and things.'

'I like the country better than the war.'

'That's 'cos you're silly. If I was bigger I'd go with Da and kill lots of Germans stone dead.'

Betsy regarded him through admiring eyes. She didn't doubt for a minute Jack would do exactly what he said.

'Quick.' They both heard the sound of a chair scraping, and fearing they would be caught eavesdropping, the two children scurried up the stairs to their bedroom where Alice and Grace were fast asleep in the other bed the room held.

When after a little while it became apparent their parents weren't going to come upstairs, Jack debated whether or not to go back to the stairs. But he was warm now and the stairs had been draughty. Betsy had fallen asleep. He could tell she was asleep even though she had her back to him because she wasn't talking. His mam said Betsy could talk the hind leg off a donkey. He contemplated the thought of a three-legged donkey for some moments before shutting his eyes and snuggling further under the covers. His da was a hero going to fight the Germans but although he would never admit to it he, like his mam, wished his da didn't have to go away. And he'd miss his granda when they went to the country. In fact he thought he would miss his granda more than anyone. Within minutes he, too, was fast asleep.

In the kitchen Hope busied herself making a pot of tea, more in an effort to control herself than because she and Daniel wanted a cup. But it helped. The shock of hearing he had joined up had been overwhelming but now it was with some bitterness she said, 'You couldn't wait to get away then? Most men hereabouts are waiting to see if they get called up eventually, but not you.'

'It's not like that.'

'I think that's exactly what it is like.' She gave a painful laugh. 'It comes to something when your husband would rather go away to war than share your bed, don't you think?'

'Stop it.'

'No, I won't stop it.' She faced him, sick to death of living a lie and hardly able to believe he'd joined up without discussing it with her first. This wasn't a marriage. She didn't know what it was but it wasn't a marriage. 'It's the truth, Daniel. Why can't you *talk* to me? You will never talk to me.'

'Try to understand. I've volunteered for you and the bairns. Someone has to stop Hitler, surely you can see that? And a mass call-up is coming, Hope, everyone knows it's on the cards. I'd rather jump before I was pushed, that's all.' He paused and his voice sank, and he repeated, 'That's all.'

A combination of pain and anger and consuming fear for him was making her tremble from head to foot. It was the look on his face more than his words that had stilled her tongue. If it had been Jack or Betsy in front of her she would have described the expression as one of desperate vulnerability, an unspoken childish plea to make whatever was wrong right again.

'Hope . . .' He hesitated. 'I love you. Please believe that. I have always loved you and I always will. And you're right, I should have talked to you.'

She knew he wanted her to say it was all right, that she forgave him and that she understood why he had volunteered. Especially in view of the fact he was going away to training camp in the morning. But it was not all right and she couldn't forgive him and this final act of shutting her out, of joining up without a *word* to her, hurt more than anything that had gone before. Right at this moment she didn't know if she loved him or hated him.

She passed him a cup of tea and then poured one for herself before sitting down at the kitchen table opposite him. 'Actions speak louder than words, Daniel. You say you love me but we only ever talk about unimportant things and we hardly ever make love these days.'

'You've been so tired with looking after Grace and Alice—'

'No.' She put up her hand. 'Don't use the babies as an excuse. And don't make out you were thinking of me. It hasn't been like that.'

She half expected him to deny it and when he didn't the niggling fear that she managed to keep buried most of the time surfaced. Without even thinking about choosing her words, she said flatly, 'Is there someone else?'

'What?' His head jerked.

'*Someone else.*' He could understand English. 'Are you in love with someone else?'

'Hell, no.' She had shocked him to the core. 'Is that what you've been thinking? Hope, I swear I've never looked at another woman. How could I? I love you.'

She felt he was telling the truth and her whole body wanted

to slump with relief but she didn't let it. Continuing to sit upright as she faced him, she said, 'Then why have you changed so much from the man I married?'

He stared at her. Some moments ticked by and then he said slowly, 'It's not you. It's never been you. But you're right, I have changed.'

'And you joining up isn't just about fighting for your country or me and the bairns, is it? Be honest.'

He blinked. 'I believe Hitler has to be stopped and that every man worth his salt should fight, Hope. I do believe that. And I suppose I think it's time I made a stand and did something with my life, something worthwhile.'

She didn't know how to interpret that. She stared at him uncertainly as he stood up and came to where she was sitting. He drew her up by her hands and then enfolded her in his arms so her face was against his throat and she couldn't see his expression.

Above her head he said softly, 'I was never cut out to push bits of paper round an office all day and I've got no head for figures like Cecil. I've felt like a round peg in a square hole for years and maybe that's what you've sensed. But don't doubt that I love you and the bairns. I do, Hope.'

But he could have left his father's office and started working with her a year ago. She had asked him. She had all but begged him. Hope opened her mouth to speak and then closed it again. He was telling her part of it but not all; she felt she still didn't know how he felt in the depths of him. 'Do you resent the twins coming along so early in our marriage?' she asked after a moment or two had elapsed.

'No, of course not.'

He had answered too quickly and they both knew it. She

shut her eyes against the warmth of his flesh as her mind grappled with what she should say.

And then he took the decision from her by moving her away from him so he could look into her face. 'You're beautiful,' he whispered. 'Beautiful and warm and too good for a man like me. Will you come to bed with me? Will you let me hold you and caress you and prove I love you?'

Hope knew she should insist they talk some more, but she found she didn't want to translate the jumble of questions reverberating in her mind into words. Not now. She felt confused and sad, but with the knowledge there was no other woman in his life had come the realisation she still loved him. And he was going away tomorrow. Only to training camp admittedly, but once that was over, who knew where he would be sent. It could be overseas, an ocean could separate them. An eternity.

She wanted to howl out her frustration at the mess they had made of their marriage but now was not the time to indulge. She had a stark choice here. She could either do what he had done to her a hundred times over the last months and years and turn her back on him, or she could try and salvage something out of their relationship to build on in the future. If there was a future.

She put her hands either side of his face and brought his mouth down on hers.

The next morning Hope tried to be strong for the children's sake but it was hard, the more so because of the night they had shared. It had been wonderful, like when they had first been married, and although she was glad of this, perversely it made her angry with him too. He had put her through torment on and off for years when every night could have been so good.

But now they were standing in Central Station with the twins, the younger children having stayed with Jinny at the house. The platform was packed with children being evacuated. So many carefully labelled little ones standing clutching small bundles of belongings and the square boxes enclosing their gas masks. The mass exodus had started some days before and Hope herself was due to leave the town at the end of the week with the twins and two younger children. She had thought Daniel would be seeing them off then; never in her worst nightmare had she imagined they would be waving him off first.

'You shouldn't have done it.' As he held her close she couldn't prevent herself speaking her mind. 'You should be here, with me, with us. We've so much to sort out between us, Daniel.'

His eyes moved over her face as he said softly, 'I'm not like you, Hope. I find it hard to express my feelings, I always have. Anyway, everything's changing, you know it is. Soon you'll be in Yorkshire with the bairns. If I'd stayed I would have been by myself at the house.'

'But you know I probably won't stay very long,' she murmured quietly so the twins couldn't hear. They'd decided some time ago there was little point in mentioning to the children beforehand that she might return to Sunderland. 'We could have been together. You knew that.'

'I did what I felt I needed to do.'

'And that makes it all right?' She couldn't help glaring at him. 'To join up without even discussing it with me first?'

'You're right. And I'm sorry. Look, I promise I'll never join up again without telling you first. How about that?'

'This is not funny, Daniel.'

'Mam?' Betsy had been silent for two minutes which was a record. 'Why is that lady crying?'

They all looked to where Betsy was pointing and saw a mother kneeling with her arms round two young boys who looked to be a few years older than the twins. In contrast to their poor mother, both boys seemed remarkably cheerful, no doubt looking on their evacuation as a great adventure. Hope's heart went out to the woman who clearly couldn't pull herself together.

'I think that lady can't go with her children to the country,' Daniel whispered. 'It isn't always possible.'

'Here's Granda!' Jack let go of his mother's skirts, calling, 'Granda! Granda!'

Daniel and Hope's heads swung round. Sure enough, Abe was making his way through the throng and as Jack reached him he bent down and lifted his grandson into his arms.

Hope's eyes had gone to Daniel and in answer to the unspoken question, he said, 'I didn't know he was coming. I thought we'd said our goodbyes yesterday when I got back from the recruiting office before I called in the house to see Mother and Annie.'

Daniel had mentioned the night before that his father had been upset, but as Hope looked into Abe's face she could see that had been an understatement. The irritation she had felt at Abe intruding on what she considered should be a time for just herself and Daniel and the twins abated somewhat. She had thought Abe looked awful in the aftermath of Rosaleen's death but that was nothing to how he looked today.

'I know I shouldn't have come.' He looked at them both

as he reached their side. 'Annie said it was a time for just the pair of you and I won't stay a minute but . . .' He couldn't continue, gulping in his throat as he hugged Jack to him.

'Where's Mother?' Daniel asked quietly.

'She's took to her bed.'

Emily's answer to all the trials of life. And then Hope felt ashamed of herself. Of course Emily would be upset at her youngest son going to war. How would she feel if Jack had been old enough to volunteer? The thought of this brought a softness to Hope's voice as she said, 'It's only training camp at first.'

'Aye, but you never know if they're going to be shipped straight off or not.' Abe bent and stood Jack on his feet before saying gruffly, 'I just wanted to say you look after yourself, lad. An' don't play the hero. You've done more than your fair share by volunteerin' in the first place.' He didn't add, daft blighter, but the words hung in the air nevertheless.

'Here's the train, Mam.' Betsy began to jump up and down excitedly. She had never been to the train station before.

'Here, give your da a kiss an' then we'll go and look at the engine before you wave him goodbye.' Abe pushed Jack and Betsy in front of Daniel. After the twins had dutifully kissed their father, Abe leant forward and hugged his son quickly before pushing him away. 'You have a minute together,' he said, taking the children's hands and leading them towards the steaming engine. Suddenly he looked like an old, old man, the contrast with the twins skipping either side of him poignant.

'He loves you very much.' Hope's eyes came back to her husband's face.

'I know, that's why—' He stopped, then made a physical

307

movement as though dislodging a weight from his shoulders. 'Come here,' he said softly.

All around them was noise and commotion. Children crying, parents shouting instructions as they put their little ones into the carriages and the odd couple, like them, holding each other tight.

'You'll write?' She clung to him.

'Every day. Oh, sweetheart, don't cry.'

'And do what your father said, don't try and be a hero.'

'Darling, like you told him, it's training camp first.'

And then the front most probably. Fear for him was a huge lump in her throat. 'Try and get leave after your training is finished.' She didn't add, before you're sent abroad, but they both knew that was what might happen.

'I will. Of course I will. Make sure you send me the address of where you're billeted in Yorkshire so I know where to come.'

'Yes, I will.' She couldn't seem to let go of him. And then he gently disentangled her fingers from his coat, slipped her arm through his and led her to the edge of the platform. There he kissed her with all the hunger of the night before, careless of onlookers, before he got into the carriage.

As Abe and the twins joined Hope, all the doors were closing and then the train began to move. She just had time to catch a last glimpse of his face at the window and then he was gone. She stood dumbly watching the train disappear, quite bereft. The last years of worrying that things had gone wrong between them, the shock of his joining up and then their coming together the night before had left her emotionally and physically drained.

'Come on, lass, let's get you an' the bairns home.' Abe's

voice was thick and as she looked into his face she saw the tears streaming down his cheeks. Amazingly, since this man was a thorn in her flesh as she was no doubt a thorn in his, she knew there was no one else she would rather have with her at this moment. It was a revelation, and for the first time she caught a glimmer of what held Daniel to his father. For all his faults there was a bigness about Abe, a capacity for love and warmth that was beguiling.

It was dangerous, too, she qualified, as the four of them left the station, she holding Betsy's hand and Abe his grandson's. And she still believed the only way forward for them as a family was for Daniel to cut his ties with Abe and for them to stand on their own feet. But overall she wasn't sorry Abe had turned up today, which showed she didn't know herself as well as she thought she did.

Three days later Hope was back at Central Station, this time with the twins and Alice and Grace. Although the numbers of evacuees had begun to diminish, the platform was still relatively full of children waiting to board trains for the country.

Abe had insisted on picking them up in the car and Hope had been thankful for this; with the children's bags of clothes, their gas masks and her own bag she felt she could do with two pairs of hands. Annie accompanied Abe, Emily apparently still confined to bed with her nerves. Hope had made her goodbyes to her aunt and Bernice before she left home. Jinny had agreed to be in charge of the front-room shop on a daily basis while she was gone, and Bernice had recently offered to help with the making of the ice cream and sweets as long as it was understood she stayed in the background. The door-to-door side of the business had been put on hold.

Hope had been pleased at Bernice's offer, as much for her sister-in-law's sake as Jinny's and the business. Bernice had stayed with her parents until her divorce settlement, which had come through recently, whereupon she'd bought a small property near Hendon Burn and moved in. For the last three months she had become something of a recluse and Hope knew her sister-in-law's lack of confidence these days was a direct result of the rape. She felt being with her Aunt Jinny on a day-to-day basis was the best medicine Bernice could have.

'Mam?' Betsy tugged at her sleeve as they all walked onto the platform to wait for the train. 'Jack says they don't have privies in Yorkshire and you have to go in a field.' Betsy, the most private of little girls in her habits, looked ready to burst into tears.

Hope glanced at her son who was grinning widely, clearly delighted with the result of his teasing. 'Lads who tell fibs get their mouths washed out with soap and water,' she warned quietly.

'Oh, he was only havin' a spot of fun, weren't you, lad.' Abe immediately came to Jack's defence as he always did, no matter whether his grandson was in the right or not. 'Trying to cheer everyone up.'

'Well, he didn't succeed with Betsy.' Annie gave Abe a glance which told him to shut up, and not for the first time Hope reflected how comfortable the two were with each other. Which was just as well, what with Emily being in bed more than she was out of it these days – unless there was a particularly nice dinner or event she wanted to attend, of course.

Telling herself not to be so bitchy, Hope smiled at Annie.

'Thanks for coming,' she said softly. Annie had been a rock all morning, taking care of the two younger children while she'd got ready and calming the twins when they got overexcited.

'Pleasure, lass. Now you make sure you write and put this one's mind at rest,' she said, nodding her head at Abe. 'Worried to death about you all, he is. Oh, here's the train now. We'll help you on with the bairns and see you settled; hopefully there'll be someone the other end to give a hand.'

It was all bustle and activity for the next few minutes but eventually they were in the carriage, their belongings on the rack overhead, along with their gas masks. Hope had noticed that Abe avoided any contact with Alice but this was not unusual. He'd been askance at them taking Constance in to start with and even more angry when she had run off, leaving Alice with them. The kindest and most loving grandfather with Jack, Betsy and Grace, he had ignored Alice from the moment she was born. This was another facet of his complicated nature that Hope had difficulty coming to terms with.

'Bye then, lass.' Abe shut the carriage door and stood back slightly as the train began to move, Annie at his side. As Jack hung out of the window, waving, Abe called, 'You mind you look after your mam, lad. All right?'

And then they were out of the station, steam from the engine floating past the window, and Jack settled back in his seat.

Hope let out her breath in a long sigh. Daniel, who wouldn't hurt a fly, volunteering to go away to train and kill other human beings; Bernice and Jinny in charge of her house and the business, and now her and the bairns on a train bound for Yorkshire to live with complete strangers. The world had indeed gone mad.

Abe and Annie left the station and got into his car, but he didn't start the engine immediately. Annie looked at him. 'What's up?'

'You mean besides Daniel rushing to put himself in the way of a German bullet and leaving his wife and bairns?'

'Don't try and be clever.' Annie's voice had lost its soft note and was tart.

'I can't understand the lad. What possessed him? He's got a wife in a million and the bonniest bairns in Sunderland.'

'Have you ever told her that?'

'What?'

Annie clicked her tongue. He knew full well what she had meant. 'Have you ever told Hope you think she's a wife in a million?'

'Don't be daft.' He looked askance.

'You should. You've given her enough grief over the years, a little praise is long overdue.'

'Aye, well, I'm not made that way.'

'Don't we know it.'

They sat in silence for a moment and then Annie said, 'Anyway, it isn't Daniel going away. There's something else, isn't there? I knew it first thing. You were all right last night so what's happened?'

He was still for a moment and then he reached into the pocket of his suit jacket and brought out an envelope. 'That came in the post this morning,' he said gruffly. 'It's knocked me back a bit.'

Annie stared at him before she opened the envelope. She

had loved this man all her life and it was rare he would make an admission like that. Whatever this letter was, it wasn't good.

> Been quiet for a bit, hasn't it, but that's not to say
> I've forgotten about you and yours. I'm just taking
> my time. Enjoying it. One down and three to go
> as I see it. Ever wondered who got your youngest
> and her fancy pals started on the hard stuff, by the
> way? There's more ways to kill a cat than
> drowning it but then you know all about that.

It was written in block capitals and there was no signature.

Annie felt sick. 'You've got to take this to the police.'

'And have them raking up Rosaleen's death and everything connected with it? Talk sense, lass. They'd get nowhere and all we'd be left with is my lass's name being bandied about like dirt. And I'm not so sure this isn't him trying to be clever and put the wind up me 'cos he's heard certain things and put two an' two together and made four.'

'Him? You mean Jim Clark? You think he's behind this then?'

'Who else?'

'But I thought the Mullens had leant on him.'

'They did but poor old Edwin copped it a while back, as you know. Some sort of growth in his stomach, the quack said. Perhaps Jim reckons Vincent's not got the clout now he's on his own.'

'And has he?'

'Don't ask me, lass. I don't know.'

'Oh, Abe.' Annie put her hand on his arm. 'Be careful,

won't you? It's you he's really after. You know that, don't you?'

'Aye, I know that, lass.' He covered her hand with his own for a moment before starting the engine.

It was rare they touched. Since the night in Scotland when they had declared their feelings for each other, there had been no hanky-panky, as Annie termed it in her mind. She sat quietly in her seat now, her mind and body aware of every little movement Abe made. It was always like this. It always would be.

She turned her head to look out of the side window of the car as her thoughts sped on. She had been terrified at first that he would stop his visits to the kitchen, that their easy relationship would be spoilt by what had occurred but the opposite had happened and she was so grateful for it. In every sense but the physical one she was now his wife and she knew it. It was her he shared every little thing with, her he had sobbed with over Rosaleen's passing and again when Bernice had been treated so cruelly by her husband. She didn't think any the less of him for crying. He was a man in every sense of the word and she didn't hold with this thinking that only women should have the relief of tears.

When, in the throes of blaming him for their daughter's death, Emily had banned him from their bedroom, she had known a peace she hadn't felt since he had begun courting Emily. He had taken up residence in a room of equal size across the landing and she knew he wouldn't visit his wife's bed again. He had never discussed this with her but she knew it just the same. Whether he would have moved out of the master bedroom if Rosaleen hadn't died she didn't know, but that didn't matter. It was enough that he and Emily were no longer intimate.

She touched the rosary in the pocket of her dress. Her guilt was constant, a result of her Catholic upbringing, she supposed, not to mention listening to fire and brimstone from Father McHaffie every Sunday. She and Abe might not have committed fornication but what they had was even more of a betrayal of the wedding vows somehow. She knew Abe wouldn't have understood that if she had mentioned it to him, but another woman would. But she would take what was dished out in the hereafter for what she had now.

She glanced at the rugged profile at the side of her and as always her heart fluttered. Barmy, at her age, but she couldn't help it, and she knew if Abe had so much as lifted a finger to encourage her into his bed she would have obliged like a shot. Which made her wanton, she supposed. Wanton, and looking like she did! A small self-deprecatory smile touched her thin lips But the passion that flowed through her for this man was all at odds with her outward appearance.

'I might have a word with Vincent, see if he knows owt. What do you think?'

'What? Oh aye, yes, do that. He might be able to say if Jim Clark is all wind and water or whether he could have had a hand in selling the drugs to the tennis crowd. Either way, I think I'd tip Cecil and Bernice off. You could just say to her what you said before, someone's got a grudge because they got the sack. And at least Daniel's clear of it for the time being.'

'If that's a hint to count my blessings, you can keep it. I'd rather have him here where I can keep an eye on him than being shot at by some fanatic from the so-called master race. Master race! And Hitler a weedy little nowt that a breath of wind could blow away.'

Abe was on his hobby horse and Annie let him rant on, glad he seemed more like himself again. But she rather thought she'd call the locksmith in tomorrow and have a couple of bolts put on the front and back doors, and on the French windows in the drawing room too.

Just to be on the safe side.

At the engineering works, Abe called Cecil into his office. 'You'd better read that. It's probably nothing more than our old friend trying to put the jitters up me, but be on your guard, lad. All right? Bernice will be told the same story as before.'

Cecil read the note in silence. 'Great. That'll put the tin lid on things with Gwendoline. She'll twist it round so it's me who's putting Edward in danger. I can hear her now.'

Abe regarded his son through narrowed eyes. 'Bad as that, is it?'

'You've no idea.'

'You don't have to say anything to her.'

'No, that's true enough.' Cecil gave a harsh grunt of a laugh. 'But perhaps I will. To tell you the truth, Da, I'm tired of being held up against her esteemed father and found wanting. Not that she'd look at it like that, of course.'

'Do you want me to talk to her?'

Cecil looked at his father for a long moment and then he said, 'No, I don't want you to talk to her but thanks for asking. Just don't be surprised if she goes back to her mam and da in the next couple of days.'

'And Edward?'

'He'll go with her of course. Why wouldn't he? Any decisions that have ever been made in our household have come via her parents.'

The bitterness in his son's voice caused Abe's eyes to narrow. 'Why didn't you tell me things were as bad as this?'

'I did, Da. Or I thought I did. Dozens of times. Perhaps you just weren't listening.' And then Cecil flapped his hand. 'Forget it. A man ought to be able to control his own household, I know that. I'm not belly-aching. And I'll keep on my toes regarding Jim Clark. Funny, but I had a gut feeling we hadn't seen the end of him.'

'Aye, so did I.'

They looked at each other for a moment.

'I'll get back to those figures for the Hutton contract.'

As Cecil left the office, Abe had the urge to call his son back but he restrained it, not knowing what to say to him. He sat staring into the outer office for a minute or two, his gaze fixed on Cecil who had his head bent over the open file in front of him.

And then the telephone at his elbow rang; he reached out and picked it up, and the moment was lost.

Chapter 23

Years later Hope was to think of the time she spent in Yorkshire as no more than the blink of an eye, although it was four weeks before she returned to Sunderland without the children. From the moment she stepped off the train in the little Yorkshire town, she had felt reassured that her bairns would be in good hands. There were none of the horror stories that had been reported in the press over the last week, that of folk haggling over which children they would take into their homes, the unattractive, sickly, bedraggled or tearful ones being shunted aside. Even several children from the East End who were infested with lice and fleas were made welcome, albeit after they'd had hot baths liberally sprinkled with disinfectant and had had their hair bobbed and combed through.

The seventy or so children and handful of mothers were all ushered into the local school and refreshed with cups of tea and bread and butter, before several horse and carts and a couple of cars began to distribute the human cargo to their waiting hosts. More than a few of the children who had made the journey without their mothers had tears running down their faces, but they wept quietly, too tired and bewildered to make much noise.

Hope and the four children were transported to their destination by horse and cart, much to Jack's delight. It clip-clopped them through country lanes where the last of the dying sun lit up small whitewashed cottages, farms and cattle grazing on green grass. It was an idyllic picture, and one far removed from the graphic warnings of the bombing on England's cities which was sure to come, according to the news reports.

Several other children accompanied them in the horse and cart, including two small boys from Newcastle about Jack's age who seemed to possess a natural cockiness and resilience, if their conversation was anything to go by. Jack was immediately drawn to them and the three kept up a running commentary about everything they passed by. Hope had expected the other children to be deposited en route but instead they all finished up at a large sprawling farmhouse where the plump farmer's wife was waiting to greet them, her teenage daughters by her side.

By bedtime, Jack and the other four little boys ranging in age from five to eight were installed in one bedroom on pallet beds with straw mattresses. Betsy, Alice and Grace, along with two sisters aged five and eight, were in the other spare room where provision had been made for Hope in the way of a put-u-up. Although basic, the accommodation was scrupulously clean, and much to Betsy's relief the privy was situated just outside the farmhouse in the yard and was sweet-smelling.

Alice and Grace were the youngest evacuees in the household, the other children all being of school age, and Eve, the farmer's wife, told Hope the little girls would be dropped off at the parish church hall every morning while the other children were in the village school. 'My married daughter's the president of the local WI and she's organised all that,' Eve said proudly.'They expect about thirty infants most days and there's a rota in place for taking care of them. The members have donated umpteen cots and blankets so the younger ones can have a nap in the day, there's nothing they haven't thought of.'

Hope found this to be true over the next few days, and within two or three weeks all four children had settled into their new lifestyle as though they'd been born to it, so much so that Hope found Betsy, complete with gas mask, in earnest conversation with a placid cow one evening before milking. The pair seemed fascinated by each other. Considering that the twins had never been further away from home than a few miles on a Sunday School outing, Hope was heartily relieved at their easy adjustment.

She, on the other hand, found time hanging heavy on her hands. Despite making herself available for any jobs round the farm, she was rarely called on. The outside work was done by Mr Walton, the farmer, and his four married sons, all of whom lived close by. The dairy was Eve's territory and she guarded it fiercely, and her teenage daughters, two big buxom lasses, could turn their hand to anything. Even when the children returned home in the evening, Hope felt redundant. The older children played outside or in the big hay barn close to the house, and Eve's daughters monopolised Alice and Grace, enchanted with the infants. The twins' heartache at leaving their pet rabbit Nugget behind was appeased by fussing the five farm dogs and umpteen cats, and already the country life had put new colour in their cheeks. Everything was new to them and all was lovely. The orchard, the hedgerows with their fat blackberries, the fields and the animals were a wonderland of joy.

And so it was that at the beginning of October Hope decided to return home alone. In spite of hospitals being cleared, mortuaries stacked with piles of cardboard coffins, and lime pits dug to cope with the dead, the expected bombing had not happened. Apart from all the new government regulations, constant exhortations and petty officialdom, the country wouldn't know it was at war and she saw no reason to remain where she was not needed when she could be more usefully employed at home. Her children were safe and happy, which was the important thing. Even if the war hotted up, that would not change.

Her leave-taking was tearful – more on Hope's side than the children's, it must be said – but she comforted herself with the fact that the special 'visit to evacuees' cheap day return tickets would make it possible for her to visit whenever she needed to. Nevertheless, as the train puffed out of the tiny market town station, Hope suddenly had an overwhelming desire to leap from it and make her way back to the farmstead, but she restrained herself. She gave herself a silent talking-to all the way home, and by the time she was once again under the familiar domed roof of Central Station, she knew she'd done the right thing.

'Hope!' As she walked into the kitchen by way of the back door, Bernice, who was busy breaking up a tray of baked stickjaw to divide into little bags, nearly dropped the lot in her surprise. 'What on earth are you doing here?'

Before she could reply Jinny, who had always had ears like an elephant, burst in from the hall. 'Ee, lass, you're a sight for sore eyes,' she beamed. 'Why didn't you send word you was comin'?'

'I kept umming and ahhing till the last minute,' Hope admitted ruefully, hugging them both. 'It was hard to leave the bairns but I was just a spare part there.'

'But are they happy?' Bernice asked anxiously.

'Supremely so. And very well looked after.'

'Bit different to Mrs Briggs' bairns then, three doors down from me.' Jinny shook her head. 'They were sent to some cottage or other that wasn't big enough to hold a bird's nest, let alone the family of eight who lived there. The three eldest were put in a crumbling outhouse on a mattress on the floor with the rats an' cockroaches, an' the two little 'uns top an' tailed with the other bairns. Eight of 'em in all in one bed, with no room to move or turn over, according to Mrs Briggs. Her eldest lad wrote her an' she was on the next train bringin' 'em back. Course, it was the eight an' six a week for each child the family had their eye on. Mrs Briggs gave 'em what for, I can tell you. Wiped the floor with 'em, she did.'

Hope could imagine. Mrs Briggs was built like a tank and there wasn't a man in the East End who would dare to argue with her.

'Have you written to let Daniel know you're back home?' Bernice asked.

Hope nodded at her sister-in-law. 'I posted the letter when I got off the train at Central Station, just in case I changed my mind about leaving the bairns at the last minute.' Her determined cheerfulness faltered. 'It'll seem strange without them.'

It *was* strange. In fact it was horrible and Hope cried herself to sleep for the first few days in spite of trying to make sure she went to bed too exhausted to think. But then a week after she was home, Daniel wrote to say he was coming to see her on a special fourteen-hour pass on leaving training camp. Hope was bitterly disappointed he couldn't stay longer but when she met him on a damp October morning at the train station, all was explained. He was to join the British troops from the Expeditionary Force already in France to bolster the French defence. Her worst fears had come true. It was meagre comfort to know Daniel had been right; a general call-up for all men over twenty had already begun and so sooner or later he would have been caught in the net.

They only had time to have lunch together at a little café tucked away in a side street near the station before they were back on the platform again, ready for Daniel to catch the train into Newcastle where he was to meet the rest of his company. Hope wanted to say so much but in the event she said very little; it didn't seem to be an occasion for words, just for holding each other tight. They sat close together, hands entwined, on one of the seats as they waited for the train which would take him away. Hope knew if she tried to speak she would break down and she was determined his last sight of her wouldn't be of her weeping.

When the train steamed in, she managed to keep control of herself, bringing all her considerable will to bear. 'Be careful, won't you?' She stared at him, thinking, what silly things one says at times like this.

'Darling, I'll be fine.' He lifted her chin with one finger and smiled. 'I'm more worried about you here with this damn blackout at nights causing havoc. If you have to go out after dark, wear a white scarf or belt, anything.'

She moved her shoulders impatiently. What did the perils

of the blackout matter compared to what he was going to have to face? 'Come back to me, Daniel. Don't take any chances you don't have to take.'

'I won't, I promise.' All amusement gone and his voice low and throaty, he murmured, 'I love you, Hope. Just remember that. I've made a pig's ear of things between us but I'll make it up to you one day. There'll never be anyone but you.' He pulled her against him, kissing her in a way which would have been considered unseemly in public before the war. But now he was a soldier in uniform and the most they received was sympathetic glances.

Then he boarded the train, the carriage doors closed, the guard blew his whistle and the train began to move. This time she was left on the platform alone. There was no Abe and no small faces to focus on.

But that was the way it was going to be from now on so she might as well get used to it. She nodded mentally to the thought, dashing the tears from her eyes with the back of her hand and sniffing loudly before she turned and left the station. It was raining outside, a cold drizzle. The summer was well and truly over.

Chapter 24

'What do you mean, you've found Bernice's young man?'
Jinny stared at her niece, consternation written all over her
plump face. 'What have you been up to, hinny?'

Hope's chin rose as it always did when she faced criticism.
And it was criticism she heard in her aunt's voice. She finished
pouring two cups of tea and handed one to Jinny. 'I mean
what I say, that's all. I know where Thomas is living.'

'How do you know? Have you talked to him?'

'No, I haven't talked to him. He's some miles away, in
Middlesbrough.'

'How can you be sure it's him then?'

Hope took a sip of her tea before she said, 'Bernice
mentioned him again one evening some weeks back, just after
the bairns had gone back to the farm again after Christmas.
She told me where he used to live when the family were
here.' She didn't say it had taken some careful manoeuvring
on her part to acquire this information. 'While I was out
selling the ice cream in that neighbourhood, I asked about

the Howards. I made out we were distantly connected,' she added, unabashed as Jinny clucked her tongue. 'An old neighbour who was a good friend of Thomas's mam was most helpful.'

'By, hinny, the things you do.' It was not praise. 'As though you haven't got enough on your plate as it is.'

Hope stared at her aunt. She'd thought she might disapprove which was why she hadn't confided in her before this. She could understand her misgivings. Whatever way you looked at it, she was guilty of interfering in someone else's life, which was always risky, as Daniel had pointed out that time. But in the months since Daniel had been gone, especially since the first bombing raid by the Germans in the middle of March two weeks ago when the Luftwaffe had attacked a naval base in Scotland, killing civilians, time had become more of a precious and temporary thing. And one fact was inescapable: that enemy attack from the skies was a foretaste of what was to come all over England.

'Look, Aunt Jinny, you know as well as I do that Bernice would never try to contact Thomas, not after what her father did to him. She's mortified he was blackmailed by her own da. And he wouldn't make the first move after that, even if he knew she was no longer married. Which of course he doesn't.'

'Aye, but what if he doesn't want to make a move, eh? You thought about that?'

'Of course. And for that reason I'd go to see him without saying anything to Bernice. The thing is,' Hope bent closer, her face earnest, 'she still loves him as much as ever. She's told me so on more than one occasion. And what if he feels the same? What then? Why should they spend the rest of their lives apart when they could be together? Bernice is a free woman now, there's absolutely no reason why she can't see another man. I know Abe got involved and, being him, managed to wangle some sort of agreement that the divorce would be on the grounds of non-consummation or something. Not that that's true of course, but it means even the Catholic Church sees her as free to marry again. That mattered to Bernice.'

'Hang on, lass. You're running before yourself here. He might be married himself, this Thomas. Or courting a lass.'

'He isn't. Or at least he wasn't when this neighbour's son last took his mam to see Mrs Howard about a year ago.'

'Plenty can happen in a year.'

Plenty could happen in a day. She was terrified the enemy were going to invade France any minute and then Daniel would be right in the thick of any fighting. He could be killed, and if he was injured he could be taken prisoner. The rumours of invasion were incessant and just the week before, Hope had invested in a wireless set so she could hear immediately something happened. If it happened. But then it was bound to. She couldn't live in false hope. She cleared her mind and said to Jinny, 'I'll never know if there's a chance for Bernice if I don't go, now will I?'

'So you've made up your mind?'

'Aye, I have.'

'What's Daniel's da going to say? He'll go barmy, lass.'

'He might.' Hope's tone suggested that was the least of her worries. 'But it's all right for him. He's got a wife and family and the business, his life is full and busy. And before you say it, I know Bernice has come out of herself a bit in the last months while she's been working with us, but she's not happy,

Aunt Jinny. Not deep down. And if the chance to have her own bairns isn't to pass her by, then she needs to meet someone soon. And the only person she'd want would be Thomas. I know that. After you've gone home to see to Uncle George's dinner in the evenings she often stays on for a bit and we talk. She's lonely, heart lonely.' And she could understand that. For the last year or two of her marriage she'd felt the same, isolated, unlovable. And if she had felt like that with Daniel with her, what did Bernice feel like living alone?

'So what are you going to do?'

'I'm going to see him tomorrow so you'll have to cover for me with Bernice. I can't say I'm going to see the bairns else she'll wonder why I didn't let Abe take me and ask her to go along.' The last couple of times she had gone to see the children, Abe had insisted on taking her in his motor car, and because he had invited Bernice, Emily and Annie along, Hope hadn't felt she could refuse. She hadn't enjoyed these visits. Abe had monopolised Jack and left the three girls to the women so she hadn't had a chance to talk to her son properly. Abe had also given broad hints that with a good number of the evacuees trickling back to the towns, it might be time for the twins and two younger children to return home. Much as Hope would like to have her children with her, she felt she owed it to them to maximise their safety and that meant the four of them staying where they were. Abe's disagreement with her on this had led to some tense silences on the journey, and she was determined the next time she visited her son and the three girls it would be alone and on the train.

As though Jinny had picked up on this, she said, 'You're not doin' this just to get at Daniel's da, are you? Going to see this Thomas, I mean? Teachin' him a lesson, so to speak.'

Hope was hurt her aunt could think this and said so, but Bernice's arrival at the house in the next moment signalled the start of the morning's work and nothing more was said about the matter. Later that evening, though, when Jinny and Bernice had gone, Hope thought about what her aunt had suggested. *Was* part of her motivation over this a wish to show Abe he couldn't control their lives? Her self-examination was uncomfortable; she had to admit to herself there was an element of confronting Abe in all of this. But the main objective was to reunite the two people who had been most hurt by Abe's actions, if that was possible, and for Bernice to know some peace and joy in her life before it was too late. In that her motive *was* pure.

Hope was gone long before Bernice and Jinny arrived the following morning. She had told her sister-in-law that an old schoolfriend of hers had recently had twins and was finding it difficult to cope, so she had promised to spend the day with her and give her a few pointers on how to make life easier for herself with two babies to take care of. This had the advantage of being true, although she wasn't actually due to see her friend until the end of the week.

She took a library book with her to read on the journey, more to keep her mind off the possible reception she was likely to get from Thomas Howard – if he was there, that was. He might have moved, he might be in the army, or, and she dreaded this more than anything, he might have met a lass in the last year like her Aunt Jinny had suggested. After she had read the same page three times and still hadn't taken a word in, she gave the book up as a bad job.

When she left the train station in Middlesbrough, she did something she had never done before and took a taxi cab to the address Thomas's old neighbour had given her. She felt too het up to waste time finding it herself. In the event the street wasn't too far from the station. In less than five minutes the car drew up outside a dingy house in a street full of dingy houses, the normal quota of snotty-nosed bairns playing their games on the pavements.

She stood outside the house for some time, so long in fact that she became an object of interest to the children. It was this that finally made her knock on the door. She knocked twice, and was just turning away, half relieved no one was at home, when it opened to reveal a small grey-haired woman in a neat black dress. The woman frowned at her. 'What are you aknockin' for? My lads are on shift work an' tryin' to get some kip.'

'Oh, I'm sorry.' Not the most auspicious of starts. 'Are you Mrs Howard?'

'Aye. Who's askin'?'

'My name is Hope Fallow.' The woman's eyes narrowed and, afraid the door was going to be shut in her face, Hope said quickly, 'I've come to see your son, Thomas. It's about him and Bernice. She doesn't know I'm here but she isn't married any more and she's never stopped loving him, Mrs Howard. I just thought he ought to know that.'

It seemed a lifetime before the woman stood back and beckoned for her to enter, saying, 'You'd better come in.'

'Thank you.' Hope stepped into the hallway, which was spotlessly clean. Thomas's mother led the way down a short passage and opened a door into what was obviously the front room. This, too, was immaculate and furnished very comfortably with a three-piece suite, a china cabinet, a large book-case and a fine wireless set in a mahogany surround. Without speaking, Mrs Howard closed the door, leaving Hope alone.

He must be here, sleeping upstairs. Hope's heart did a fandango. What if he objected to her meddling in his private affairs? What if he turned nasty? This was a nice house. Her thoughts were leaping from one thing to another. Mrs Howard kept it beautiful. You wouldn't have thought it would be so nice from the outside. This must be him coming now.

The door opened and a tall, well-built man with a craggy face and greying hair walked in. Without any preamble, he said, 'My mother tells me you have news of Bernice.'

'Yes. No. What I mean is, she doesn't know I'm here. I'm her sister-in-law but we are also good friends. She's not happy, Mr Howard. I don't think she's been happy since the day you left. Not that leaving was your fault of course, but she didn't know her father drove you away until after she was married. She thought you had just walked out on her.'

He was staring at her in much the same way one would view an escapee from the asylum and she couldn't blame him. She was saying this all wrong.

'Please sit down, Mrs Fallow.' When she was seated on the edge of one of the armchairs, he sat down himself, and it was only then he said quietly, 'Perhaps you should start at the beginning.'

And so she did, from as far back as when she'd met Daniel and his father had objected and Bernice had advised them to marry in secret. She told him almost everything, only leaving out the detail of the night Bernice was raped by her husband. She felt that was something for her sister-in-law to decide whether she wanted him to know. Nevertheless, she said enough to make it clear Rupert had been violent that night and the aftermath had been dreadful.

Thomas did not interrupt or ask any questions. Hope had no idea what was going on behind the steady gaze until she came to the point in her story about the night Bernice was attacked. Then Thomas's face darkened and a muscle jumped in his jaw.

When she'd finished speaking, silence reigned for a moment or two. Then, clearing his throat, he murmured, 'Bernice is fortunate to have such a loyal friend.'

'She has been a wonderful friend to me when I needed one.'

'She's a wonderful woman.'

'I think so. That's why I had to come and see you. But as I've already said, she doesn't know I'm here so if you can't see your way to renewing your friendship, she'll never know I've met you.' She was aching to ask him how he felt but warned herself not to rush in where she didn't belong.

'There are a few things I need to see to. My mother will get you a cup of tea and something to eat.'

He stood up and Hope rose with him. She found herself asking the question she'd promised herself she wouldn't voice. 'What are you going to do?'

'Do?' For the first time since she had met him he smiled. Hope saw immediately what had attracted Bernice to this man. 'I'm coming back to Sunderland with you, of course.'

'You are?' She stared at him stupidly. 'Now?'

'It might take half an hour.' The smile widened and she smiled back. 'Make yourself comfortable. My mother will look after you,' he added as he left the room, closing the door behind him.

When Mrs Howard bustled in a few minutes later with a tray holding a cup of tea and a plate of hot buttered girdle

332

scones, Hope said immediately, 'I'm sorry to put you to any trouble, Mrs Howard.'

'No trouble, lass.' The bright eyes in the little wrinkled face were cheery. 'Not with the news you've brought. I've prayed to the Holy Mother night an' day since we left for this, 'cos I tell you one thing, lass. My lad's a one-woman man. An' I didn't want to depart this mortal plain without knowin' he'd got a good lass alongside of him. He tells me you had a run-in with that old devil an' all.'

So that was why she was so friendly. Hope smiled but said nothing. Curiously she found she wanted to defend Abe but as that was not an option with the mother of the man Abe had treated so badly, she decided least said, soonest mended.

'I hope he burns in hell, lass. I tell you straight, I do. Wicked old blighter.'

Oh dear. Hope took a bite out of one scone. 'These are delicious, Mrs Howard, but you shouldn't have used your butter ration on me.'

'Aw, go on with you.' The tactic worked. 'Least I can do with you comin' all this way.' Smoothing down her dress, Thomas's mother lowered her voice. 'Had a rough time of it, did she? With the man he forced her to marry?'

Hope nodded, her mouth thankfully full of scone.

'Marriage can be a blessin' or a curse, that's sure enough. For me it was the former an' I've seven bonny bairns an' six grand-children to show for it. Thomas an' two of his brothers still live at home but me three lasses an' one lad are married. All me lads are in work an' earnin' well. I'm set up better than I've ever bin.'

'I'm glad.'

'So if he,' Mrs Howard cocked her head towards the door, 'decides his place is in Sunderland with the lass, I'll be all right, see? I've already told him that. He did his share when he fed an' clothed the lot of us for years. Now it's his turn to have a bit of happiness.'

Hope decided she liked Thomas's mother.

She found she liked Thomas too as they chatted on the journey back. They arrived in Central Station at four o'clock and went straight to Hope's house, entering by the back door. Thomas waited in the scullery while Hope went through to the kitchen.

'Hope.' Bernice was putting away some cooking utensils and she straightened. 'How was your friend?' And then, without waiting for an answer, she added, 'Jinny's gone home early. One of her daughters sent a message to say she'd gone down with a stomach upset and could Jinny take care of her children.'

Perfect. Hope didn't spare a thought for her cousin's discomfort.

Something in her face must have alerted Bernice to the fact all was not as it should be, because her sister-in-law now said, 'Are you feeling well? You look . . . Sit down, dear. You've been doing too much.'

'I didn't go to see my friend, Bernice. I've been to Middlesbrough.'

'Middlesbrough? Why on earth would you go there, Hope?'

'To see someone. Someone you used to know.'

'Someone *I* used to know?' Bernice wrinkled her brow. 'I have never been to Middlesbrough that I know of.'

'Prepare yourself for a shock. No, not so much of a shock as a surprise. Look, sit down.' Hope pushed her sister-in-law into one of the kitchen chairs and when Bernice was sitting, she said, 'When Thomas left Sunderland he went to Middlesbrough, Bernice.'

The colour drained from her sister-in-law's face but she made no sound or movement.

'I went there today and I talked to him. I told him you were no longer married.'

'You . . . talked to Thomas?' Bernice's hand went to the collar of her dress and she touched the small locket Hope could see beneath the lace. 'Is . . . is he well?'

'He came back with me. He's waiting to see you if you want to see him. He's been waiting years, like you.'

'Thomas is here?'

Bernice's eyes were dry but the look on her sister-in-law's face reduced Hope to tears. Almost blindly she went to the scullery door and opened it, beckoning Thomas into the kitchen and then stepping into the scullery. She shut the door behind her but not before she heard an inarticulate sound from Bernice that said more than any words could have done.

In the small backyard Hope looked up into the darkening sky. It was the first week of April and although the northern air still had the bite of winter, the skylarks would already be building their nests where she used to walk years ago and where she had first met Daniel. She had a sudden longing to hear their beautiful exuberant song as they hovered and soared in the heavens, her mind recapturing the euphoria she'd felt when the joyous liquid notes had reached her ears.

She stood with her face lifted to the sky for some time. She was still standing there when the back door opened and Bernice, her face alight in a way that gave her a kind of beauty, reached out her arms to her, saying over and over, 'Thank you, thank you, oh, thank you.'

Chapter 25

He was a damn fool. If ever there was a fool, he was it. Daniel stared morosely into the mild May night, the darkness flavoured with the scents of grass and wild flowers and budding hedgerows from the fields in which his company were camped.

Why hadn't he written to Hope before now with all that was in his heart? He had meant to, umpteen times, but instead his letters invariably turned into the mundane, surface issues they were both facing in their separate lives. Was he frightened that if he admitted he'd used her as a scapegoat for years to cover up his own inadequacies, she'd think less of him?

Aye, he damn well was, he thought bitterly. Getting right away from Sunderland – or, to be more specific, his father – had enabled him to take a long hard look at himself and he hadn't liked what he'd seen. He had never considered himself a stupid individual, but he was, weak too. He should have left the family business the morning after Lonnie Kirby spewed his venom. Nothing had been right after that. If he'd been a man then, steered his own course, done whatever it took to put a crust in their mouths, they'd have pulled through, together. Cecil had been right that day, he was a hypocrite. But no more.

He straightened, flexing his shoulders. He'd always love his da and he knew his da loved him but there couldn't be two heads of one house. It was as simple as that. His father's form of love was strangling the life out of him, his marriage, his manhood. The last few years he hadn't known himself. And why? Because he'd stopped fighting to break free. He now realised that subconsciously he'd been fighting against the charismatic and complex man who had sired him most of his life, certainly since he'd reached puberty. The stark virility and passion for life that made his father so masterful and strong wasn't a bad thing in itself, it had got him where he was now, successful and respected, but it was too much for those close to him. It consumed, sucked the life out of lesser mortals.

He shook his head, faintly embarrassed by the intensity of his thoughts. But it was true right enough. It had taken this time and distance between them for him to acknowledge he'd always had a fear of becoming like Cecil, a walking, talking shadow of their father, without substance or even any real personality of his own. And yet his da's heart was big. The need to defend him was there and he shook his head again, this time in irritation at the old guilt rearing its head. He had to stop feeling like that. He was seeing things clearly, that was all.

One of the sleeping men a little way away from him passed wind, long and loudly, before giving a contented little grunt and continuing with his snoring. Daniel's upper lip lifted with distaste. That was one of the worst things about army life, the close proximity twenty-four hours a day to his fellow man.

It was also one of the best. He knew full well if it wasn't for the rough camaraderie and grim dry humour of some of the men around him he'd be a gibbering idiot by now.

None of them understood this sudden move from the defensive positions they'd spent the bitingly cold winter so arduously preparing, but the talk was they were moving forward to join the Belgian army to form a line running along the Dyle and Meuse rivers to stop the German invasion which had started at the Dutch frontier. All Daniel knew was that the Luftwaffe's constant dive-bombing – and more especially the nerve-shaking howl which accompanied it – was stretching even the most stoical among them to breaking point. He hadn't been the only one to bring up the contents of his stomach a couple of days ago when Charlie Stamp had been blown to smithereens ahead of them. One minute he'd been there, the next, pieces of mangled flesh and bone had formed a grotesque rain. They'd lost others since to the Luftwaffe's bombs and machine guns, but nothing affected him the way Charlie Stamp's death had.

So why didn't he put things right with Hope before it was too late? He groaned within himself. Well, there was no time like the present. He reached out and drew his kitbag to him, fumbling about in the darkness for paper and an envelope and his pencil.

The moon gave a little meagre light but half the time he was writing blind. Somehow, though, perhaps due to the darkness and inability to see clearly what he had written, he found the words flowing so fast, his hand could barely keep up with his mind. He didn't try to justify himself. There was no justification for how he'd treated her. And he was brutally honest, revealing his innermost thoughts and feelings about the past, the present and how he saw the future. He hoped the latter would make up for the former in some way. If there was a future for any of them.

Once the letter was written he felt more at peace with himself. He needed to sleep. Hell, how he needed to sleep. It had been slow going today, the roads choked with refugees fleeing from the enemy's advancing infantry. Terrified men, women and children who of necessity had been herded out of their way like rogue cattle.

But he couldn't allow himself to think like that. Compassion was a luxury he couldn't afford. What he had to do was concentrate on trying to stay alive until this madness was over and he could return to Hope and the family. Stay focused. That was their corporal's signature tune. He drummed it into them ten times a day, stroppy little fighting cock that he was. He'd numbed all their ears at first with his shouting and cursing but in spite of the fact that he could only communicate in a bawl, he wasn't a bad bloke to have standing with you in a tight spot. And they were certainly in a tight spot.

Daniel lay down and pulled his army blanket over him, the movement making him aware he smelt to high heaven like they all did. His clothes would stand up and walk to a wash tub themselves, given half a chance.

He felt for the letter he'd stuffed in the pocket of his tunic. He'd try and get it posted somewhere on the march tomorrow, there might be some village or town where someone would oblige if he made it worth their while. And it was like that, his hand still resting on the letter to Hope, that he finally went to sleep.

★　　★　　★

Over the next days it became apparent to even the most inexperienced soldiers among them that the Allied armies had been tempted forward from their previous strategic defensive positions into a German trap. Bungled tactics by those in command, along with severe underestimates of the enemy's power and cunning, meant Daniel and his division were attempting to stop an unstoppable tide.

The German army flooded into France, their panzers bulldozing their way forward, preceded by a cloud of screaming Stukas which were covered against attack from British or French fighters by marauding Messerschmitts. Daniel saw men he had trained and marched with for the last seven months fall to his right and left, some of them barely more than boys. He witnessed at first hand the slicing power of shrapnel on human flesh and very soon began to pray not that he would survive the mayhem and carnage – for who could hold out in the midst of such hell? – but that when his turn came, the end would be quick and clean.

Every day they retreated further, fighting like Trojans, and every night he dreamt of Hope and home even though that other world held no reality for him now. Real life was noise and dust and men's intestines strewn on the ground. But every so often, in an occasional lull in the bombing or when they were snatching a few hours' sleep in a farmer's barn or under hedgerows, he'd hear a bird singing somewhere or cattle lowing and the everyday sounds would bring a lump to his throat.

By the last week of May it was common knowledge that the remaining British brigades were being withdrawn to the north, a rapid retreat to the coast and evacuation to England their only hope. When they reached the beaches on each side of Dunkirk, their corporal strutted around chivvying the debilitated and demoralised men with talk of home. Daniel watched him as night set in. The man was inexhaustible, he'd been born to be a soldier and be where he was right now. He kept his eyes on the corporal as he knelt by the side of a young lad who had been shot up pretty badly earlier that day. He couldn't hear what he said to the lad but by the time he stood up again, the lad was smiling.

What had he been born to do? Daniel wondered. Not this, never this. He didn't know which turned his stomach more, watching men being annihilated or maimed beyond recognition, or the fear that he was becoming numb to the slaughter.

He rubbed his face and leaned back against a sand dune. He watched some ants scurrying about searching for food. They knew what they were doing, too. No hesitation or doubt, even though their brains were minuscule. He smiled darkly to himself. Was he envying the ants now? He'd better not tell anyone. They'd think he'd cracked, like poor old Horace Bell who had broken rank and run screaming down the middle of the road until a German plane had made mincemeat of him.

No, he hadn't cracked but he was doing what he'd always done, dreaming dreams, thinking, soul-searching. He hadn't realised he was a dreamer until he'd joined the army but the machine had a way of bringing you into stark confrontation with yourself. He wasn't a doer, not like his father, or Hope for that matter. They were both doers, possessed of some driving force he knew he didn't have. And that was why, although he'd fallen in love with Hope, had been fiercely attracted to her from the minute he'd set eyes on her, he'd always felt that part of himself was in opposition to her too. He'd subconsciously feared that if he let her have her head, if he agreed to go in with her and work with her, he would have been smothered by her like he'd always been smothered by his father. Flawed thinking. Because Hope wasn't his da. She didn't want to control him. She'd been offering him the chance to help her create something lasting and worthwhile for the two of them and their bairns, that was all.

'You all right, Fallow?'

The corporal was looking down at him, his thin rat-like face inquiring.

Daniel felt a stab of affection for the loud little individual who had been mother and father to the lot of them for months. 'Aye, Corp. Just thinking of home, the wife and bairns. You know.'

'That's the ticket. Keep your pecker up until the wife can get it up for you, eh? Makes the world of difference, your state of mind. Believe you're going to get home and you will.'

He moved on to a group of men some yards away without waiting for a reply, but as Daniel stared after him he felt the significance of the corporal's words hit home. There were endless columns of British troops on the beaches and in the harbour waiting for the ships that would take them home, but German heavy armour and tanks couldn't be too far away. And all day they'd watched the Luftwaffe bombers and fighters attempting to annihilate the men in the water and on the beach. The RAF did their best to provide some defence but they were hopelessly outnumbered.

Did he really believe he was going to make it when it was his turn to try for the ships? That's if he hadn't got blown to bits before then. But no, he wouldn't think like that. He'd got this far, hadn't he? Against all the odds, he still had two arms and two legs and his mind intact which was more than could be said for some of the poor blighters around him. He'd make it. If those little craft from home were prepared to risk life and limb to come and take them home, he'd be on one. They had expected the Royal Navy anti-aircraft cruisers and the like, but none of them had anticipated the vast fleet of small boats manned by civilians. It proved they hadn't been abandoned and hung out to dry.

'I could eat a horse, man. How about you?' One of the men Daniel had trained with who hailed from Newcastle plumped down beside him on the sand. Groaning, he eased his grossly swollen foot out of his army boot. He had marched thirty or so miles each day for the five days it had taken them to reach the coast with a machine-gun bullet lodged in his foot. 'Failing that a plate of me mam's panackelty'd go down a treat.'

Daniel nodded. None of their contingent had eaten for over three days now and he had dreamt of food the night before.

'Think it'll be our turn tomorrow, Dan?'

Again Daniel nodded. 'They got plenty away today.' Neither of them referred to the bodies left floating in the water or washed up on the beach. Several boats had been sunk by Stuka dive-bombers too and the debris from these littered the sand in places.

'There were lads of no more than fourteen or fifteen manning some of those little dinghies and rowing boats,' his friend said quietly. 'Makes you proud to be British, don't it?'

'Aye, it does, Walt. You're dead right it does.'

They talked some more before drifting off into uneasy sleep through sheer exhaustion, but come morning light they were standing waiting along with hundreds of other soldiers. More were being added to their number all the time and through some of these word filtered in that Allied troops were still fighting furiously and covering the embarkation of their comrades.

It was late afternoon by the time Daniel and Walt and a good number of their company were told to wade out into the water to board three barges that an old tug was towing. They didn't need telling twice in spite of the barrage from the blue skies above.

As luck would have it there was a slight lull in the bombing just as they ploughed through the icy waves. Their frantic progress was hampered by their uniforms and the guns and kit they were carrying. With hearts pounding like sledgehammers they fought their way through the water until they reached the barges and eager hands pulled them on board.

'That's it, lads.' A gnarled old skipper with a face as tanned as leather and a long white beard grinned at them, his wispy white hair blowing in the salty wind. 'Me and some other folk thought it was a nice day for a jaunt across the Channel. You on for it, lads?'

Eventually the three barges were packed and they were off, other boats of varying sizes passing them to reach the beach they'd just left. The Stukas were back in force and somewhere not far behind them there was a mighty explosion and the sound of shouts and screams. They looked back at a scene of carnage.

'I hope Jerry rots in hell.' Walt turned away, his face grim. 'And if it was left up to me I'd make room for that snake in the grass Leopold an' all. He knew if he surrendered it was like giving Hitler an invitation to wipe us out.'

Daniel said nothing. He agreed with Walt. Belgium's recent

armistice with the Germans had left a large gap in the front line through which the enemy had poured, but right now this wasn't as important as concentrating on getting the hell out of France.

The tug seemed to chug along painfully slowly but eventually they were out to sea, the sights and sounds of the beach fading. The sea was choppier the further they got away from land, and a salty wind whipped his face. Daniel shut his eyes for a moment. No one was talking. Perhaps, like him, they couldn't quite believe they were going home when so many of their comrades had died in the retreat to the coast.

When he opened his eyes again he saw the enemy plane making straight for them.

There was nowhere to go and nothing to do. All he and the other men could do was watch in fascinated horror as it came. And then, from seemingly nowhere, a lone Spitfire was on the Stuka's tail. Walt clutched his arm but otherwise everyone had frozen, mind and body concentrating on the metal deliverer of death.

The Spitfire wasn't going to be able to deflect the Stuka in time. The thought came a few moments before Daniel saw the bombs drop. For a second of time the world stood still, the bombs seemingly moving in slow motion, and then barge and sea erupted in a noise that was all-consuming.

Daniel never knew if he passed out in the explosion but his next conscious thought was of being underwater and sinking away from the greeny-blue light above him. Aware his gun and other equipment were pulling him down to Davey Jones's locker, he frantically tried to lose them along with his army boots, twisting like an eel as he rid himself of everything he could.

He fought his way to the surface and emerged to see debris scattered all around him. He knew his only chance was to grab something and hold on. He'd never regretted anything so much as not learning to swim.

The salt water was burning his eyes and throat and there were bodies and bits of bodies floating around him, but just in front of him was a piece of wreckage. Splashing wildly with panic he attempted to reach it. Once he'd grabbed it he hung on like grim death, sobbing rawly in his throat, and then he managed to hoist himself half across it and then fully on where he lay spreadeagled, his lungs and throat on fire.

Don't sink, don't sink, don't sink. The refrain was beating in his head with his heartbeat, and then he nearly did just that when the makeshift raft was grabbed on one side and he almost toppled back into the water.

'Here, pull him up alongside of you.'

He saw the corporal was towing a seemingly lifeless body and it was a moment before he recognised Walt. Between them they managed to get Walt onto the wood. Walt opened dazed eyes. Keeping one arm round his friend to prevent him sliding off, Daniel gasped, 'You come on too, Corp.'

'No, three'll sink it, lad.' The corporal was holding on loosely and now he turned his head to look back over the scene from hell. 'Them poor devils in the first two barges didn't stand a chance, direct hit they took. There's not many left from ours either. Look, you make for shore, lad, and I'll follow. I'm a good swimmer. Paddle with your hands as best you can and I'll kick with me legs. All right?'

'Back to shore?' Everything in him wanted to try for England, impossible though their chances might be.

'Only thing to do.'

Daniel nodded. He was in no position to argue.

They had only gone a few yards when Daniel felt the current beneath them take the wood. He heard the corporal swear and then say, 'Hold on, lad, and keep him with you if you can.' And then they were moving much faster, as though a giant hand was pulling them. Dumb with fear, Daniel tried to keep himself and Walt on the wood which was lurching and slowly spinning. He hooked one leg over his friend and stretched his hands either side of the wood as though he could steady the frail piece of flotsam. It was some minutes before he realised the corporal was no longer with them. All he could hope for was that somehow the man had managed to keep afloat. He had seemed a strong swimmer.

He felt Walt stir beneath him, moving as though trying to dislodge the weight holding him down, and through gritted teeth he ground out, 'Keep still, man, if you want to live. You hear me, Walt? It's Dan. Keep still, don't move.'

Whether Walt fully understood him or not he wasn't sure; he didn't speak, but he did stop squirming which was the important thing.

On and on they went, the wood moving in a kind of mad dance, and now added to the blinding fear was the physical discomfort of vomiting. Daniel choked and retched. It was only salt water, he hadn't eaten for days, but it kept coming and coming until his head was swirling and he was exhausted and at the end of himself. And still they kept afloat.

He didn't see the rock. When the raft hit it he was aware of being flicked off as if he was a rag doll. Instinctively he made a frantic grabbing motion with his hands and felt his body hit unyielding stone. His fingers clasped a ridge as his knees slammed against the rock, and his feet scrambled over the harsh surface covered with hundreds of tiny barnacles. And then his toes, too, found the smallest of ridges in the stone, which, had he had his boots on, would not have been enough for him to gain a foothold.

He hung on, too scared to move a muscle for a while. As his breathing steadied he expected a wave to crash over him and take him down into the water any moment but this did not happen. Eventually he steeled himself to move his head slightly and glance about him. The force with which the makeshift raft had hit the rock had flung him above the water level, and he was spreadeagled against the murderously rough surface of the rock. Of Walt and the wreckage there was no sign but there was no possibility of his friend surviving in the water, the state he'd been in, and he grieved for him. He had let him die. He had wanted to save him but he'd let him die.

Gradually over the next minutes the physical pain kicked in. The barnacles covering the rock had taken strips of flesh from his arms and legs, especially his hands and feet, and his face felt raw. When he moved his head slightly he saw the rock underneath was red with blood. The agony was acute. But you had to be alive to feel agony. How much longer he'd remain alive, wedged as he was on a rock out to sea with no hope of rescue, was another question, he thought.

I love you, Hope. Wherever you are, whatever you are doing at this moment, feel my love. I've made you unhappy and I never wanted to do that. Don't ever forget me, and don't love anyone else like you loved me.

He frowned at himself, the movement causing him to wince with pain as his lacerated skin protested. Wasn't approaching death supposed to make one noble? Unselfish? Shouldn't he be praying she would go on to find a new love, a man she could be happy with? But the thought of Hope with another man caused his stomach to form a giant knot. Anyway, he reasoned painfully, whether he wanted it or not, it would happen. She was too beautiful to live the rest of her life alone. He shut his eyes, too exhausted to think any more.

Over the next hour he grew so cold and was in such pain the thought of just letting go and allowing the sea to take him lost its terror. But gradually he became aware that things were changing, the sea was doing something strange. When he realised what it was, he almost laughed out loud. The tide was going out. He must be close to a beach somewhere because the water was definitely going down, though the approaching darkness made it difficult to ascertain exactly how deep it remained.

He didn't dare try to climb further up the rock to attempt to peer over it, but he could see he was much further above the water now. Could he try and climb down towards the sea? It was the only way he was going to get off this accursed thing, but what if the water was still too deep for him to touch bottom and the current took him again? Would there still be a current if the sea was withdrawing? He didn't know.

His first movements caused such acute pain it took his breath away. His raw knees had stuck to the stone and he felt the blood begin to run down his legs as he slowly felt for hand- and footholds. Slowly, very slowly he began the descent but inevitably he lost his feeble grasp on the rock and ended up in a skin-shredding slide straight into the water.

He went right under at first and it was only after panic-filled moments that he realised he could touch bottom and keep his head and shoulders out of the water. He splashed and stumbled round the rock and there was the beach stretching endlessly in front of him. It wasn't Dunkirk. He didn't know where the current had brought him, but it was not Dunkirk.

Slipping and sliding under the waves time after time, he made slow progress up the beach, hardly able to walk. The cold water had numbed the pain in his feet to some extent so he was barely aware of the rocks and shingle beneath them. When he was thigh deep in the water, he realised his clothing was so shredded he was practically naked.

There were a few fishing boats pulled up on the sand in the distance, he could see the shape of them in the darkening twilight. And where there were fishing boats there was likely to be habitation.

His teeth were chattering with a mixture of cold and shock, and he had to force himself to keep walking. If he collapsed now, out here in the open, he wouldn't last till morning. He passed the boats and then the sand dunes beyond them, and reached a rough road which was little more than a track winding away towards what looked like a small village some couple of hundred yards in the distance. There looked to be an inn of some kind and beyond that a cluster of small white-washed cottages and other buildings.

Beyond thinking now, he headed for the inn, telling himself he couldn't pass out, not yet, not till he was safe.

He was still some fifty yards away when a German voice came out of the shadows, telling him to halt. He didn't react immediately, stumbling forward a few more steps before it came again, more harshly this time. He stopped and turned. Two young Germans in uniform stood holding Luger pistols pointed at his heart.

He stood swaying stupidly, his eyes trying to focus on the soldiers walking towards him. Behind them he could see a couple of armoured vehicles and more German uniforms. He had walked straight into occupied territory.

One of the young soldiers barked an order. Daniel gathered that he wanted him to put his hands in the air, but it was beyond him. It was all he could do to remain upright. If they shot him, they shot him.

They didn't shoot. If he hadn't been beyond feeling anything, Daniel would have been amazed that when they took hold of him, their grip was supportive rather than restraining. He was not to know that virtually skinned raw as he was, he presented an appalling sight, even to men used to appalling sights.

The next few days were lost in a haze of drugged agony. He was vaguely aware of a German doctor tending to his lacerated flesh and stitching a number of wounds that ran deep. Whether it was the medication or the bang on the head he had received when the bomb struck he didn't know, but it was not until five days later that he realised all his efforts to escape the sea had been for nothing. If he survived his injuries, all he had to look forward to was a German prisoner-of-war camp.

This dark frame of mind continued for a short while until he joined other prisoners waiting to be shipped out of France. As he clambered into the lorry that was taking them away, trying not to groan as the tender new flesh beneath the scabrous surface began to bleed, his tortured eyes met those of Walt's.

'Dan!' Walt's face split into a wide grin as he moved to sit beside him. 'Man, I thought you were a goner.'

'You thought *I* was?' In spite of his pain, Daniel was smiling. 'By all the laws of blighty, you shouldn't be here, Walt. You were unconscious when we hit that rock.'

'What rock?'

'The rock that pitched us off that bit of wood.'

'Man, I don't remember no bit of wood. All I recall is waiting for them bombs to hit and then waking up on a fishing boat as sick as a dog. Unfortunately for us all, there was company on the beach when we landed.'

'I don't believe it.' Suddenly the world was a better place, a place where miracles did still happen. 'You're a sight for sore eyes, Walt.'

'Likewise, Dan.' Walt bent his head closer. 'You know where they're taking us?'

'Germany.'

'Aye, man, I know it's Germany. You know which camp? Word is it's a place near Berlin.'

Daniel shrugged. 'One camp is the same as another, I'd imagine.'

'Aye, mebbe.'

'It'll be all right, Walt.' Daniel tried to bring reason into the equation. 'I haven't been treated too bad. How about you?'

Walt looked at him. 'These blokes are ordinary soldiers, man, like us, even if they're on the wrong side. Them camps are different.'

Different or not, he was determined to survive, come what may. One day he was going to see Hope again, and in a free England. To even contemplate anything else was unthinkable.

★　　★　　★

It was a full two months later before Hope received a telegram informing her that Daniel was not dead as had first been assumed, but was, in fact, a prisoner of war.

She opened the ominous brown envelope with trembling fingers, her heart beating so loudly it filled her ears. She read the few short lines, the words dancing before her eyes as she endeavoured to take them in.

'Hope?' Jinny had heard the knock on the door and now stood silently watching her from the kitchen doorway. 'What is it, lass? Not more bad news?'

Hope sank down onto the bottom tread of the stairs. 'He's alive.' Hope held out the telegram, her face alight even as the tears rolled down her cheeks. 'Daniel's alive. He's a prisoner of war but he's alive.' She fumbled in the pocket of her dress for his letter. From the moment she had received it just a week or so before he'd been reported missing, presumed dead, she'd kept it about her person, day and night. It was her link with him; his handwriting was part of him and precious. Strange that one letter could heal all the hurt of the last years so completely. She held on to it now, feeling she was holding on to him.

Jinny took the telegram and read it swiftly. 'I'm glad, hinny.'

Jinny's youngest two boys, Dennis and Norman, who had still been living at home when war broke out, had volunteered shortly after Daniel. Neither had survived Dunkirk.

Thinking of this, Hope said, 'Oh, I'm sorry, Aunt Jinny. I wish Dennis and Norman were here for you. I don't know how you stand it.'

'No, lass, no, don't you think like that. Don't you feel bad 'cos your man's still alive. They're gone and nowt can bring 'em back, bless 'em, but it'd be a poor do if we can't rejoice

353

with them that rejoice.' Blinking hard, Jinny reached for her niece, drawing her up off the stairs and hugging her. 'How about I make us a nice cup of tea, eh? To celebrate? Like old times, hinny.'

Old times. In the kitchen, Hope glanced down at the letter in her hand and then at the telegram her aunt had placed on the kitchen table. Would the old times ever come back? She doubted it. This war was changing everything. *But Daniel was alive.* If only he could come back to her she would never ask for anything else for the rest of her life.

Keep him safe, she prayed silently, her eyes wide open. Please, please keep him safe.

Chapter 26

Three years of war had brought great change to Hope, as they had to the town itself.

The first bombs fell on Sunderland in the middle of 1940, and by the same time the following year many famous landmarks in the town had been blitzed and the once familiar landscape gone for ever.

With the coming of the Luftwaffe and civilian casualties all over Sunderland, Hope had been glad she'd remained firm in her decision to keep the children in the country. Although Abe never said she had been right, from the first bombing raid he had stopped pestering her to bring Jack and the girls home. He took her to see the children often, and Hope had given up asking him how he obtained the petrol when it was being severely rationed, because he would never give her a straight answer. Neither would he agree to her travelling by train. For the sake of family harmony, she held her tongue. Gwendoline's parents had taken their daughter and grandson to stay with friends in Buckinghamshire, and although Cecil had visited his wife and child once or twice, Abe did not accompany him.

At the end of 1941, just before the New Year, Bernice married her Thomas. Abe and Emily attended the wedding but relations between Thomas and his in-laws were tense, and the situation was not improved when Mrs Howard made plain her feelings about Abe's part in preventing the marriage the first time round. All in all, once the happy couple were on the train to Middlesbrough where they planned to live, Hope was not the only one who gave a sigh of relief that the day was over.

Just a short while after Bernice had left the town and with rationing beginning to bite, Hope decided to close her business until the war was over. The call had gone out for women to work in the town's shipyards, previously a sanctum of purely male labour, and although the work was hard and carried out under dangerous conditions, Hope took to it like a duck to water. She'd joined Austin's shipyard, the one closest to home, and after training she began work as a crane driver. The long hours were tiring but she welcomed this, hating the moment when she would return to an empty house devoid of her family. The camaraderie of the other women eased her loneliness during the day but the evenings consisted of endless bitter-sweet memories – of baby hands reaching out to her, Betsy's giggle, Jack's frown, Daniel's smile. However busy she tried to keep, it wasn't enough.

And then in May 1943, in what was to be the last raid on Sunderland, something happened that changed her solitary state. George was on fire-watching duty when Fenwick's Brewery in Long Row was hit, and part of a wall fell on him, injuring him badly. He lingered for some hours in the infirmary but died in Jinny's arms.

The change this brought about in Jinny was dramatic. She

had weathered the loss of her two youngest boys with forti-
tude, and had learned to live with the worry of Bart and
William being called up and sent to the front, but with her
husband's death it was as though her own lifespring had
snapped.

Several evenings running after the funeral Hope found her
aunt sitting in a dark kitchen without having eaten or apparently washed or slept. Taking matters into her own hands,
Hope took Jinny home with her. After putting her to bed
she called the doctor who prescribed a sedative, after which
Hope fed her aunt a bowl of soup and then sat with her until
she fell asleep. One of Jinny's daughters agreed to come to
Hope's house and sit with her mother during the day, and
Hope took over in the evenings.

She never went to bed herself until she was sure Jinny was
comfortable and asleep. The doctor's diagnosis of a mental
breakdown might have been right, but within a short while
it was clear something was wrong physically too. Kidney
failure, the doctor pronounced. Broken heart, Hope called it.
Whatever, the day after Italy completed a military about-face
by declaring war on Germany, her ally until little more than
five weeks before, Jinny died peacefully in her sleep.

When Hope went into the bedroom the next morning
with her aunt's breakfast tray, she didn't realise at first that
Jinny had gone. After drawing back the blackout curtains and
letting the dull October light spill into the room, she said,
'It's trying to sleet again, we're going to be in for a bad winter
this year. You're in the best place this morning, Aunty. The
wind's enough to cut you in two out there.'

When no response was forthcoming, she turned and looked
at the figure propped up on the pillows. Jinny was lying with

a slight smile on her lips, her hands folded on top of the pink eiderdown and her once fat body barely making a mound under the covers.

Hope stared at her. The moment she had been dreading had arrived and although she had tried to prepare herself for it, she couldn't. 'No, oh no, Aunty.' Her hand to her mouth, she remained frozen by the window. 'Please don't leave me yet. Please don't go.' This was her aunty and mother and best friend, her rock and beloved confidante.

She made herself walk over to the bed, numb with shock. She sat down and took her aunt's hand. It was cold, stiff, the life long since departed. She sat for some time, silent and bewildered, her eyes roving aimlessly round the familiar surroundings. She felt like a very small child again, lost, lonely, but this time there would be no Aunt Jinny marching in and whisking her away home.

She wanted her back. Oh, she did, she wasn't ready to say goodbye. She wanted to hug her and be hugged in return, to tell her she loved her and appreciated so much all she'd done. Hope looked into the dear face which had grown gaunt in the last months but to which death had given a relaxing peace that made her appear more like the old Aunt Jinny.

She couldn't wish her back. Not to pain and discomfort and the sorrow of missing Uncle George the way she had. Tears coursed down her cheeks. 'You're with him now, Aunty,' she whispered. 'Happy again. Free from pain and sorrow. But I'm going to miss you so much. I love you, you know that, don't you? How am I going to bear it not having you around?'

Of course she did bear it, constantly telling herself that people were suffering much worse losses than her own. Her children were safe and well and there was still hope Daniel was alive, even though she had heard nothing from him or about him since the telegram telling her he was a prisoner of war. Like many other POWs he appeared to have vanished from the face of the earth once he crossed Germany's borders. How she hated the Germans. Sometimes she thought it was the power of hate, rather than the love she felt for her family, that kept her going.

As Christmas approached, Abe arranged a date when he would take her to stay with the children for a few days. She had done this several times since they had been staying in Yorkshire and Eve always made her very welcome but the agony of saying goodbye when she left got worse, not better, as time went on. They were growing up without her, that was what really hurt, and she could never get the days back. At times she felt so desperate she didn't sleep for nights on end, but then she would go and visit them and see their rosy cheeks and happy faces and it would sustain her until the next occasion.

They were due to leave Sunderland on the morning before Christmas Eve; she hadn't been able to get leave from work any earlier. She was just packing a few things into her bag when a knock came at the front door. It was bound to be Abe. He had been jumpy of late. Cecil's house had been broken into twice in the last six months when he hadn't been at home, and Abe had taken to calling round to see her in the evening on his way home from work to make sure she was all right. Hope found herself looking forward to seeing him. They would sit and have a cup of tea together, talking about Daniel and the bairns often as not, and she would find herself telling him all sorts of things about her day, feeling a sense of achievement when she made him laugh. She couldn't remember her father, and her Uncle George had always been a comfortable but somewhat remote figure in the household when she was growing up. Abe was different.

But when he left the house she always reminded herself that there was another side to him. Everything was fine at the moment and they were getting on well, she admitted it. Furthermore she had developed a real affection for him these last years, and since Daniel had gone away he couldn't have been a better father to her than if she'd been his own daughter. But once, pray God, Daniel was home and the bairns were back, she knew he wouldn't be able to resist interfering. Not that he'd call it that of course.

She smiled to herself as she went to the door, wondering why Abe hadn't used the key she had given him some months before after Cecil's break-ins.

'Hello, Mam.'

She stared at Jack's grinning face and then at the three girls standing behind him, so taken aback she couldn't react for a moment. And then she flung wide her arms and gathered them all to her. 'My bairns, my bairns. What on earth are you doing here? Who brought you? Where's your granda?'

'Granda didn't bring us, we came by ourselves.' As they spilled across the threshold and into the hall, Jack continued, 'We've had enough of the farm, Mam, and Archy's mam wrote him to say they haven't bombed here for months, not since the summer.'

'You came by yourselves?' Hope stared at the children, horrified.

Jack nodded. 'On the train.'

'Where did you get the money from for the tickets?'

'Jack's got lots of money.' Betsy piped up. 'Him and the

360

others do lots of odd jobs and things, don't you, Jack, only him an' Archy are being blamed for stealing Mrs Murray's chickens and selling them off and the constable came and everything.'

Jack turned and glared at his sister. 'It wasn't us.'

'Who's Archy?' Hope asked faintly.

'Archibald Benson. He's one of Jack's gang and he lives with Mrs Turner in the village although his real home is here in Sunderland in the East End,' Betsy said importantly, ignoring her brother. 'He came back with us an' all.'

'What about Eve, Mrs Walton? Does she know where you are?'

'I left a note.' Jack looked up at her, his angelic face with its crown of blond curls imploring. 'Mam, we don't have to go back, do we? We want to stay here, with you. If there's no more bombs falling, it's safe, isn't it? Alice an' Grace cry for ages every time you go,' he added with seeming innocence. 'They wanted to come home, didn't you?'

Alice and Grace, who each had their arms wrapped round Hope's legs, looked up at her and nodded.

'You cry?' Hope murmured. She hadn't seen a trace of tears.

'Aye, they do,' Betsy affirmed. 'But Mrs Walton said we mustn't cry in front of you 'cos it'll just upset you and put you off coming next time.'

'I . . . I think I need to sit down. Come on through to the kitchen and leave your bags in the hall.' She could hardly believe the four of them were here, and to think they had made the journey by themselves. Anything could have happened. The train could have been bombed, they could have got lost, anything.

The next few minutes were pandemonium but eventually the four were sitting with a slice of sly cake and a beaker of milk in front of them. Hope feasted her eyes on them. She couldn't help it. She was furious with Jack for bringing the girls home like he had, and she was sure there was more to his story than Alice and Grace being homesick, but nevertheless they were here. Home. The house was alive again. She felt like all her Christmases had been rolled into one.

Much later, when Alice and Grace were fast asleep in her bed, curled under the covers like little hedgehogs, she sat the twins down in the kitchen in front of her. They were in their pyjamas, hair damp from their bath and their big brown eyes fixed on her face. 'Now I want the truth.' She spoke to Jack but glanced at Betsy too. 'Did you have anything to do with these chickens going missing, Jack? You and this gang of yours?' She didn't like the idea of him being involved with a gang of any kind.

He looked straight at her and shook his head. 'No, Mam.'

Out of the corner of her eye Hope saw Betsy give a little wriggle. She knew that action. Turning to her daughter, she said, 'This is serious, Betsy. Did he?'

Betsy glanced at her twin and then shook her head.

'They're always blaming me an' the lads for everything,' Jack put in, and Hope thought she detected relief in his voice. 'Just 'cos we went scrumping in the summer in Mrs Robson's orchard, she sent Constable Hicks to the farm again.'

'Aye, but you an' the others shouldn't have sold the apples round the doors,' Betsy put in, receiving a kick for her trouble.

'Stop that.' Hope spoke sharply. 'And what do you mean *again*? How many times did the constable come with complaints about you and this gang, Jack?'

'I told you, we get the blame for everything.' He scowled at his sister as though it was her fault.

'I'm going to ask you one last time, Jack. Did you help this Archy take the lady's chickens to sell somewhere?'

He shook his head, his face sullen now.

'Then why did they think you did?'

He shrugged. 'I dunno.' Then, his face brightening, he slid off his chair and came and put his arms round her. 'Can we stay, Mam?' he pleaded. 'Please? None of us want to go back. We miss you, don't we, Betsy?'

Hope knew when she was being charmed. She also knew he was very good at it. He took after his grandfather in more ways than one. But he had been away for a long time and however good Eve and her husband were, they had the farm and lots of other children to look after. Whether he had been up to mischief or not, he clearly needed a firm hand and some discipline mixed with love. Now they were back she couldn't bear to send them away again, she just couldn't. And since May they hadn't seen hide nor hair of the Luftwaffe. Sunderland was as safe as Yorkshire probably.

After Christmas she'd sort out this matter of the missing chickens as best she could and they'd start afresh in the New Year. Jack would be in a new school with different friends, everything would be fine. She would make sure it was fine.

Hope hugged her son to her, ruffling his curls and putting out her arm to draw Betsy into the embrace. Her precious bairns. Tomorrow she'd have to make some practical decisions because Jack was now too old to share a bedroom with the girls. Maybe Abe would help her move a bed downstairs to the front room and she could sleep there. The girls could have her bedroom, leaving Jack across the landing in their old room.

She'd have to see about their schooling, inform the local authority they were home again, sort out the ration books, things like that. Alice and Grace would still be receiving a child's ration book, not being six years old yet, but the twins would need to be added to a general one with her. At least with the children home again it would mean that everyone's bit of ration would combine to make enough for a decent meal. She hadn't felt like bothering much when she was on her own, and the tiddly little portions for one were impossible to do anything with anyway. Now everything was different. Tomorrow they'd get the box of Christmas decorations out from under the stairs, the bairns would love that. Oh, it was going to be a special Christmas regardless of the war; her babies were home.

It was wonderful waking up with the children on Christmas Eve although their presence in the house served to emphasise the absence of the other adult member of the family. Hope found herself missing Daniel more than ever and the emotive time of year didn't help either. She'd gone to stay with the children at the farm for a few days over Christmas the year before, the different surroundings going a little way to taking her mind off the fact that Daniel was far away, possibly in one of the terrible camps they kept hearing about on the news.

Abe had called round after the children were in bed the previous night and had come back first thing that morning to see them and help Hope rearrange the sleeping accommodation. After he'd gone to work, she and the children went out into the snowy day to do some emergency shopping. Although she'd been putting away the odd tin of this and that with her coupons since the summer to take to the farm at Christmas, she didn't have enough in the house for four extra healthy appetites.

The newspapers had reported there were only enough turkeys for one family in ten this Christmas, but when they arrived home after their shopping trip – which had taken a good part of the day because the children had wanted to see all the big shops in their Christmas finery and wander round the Old Market thronged with shoppers – it was to find Father Christmas had come early.

A monster of a turkey was sitting plucked and prepared in a huge roasting tin on the kitchen table, surrounded by a bag of potatoes and another of mixed vegetables. Even a large Christmas pudding was there with a bowl of brandy sauce beside it. There was a note propped against the food.

Emily has suddenly decided to take herself off with Cecil to see Edward this Christmas, so thought this might come in useful with the bairns home. Annie and I wouldn't say no to sharing it with you the morrer. Annie says to tell you the pudding's got carrots in it which makes it look light, but cook it long enough and they turn dark. Abe.

This wasn't the end of the surprises. When they went into the front room, a small Christmas tree decorated with fancy tinsel and baubles was standing on a little table by the window. Gaily wrapped parcels were piled beneath it, along with a bowl of oranges, a couple of enormous boxes of chocolates and bags of walnuts and chestnuts. Hope didn't doubt for a minute that most if not all of what had been provided had come via the black market, and as Abe had also made it his business to become friendly with the GIs from a nearby US base, the oranges and chocolates might be courtesy of their allies. Usually she flatly refused to accept Abe's contraband, fearing it had come from contacts like the Mullens and other gangster types, but today her eyes softened on account of the effect it was having on the children.

They were ecstatic, dancing around the front room and getting so excited that Grace made herself sick.

When she had calmed them down, Hope put the wireless on and they listened to Christmas carols, singing along to the warm familiar words as Jack and the girls made paper chains to string across the ceiling. After a tea of chitterlings and bread and dripping, followed by a plateful of teacakes fresh from the oven which disappeared in two minutes flat, Hope shooed the children off to bed so she could wash up and prepare the vegetables for morning. For the first time in a long, long while, she sang as she worked.

She went into the girls' room first to say goodnight. Grace and Alice were almost asleep, worn out by all the excitement but still desperately trying to keep their eyes fixed on their stockings hung at the end of the bed ready for Father Christmas's visit. 'He won't come until you're asleep,' Hope chided, kissing them both and then humming some lullabies until they drifted off, snuggled under the covers.

As soon as the little ones were asleep, Betsy, who had been lying quietly holding her mother's hand, whispered, 'Mam? Where's Alice's mam gone? Why did she have to go away and why didn't she take Alice with her? An' where's Alice's da?'

It had to come one day. No doubt it would have happened sooner if they had been living at home the last three years.

Speaking very quietly, Hope said, 'Does Alice ask about your Aunty Constance or her da?'

Betsy shook her head.

But she would eventually. Thinking carefully, Hope murmured, 'Aunty Constance had to go away to find work because there was none here and she thought it better to leave Alice with you and Jack and Grace because you're like her sisters and brother. Me and your da thought that was best too.'

Betsy thought about this. 'What about her da? Why couldn't he have her? Did he go with Aunty Constance too?'

'Her da died before she was born.' Well, he had in a way. Lonnie Kirby, if he *was* Alice's father, which wasn't certain, was as good as dead to the little girl.

Betsy nodded, apparently satisfied. 'She doesn't need them if she's got us, does she?' she said with the matter-of-factness of children.

'No, she doesn't need them, Betsy. We're her family.'

'I'm glad we're home, Mam,' Betsy whispered after a moment. 'Jack wouldn't listen to me at the farm but he'll listen to you.'

Calmly, Hope said, 'What wouldn't he listen to you about?'

'Things.'

'Things?'

'Just things.'

Clearly Betsy was not about to betray her twin by saying anything more. Hope nodded. 'Don't worry about Jack, hinny. He'll listen to me or I'll want to know the reason why. All right?' She tweaked her daughter's little nose. 'Now, sleep for you or Father Christmas will never come.'

'Oh, Mam.' Betsy wriggled. 'You know he's just make-believe for the little 'uns, like Grace and Alice.'

Hope stared at the small face. They had grown up and she hadn't been there.

She bent down and held Betsy tight for a moment, then kissed her. Keeping her voice light, she said, 'Make-believe or not, I dare say you'll still want your stocking filled? So sleep, madam.'

'All right, Mam.' Betsy smiled a sleepy smile. 'I love you.'

'And I love you, hinny. More than you'll ever know till you have bairns of your own.'

Jack was reading one of his comics when Hope entered his room. He had been highly delighted to learn he would have a room all to himself, and had immediately transported everything belonging to the girls into their new bedroom. Then he had spent a happy hour sorting out his books and comics. Hope noticed that instead of the *Dandy* he had loved before he'd left for Yorkshire, he was now reading a more worthy weekly called *Scoops* which apparently dealt with science and the wonder world of tomorrow. The knowledge that the twins would be ten years old on Boxing Day, a move into two numbers and the end of an era, caused her to swallow hard.

'This is great, Mam.' He looked up at her, his eyes shining. 'All about the launch of a spaceship. Do you think they'll ever really put an aircraft into space?'

'I shouldn't think so,' she said, smiling as she took the comic and placed it on the pile on the floor by the side of the bed. She kissed him goodnight. 'Sleep, young man.'

'If they do, I'd want to go.' He slid down under the eiderdown. 'Or I might be a pilot.'

'Right.' She nodded and switched off the light.

'Or I might be like Granda.'

'Granda?' She paused in the doorway.

'Aye, Granda. He lives in a great big house and has lots of money and men working for him, and he told me you have to start young if you want to get anywhere. Money is the key, that's what Granda said. He had two jobs when he was still at school, Granda did. He said there's always ways to make money if you look for them and keep your wits about you.'

'Did he.' She was glad of the darkness. 'And when did Granda say all this?'

'I dunno, ages ago, when you came to the farm one day and me and Granda went for a walk. I told him about—' Jack stopped abruptly as if he'd just remembered who he was talking to.

'You told him about what?'

There was silence for a moment. 'I don't remember.'

He remembered all right and she'd bet her last farthing it was something like selling the apples round the doors or stealing chickens. Up to this moment she hadn't been absolutely sure Jack had been involved in that, or at least she'd told herself she wasn't sure, but now there was no question in her mind. It was just a matter of what else he'd been up to. How she wished Daniel was here to talk this through with.

She made herself say evenly, 'There's lots of time for you to decide what you want to do when you grow up, but for now you are still nine years old and it's time for sleep.'

'I'll soon be ten.'

Yes, he would soon be ten. She closed the bedroom door and stood on the landing for a long time. When she finally walked down the stairs, her shoulders were bowed.

Chapter 27

'I don't think you ought to be bringing the bairn along, that's all I'm saying. His mam'd go mad if she knew.'

'Aye, well, she don't know, does she, and she's not likely to.'

'I don't see why you want him tagging along.'

Abe stared at his son. He and Cecil were sitting in the office; everyone else had long since gone. 'What have you got against the lad?' he asked quietly.

'Against him?' Cecil's chin poked forward. 'Why do I have to have something against him not to want him involved in stuff that's men's business? He's a bairn, Da, don't you understand? One slip of the tongue and it won't be just Hope he lands us in trouble with.'

'There's no question of that.'

'Oh, for crying out loud.' Cecil jumped to his feet, sending his chair sliding back with his legs in an angry gesture that thinned Abe's mouth. 'He's ten years old.'

'He's a canny lad and older than his years. He's coming.'

As Cecil shook his head, Abe added, 'He's like I was at that age, Cecil. Bright as a button. And he knows when to keep his mouth shut. His mam'd wrap him up in cotton wool but it won't do him no favours in the long run. In the real world you have to have an edge if you want to get on. That's all I'm showing him.'

Cecil had gone to stand at the window with his back to the room. 'Taking over the boy won't bring his da any closer,' he said flatly, staring out into the hot August evening.

'I know that.' Abe's voice was sharp. 'And I'm not taking him over, not like you mean. He likes to be with me, that's all. And with his da away, it's only natural to my mind. He lives in a house full of females, poor little devil. He needs a man's influence, the age he is. You wouldn't have him growing up all namby-pamby, would you?'

Cecil turned. He looked at his father for a long moment. Then, without answering him, he said, 'He's just coming through the gates now. Do you want me to go and meet him?'

'No, no, I'll go,' Abe muttered. 'You close up here and follow me down.'

Abe walked through the larger outer office and into the corridor outside. At the end of this a staircase led down to the factory beneath, the main doors of which opened up onto a big yard. These were bolted, but a narrow side door next to them opened just as Abe reached it and his grandson stepped through.

'Hello, Granda.' Jack turned his bright gaze up to the man he adored.

'Hello, lad.' Abe ruffled the blond hair that of late Jack had insisted he wanted cut close to his head to stop it curling. 'You get away all right?'

Jack nodded.

'What did you tell your mam?'

'That I'm coming to tea with you an' Grandma.'

'Aye, well, you are.' Abe grinned.

'Where are we going first, Granda?'

Abe touched the side of his large nose. 'Bit of business, like I told you a couple of days ago. You've not mentioned it to no one?'

'Course not, Granda.'

'Not even to Betsy?'

Jack shook his head. 'She got the hump 'cos I wouldn't let her come, though.'

His tone indicated he didn't like being at odds with his twin and Abe picked up on this. 'It's for the best, lad,' he said softly. 'Your sister's a little lassie still but you're a young man. You've got a head on your shoulders, Jack, and it's not too soon to use it.' Then he repeated what he had said to Cecil minutes before. 'You're a canny lad and older than your years, like I was at your age.'

Jack beamed. He liked nothing better than being compared to his granda. Cecil joined them at this point, smiling at his nephew. Jack smiled back but said nothing. He was wary of Cecil. His uncle had always been nice to him but he felt his da's brother didn't like him and he didn't know why. He had said as much to his mother but she had poo-pooed the idea. Nevertheless he felt she agreed with him at bottom. He wondered if it was something to do with the fact that Edward lived so far away with Aunty Gwendoline and his other granda and grandma, but that wasn't *his* fault. He had asked his granda a few weeks ago when Edward was coming back, and his granda had said he might not. Aunty Gwendoline and her mam and da liked the country better than the town, he'd said.

'We'd better get going.' Abe gestured for his grandson and son to precede him out of the side door and he locked up. They walked over to the reserved spaces in one corner of the yard where their two cars were parked. Cecil climbed into his and Abe opened the door for Jack to clamber into the passenger seat of his car.

This Jack did with alacrity. No one in his class at school had a granda with a car and every time he rode beside Abe he hoped one of his friends would see him. When he'd first started at the school after Christmas no one had believed his granda was rich and lived in a great big house and had a car. Then his granda had come and picked him up one night and everyone had seen for themselves. That had been very satis-fying.

Jack hugged the memory to himself, the warm feeling it gave him colouring his voice as he said, 'I love riding in your car, Granda.'

'Good. I like having you with me.'

Their eyes met in perfect accord and the two smiled at each other. Abe started the engine and followed Cecil out of the yard. Both cars stopped in the road outside and Cecil got out to close and padlock the ten-foot-high iron gates set in the brick wall surrounding the works.

When both cars set off again, Abe was in front. After a minute or two, Jack said again, 'Where are we going, Granda?'

'You know I told you about how things are in short supply because of the war but that you can't just sit on your back-side and hope everything comes to you? Well, I'm seeing someone, a friend. He helps me out sometimes. Things that have fallen off the back of a lorry.' Abe winked at his grandson.

The black market. Jack knew all about that. Even in Yorkshire there had been shortages of certain things but he knew in the towns it was worse. Archy's mam said you could make more on the black market in one night than working a month of Sundays in a factory, and Archy's uncles were up to their eyes in it. He'd been round Archy's house the other day when one of his uncles had come by with some stuff for his mam. At least Archy called them his uncles but they weren't really, not like his Uncle Cecil was to him. They were Archy's mam's friends. Jack looked at his grandfather. 'What are you getting, Granda?'

'Half a pig, among other things, lad. And a few bits to sell on. Sell them for the right price and you end up paying nowt for what you've got yourself. See?'

Jack saw. He thought about how his mam came back from the shipyard too tired to eat her evening meal some nights and felt a dart of irritation at her stupidity. She knew his granda was able to get things and knew people, she didn't have to work so hard. But she'd got a thing about his granda, about taking short cuts in general. That's why he'd stuck to his guns about Mrs Murray's chickens; his mam would never have understood he was just looking after number one. And that's what you had to do if you wanted to be better than the rest of them. His granda understood that.

He looked at the hard profile again. He didn't intend to slog his guts out for the rest of his life working for peanuts, like most of the folk round here. He wanted to be like his granda.

374

They passed Lambton Drops and turned into a road close to Hetton Staits on the river. They stopped at the back of the bottle works. There was a lorry parked a little distance off and a man was leaning against it, drinking a bottle of beer. Abe switched off the engine and immediately Jack said, 'Can I come with you, Granda?'

'No, lad. You stay in the car and keep the doors locked till I say, all right? Your Uncle Cecil and I won't be long. You keep your eyes peeled and if you see anyone about, press the horn.'

Jack thought about this. His face brightened. 'Am I the lookout, Granda?'

Abe chuckled. 'You're a canny lad. Aye, Jack, you're my lookout so do a good job.'

Jack nodded, beaming. He'd be the best lookout in the world for his granda. He'd do anything for him, anything.

He watched as his grandfather joined his uncle outside the car. They said something he couldn't hear and then walked over to the man beside the lorry.

True to his word, Jack knelt up in his seat so he had a clear view of his surroundings. His gaze moved back and forth until he saw his grandfather and uncle walking back towards him after they had peered in the back of the lorry. He slid down in his seat again. As his grandfather opened the car door, he said, 'What's happening, Granda?'

'Just need to move the car closer.'

So they could load up the boot without anyone being any the wiser, Jack thought, seeing his uncle climb into his own car and then reverse towards the lorry.

When the two boots were loaded, Jack watched as money changed hands and then within minutes they were back on the road again. Back at his grandfather's house, he helped the two men carry the sacks into the garage. They were heavy and there were lots of them.

When the cars were empty and his grandfather had closed the garage door, he said, 'You coming in for a bite, Cecil?'

'Not tonight.'

'Why? Annie's made plenty and you've only an empty house to go back to, haven't you?'

'I've things to do but thanks all the same.'

His uncle wasn't going to stay because he was here, Jack thought. He stared at his father's brother and he knew he wasn't imagining how his uncle felt about him.

'What things?' His grandfather's tone stated he didn't believe the excuse either.

Cecil began to walk to his car. 'Personal things,' he said crisply over his shoulder. 'Amazingly, I do have a life outside of Fallow Engineering.'

But Cecil did not head for his home – which of late had begun to feel more and more like a mausoleum – but towards Newcastle. He'd discovered several public houses there where the women were friendly, more than friendly on occasion. And on the whole they were ordinary women, factory workers and the like on nights out. It would never have been that way before the war; then it was only women of questionable character who would drink without a man, but the last few years had changed everything.

He parked in a side street adjacent to his favourite hunting ground, an old inn with diamond leaded windows that went by the fancy name of the Lord's Falcon. He had long since stopped feeling guilty about frequenting such establishments to meet a woman who would relieve his bodily frustation. Gwendoline had made her choice and as far as she was concerned all she wanted was the continuing façade of marriage while she brought Edward up with her parents. He had never sunk so low as to pay for it; these nights were merely brief encounters which suited both the woman in question and himself. A few short hours of pleasure for a woman who had been without a man for months or years because of the war, and for himself an ease to the burning in his loins which had him walking the floor some nights.

In the pub he found it was one of the nights when the GIs were out in force. Cecil groaned inwardly. With their snazzy uniforms and Yankee chit-chat they bowled the women over every time. He wouldn't get a look in. At bottom he didn't really blame the local girls, the Americans were a friendly bunch and they brought a splash of colour and glamour to dull lives. Mind, it was the nylon stockings and nail varnish that attracted the women too, along with the cigarettes and other luxuries the GIs bandied about. Some of the women hereabouts would sell their bodies and likely their grandmothers too for a bottle of perfume and a fancy lipstick.

Cecil made his way to the bar. As he had expected, the women didn't give him a second look. After paying for his drink, he found a table in the far corner of the pub and sat down. He took out a packet of Chesterfields, one from a box of fifty his father had slipped him a few days before, courtesy of the American base. Lighting up, he surveyed the scene in front of him through a cloud of smoke, his eyes half shut. One drink here and he'd move on.

A moment later a bright voice said, 'Cecil? It *is* you, isn't it?'

'Constance?' He jerked upright in his seat, staring at the peroxide blonde in front of him. 'Good grief! What are you doing in Newcastle?'

'I work here, in this pub, as of last week.' She was smiling but there was a wary look to her face. 'I saw Dora serve you a minute ago and I thought you might be ignoring me.'

'Ignoring you? Why would I do that?' Cecil knew his face was burning but her low-cut blouse was making it difficult to concentrate. 'I didn't see you, that's all.'

'Right.' She nodded. Then, bending over him, she murmured, 'Cecil, don't tell Hope and the others I'm back in these parts. I . . . Well, I ran into a bit of trouble down south and decided to move back some months ago. I was working in a pub in Scotswood but this pays more and it's near my flat. It's better Hope thinks I'm still down south. I've got my own life now and I wouldn't fit in at home any more. You know?'

Easing his tie loose, Cecil said, 'Whatever you say, Constance.'

'Thanks.' She straightened. 'Look, I've got to work now, the boss is a tartar, but hang on till I finish, would you? You can fill me in on what's been happening at home over a bottle of gin. My flat's just a stone's throw from here. If you've time, that is.'

'Aye, I've time.'

'Good.' She fluffed her hair, the movement bringing the white mounds of her breasts into more prominence.

Cecil swallowed. He watched her progress back to the bar and he didn't miss the familiar pats on the bottom one or two of the customers gave Constance or the smiles she flashed at them. He continued to watch her all night. She was a popular girl, there was no doubt about that. A little too popular? Still, it was her life and who was he to judge? If anyone had made a pig's ear of their life, he had. Playing second fiddle to Daniel all his life and now to a ten-year-old child, to add insult to injury. He had been the one to play it straight down the line and fall in with whatever his da wanted, and what had he got out of it? An iceblock of a wife who even when she'd been with him had only let him near her on high days and holidays, and a son he didn't know and who didn't want to know him.

He continued to brood all evening and by the time he met Constance in the alley at the back of the public house, the chip on his shoulder was weighing heavy. She linked her arm through his, the flowery scent of her perfume over-powering, and for a moment he wanted to pull away and tell her he had changed his mind and was going home. But he didn't.

Her flat was a surprise in that it was spacious, being the ground floor of a three-storey house, and furnished expensively, if a little gaudily.

'Like it?'

Her mascaraed eyes were watching him and he made himself smile and say, 'It's grand, Constance. Must have cost you a fortune.'

'Aye, it did, but I like nice things.'

She couldn't have got all this on a barmaid's wage, but then he had already gauged how things were, hadn't he? Wasn't that why he had come back here with her?

'I'll get us a drink in a mo when I've changed out of these

clothes. Sit down and make yourself comfy. There's plenty of food in the kitchen if you want to make yourself a sandwich or something.'

He was hungry but not for a sandwich.

His face must have revealed what he wanted because she kissed him full on the mouth, long and hard, before she turned, saying, 'I'll be back, don't worry,' with a gurgle of laughter.

He was to remember the night that followed for the rest of his life. It was a revelation to him. In the last two or three years he had been with a few women when the need pressed, but they had been what he would term ordinary girls. Constance was not ordinary. The things she had done to him and instructed him to do to her were beyond amazing, and even though he knew they had to be acts she had learnt whoring, it didn't lessen the sheer ecstasy. And she was voluptuous, soft, tasty, everything Gwendoline wasn't, and so at ease with her own body. In all their married life he had never seen his wife fully naked and yet here was Constance revelling in showing herself.

Three times they did it and each time it wasn't just a quick tussle and then finished, but a slow exploring and tasting that made him as hard as a rock the whole night. The first rays of dawn were breaking through Constance's bedroom window when he rolled off her for the last time. Propping herself on her elbow and as naked as the day she was born, she said, 'By, lad, you needed that, didn't you? Something tells me all's not well between you and Gwendoline.'

He didn't answer this directly, saying instead, 'That was . . .' But he couldn't find words to describe what it had been.

Constance smiled. 'Likewise.' She traced a path through the hair on his chest with one finger. 'You're a big boy, Cecil.'

He blushed. Ridiculous, after what they had shared, but he couldn't help himself. He had never known a woman talk in such an earthy manner.

'So?' She sat up and reached for a packet of cigarettes on the little table next to the bed. She lit two and handed one to him. 'What gives with you and Gwendoline?'

She hadn't asked after her child. The thought brought his eyes narrowing. It made him feel uneasy, reminding him of the life she had chosen. He did not comment on this, however. 'Gwendoline left at the beginning of the war. She and her parents took Edward down south. The last time I visited I was informed that's where they're staying when the war's over too.'

'How do you feel about that?'

He shrugged. 'The marriage was in name only for some time before she left, to be truthful, so it's no odds.'

Constance looked at him intently. 'She must be mad.'

He didn't know what to say to this.

'I mean it,' she persisted. 'Some women don't know which side their bread's buttered. If I'd met someone like you years ago, someone who was decent and good and a stallion between the sheets, I'd have spent the rest of my life making him happy.'

He stared at her. He felt warm and it was nothing to do with the humid August air.

'Some people get all the breaks,' she said, drawing on her cigarette and letting the smoke curl out of her mouth. 'Like my dear sister.'

'Hope?' He was surprised. 'I thought you and Hope were close. Before you left Sunderland, I mean.'

'Not really.' She lay back against the pillows, the heavy domes of her breasts with their big pink nipples exciting him so he pulled the sheet over the lower half of his body. 'She was always the favoured one, you see, with my aunt and uncle, with everyone. Couldn't do no wrong, Hope couldn't.'

'Like Daniel.' It was out before he thought about it but once spoken he found it easy to go on. 'My father fairly worships him and he dotes on Jack too because he's Daniel's son. Did you know Daniel's a POW?'

'No. Really?'

He nodded. 'You'd think he was the only man who had ever fought for his country but then right from when he was born he was the blue-eyed boy.'

'Have you been in the forces at all?'

Cecil shook his head. 'I had scarlet fever as a child, it's left me with a weakness in my chest. The quack wrote saying I wasn't fit enough to fight.'

'Their loss, my gain.' Then she bit her lip. 'I've been putting off asking, but . . . how's Alice?'

So it wasn't that she didn't care about her daughter. He felt a sense of relief out of all proportion to the situation. 'She's bonny and happy,' he said quickly. 'And doing fine.'

Constance nodded. 'I knew she would be. It was the right thing to do, to leave her with the other bairns an' all, but it was hard, Cecil.' She dropped her head just the slightest. 'Very hard.'

Didn't he remember Daniel saying she'd left a note saying she hated motherhood or something similar? But he could be wrong. It was a long time ago.

Then her manner underwent a lightning change. She stubbed out the cigarette and moved closer to him, putting an arm across his chest as she fitted herself into the side of his body. 'Tell me all the news from home then.'

Somehow he found himself staying for breakfast.

And by the time he left they both knew he would be back.

PART FIVE

1945 – Wheels Within Wheels

Chapter 28

It was over. It didn't matter that it was wet and thundery; the war was finally, officially over. Hope and the children stood with the thousands of other folk jamming Fawcett Street. After a fanfare of trumpets from the police brass band, the Mayor made the announcement and then everyone sang the national anthem with great fervour.

'Mam?' Grace tugged on Hope's sleeve. 'Why is everyone crying?'

'Not everyone is, hinny,' Hope whispered, 'and those that are are crying with happiness because there'll be no more fighting soon.' Pray God victory over Japan would follow quickly.

'So Da will be coming home?'

How did she answer that when they still didn't know if he was dead or alive? 'I hope so, pet.'

'Are we going to the street party now?'

'Soon, hinny.'

'We're going to have a lovely time, aren't we, Mam?'

They did have a lovely time although the celebrations in Roker and Fulwell were halted briefly when some sailors fired off a gun on a ship berthed in the Wear and a dozen anti-aircraft shells damaged some houses. All in all, though, the day was a good one, if a little soggy.

At nine o'clock in the evening a hush fell over the street as those households with a wireless filled with folk to hear the King give thanks to God for what he called a great deliverance. The King's broadcast only briefly interrupted the street party. Shortly afterwards the effigy of Hitler was lit on the bonfire and homemade fireworks fizzled and banged in the gathering darkness. Hope had her work cut out keeping an eye on Grace and Alice as they ran hither and thither, waiting for the potatoes that were being cooked in the ashes of the bonfire.

At ten o'clock, old Mrs Duckworth's piano was carried out into the road and she sat down and began to play a medley of popular songs. 'Roll Out the Barrel', 'The Lambeth Walk', 'Tipperary', 'Daisy-Daisy', she played them all, and everyone sang along and laughed and cried as the mood took them.

It was the lights burning in every window that seemed to thrill the children most, though, but then they'd spent most of their young lives living under blackout regulations so perhaps it wasn't surprising.

Eventually, at about midnight, people started to drift off into their own houses. Hope managed to find Jack and Betsy among the throng still celebrating and persuade all four children that VE Day was over.

By the time the children were asleep, she felt so tired she didn't know what to do with herself. The strain of being bright and cheerful all day had taken its toll. If she'd known Daniel was safe and coming home to her, to them all, it would have been different, but she didn't. The flood of ex-POWs that had begun weeks before had steadied to a trickle, but there had still been no word. She was frightened, desperately frightened that Daniel would be one of the thousands of names lost in a nameless grave on foreign soil somewhere. The things they had heard and read in the papers were horrendous, unbelievable, but they had happened, and she just prayed Daniel hadn't been tortured or beaten to death, but it was the strain of not knowing that was worst.

She glanced round the quiet kitchen. All the years of them being apart would be worth it if he could come home. And if he did, at least he would know she had waited for him. There were so many soldiers' wives, even one or two in this street, who had dated other men while their husbands had been gone. She couldn't say the loneliness hadn't tempted her at times because it had, but she'd felt deep inside that if she stayed faithful to him God would bring him back. Daft, maybe, because you couldn't bargain with the Almighty, but that's how she had felt.

She sat at the kitchen table looking at the pot of tea she had made but which she didn't want. Then she stood up and walked out into the little backyard where Nugget's empty cage still stood. The rabbit had died just after the children had returned home, and she found she still missed him. While they had been living in Yorkshire he'd been her only companion, and she had spent many an evening sitting in the kitchen with the rabbit on her lap, listening to the wireless. His warm, furry body had been comforting and he'd been a link with the children too. But now he was gone.

She stood for a long time looking up into the night sky. It was quiet now, the last of the revellers had gone indoors, but although the air was cool it wasn't raining.

The empty cage led her thoughts on. She remembered her beloved Aunt Jinny who had not lived to see the end of the war; dear Uncle George; her four male cousins, not one of whom had survived; her one-time hopeful beau, Clarence Irvin, the vicar's son, who had vanished without trace when the troopship he was on had been sunk by the Japanese; Mrs Duckworth's only son, Neville, who had been shot while trying to escape from a prisoner-of-war camp. But most of all she thought of Daniel.

When the cold began to make her shiver she went back indoors, mounting the stairs to Jack's bedroom. He was lying with one arm clutched round the book of fighter planes Abe had given him a few days before, the covers kicked off his legs and a lone wispy curl falling across his forehead. He looked much younger in sleep than he did in the day and she gazed into his face for some minutes, thankfulness flooding her heart.

Her son wouldn't have to fight. He was safe. His life lay before him in a world at peace.

Finally she felt she could go to sleep.

The following Sunday was one of sunshine and warmth, rare in the north in the first couple of weeks of May. When they'd had breakfast, Hope looked round at the four faces sitting at the kitchen table. 'How about a picnic in the country? I can show you where your da and I first met if you like.'

The three girls' response was enthusiastic, Jack's less so. 'I was going to Granda's later,' he said slowly. 'We were going for a ride in his car.'

Hope looked at him keenly. She had her own ideas about these trips which never included Betsy or the others, but to date she hadn't been able to prove her suspicions. Nevertheless she was as sure as she could be that Abe was virtually grooming his grandson to join the business when he was old enough and she hated the thought of it. She didn't want Jack to turn into another Cecil, so dominated by Abe he had to ask permission to breathe. But perhaps that wouldn't happen. Jack certainly had a mind of his own, that was for sure, and although he saw his grandfather through rose coloured glasses now, that might change. She knew Jack's nature well enough to realise that if she tried to stop him seeing so much of his grandfather, he'd just dig his heels in, and so she always trod carefully these days.

'I'd like you to come,' she said quietly. 'I'd like to show you the spot where Da and I met. I feel it will bring him closer somehow, or is that silly?'

'No, course not, Mam.' In one of his mercurial changes of heart, Jack came to her and touched her arm. 'I'll come, it won't matter. Granda won't mind.'

It was a merry little crew that left the house half an hour later, Hope carrying their picnic lunch and bottle of water in a big cloth bag, and Jack with a blanket over his arm in case the grass was wet.

'Where are you off to, hinnies?'

Mrs Duckworth was clearly going to church; her Bible was tucked under her arm. She smiled at Alice and Grace who were skipping in front of the others.

'Mam's going to show us where she met my da.' Grace beamed up into the wrinkled old face.

'It won't matter missing church for once.' Hope came abreast of the old lady. 'It's such a beautiful day.'

'It is that, lass. And God's the same whether you're worshipping him in church or elsewhere.'

Hope thought of Mrs Duckworth's words when she and the children reached Tunstall Hills. The town they had just walked through showed the ravages of the last six years but here on the outskirts, nature was unchanged. The sunshine through young leaves and the twittering of the birds were the same as they had ever been and hedges of whitethorn and banks of primroses and violets had Alice and Grace gathering posies. The skylarks were swooping in the blue sky, catching insects for their fledglings no doubt. Hope shaded her eyes as she looked up at them. 'Come home to me.' It was the faintest of whispers, her lips barely moving. 'Please, please let him come home to me.'

She felt her hand being clasped and she looked down to see the twins either side of her. 'It'll be all right, Mam,' said Betsy, and Jack nodded.

'Archy's da was a prisoner of war and he only came back a couple of days ago,' Jack volunteered. He didn't mention that after a couple of the neighbours had had a word with Archy's da, the roof had nearly gone off the house. Something to do with his uncles, Archy had said.

'I know it will.' Hope smiled down at her beloved bairns. She didn't want to spoil the day which was ripe with apple blossom and honeycups. They would face what had to be faced when it was necessary.

They had a lovely day, the sort of day that remains in the memory even when the mist of time blurs the edges. Even Jack, such a live wire, seemed to relax, lying on his back among the buttercups and daisies after their picnic lunch and reading the book he'd brought with him until Hope noticed he'd fallen asleep.

Twilight was falling when Hope decided she had to wake him so they could make their way back to town. With the setting of the sun it was suddenly chilly but the warmth of the day must have brought out a lot of insects because the skylarks were whirling overhead, singing and calling as they hunted in the evening air. They were a beautiful sight against the red and mauve sky and the years fell from Hope as she stood watching them. Suddenly she was a young girl again, she'd escaped from the East End and her Aunt Jinny's crowded house and was revelling in the brief freedom of the fresh outdoors. Life was open before her, anything was possible, everything was an adventure.

And then she saw him.

Against the backdrop of the sunset and the birds, a lone figure in uniform was slowly walking towards them. Thin, gaunt, and still too far away for her to see the man's face clearly, but she didn't have to see his face to know it was her love.

She remained transfixed for another moment, the girls utterly unaware of what was happening as they continued to pack up and Jack still fast asleep on the blanket at her feet.

And then, like one of the skylarks in the heavens above, she was winging her way towards him, rapidly closing the distance between them. He had stopped as she had begun to run, but then, after a moment or two, he dropped the kitbag he had been holding and began stumbling towards her, his jerky unsteady gait telling her what it must have cost him physically to climb the hills to them.

And then she was in his arms, their lips meeting in an endless kiss that was salty with their joined tears. She didn't know if it was her legs or his that had given way but somehow they were sitting on the grass, wrapped close, murmuring incoherently between kissing and touching each other's faces.

'You're home, you're home, you're home.' She didn't seem to be able to say anything else as Jack and the girls joined them, falling down beside them and hugging Daniel and herself so the six of them were joined together in one joyous package.

It was some time before they separated, and the nature of the reunion had taken away any shyness the children might have felt about the father who was almost a stranger to them. Grace and Alice were a little bemused, Hope felt, as they sat on her lap watching Jack and Betsy, who were now sitting either side of Daniel, bombarding him with questions.

'Enough, enough.' She was laughing but her voice was still unsteady and husky. He looked so ill, so terribly frail. Little more than a walking skeleton, and she had noticed he had tucked his hands under his knees to hide their shaking. 'Give your da time to breathe.' And then she tipped Alice and Grace off her lap and stood up. 'You four go and bring everything, we're going home. Da and I will wait here while you make sure nothing's left.'

As the four scampered off, she helped Daniel to his feet. She put her arms round his waist and looked up into his face 'How did you know where we were?'

'Mrs Duckworth.' He smiled at her. 'Nothing changes, does it? I'd forgotten how everyone knows everything about everyone within a ten-mile radius.'

Nothing changes . . . She reached up and brushed the hair out of his eyes. It had been rich with colour when he had left England, now it was completely grey and much thinner.

Brittle. Like he looked. 'I didn't know you were coming, I've had no word, nothing.'

'I was in one of the last camps to be liberated in north Germany and those that were able to leave they flew straight out. I've probably arrived before the telegram.' He didn't mention that of the two thousand men in the camp, only a third were still living when they were rescued and of them no more than half were fit to be moved. When he and Walt had made a bid for freedom on the journey to Germany, they had been separated from the other prisoners of war and taken to one of the infamous concentration camps to 'teach them a lesson'. The camp had been situated in the middle of nowhere, and after the Nazi guards had recognised defeat was round the corner and the Allies were invading, they had gone on an orgy of killing before they had fled. For the last two weeks before they were rescued, there had been no food and little water. Those that had survived the massacre had dug in the camp vegetable plot for any odd potatoes or carrots they could find, and they ate grass, weeds, worms, anything to keep them alive.

But he and Walt had made it. Against all the odds, they'd made it. For five years they had watched each other's backs and shared their rations and any extra they could get from stealing from the vegetable plot and catching mice and bugs with the little traps Walt made. He wouldn't be here now if it wasn't for Walt. He hoped his friend's homecoming was as good as his.

Hope's eyes were swimming with tears again. 'You look . . .' She couldn't continue.

'I know.' He smiled to reassure her. 'But a few of your meat puddings and I'll fatten up in no time.'

'What was the camp like? We've heard such things—'

'Not now.' He stopped her questions with a gentle finger on her lips. 'We'll talk about it all one day but not now. Now I just want to go home.'

They turned and looked to where the four children were running pell mell towards them, and Hope slipped her arm round his waist. 'Home,' she said, and the word was like a promise.

Chapter 29

Three months later VJ Day came and went amid scenes of celebration which eclipsed those of VE Day in the north-east, possibly because many local servicemen had been POWs of the Japanese. Wearsiders partied like they were 'first footing' on New Year's Eve, even though it was August, and the next day half the town woke up with a headache.

Hope and Daniel spent the day quietly enough. They'd invited Walt over to join them when they'd heard his wife had left him. Apparently Edith had been working delivering milk from a horse-drawn float throughout the war, and had become independent and free thinking. Part of this free thinking had led her to have plenty of gentlemen friends and she had gone off with an American shortly after she and Walt's house had been bombed out. She'd left a letter with one of the neighbours explaining everything in case he came back from the war; now they were getting a divorce.

'Probably all for the best.' Walt refused to be downcast. 'I'm back with me mam and she always was a better cook than Edith.'

Hope and Daniel smiled, as he meant them to, but they felt terribly sorry for Walt. All those years fighting to stay alive and he had come home to no wife, no home and no possessions other than his demob suit. And he was by no means the only one. For most folk there was a deep disquiet about what lay in the future. Would there be jobs for the demobbed, homes for the bombed out, a fair living wage for the masses? Abe had been urging Daniel to take his old place in the firm when he was well enough; Hope knew this although as yet she and Daniel hadn't discussed it. She knew they would have to. But not yet.

There were still many nights when Daniel would wake up screaming in the early hours, soaked with sweat as the nightmares brought back the unspeakable horrors he had seen, and she didn't want to put him under any pressure and perhaps slow his recovery. He had told her a little of what he had been through but she knew there were many things he had kept from her simply because to voice them was impossible as yet. And so she tried to carry on shouldering the responsibilities she had dealt with over the last few years – job, children, home, and now sick husband.

There was one thing she couldn't protect Daniel from however, and that was the closeness their son had formed with his grandfather. Abe had supplanted Daniel in Jack's affections; it had started before Daniel had gone away to fight and the intervening years had only strengthened the bond between grandfather and grandson. Daniel's homecoming highlighted the amount of time Jack spent with his grandfather and even when Hope asked Jack to keep his father company, the boy would make some excuse or other to escape the house. She knew that of the four children, Jack was the most stubborn. He always thought he was right and the things he said at times startled her with their maturity. For those reasons she hesitated to try to force him, that and the fact that she felt she had enough on her plate as it was. Which was selfish, she knew it, but at times she felt her head would burst with all she was trying to juggle.

The months sped on. By Christmas Hope had lost her job at the steelworks due to the returning POWs and soldiers, but she had managed to obtain a very good position as manageress at a local laundry, thanks to her experience in the past. They could make ends meet on the wage she brought in and the allowances Daniel could get. Continuing shortages and rationing were frustrating for everyone, it didn't feel like England had won the war, but Hope's main concern was holding her family together. The relationship between Daniel and his son was strained and it got worse, not better, as Daniel recovered. She knew Jack didn't do it on purpose but all the time it was 'Granda said this or Granda said that,' and now when Abe visited or they visited Abe's, she could see Daniel beginning to resent his father.

Daniel had put on two stones since he had been home and although he was still severely underweight, the worrying grey tinge in his face was giving way to a more healthy colour. He slowly began to take his place as the man of the house once more, and therein lay the conflict with Jack. Several times recently, when Daniel had insisted Jack stay home at night and do his homework rather than disappear off to his grandfather's the moment dinner was finished, there had been angry scenes out of all proportion to the matter in question.

Hope had talked to Jack, Daniel had talked to Jack, calmly and reasonably, but nothing worked. It made for an uneasy atmosphere in the house which was telling on them all.

After one particularly bad confrontation in the New Year, Hope took it upon herself to have a quiet word with Abe. She called him at the office and met him during her lunch break at a small cafe. She was waiting for him when he entered the cafe, and she saw immediately he was wary.

'Well, lass?' He smiled with his mouth only as he sat down at the little table. He nodded his thanks for the pot of tea and plate of bacon butties she had ordered for them both. 'What is it?'

Hope didn't know where to start. Like most folk, she and Daniel had little spare cash for luxuries, nor would they have until she could start her business again and that didn't look likely for years yet the way rationing was going. At Christmas they had carefully budgeted to buy the children a comic book each and one toy, along with the usual sugar mice, orange wrapped in shiny foil and a gleaming half-crown each. Then Abe and Annie had arrived on Christmas morning with armfuls of brand new toys for the children, and a bicycle each for Jack and Betsy. It was kind, so very kind of Abe; she knew it was done out of a heart full of love for his grandchildren, and these days he seemed to include Alice under that banner, but the excessive generosity was not good for Jack or Daniel. To the former it was proof that his grandfather was able to buy him anything his heart desired, and to the latter it emphasised he was a failure. She knew this because Daniel had said so and it had broken her heart.

After pouring Abe a cup of tea and placing a sandwich on his plate, Hope said carefully, 'I want to talk to you about

Daniel. I'm sure you understand he's found it difficult to be home and so unwell.'

'But he's improving all the time.'

She nodded. 'Nevertheless he still tires easily and has recurring infections.' And then she waved her hand. She didn't want to talk about Daniel's physical problems. 'The thing is, he and Jack are not getting on and I know it bothers him a great deal.'

'Nonsense. The lad thinks the world of his da. It was bound to be a bit sticky when Dan first came back, though. Jack's been used to being the man of the house, after all.'

'But that's the thing. Jack was never the man of the house. You were. And I appreciate all you did for us when Daniel was away. I mean that, I don't know what we would have done at times without you, but perhaps it's time for you to take a bit of a backward step and let Jack get to know his da again.'

Abe leant back in his seat, his chin going into his neck as he frowned at her. Hope knew that look. It was intimidating but she wasn't about to be browbeaten. He didn't speak for some moments and neither did she. Then he said, 'You sure this is not so much about Dan as you?'

'I'm absolutely sure.'

Abe gave a small smile. 'You're more like Annie than her own daughter would have been, do you know that?'

Hope didn't answer this. 'You must see that your influence over Jack is undermining Daniel. There were several occasions over Christmas when you were very unwise.'

The smile had gone. 'Name one.'

'When Daniel told Jack to finish his meal before he got down from the table and went out on his bike.'

'I merely said it was Christmas, that's all.'

'And Jack was down from the table like a shot and out of

the door, pretending he didn't hear Daniel call him back. And that was just one thing. There were so many others.'

His voice a growl, Abe said, 'I love my son, Hope. I love the others too but Dan . . . And you're saying I'm deliberately cutting the ground from under him?'

She looked at him, her eyes unblinking; then she bit her lip and bowed her head. 'I know you love him,' she said softly. 'That's why I'm talking to you like this.' Raising her gaze, she shook her head. 'Don't look like that.'

'How do you expect me to look?' Pushing his plate aside, he glared at her. 'You'd have that lad still in nappies if you could, that's what this is all about, not Dan. You want Jack tied to your apron strings, now don't deny it, same as right from when you met Dan you wanted him to break off with his family. He was perfectly happy working for me before he met you.'

Hope stared at the angry man before her. 'That's not true and you know it,' she said hotly, her own temper rising. 'He was never happy to come into the family business, never.'

'That's not the way I remember it.'

'Then you have a very selective memory.'

'The hell I do.' Red with rage, Abe got to his feet. He flung a ten shilling note on the table and said, 'That'll cover the lunch.' He stomped out before she could react.

Hope sat quietly for a few moments, conscious of the veiled but interested glances from other customers at the tables around her. She made herself drink her cup of tea as her colour subsided and her hand stopped shaking. Well, that had gone well, she thought with dark humour. What was it about the Fallow males that made them so difficult?

★   ★   ★

If Hope had but known it, some miles away her sister was asking herself the selfsame thing. Constance was sitting at her dining table in her nightdress, having slept in late, and she was staring at a letter she had received in the morning post. Cecil was cooling off, she knew he was. This excuse of having to work late for the next week or so didn't ring true. He must think she'd been born yesterday.

She lit a cigarette and inhaled deeply, staring at her red taloned hand for a few moments as her thoughts sped on. It was because she'd been pressing him to ask Gwendoline for a divorce, that was it. And it wasn't on any religious grounds he was digging his heels in, whatever he said. He was worried his da would oust him if he knew he had taken up with her, that was the reason. Especially now Daniel was back.

She rose, pulling her thin negligee over her shoulders before she went to stand at the window. She looked down into the street below, her mouth tight. All the men that hadn't come back from the war and Daniel had to turn up as right as rain, or nearly. But that was her sister all over. Drop Hope in a dung heap and she'd come up smelling of roses. But not this time, not while she had breath in her body.

She returned to her seat and drank a cup of now cold coffee. She lit another cigarette. Cecil was his da's right-hand man, he was her ticket out of this life and into one of ease and she didn't intend to let that fizzle out. Not after all the effort she'd put in keeping him happy. A big house and a good going-on was all she wanted and she'd do her bit to keep him satisfied. As the elder son he was positioned very nicely, even if he couldn't see it. All she had to do was make sure Daniel didn't take up his old job with his da once he was well enough and she knew exactly how to accomplish that. She had something up her sleeve that could cause a blow-up between Daniel and his da that would never be healed, and then Cecil would be sitting pretty when he told his da about her. Abe was no fool, he needed Cecil. He wouldn't cut his nose off to spite his face, not Abe. He was too sharp for that.

She settled back in her seat. She had to play this just right, though. The last thing she wanted was for Cecil to click on she had told his brother about Abe involving Jack in his dirty deals. If it went wrong, she could well find herself with no Cecil, and if he told Hope and Daniel where she was, she might have Alice dumped back on her too. That wouldn't matter if she was sitting pretty with Cecil and had a house-keeper to take care of the brat, but there was no way she was having a kid hanging round her skirts here.

She narrowed her eyes through the haze of cigarette smoke. It would have to be anonymous, written in such a way it'd look as though it had come from folk Abe and Cecil had upset. And she bet they'd upset more than a few, what with their black market scams and everything else. And she would write to Cecil too, a nice sugary sweet letter saying she was counting the minutes until they were together again, some-thing like that.

Smiling, she pulled out a pad of paper and matching envelopes. She addressed the envelopes to the two brothers first then settled down to concentrate on the letter to Daniel. When she'd finished, the letter to Cecil was done in no time.

After sealing both envelopes, she lit her umpteenth cigar-ette of the morning. Cecil had bitten off more than he could chew if he thought he was going to get rid of her so easily, and she was doing him a favour anyway. He'd got a chip on

404

his shoulder that weighed a ton about his da preferring Daniel to him, but once the lid went off this little lot, it would be Cecil who was the blue-eyed boy. Aye, the future could be very rosy, all told. Very rosy indeed.

'Who the hell could have sent it and how come you got it instead of Daniel?' Abe was white-faced and tight-lipped as he read the letter Cecil had just handed him. He had already had a barney with Annie before he left the house that morning and he was still furious with her for taking Hope's part when he had told her about the meeting the day before. Unreasonable, she'd called him. *Him*, unreasonable. He didn't understand women. The whole jam pack of them were a race apart and barmy with it.

'If I knew that, I'd be a mind-reader. It's anonymous, isn't it?'

Abe glared at his son. 'It has to be our old friend trying to cause trouble. Damn him, he don't give up, does he? I thought the last time I got Vincent and the lads to lean on him he'd learnt his lesson.'

'Aye, but mebbe he feels a bit braver with Edwin gone and blokes like Lonnie Kirby having the needle against us.'

'It don't explain how you got it instead of Daniel, and how come he knows about Jack coming on the odd job. "Grooming him", that's the words he's used.'

'I don't know how he knows,' said Cecil irritably. 'Same way he knew about Rosaleen, I suppose. I've told you before, the underworld talks. It's a stroke of luck me getting it instead of Daniel, however it's happened. But this proves what I've been saying for some time. You're meddling in the black market and there's people out there who have taken umbrage at us being on their patch. If it wasn't that you're pals with Vincent and his gang, we'd have been found in the river one morning with concrete boots.'

'Aye, well, I am pals with Vincent, aren't I, so stop your griping.' Abe read the letter again. 'Interfering so-an'-so. He can't let go of the fact his old man died, can he? He's determined to ruin my family one way or another.'

'What are you going to do?'

Abe plumped down in his big leather chair, his hands flat on the desk in front of him. Looking down at his short square nails, he said, 'Whatever I have to.'

'You don't mean . . . I mean you wouldn't . . .' Cecil found it impossible to go on.

'Hell's bells, man, I don't know.' Abe slammed both fists onto the desk, making his papers jump. 'But ransacking your house a few times along with the other pranks he's got up to is one thing, this is something else. I thought it was all wind and water about Rosaleen but maybe it wasn't. Maybe he did have a hand in all that drug business, and if he did, then it was murder, now wasn't it? She died, Cecil. Don't forget that. And he crowed about it. He's trying to take my bairns. One way or another, he's trying to take you all.'

Cecil stared at his father. 'I don't like this,' he said slowly.

'And I do? Someone's watching us, Jack an' all.'

'We ought to go to the police.'

'Now you're talking out of your backside.'

Helplessly, Cecil murmured, 'You could get Vincent to ask around rather than pointing the finger immediately, couldn't you? You could do that.'

'Aye, I could do that.' Abe nodded. 'But what when he comes back and tells us what we already know?'

'Then I suppose we have to . . . deal with it.'

'Aye, we do, 'cos I'm not having the lad put at risk.'

Jack again. As far as his father was concerned, he only had one grandson. Bitterness like bile in his mouth, Cecil said, 'Get Vincent to nose around first anyway. We don't lose anything by doing that.'

Abe ran his hand over his face. 'Aye, all right, although who else could it be but Jim Clark? There's spite in this, Cecil, and it's directed at me. I used to think he'd give over in time but I don't reckon this'll finish until one of us is six foot under. If I'd have known all the trouble that damn contract was going to bring I'd have let Clark's have it and be damned.'

Cecil didn't say, 'I told you at the time what Jim Clark was like.' Instead he said, 'We didn't know the old man was going to collapse and the business fold. It was just a contract, Da. Business.'

'It's been anything but business since.' They stared at each other for a moment and then Abe reached for the telephone on his desk. 'I'll ring Vincent now. No time like the present. But just watch your back for the next day or two until he finds out what's going on, all right? And we'd better keep Jack out of it for the present.'

'He won't like that. You've made him feel important.'

'Like it or not, he won't be coming with us tomorrow when we pick up them bits at the docks.'

Cecil nodded. He went back to his desk and stared at the papers in front of him without really seeing them. Damn funny business this, especially him receiving the letter that was meant for Daniel. There was more to this than met the eye, he felt it in his water, and whatever Vincent unearthed, it would mean more unpleasantness. Should he have a word with Daniel?

He raised his eyes and glanced at his father through the glass. Abe had just put the phone down and was now bent over his desk, writing something.

No, he couldn't say anything to his brother, not without mentioning Jack, and his da would go demented if he let on about the lad. Besides, he didn't owe Daniel owt. No, he'd say nothing and wait and see what Vincent ferreted out but he hoped his da had made it clear this was a priority.

Hunching his shoulders he picked up a complicated report his father had asked him to check and prepared to focus his mind. One thing was for sure, Jack wasn't going to take being shunted aside quietly. His da was right in one thing, the lad was the spitting image of him.

'Oh, Daniel, this is lovely, Bernice is expecting a baby.' Hope raised shining eyes from the letter in her hand. 'Daniel? Did you hear me?'

'What?' Daniel looked at her and his expression alarmed her.

'What's the matter? What is it?' She glanced at the letter he was holding which had come in the morning post, along with the glad tidings from Bernice.

'Read this.' He thrust the letter at her. 'Tell me I'm not going barmy.'

Hope took the letter as though it was going to bite her. The writing was vaguely familiar, although she couldn't think from where, but the words themselves caused her to sit up straight with a little exclamation of shock.

My darling one,

I shall miss you so much this week but I understand about you having to work, even if it is never appreciated, but that's a different story. Please come to me as soon as you can. Every hour we're apart always seems like a lifetime and I can't wait to feel your body next to mine again. The things you do drive me crazy but you know that, my big boy. Think of me every night. I shall think of you and imagine you touching me and kissing every inch of me. I want you right now, can you feel that? I'm stroking my breasts and imagining it's your hands on them, and I'm . . .

The rest of the letter was so explicit it brought fiery colour into Hope's cheeks and made her feel hot all over. It was signed 'Your Lollipop', with dozens of kisses scattered all over the page.

'Who on earth could have written this?' Her voice was high and indignant and caused all four children to stop eating and stare at her. 'Let me see the envelope.'

He passed it to her and there was his name in black and white, along with their address.

'Needless to say, I have no idea who or where this has come from and half the things described would be physically impossible, the state I'm in.' This did not bring a smile to her face. Daniel glanced at the children and said, 'Upstairs and get ready for school, chop chop.'

'Aw, Da, I want some more toast.'

'You've had two slices, Jack, and I want to talk to your mam. Skedaddle.'

When the children were out of the way, he came and sat next to Hope, taking her two hands in his. 'Someone's played a joke, a somewhat sick one admittedly, but don't take it seriously.'

'Don't take it seriously?' She tugged her hands away. 'It's horrible, Daniel.'

'Well, actually, I'm rather looking forward to doing some of those sorts of things in the near future.'

'You know what I mean.' She let him take her hands again. 'And it's not funny.'

'No, it's not, but it's obviously from a sick mind, someone whose husband didn't come back from the war most probably and who has become mentally ill. Look, if we get another one I'll take it down to the police station and ask them to look into it, all right? Or do you want me to take this one?'

'No.' She couldn't bear the thought of anyone else looking at the letter and thinking Daniel could possibly be the man in question. 'No, we'll see what happens.'

'I love you.' He took her face in his hands. 'So very much. And we're so lucky, Hope. We survived, both of us, and the children too. We even have our home intact. Some folk lost everything – family, home, memories. We have it all and the future in front of us. Our own business, working together at something we can make a success of.'

It was the first time he had mentioned the future in such terms and for a moment her heart seemed to stop beating. 'You don't intend to go back to working for your da?' she asked softly.

'Not for one hour.' He kissed her, long and passionately, and when he took his mouth from hers, he murmured, 'I meant every word in that letter I wrote to you all those years ago, my love. I was a fool but we survived it. You survived it. From now on it's me and you, and the children of course.'

'Your da won't like it, Daniel. He'll try to persuade you, like he's doing with Jack.' She stopped abruptly, she didn't want to say too much, not when they were really talking for the first time since he had been home.

He didn't take offence though. 'Hope, he means well.' He sighed. 'But he's like a bull in a china shop half the time. But perhaps we might have to think about moving away before Jack is too much older. We need to . . .' He paused. 'We need to bring things back under our control.'

The relief of hearing him talk this way, of feeling that he was mentally fit enough to have thought it all out and made such decisions, was overwhelming. She knew how his mind could torment him on occasions, especially when physically he was still so very low. Only the night before a nightmare had brought him awake drenched with sweat and muttering about an atrocity he must have seen in the camp. She hadn't understood half of what he had been saying in his sleep, but it had been enough to make her blood run cold and feel nauseous.

'I think moving away would be good.' She smiled at him. 'We needn't go far, just . . . far enough.'

'And I intend to look for work in the next week or two.'

'No, Daniel,' she said quickly. 'The doctor said not for months—'

'I need to get out of the house.' He let go of her hand and took a handkerchief out of his pocket to wipe his face where the sweat had broken out again. 'I have too much time to remember here, Hope. I need to keep my mind occupied. I don't care what I do but I need to do something to keep the pictures out of my mind, you know?'

'Oh, Daniel.'

'And don't look like that. I'm ten times better than I was even a month or so ago, but I'd rather work than see one of those damn psychiatrists the doctor was on about. You're my psychiatrist, you and the bairns and our home.'

She fell against him, her arms going round him tightly, and they held each other close without speaking until the clatter of feet on the stairs told them the children were coming down. Hope always dropped the younger two off on her way to the laundry. She rose and quickly got ready. The letter didn't matter. She felt they had turned a corner in the last hour and that was all that mattered. And Daniel was right. As long as they and the bairns were together, everything else could be worked out. They had the rest of their lives in front of them, after all.

Chapter 30

'So he's saying Jim's not involved?'

'I didn't say that.' Abe's voice expressed his impatience. 'Vincent said he couldn't pin him down about it. That's different. But it's got to be Jim and his cronies.'

Cecil stared at his father. 'So what did you say to Vincent?'

Abe shrugged. 'Not a lot.'

'You've told him to lean on Jim?'

'Don't worry your head about it. Let's just say I made it clear I don't want the sort of letter we got yesterday dropping through the letterbox again.'

The two men were walking down the stairs leading from the offices, the rest of the office staff and employees having left some time before. Outside in the yard, Abe said, 'I'll follow you to the docks and we'll do that spot of business as quickly as possible. Your mam's got half the town council coming to this dinner party tonight. I could have done without it but you know your mam.'

Aye, he knew his mam and he knew his da as well. Whatever

he said, his da nurtured the contacts these dinner parties brought and capitalised on every one.

It was snowing heavily and the wind was biting in the yard, cutting round the corner of the building and bringing the snow in mad flurries which stung flesh and made eyes smart. As they walked towards their cars, Cecil nudged his father. 'You've got a visitor.'

'Jack?' Abe took in his grandson who was sitting on a pile of scrap metal to one side of his car. He resembled a small snowman. 'What are you doing here? I told you you're not coming, didn't I?'

'But why, Granda?'

'I told you, lad. You've homework and things to do after school and your mam an' da want you home nights. The weekends are different.'

Cecil glanced at his father. Clever. So he'd laid it all on Hope and Daniel, had he?

'You look frozen to death.' Abe stared at his grandson. It was true, Jack's lips were blue with cold. 'How long have you been waiting out here?'

Jack shrugged in a manner that was so like Abe, Cecil almost smiled. 'Don't know.'

'Too long.' Glancing about him as though the whirling snow would provide an answer to his quandary, Abe said, 'I suppose you better get in now you're here but I'm telling you, this is the last time for a while, all right? Your mam wants you home with the weather so bad and I don't blame her. Come the warmer evenings, we'll think again.'

'Promise, Granda?'

'Aye, I promise. Look, we're going to the docks and I want you ducked down and as quiet as a mouse. No lookout this time. I don't want anyone to see you. I mean it, Jack.'

'Aye, all right, Granda.'

Cecil sighed. The moment he had seen his nephew he'd known what would happen. His father might not realise it but Jack was just as stubborn and determined as he was at getting his own way. There would be more nights like this, winter or no winter.

They drove as fast as the atrocious conditions would allow to Hudson Docks. As they approached the East End, Abe told his grandson to slip off the seat and onto the floor of the car, which Jack did promptly, his bright face showing his delight in the cloak and dagger nature of the evening. Abe couldn't help grinning at him. He was a lad and a half, no mistake. Fancy turning up when he'd told him not to. There'd be no flies on him when he was older, that was for sure.

Abe turned into Prospect Row and drew up by some warehouses and transit sheds. Even the freshly fallen snow and gleaming whiteness couldn't disguise the squalor of the district, but the air was sweeter than in the spring and summer. 'Now you wait here and keep low.' Abe didn't look at his grandson as he spoke. He climbed out of the car and banged the door shut. Cecil joined him, and the two of them walked off into the whirling whiteness.

Jack knelt up and peeped over the bottom of the window. He saw his grandfather and uncle in the distance and then a shadowy figure joined them and they all stood still for a moment before disappearing into one of the warehouses. It was very quiet.

It was not quiet in the warehouse.

As Abe had followed the man through the narrow door he had glanced around him, surprised to see other men standing about. Then his arms were grabbed from behind and he heard a skirmish which told him Cecil had been treated in the same way. At that point the other men turned round and he immediately recognised Jim Clark, along with the big gorilla type who had threatened him that day in the East End so many years ago.

'Abe.' Jim strolled over to him. Abe didn't bother to try and struggle against the hands holding him, they were like steel, but he glanced round to see where Cecil was and saw his son had one arm twisted behind his back by a thuggish-looking brute and that Cecil's eyes were wide with terror. He wanted to reassure him but Jim Clark was saying, 'I hear you were wanting a word with me. Is that right?'

Abe stared into the face of his old enemy. Gone was the relatively young man he remembered and in his place was a stout, even prosperous-looking individual with hard eyes and an even harder mouth. 'Who told you I wanted a word with you?'

'Our old friend, Vincent.'

'If Vincent said I wanted a word with you, he was mistaken.'

'Oh aye?' Jim's eyes moved to the two men holding Abe's arms and then to the one who had Cecil, and it was to them he said, 'Vincent was mistaken.' He turned and looked at his henchman. 'What do you say about that?'

'He was mistaken all right.'

All the men sniggered, as though the statement had been particularly witty, but Jim did not smile. His eyes returned to Abe. 'You've annoyed a lot of people, poking your nose where it shouldn't go. There are rules, see? Villains are villains and businessmen are businessmen and even when the two cross over, certain things aren't done. Now when you put the screws on me da, that could still have passed for business. I didn't like it, but it could have passed for business. But you got cocky, didn't you? And with pals like the Mullens, mebbe you felt your back was covered whatever you got up to. Is that how it was?'

'I don't know what you're talking about.'

'No? Then let me put it in plain English. When you sent them to work me over years ago they did a good job, but then you know that. And it sent out a warning to others, which was no doubt part of the plan, and left you able to cast your net a little wider. But things change, Abe. That's what you've forgotten. Vincent's brother was the power behind the Mullen throne; when he went, their reign ended. And others were quick to step into their shoes.'

'Like you, you mean?'

'Oh, I don't pretend to be one of the real hard cases, Abe. But I work for a couple of them. Me and my blokes.' He glanced at the other men. 'And your black market activities have been duly noted. It wasn't so bad when you were just dabbling but certain folk think you've got a little too adventurous, if you know what I mean. Add that to the fact the word was out you were on my back again and ↑ . . Well.' He smiled. 'Let's just say that's why you and the lackey are here tonight.'

'If I was on your back, as you put it, it was because you wrote that letter and you know it.'

Jim stared at him. 'Letter? That was years ago, when your kid died, and it was just a wind-up.'

'The one this week, the one meant for Daniel, only it reached me instead.'

'I haven't the faintest idea what you're talking about. All I know is that for reasons of your own you put the word out to lean on me again, and it was once too often, Abe. I might have been prepared to let bygones be bygones before that.'

There was something wrong here. Abe's mind was racing. He could recognise flannel when he heard it but Jim was telling the truth about the letter. If he hadn't sent it, who the hell had? 'Look, there's been a mistake.'

'Aye, an' you've made it. You and Vincent. He acknowledged that, didn't he, lads, before we sent him to join his brother.'

Abe stared at the man in front of him and now fear swept over him like a wave, causing his flesh to shrink. He licked his dry lips. 'Your quarrel is with me, not my son. Let Cecil go.'

'And he would keep quiet in view of what's going to happen to you?' Jim looked past him. 'Would you, eh?' When Cecil made no reply, he said, 'Course you wouldn't, same as I wouldn't for my da. But my da's not here, is he? And there we have it, full circle.'

'There's no need for this.' Abe knew it was useless but he had to try.

'Even if I agreed with you, it's out of my hands. I'm acting on orders, Abe. I thought I'd explained that. And when you get orders from the sort of men you've irritated, you don't ignore them. There's just one thing.' Jim's bullet eyes narrowed. 'Vincent mentioned something about your grandson tagging along these days. Is he with you tonight?'

Abe's blood ran cold.

Before he could say anything, the man who had met them outside said, 'There was just the two of 'em in their cars from what I could see.'

418

'Aye, well, best check. We don't want any loose ends, do we?'

What happened next happened so fast it took all of them by surprise. Cecil had been standing silent and still throughout and whether his docility had caused the man who was twisting his arm behind his back to relax his hold slightly was unclear. What was clear was that as Cecil swung his fist straight into his captor's face, he was totally unprepared for it. The blow probably wasn't as powerful as others the man had taken in his life if his broken nose and cauliflower ears were anything to go by, but hitting him straight between the eyes was enough to knock him to the floor.

Cecil did not hang about. He leaped for the door, wrenched it open and sprang outside. The man who had ushered them in minutes before made an attempt to stop him but ended up sprawling when he tripped over the man on the floor.

In the few seconds before they were on him, Cecil made no effort to run, knowing he wouldn't get very far. Instead he shouted at the top of his voice, 'Jack! Jack! Get away! They're coming for you! Do you hear me? Run for it!'

He saw the car door open and a small figure jump out just as he was grabbed from behind. His nephew just stood there and again he shouted, 'Go! They're coming to hurt you!' He just had time to see Jack sprint away before it seemed as if the world had exploded in the side of his head. And then he knew nothing more.

When they carried Cecil's body back into the warehouse, Abe stopped his struggling. He knew immediately his boy was dead; the lolling head would have told him without the fact that half his skull had been smashed away by the iron bar the man who had been holding him was carrying. Abe stood very still, and in that moment he loved Cecil as he had never done when he was alive. This was his firstborn; he had been overcome with joy the day Cecil was born and he knew he had a son to carry on his name. And he'd been a good lad, staunch and true. Aye, he had. Cecil. Oh, Cecil, Cecil. What had he brought his lad to?

'The nipper?' Jim asked.

'Harry's gone after him but the kid had a head start. I suggest we get the hell out of here.'

'Not before we've finished the job. You know what the Kirbys are like.'

'You filthy bit of scum you.' The murderous rage burnt up Abe's fear and he spat full in Jim Clark's face. 'My lad never did a thing to you. Your old man must be turning in his grave to know what he spawned but then he'd always got a good idea. Ashamed of you from when you were a lad, he was.'

Jim had gone white. 'Shut up.'

'And you knew it at bottom. That's what all this has been about all along. Even when you were at school and mixed up with that crew you got into trouble with, he was hanging his head in shame. It was against his better judgement when he let you get a foothold in the business but he was hoping it'd set you on the straight and narrow.'

'I said shut up.'

Jim's fist lashed out and Abe felt his nose crack. Blood gushed into his mouth as he spluttered, '"I'd have sooner been incapable like one of them eunuchs than have our Jim." That's what your da said to me. Whatever you and I might be, your da was as straight as a die and you let him down.'

With a cry that didn't sound quite human, Jim launched himself at Abe. The two men either side of Abe continued to hold him fast as Jim hit over and over again with a strength increased by fury, until Abe was covered in blood. When Abe was sagging and all but unconscious, Jim stepped back, red in the face and sweating like a pig. 'Finish him,' he said.

When the two let go, Abe fell to the floor and they used their feet on him, laughing as they slammed into the now inert body time and time again. They were still having their fun when the door flew open and the man they'd called Harry burst in. His eyes took in the blood-splattered scene in front of him and he gasped, 'The kid got away and the other 'un's shouting has roused a few folk. If we don't go now, we're liable to be caught like rats in a trap.'

Jim glanced down at the two still bodies on the floor. 'We're finished here in any case. No, don't try and bring 'em, they'll only slow us down. We can nip away round the back by the barracks. It'll save having to dump 'em in the docks, if nowt else.'

'Come on, man. I'm telling you, the place'll be crawling in a few minutes, the row that 'un was making.'

'Aye, all right.' With one last vicious kick at the unrecognisable figure at his feet, Jim turned, wiping his bloody hands on a handkerchief as he left.

It was getting on for seven o'clock the same evening and Hope was angry. When she had returned home from work to find that yet again Jack hadn't come straight home from school with the girls, she had been annoyed, especially as the night before she and Daniel had given their son a pep talk about getting his homework done before he went out to play. But on top of this disobedience, Jack knew dinner time was half past six and that they all liked to eat together. She checked the mutton stew which had been simmering for over three hours and decided to start dishing up. And she wouldn't save a plate for Jack either. He could have bread and cheese when he came in and like it.

The snow was falling thickly outside but the warm glow from the range and the smell of the stottie cake she had made to go with the stew gave the kitchen a cosy comfort. She looked at Daniel who was sitting in an armchair in front of the range, toasting his toes on the fender. 'He's a monkey, your son,' she said, walking over to the table with the wedge of stottie cake.

'My son?' Daniel grinned. 'He's your son when he plays up.'

'Ten to one he'll come in soaked to the skin.'

'He's a boy, what do you expect?'

'That he listens to us now and again. I think—'

Daniel never did learn what she thought because the next moment a sobbing Jack came bursting into the kitchen from the backyard. '*They've got Granda and they're chasing me.*'

Hope had dropped the stottie cake with the start she had given. It bounced on the table as Daniel jumped to his feet. 'Jack, calm down. What's the matter?'

'They've got Granda and Uncle Cecil. You have to come.' As Jack started to try to pull his father towards the back door, Daniel restrained him with some difficulty.

'Sit down.' Hope pushed her son onto one of the hard-backed chairs. 'Now tell us what's wrong.'

Through his tears, Jack gabbled out what had happened and before he had finished Hope and Daniel were pulling on their coats and boots. Calling Betsy from her bedroom where she had been playing with Alice and Grace, Hope told her to look after things until they were back. When Betsy asked where they were going, she did not answer her.

Outside in the freezing night, their progress was slow. The snow was thick but it had fallen on previous snow which had melted slightly and then frozen, and it made the ground lethal. Jack was still crying but now his sobs had reduced to hiccuping gasps. It was taking all Daniel's breath to walk, but as they neared the docks, he murmured, 'I don't want you anywhere near this warehouse, Hope. Understand? This might be a storm in a teacup but we don't know.'

'I'm not letting you and Jack go in there by yourselves.' Hope was holding his arm but his breathing was painful to hear. If his recovery was put back because of Abe and Jack, she would have something to say to Abe, she really would. 'Look, Enid and Rachel's husbands will be home by now and Enid's lads too. It will only take a second to knock and ask them to come with us.'

'No, no.' Jack was frantic. 'I told you, Granda says this has to be secret.'

'Secret or not, if Uncle Cecil told you to run away, something might have happened,' Daniel said grimly. 'We're doing what your mam says. Enid and Rachel's houses are only a stone's throw from the docks so it won't take a minute.'

As it happened, in Prospect Row there was no need to call on Enid and Rachel's husbands' services because there was a large group of householders standing at the end of the street close to the entrance to the transit sheds and warehouses. Her heart in her mouth, Hope saw a constable too, and as they neared the crowd, she saw other policemen outside the buildings.

As they reached the constable, he barred their way. 'Sorry, you can't go through there.'

'It's my father.' Daniel's face was as white as the snow all about them and this had the effect of making his eyes appear even more sunken in his thin face. 'My son was with my father and brother and he came home a short while ago saying some men had attacked them.'

'Your father?' The constable peered at them before calling a colleague. 'These say they know the victims.'

Victims. Hope's stomach heaved. What had happened?

One of the policemen took Jack to sit in the police car parked some distance from the entrance to the warehouse. Another escorted Hope and Daniel to the building. This constable quickly explained who they were to the plain-clothes policeman who met them at the warehouse entrance and introduced himself as Inspector Franklin.

Inspector Franklin glanced at Hope before saying, 'An iden-tification at this stage would be most helpful, sir, but it's not a pretty sight. I suggest the lady stays with my constable.'

'I'm coming with my husband.' There was no way she was leaving Daniel to face whatever was in this building by himself.

The inspector nodded. 'Then prepare yourselves.'

No amount of preparation could have helped to lessen the impact of the scene which met their eyes. Someone, a police doctor, Hope assumed, was kneeling by two figures on the floor. The top half of one man was covered by a blanket and there were pools of blood everywhere.

Hope's immediate reaction was one of horror mixed with relief. The grossly swollen, blue-black figure on the floor wasn't either Abe or Cecil. And then someone gently drew back the blanket to reveal the top half of the other man and Hope fought the sickness swelling her throat. It was Cecil lying there and Abe wouldn't have left his son to the mercy of whoever had done this and scarpered. The thought was there a second before Daniel pointed to the first man and said faintly, 'The ring. It's my father's ring. That's my father.'

'Is . . . is he alive?' Hope asked weakly, glancing at the inspector.

'Only just.'

The inspector clearly wasn't a man to pull his punches.

'But he *is* alive.' Hope swung round to the doctor, unaware how her face was begging him to say something, anything to take away the terrible look in Daniel's eyes.

The doctor nodded. 'Aye, lass, he's alive, and where there's life, there's hope,' he said quietly. And then he jerked forward, bracing himself to take Daniel's weight as he folded against him in a dead faint.

Chapter 31

Abe remained in a coma for some weeks. When he finally regained consciousness he started talking. He kept nothing back, thereby prompting the sort of questions from the police which could have consequences on his business as well as ensuring Jim Clark and his cronies were put behind bars. Abe remembered the Kirbys had been mentioned and the police seemed to find this particularly interesting. Abe offered to testify against the men who had murdered his son and Vincent Mullen, but, paralysed as he was from the neck down, it was Jack who went into the witness box, fighting back the tears as he described the events of that fateful night. It took the jury no time at all to bring in a verdict of guilty against Jim Clark, although the Kirbys' solicitor secured the two brothers' release by arguing they hadn't been present at the scene and knew nothing of the affair.

Emily had taken herself off to Gwendoline and Edward in Buckinghamshire shortly before the trial, declaring she had no intention of returning to Sunderland now she could no longer hold her head up in the town. She maintained she had known nothing of Abe's activities and was not accountable for anything he had done.

Annie had barely left Abe's side since he had been moved to a small side room at the infirmary. Such was the force of her determination to stay with him that visiting hours and other such niceties went completely by the board.

Hope realised shortly after the attack on Abe how Annie felt about Daniel's father. You only had to see Annie's face as she sat by the bed hour after hour holding Abe's limp hand to understand. But Daniel seemed oblivious of Annie's feelings which went far beyond the concern of even the most devoted housekeeper. Worried as she was about Daniel and Jack – who was inconsolable – Hope said nothing about her suspicions. Even when Abe regained consciousness and Annie began to talk about nursing him at home in the future, Daniel was unaware. He was there on the dot at each visiting time and left only when the bell rang, but he didn't seem to question Annie's constant presence at his father's side and Hope was glad of this.

The day after the trial and the guilty verdict, Hope and Annie finally talked. It was a bitterly cold afternoon in late March. Daniel was with his father and Hope suggested to Annie she might like to get a breath of fresh air while Abe had someone with him. Bernice was due to visit that afternoon too, and although the matron might turn a blind eye to three visitors instead of the stipulated two, there was no way she was going to countenance four around the bed.

In the hospital grounds, Annie looked at her keenly. 'You know, don't you?'

'Know?' Hope pulled her scarf more closely round her neck, the wind was enough to cut you in two.

'About me and Abe.'

'I can see you're close, if that's what you mean,' Hope prevaricated, wondering what Annie wanted her to say. She had been a rock for Abe and the last thing Hope wanted to do was say or do something to upset her.

'We love each other,' Annie said simply. 'We have for years. Not that we've ever . . . you know.'

'Annie, you don't have to tell me all this. As far as I'm concerned, the Fallows have been very lucky to have you in their lives, all of them.'

'Thank you.' Annie smiled. 'But I've seen you looking once or twice and I wanted you to know, that's all. I'm going to get him home, Hope. I'm determined on that. He'll be much better in his own home, anyone would be.'

Hope said nothing to this. When she had first realised Abe was paralysed with no hope of getting better, she had felt as bad as if it were Daniel or Jack lying in the hospital bed. Abe was strong and vital and alive, it seemed inconceivable that he would never walk or move his arms again. For most people it would be horrific, but for Abe . . .

'You know we'll be there for you,' she said gently after a few moments. 'Anything we can do, anything at all. You only have to ask.'

'I appreciate that. He'll need Daniel, he always has. Funny, he had four children and he loved them all, but it was only Daniel he had a heart for. And Jack of course.'

Hope nodded, a weight settling on her as the tentacles holding her to the north-east tightened. And it wasn't just because of Abe she felt heavy-hearted. Jim Clark had screamed out threats against Jack from the dock when he was convicted, warning him his days were numbered. She didn't know if she believed he would be able to harm her son from prison, but she didn't want it to be put to the test. And Daniel was worrying about that too, she knew he was. The nightmares had come back with a vengeance in recent weeks but now it was Jack's name he cried out. She had heard him talking to Walt one night when Walt had come for dinner and they hadn't known she was listening, and what he had said had been a reflection of her own fears.

When they got back to the little room off the ward, Bernice was already there and she was blooming. Her pregnancy had brought a softness to the Fallow features and she looked, if not attractive, then less plain than usual. Thomas was calling for her at the end of visiting time, having had some business to do in the town, according to Bernice. No one really believed this but everyone pretended to.

Shortly before the bell was due to ring at the end of visiting time, Abe looked directly at Daniel and said, 'Why don't you take your sister down to meet Thomas? It'll save him having to come up here. You too, Annie. Stretch your legs. I haven't seen much of Hope today and we could do with a little chat. Isn't that right, lass?'

Hope smiled at the shrunken face on the pillow. As the swelling had begun to go down and the black and blue bruising covering his body and face had begun to fade, Abe had seemed to melt away before their eyes. 'As long as you don't ask me to get you a double whisky like the last time you wanted a chat,' she said lightly. She had seen the questioning glance Annie had thrown at him and the way Abe had responded. This was no idle chit-chat he had in mind. As ever, Annie did what Abe wanted and within a minute or two they were alone.

'One of the nurses showed me the article about the trial in the *Echo*,' Abe said when the door had closed behind the others. 'The lad did well.'

'Yes, he did.' Hope nodded. 'You would have been proud of your grandson.'

'How did he take Jim sounding off against him?'

'He didn't hear that, he wasn't present for the verdict,' Hope said quickly.

Abe fixed her with his eagle eyes and for a moment it was like the old Abe. 'But he'll hear of it from someone,' he said after a moment. 'A schoolfriend, someone like that.'

This was Hope's fear and she didn't answer him. There was nothing to say.

'The quack told me straight I'll never get any better than I am now,' Abe said, labouring for breath slightly as he always did if he said more than a few words at a time. 'You'd put a dog down if it was like me, wouldn't you?'

'Don't talk like that.'

'Why? I've had a good life, lass, which is more than can be said for my Cecil. He died saving your lad. You know that, don't you? I wouldn't have given him credit for it before but that's what he did, so it just shows how much I knew me own bairn. And he didn't want Jack involved from the start, said he was just a young bit of a bairn and it wasn't right. It weren't neither. I should have listened to him.'

'Don't upset yourself.'

'Upset meself? Lass, you'll never know. I lie here hour after hour thinking, thinking. Rosaleen, Cecil, even Bernice. I had a damn good try at ruining her life an' all. Thank God Daniel met you, and I mean that, lass. I thank God he met you. You're the best thing that ever happened to my lad.'

She was seeing him through a haze of tears now, her voice broken when she murmured, 'It'll all work out. Things seem black now but you'll get better whatever the doctors say. I know you, Abe Fallow.' She bent and kissed the leathery cheek and felt the moisture from his own eyes on her lips. 'You'll win through.'

'Not this time, lass. They broke something in me spine with their boots, that's what the old quack says. Something that can't be mended.' And then, a touch of the old impatience in his voice, he said, 'Wipe me face, lass. I don't want anyone to see me like this.'

Her heart full, she did what he asked, touching his cheek as she said, 'Better, Da?'

He stared at her. 'You've never called me that before.'

'I should have.' And she meant it. There was no room for recrimination or grudges any more. He had made mistakes, big ones, that could have harmed her family but then everything Abe did, good or bad, was bigger than the average man. That was just who he was. And she loved him.

'I want you to do something for me, lass.'

She nodded. 'I will if I can.'

'I want you to get Jack as far away from Sunderland as you can because you'll never know a moment's peace while he stays round these parts and neither will I. It's not even Jim Clark who worries me most but the blokes he worked for. They won't like the damage the court case did to their standing and the paper said a couple of the men with Jim squealed like stuck pigs about some of their goings-on. They'll be looking to make a scapegoat of someone, you mark my words.'

He was voicing what she felt. Nevertheless, she said, 'If they want revenge, they'll target those men who talked.'

431

'I'd like to think so but I can't be sure and neither can you. He needs to be got away, lass.'

'But . . .' She stared at him. Abe worshipped Jack, Jack and Daniel. They were his world, all the more so now that his world had narrowed to a hospital bed. 'You'll miss them.'

'Aye, I will, but I'm not long for the top, lass. We all know it but no one is coming out with it. But while you're hanging about waiting for the weeks or months it takes this body to give up, who knows what could happen.'

'You're frightening me.'

'Aye, I frighten meself an' all, every time I look in the mirror.' His grin was reminiscent of the old days. 'But I mean it. You get yourself away, you and Dan and the bairns. I can help out, I've got a bit stashed away.'

She shook her head. 'Daniel would never leave you like this. You must know that.'

'You could persuade him.'

'No, I couldn't.' She smiled sadly. 'He loves you very much. We all do.'

'I'll tell him to go.'

'That would make no difference. He's your son. He can be as stubborn as a donkey when he wants to be. Besides,' she touched his face again, 'I wouldn't want to leave you like this either.'

He blinked. 'Thanks for that, lass.'

'I mean it.'

'Aye.' His voice was soft. 'I know you do. Now dry your eyes and blow your nose. If I know anything about Annie she'll be back in a minute and if you're blubbing I'll have the third degree once we're alone.'

There was a great hard lump in her throat but she did as

he said. The bell rang for the end of visiting in the next moment, just as Daniel and Annie entered the room again, and in the moments it took them to say their goodbyes, Hope avoided Annie's gaze. She had seen the sharp glance Annie had given her when she had walked in and she didn't feel up to any questions. If Annie wanted to know what had been said, she'd have to ask Abe.

Annie did ask Abe, and he was waiting for her. After telling her exactly what had transpired, he said, 'So that leaves me with one choice, lass, and I have to say I'm not sorry except for one thing and that's leaving you.'

'Leaving me?' Annie's brow wrinkled and she gave an uncertain smile. 'Where do you think you're going then?'

He stared at her. 'I'm as helpless as a babe, Annie. I can't wipe me own backside or feed meself. I can't even blow me own damn nose. And the pain . . . well, it makes me sweat a bit. There's times I'm damn near choking for breath and that's getting worse, you know it is. I don't want to leave this world gasping and choking or screaming in agony. I want to go with a bit of dignity and while it'll serve some use. Dan won't leave these parts while I'm alive, the lass is right. So . . .'

'No.' Her hand had gone to her mouth. 'You're going to get better, I know you will. You'll come home with me and I'll look after you. We'll be all right—'

'Lass, I won't get better. Every day I get a bit worse. I'm going bad inside, I can feel it. I need you to help me, Annie.'

'No.'

'Please, lass.'

'Abe, do you know what you're asking?'

433

'Aye, I do, and I'm sorry. If I could do it meself I would. But I can't.'

The tears were streaming from her eyes and when she fell on her knees beside the bed, her arms going round him, she said, 'I wouldn't be able to bear it without you, don't you understand that? Without you there's nothing, just emptiness. I don't care about anything or anyone else, I never have. You're everything to me, everything. How can you ask me to do that if you have an ounce of feeling for me?'

'I've got more than an ounce, lass, a darn sight more. But again I'll say it, I want you to help me.'

She made a deep sound in her throat, moving her head against his chest. It was some moments before she said, 'When? How?'

'Now. With the pillow.'

She raised her eyes to his, and when he smiled and said, 'That's my girl,' the feeling inside her chest was comparable to nothing she had felt before. Never to hear his voice again. Never to joke and laugh and spark off each other. Never to see him smile at her. She was ugly and yet he thought she was beautiful, his eyes as well as his mouth had told her that so many times. She would never see anyone look at her again like he did. She wouldn't want anyone else to.

'I love you,' she said faintly. 'I always have.'

'I love you. I always should have.'

She bent and put her lips to his and for a long moment they remained thus. And then she straightened and gently removed the pillow from under his head, stroking the hair from his forehead as she murmured, 'My own dear love. Always.'

When it was over, a curious numbness came to her mind.

434

Mechanically she placed the pillow under his head as before, straightening the coverlet and again brushing the hair from his brow before leaving the room.

She left the hospital without talking to anyone and walked home. She entered the house and went straight to the bathroom at the top of the stairs where she opened the little cupboard. Emily's sleeping tablets, the ones she had had for some time after Rosaleen had died, were at the back of the shelf and it was a new bottle, scarcely one was gone. Carefully she emptied the contents of the bottle into a glass and half filled it with water, swirling the tablets about for a long time until they were all but dissolved.

After she had drunk the mixture down, she rinsed her mouth with cold water to get rid of the bitter taste. Then she went across the landing and opened the door to Abe's room. It was just as he had left it the morning he had gone out and never returned, except she had tidied his clothes away. She drew back the covers and lay down, the faint scent of him enveloping her.

The numbness was still holding and for this she was thankful. She shut her eyes and went to sleep.

Chapter 32

Emily did not attend her husband's funeral. She had, she said in the letter she wrote to Bernice, washed her hands of the north-east once and for all. Bernice and Thomas were welcome to visit her in Buckinghamshire, and they could extend this invitation to Daniel and Hope if Bernice so wished, but she would not be returning. The solicitors could deal with all the financial implications of selling the business and the house and she would see Bernice and Daniel, as the two surviving children, got their share of the proceeds. That was her duty, and no one could say she didn't do her duty.

Eyebrows were raised by some at the fact that after Abe Fallow died in his sleep at the hospital, his housekeeper was so cut up about it she went home and took an overdose. And hadn't she sat by his side at the infirmary from the moment he was brought in? The wife hadn't got a look in. Something had been going on there, you could bet your boots, and that's why the wife had disappeared in a huff to foreign parts. Aye, there had been hanky-panky there all right, in spite of the fact the woman had looked like the back end of a tram.

Daniel and Hope were aware of what was being said, but such was their grief at Abe and Annie's going that it washed over them. Added to Hope's distress was the weight of the conversation she had had with her father-in-law the day he had died. It seemed a huge coincidence that within hours, if not minutes, of their leaving the infirmary, Abe had passed away in his sleep. And Annie, going home and doing what she'd done? Something was wrong, badly wrong. Hope thought about it every minute of every day but she knew she couldn't share her suspicions with Daniel. He had been through enough in the last six years for several lifetimes. What purpose would it serve now to divulge that she believed his father had asked Annie to help him end his life, the prime objective being a wish to protect his grandson by cutting the ties which held him to Sunderland? And Annie, loving Abe as she did, hadn't been able to continue without him.

No, she couldn't do it. This was one burden she had to shoulder alone, hard though it was. And Jack . . . She was deeply concerned about her boy. He was so full of anger and bitterness. Several times he had talked rashly about getting even with the men who had murdered his grandfather. When she and Daniel had tried to reason with him, pointing out the perpetrators were already in prison, he had rounded on them. Granda had told him there were always small fry and big fry, he'd shouted, red in the face, and that the big fry invariably got off scot-free, and he'd been right. Just because the Kirbys had a clever lawyer they had walked away laughing and it wasn't right.

Hope agreed with her son, it wasn't right, although she

did not say so to him. What really frightened her was the fact that the Kirbys could be watching Jack now, which meant every day Jack remained in these parts was a day too long. But Daniel's grief at losing in one fell swoop his father, his brother and the woman who had been a second mother to him had put his recovery back months, added to which all the legal formalities had to be completed. All she could do for the present was watch over her son like a hawk.

In July, when Britain's housewives were reeling from the announcement that bread was going to be rationed and that there wasn't enough coal to see the nation through the winter, Constance came to see Hope. The week before, Daniel and Bernice had received reasonable but not generous settlements from Emily. Daniel's mother had made it plain that considering Abe had left everything to her, she felt her son and daughter were fortunate to receive anything at all.

The day had started badly. Jack had become more and more surly and hostile in the weeks since his grandfather's demise, particularly towards Hope. It was as though he held her personally responsible for Abe's death. When she said this to Daniel, he told her she was imagining things. But Hope did not think so. And this morning had proved it. She'd made a casual remark about his homework at the breakfast table, and before she knew it a scene erupted which had the girls in tears and Daniel threatening to skelp his son's backside.

'I don't care!' Jack was scarlet-faced as he leapt up from the table, surveying them all from the doorway into the hall. 'I don't care about any of you and what does homework matter with Granda gone? And you're glad.' He turned his wild gaze on Hope, the enmity in his eyes piercing her through. 'You're glad Granda's dead. You hated him, I know you did.'

'That's not true, Jack.' Hope motioned with her hand to stay Daniel who had begun to advance towards his son. 'I loved your granda.'

'No you didn't! You never wanted me to see him, never. You were always against him and I hate you. I really hate you.'

Daniel wouldn't be held back any longer. He had hauled Jack into the front room and shouted at him in a way Hope had never heard before. Quite what transpired after that she didn't know because before the pair of them emerged she had had to leave for work.

She walked to the laundry in bright summer sunshine, fighting back the tears. Her family was falling apart and she couldn't stop it. Jack hated her, she'd felt it for weeks, and he wouldn't have anything to do with any of them, even Betsy. She knew Betsy was crying herself to sleep every night over her brother's treatment of her.

Hope didn't know what to do any more. She stood outside the entrance to the laundry for some moments before she could steel herself to go in and be the brisk cheerful manageress they paid her to be. There was no reaching Jack and he was getting further and further away from them by the day.

Oh, Abe. She looked up into the blue summer sky far above the mean dusty streets, her whole being aching. Do something. You loved him, I know you did, so do something now. Get through to him in his mind, because I can't.

And then she shook herself. Abe was gone and she was here. It was she who had to try and steer her son out of this maelstrom of rage and resentment, but everything she said or did seemed to make things ten times worse between them.

He was awkward with Daniel too, but with her he took it to another dimension.

But now she had to work. She opened the door of the laundry and went inside.

Constance was waiting for her in the street outside the building when Hope emerged that evening. She was tired and hot and already much later than usual, due to one of the machines going wrong and throwing the whole workload for the day into disarray. One of the girls had burnt her hand badly and had had to be taken to the hospital, and another had announced she was leaving that day and had walked out without so much as a by your leave. All in all it had been a nightmare.

Dreading how things would be at home with Jack, Hope walked straight past the peroxide blonde in the low-cut blouse standing on the pavement. And then she heard her name called and she turned. Her eyes widened. 'Constance?' she said. Forgetting the past, she hugged her sister close, saying, 'Oh, Constance, Constance, I thought you might not have come through the war with all the bombing down south. Why didn't you write and tell me you were all right? You must have known we'd worry. Oh, I'm so glad you've come back.'

Extricating herself from the embrace, Constance smiled. 'I couldn't write, there were circumstances . . .' She flapped her hand then linked her arm through Hope's. 'Let's go and have a cup of tea and catch up.'

She was speaking as though they'd last seen each other a couple of weeks before. Hope stared at her sister, hardly believing she was actually here in front of her. She nodded. 'You must stay for dinner,' she began, and then, as Constance's face changed, she said, 'What's the matter?'

'I was thinking we'd go to a cafe and have a chat. Look, you might as well know straight off I'm not in a position to have Alice. I live by myself and there's no room for a bairn, besides which I work nights.'

'You don't have to take Alice.' Hope didn't add that now she had really looked at her sister and taken in the painted face and large expanse of cleavage, she'd have been concerned if Constance had wanted to. Instead she said, 'Don't you want to come and see her for a bit though?'

'It might upset her.'

'No, I'm sure it wouldn't. She's a very placid little girl. But if you'd rather not . . .'

'Truthfully?' Constance shrugged. 'I haven't got a maternal bone in my body and I can't help that. I don't like bairns and they don't like me.'

Hope stared at her, utterly nonplussed. Shock at Constance's sudden appearance combined with bewilderment as to why her sister had turned up if it wasn't to see Alice made it difficult to think. 'Constance . . .' She stopped. 'I don't understand.'

'Come and have a cup of tea and a cream bun or something, my treat.' Constance slipped her arm through Hope's again, her manner now girlish as she giggled, 'I love cream buns although I ought to watch my figure. Still, there's plenty of men only too happy to do that.'

She continued with her flippant talk until they were seated in a small cafe tucked away in a side street off High Street West. Constance had chosen a window seat and with the bright July sunlight streaming through the window, Hope saw her sister was beginning to look her age under the thick make-up. She waited until they had been served by a somewhat bored–looking waitress before she said, 'What's this all about, Constance?'

'Same old Hope, no beating about the bush.'

Hope stared at her. There was an edge to Constance's voice. Quietly, she said, 'I'm glad to see you.'

'Are you?' Constance narrowed her eyes at her and then shrugged. 'Well, whether you are or you aren't makes no difference. I'm here, aren't I? Look, I know all about what's happened, the court case and everything.'

'You do?' Hope was surprised. 'Was it in the papers down south too?'

'I've been in Newcastle for a while.'

She had been so close and yet she hadn't called or made contact in spite of the awful situation. Hope felt a sharp stab of disappointment and hurt even as she told herself not to be so silly. Constance had cut all the threads long ago.

'And you might as well know. I was seeing Cecil before he was done in.'

'Seeing him?' Hope's brain couldn't take it in.

'Aye, seeing him.' Constance leant forward slightly and lowered her voice. 'He was going to divorce that scrag end of a wife of his and marry me, if you want to know. We were engaged, unofficially like.'

This had to be one of Constance's stories.

Whether her sister read her mind, Hope didn't know, but Constance's voice was harsh when she said, 'We were. We'd been together ages and he'd had enough of Gwendoline long before he met me. Look, I can prove it. That letter you and Daniel got about Jack and Abe? It was me, I wrote it.'

'Letter?'

'He must have shown it to you.'

'Constance, I haven't the faintest idea what you're on about.'

'You mean he didn't show you? The dirty swine, keeping something like that back.'

There was a little bell ringing somewhere in the back of Hope's mind. Slowly, she said, 'There was a letter.'

'There, I knew it. What did you deny it for?'

'But it wasn't about Jack. It was . . .' she could feel herself reddening, 'a love letter.'

'A love letter?' Constance laughed. 'Daniel got a love letter? The sly old fox. I didn't think he'd got it in him.'

Hope repeated the one thing that had stayed with her even after the main content of the letter had faded from her mind. 'It was from someone called Lollipop.'

Constance had been about to drink her tea but her hand stopped halfway to her mouth. Their eyes held for a full ten seconds and then Constance slowly put her cup back on its saucer without tasting the tea. 'Oh hell,' she said. 'I must have put them in the wrong envelopes.' She raised her caked eyelashes. 'Which means Cecil got yours. That must have put the willies up him.'

Hope felt she was wading through treacle. 'Why? What was in it?'

'I felt it was time you knew about Abe, that's all. Him and Cecil had started taking Jack out with them when they saw people. People who sailed close to the wind, you know?'

'Yes, I do know. Abe admitted everything.'

'And you and Daniel forgave him? Well, you would, wouldn't you.'

The tone was not pleasant. 'What does that mean?'

'Abe was a rich man. With Cecil and the other daughter

gone, that left Daniel and Bernice sitting pretty. I assume you thought it wise not to fall out with him, that's all.'

'He was dying, Constance.'

'Exactly.'

She didn't like her sister. All these years and she had never admitted it to herself but now she couldn't ignore it any longer. They were born of the same parents, they had the same blood running through their veins and she didn't like her. There followed some moments of uneasy silence while they both drank their tea.

Then Constance placed her cup on the saucer and leant forward. 'The thing is, with me being Cecil's intended, so to speak, I reckon I'm due something.'

'*What?*'

'I'd have got it all if I was his wife.'

'He had a wife, Constance. And a child.'

'That scrag end? She was never a wife to him. Anyway, if not from his estate then from his da's. Daniel got a bit I'll be bound and Cecil was the eldest.'

Hope stared at her sister as though she was mad. And in truth she thought she must be. 'Abe left everything to his wife. She felt she wanted to give Bernice and Daniel something but that was up to her.'

'I reckon I ought to talk to them and tell them how it was. Cecil would have wanted me to be looked after.'

Hope could hardly believe her ears. She had always thought Constance was quite bright, certainly not dim anyway. She had done all right at school. But here she was, admitting to an affair with a married man who had a wife and child and then declaring she ought to be paid something for her trouble. Because that was what this amounted to. And she seriously thought Daniel and Bernice would agree to give her money?

'There is absolutely no way any of the family would give you a penny, Constance, so put that idea out of your head.'

'How do you know if you don't put it to them? And you could say you agree with me, you being Daniel's wife. That'd carry some weight.'

Hope leant forward and now her voice was low and cool. This conversation had been an eye-opener in more ways than one. 'I wouldn't do that because I don't agree with you. And while we're on the subject, don't try to contact Gwendoline and Edward or anyone else in the family. They will be allowed to remember Cecil as a good husband and father and brother, Constance. You won't spoil that. The letter you wrote to Daniel which ended up in Cecil and Abe's hands was what started all the bother which led to their deaths. I don't know all the ins and outs of it, but that much became clear during the trial. Go back to wherever you've come from and let this be an end to it, or you could just find yourself in hot water with the law.'

As Hope rose to her feet, Constance said, 'You can't threaten me, Hope,' but her voice carried no conviction.

'I'm not threatening you. I'm stating facts. You try anything clever and you could find yourself up before the bench and I swear I won't lift a finger to help you.' And then Hope walked out of the cafe and into the warm sunshine.

She walked some way before she paused and leant against a wall. Suddenly she wanted to cry. She'd often thought of Constance in the years since she'd left, and now they had met, only for it to end in an ugly scene. She bit down hard on her bottom lip.

Then she straightened. At least now when she left the town

445

there would be no unfinished business. Today she'd discovered her sister had not only survived the war but that she was more than capable of looking after herself. Suddenly the need to see Daniel and her family was overwhelming, and she began to walk swiftly.

It was time to talk to Daniel about leaving, not just the town as they'd discussed before but the country. They had to get Jack right away from the Kirbys' sinister presence, and with her nest egg in her bank account and now Daniel's inheritance they had enough money to get started elsewhere. They mustn't delay; every hour, every minute was vital. In a different country, New Zealand perhaps, they could begin the ice-cream business once more, buy shop premises this time and make a real success of it. It would be tough but if they all pulled together they could do it.

The pavements had cleared of all but the last shoppers and this made Hope realise how late she was, but her mind continued to buzz as she hurried on.

Constance coming to see her like this was a sign. It was as if the last full stop on the old life had been put in place; it was time to lift their eyes to new horizons. And now she wouldn't feel guilty about taking Alice far away where there was no chance she would see her mother. Constance herself had said she wanted nothing to do with the child. If, when she was older, Alice wanted to try and find her mother, she wouldn't stand in her way, but hopefully by then Alice would be a strong young woman who knew she had a loving family behind her and whatever reception she got from Constance it wouldn't hurt too much.

She would tell Daniel tonight that Abe had wanted them

to take Jack as far away from the north-east as they could. It was the truth and it would add weight to the urgency she felt about ensuring her son's safety. Of course how Jack would view things was a different matter. No doubt this would be added to the list of crimes against her in his mind. All the emotion she had been forcing herself to keep under wraps for the last months was threatening to surface in tears of self-pity, and she fought against them. She mustn't think she was losing her son, that would help no one. She had to be strong. She couldn't cry or show any weakness because what would happen to her family then?

Just before she reached the top of Frederick Street, she saw Jack standing at the corner. Twilight was falling, the fierce heat of the day over, and she watched him as he came to meet her, all lanky limbs and big hands. Her throat swelled with love for him. She supposed his father had told him to say sorry to her and he wanted to get it over with privately. He was so like Abe. Not in his looks, they were purely from her side, but in his nature. He was such a mixture of vitality and bumptiousness and arrogance and pride, with a passion that was the same whether he loved or hated. She had just never thought he would hate her.

She wanted to make it easy for him and so as he drew near she said, 'I'm sorry about this morning, Jack. I didn't mean to go on about your homework.'

His face was straight and tense and when he stood in front of her she realised, with a little lurch to her heart, that he was as tall as she was. When had that happened? He went to speak, his lips moved but he had to swallow his spittle before he said, 'You're very late. Da's worried.'

'Is he? I'm sorry. I got delayed at work. A machine broke

447

down . . .' Her voice trailed away. He still hadn't moved. Tentatively now, she said, 'Is everything all right?'

'I was worried too.'

'I'm sorry.' She had to stop saying that. 'There was no way I could let you all know.'

'Mam.' He stopped.

'Yes?' He was frightening her now; her mind was whirling with thoughts of what could possibly have happened while she had been gone.

'Mam, I'm sorry.' It was wrenched up from somewhere in the depths of him and was no trite thing. 'I'm so sorry, Mam. I love you, you know that, don't you?' The tears were coursing down his thin cheeks and as he took her in his arms she could feel his heart pounding in the narrow boyish chest. 'I'll always love you. I've been horrible, I know that, but I couldn't help myself. Since Granda went . . . And it was all my fault.'

'What?' She knew the state he must be in to break down in the street, and as she strained back to look into his face, her own was wet. 'Of course it wasn't your fault.'

'I should have got help sooner. If I'd had me wits about me I could have knocked on doors close by, anything, but I just let them beat him into a pulp.'

'No, no, listen to me.' She took his young face in her hands. 'It wasn't like that.'

'And Uncle Cecil was killed because he called out to me. If I hadn't been there, they'd still be alive.'

'Of course they wouldn't, my darling. They wouldn't. The only difference in you being there was that people were alerted to what was going on. Those men had planned to kill your granda and Uncle Cecil all along. Because of you being there it meant your granda wasn't left on the floor of that warehouse all night long to die. You being there meant he had more weeks when we could all tell him how much we loved him and he could die without pain and with people who loved him. You must understand that, Jack.'

'Oh, Mam, Mam.' He was sobbing unrestrainedly, the anguish and guilt pouring out of him in a flood, and now it was she who was holding him. 'I want him back. I miss him, Mam.'

'I know, darling, I know. We all do.'

'And at school they want to talk about it all the time in the playground and some of 'em were saying things about Granda and Uncle Cecil. I had a fight with Toby Griffiths and he broke his finger and now his da is coming up the school tomorrow.'

'Don't you worry about that, your da will sort out Toby Griffiths's da.'

She hugged him close again, pressing him fiercely to her, overwhelmed with thankfulness they were talking again.

Eventually it was Jack who pulled away. He reached in his pocket for his handkerchief which he handed to her with a shaky smile. 'I'm sorry I've made you cry. Da'll go mad at me.'

'I needed to cry. We both did,' she said, wiping her eyes.

For a moment their eyes met in perfect understanding. 'I do love you, Mam.'

'I know you do, hinny. I know.' The tears were welling again and to combat them she said, 'How would you feel about moving right away from here? Even to another country perhaps? Just me and da and you and the girls?'

His eyes widened. 'How would we go? On a boat or a plane?'

He was such a baby still. The lump in Hope's throat was enormous. And yet so grown-up in some ways. 'I don't know,' she said, swallowing hard. 'We could sort all that out. But would you want to go?'

He thought for a moment and then nodded. 'Would I be able to have a dog where we'd live?' She had always insisted it wasn't fair to have a dog where they were now and with them out most of the day.

'Yes, you could have a dog. I haven't talked to your da properly about this but I think we'd be starting our own business, so aye, you could have your dog.'

'We'd be a long way from Granda's grave.'

'He's not in the grave, Jack. Not really. He's in our hearts and you'll take him with you wherever you go. You'll be able to tell your bairns and your bairns' bairns about the amazing man who was your grandfather, and that way he'll be with you for ever. Wherever heaven is he'll know you're doing that and he'll be pleased. If I know anything about your granda, he would come back and haunt us if we tried to shut him out of our lives,' she added, trying to lighten the moment.

It worked. Jack grinned shakily, rubbing his nose as he said, 'He would an' all.'

It was going to be all right.

They began to walk arm in arm and as they turned the corner of the street, she saw Daniel was standing on the pavement outside the house with the three girls, his figure a dark silhouette against the sky which was streaked with pink and mauve and silver. He lifted his arm and waved as he saw them, and the three girls began to run towards her. Just before she gathered them into her arms, a lone skylark flew overhead, making for the country, singing as it went.

Author's Note

'England's Ice Cream'

All research is important, but to those of us who set their stories many decades ago it is vital. I draw on various channels to get my facts and figures spot on, but once in a while something comes to me like a nugget of pure gold and that's what happened with *Skylarks at Sunset*.

My heroine, Hope, starts her own ice cream and toffee apple business from the front room of her little terraced house in an effort to make ends meet for her family, and that is exactly what my maternal grandmother did. Grandma England was a tiny little woman, well under five feet tall, with the sweetest angel's face and the steel will and determination of a dozen men. My dear mum has countless stories about the powerhouse that was her mother, including the one when my granddad came home from a long stay in hospital to find – unbeknown to him – my grandma had moved the family lock, stock and barrel to a new house in a different part of town. No mean feat in the days of flat carts and shanks pony! Apparently he took it all in his stride. But on to the ice cream venture . . .

In *Skylarks at Sunset*, Hope is given the special recipe for her ice cream from the Italian lady who sells her the hand barrel and necessary equipment, but in real life my grandma's superb recipe was her own. 'England's Ice Cream' was well known in the streets and lanes surrounding her home and had a reputation for being second to none.

As you can imagine, with no fridges to use speed in selling was of the utmost importance, but Grandma's ice cream was so popular it never had time to melt before it was all sold. When she got more successful she graduated to selling from a horse and cart, but at first Grandma did just as Hope does and walked the streets pushing her hand cart, children in tow. The locals would come with their cups and bowls and Grandma would spoon the ice cream into their dishes.

Grandma jealously guarded the recipe for her delicious ice cream, but it involved custard powder, cream, vanilla essence and a couple of ingredients only she knew about. She'd collect blocks of ice from a local butcher and cart them home, churning and mixing her lovely concoctions before marshalling her brood of children and going forth to sell.

Grandma also made toffee apples and huge slabs of toffee that she would break up and sell in little brown paper bags from her front room. Needless to say, the England children were never short of pals, and my mum remembers Grandma always had a piece of toffee to spare for any young visitors to her kitchen.

Eventually family circumstances forced Grandma to sell her little business. An unfortunate move in hindsight. The business continued to grow in leaps and bounds under new ownership, blossoming into a factory-run endeavour. I like to think Hope would have made an equally big success of things with Daniel and the children supporting her. In fact, I'm sure she would.

Rita Bradshaw
Born to Trouble

All she wants is a better life ...

Born in Sunderland's filthy, crime-ridden East End,
Pearl Croft's childhood is desperately troubled. When
her violent, drunken father is killed in a fight and Pearl's
elder brothers are sent to prison, she is left to care for
her baby brothers. Then Pearl's mother brings a 'client'
to the house who has a penchant for little girls. Terrified
and hurt, Pearl runs away from home and is found,
feverish and near death, by Romany gypsies. But this is
far from the end of her struggles. Years pass and as Pearl
reaches womanhood she wonders if she will ever
find happiness?

Available now from

HEADLINE